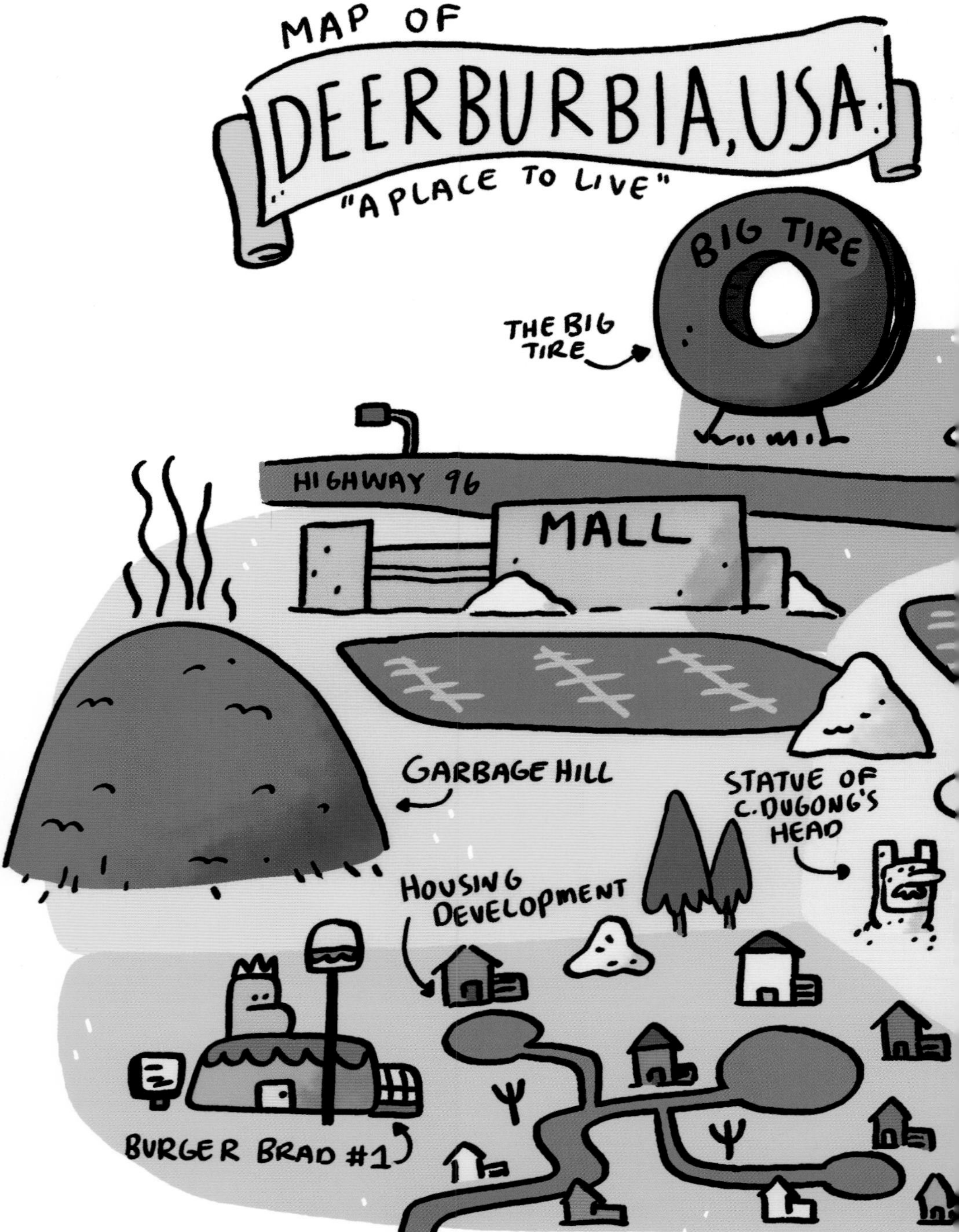
MAP OF
DEERBURBIA, USA
"A PLACE TO LIVE"
BIG TIRE
THE BIG TIRE
HIGHWAY 96
MALL
GARBAGE HILL
STATUE OF C. DUGONG'S HEAD
HOUSING DEVELOPMENT
BURGER BRAD #1

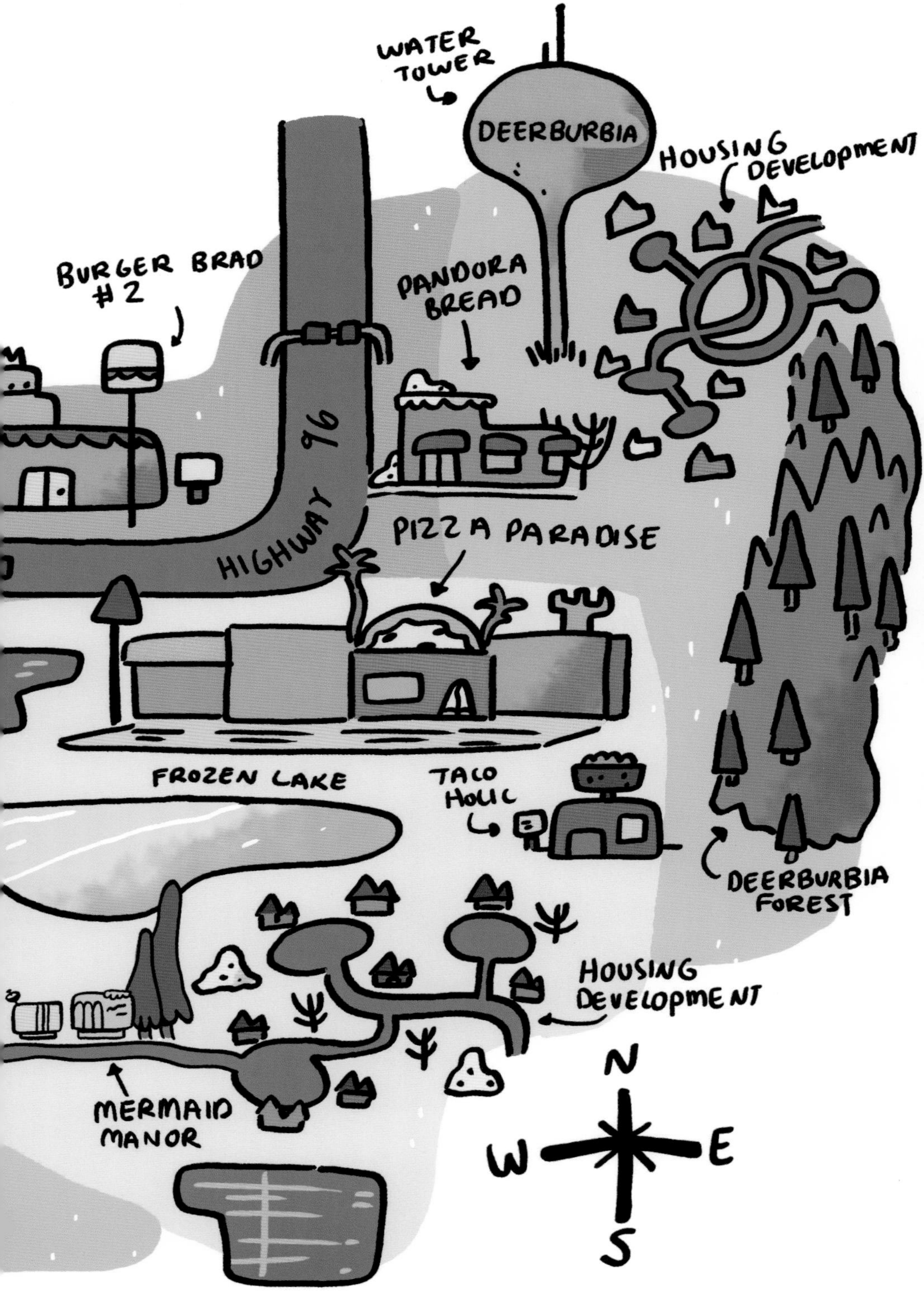
WATER TOWER
DEERBURBIA
HOUSING DEVELOPMENT
BURGER BRAD #2
PANDORA BREAD
HIGHWAY 96
PIZZA PARADISE
FROZEN LAKE
TACO HOLIC
DEERBURBIA FOREST
HOUSING DEVELOPMENT
MERMAID MANOR
N
W
E
S

DOLPHIN GIRL

GIRL

Trouble in

PIZZA PARADISE!

DOLPHIN GIRL

Trouble in
PIZZA PARADISE!

WRITTEN AND ILLUSTRATED BY
ZACH SMITH

COLOR BY LETICIA LACY

PIXEL✚INK

PIXEL+INK

ALL RIGHTS RESERVED
PIXEL+INK IS A DIVISION OF TGM DEVELOPMENT CORP.
PRINTED AND BOUND AT TOPPAN LEEFUNG IN CHINA, 2020.

DOLPHIN IMAGE ON PAGE 12: IRINA NO/SHUTTERSTOCK.COM
TV STATIC IMAGE ON PP. 18-20: VERVERIDIS VASILIS/SHUTTERSTOCK.COM
FIRE IMAGE ON PAGE 21: WEERACHAI KHAMFU/SHUTTERSTOCK.COM

WWW.PIXELANDINKBOOKS.COM

FIRST EDITION
1 3 5 7 9 10 8 6 4 2
CATALOGING-IN-PUBLICATION DATA IS AVAILABLE
FROM THE LIBRARY OF CONGRESS

HARDCOVER ISBN: 978-1-64595-017-2
PAPERBACK ISBN: 978-1-64595-018-9

DOLPHIN GIRL IS THE SUBJECT OF A COEXISTENCE AGREEMENT BETWEEN TGM DEVELOPMENT
CORP AND ZACH SMITH, ON THE ONE HAND, AND PATRICK MORGAN, TAESOO KIM AND
ED ACOSTA, THE CREATORS OF WHALEBOY, ON THE OTHER, AND APPEARS IN THIS BOOK
SUBJECT TO THE TERMS AND CONDITIONS OF THAT AGREEMENT.

FOR QUINN & ZADIE
MY WONDERFUL, WEIRD,
HILARIOUS KIDS.
MAY YOU ALWAYS THINK
FART JOKES ARE AS FUNNY
AS YOU DO RIGHT NOW.

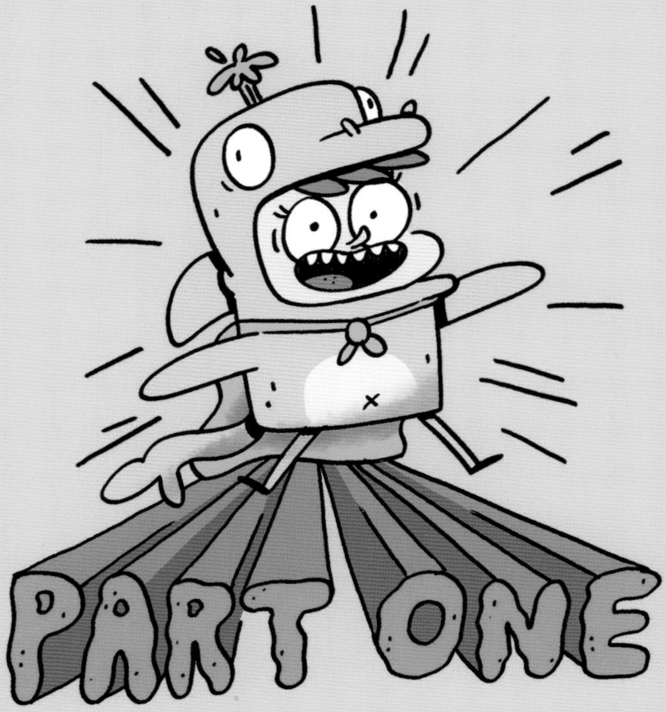
PART ONE

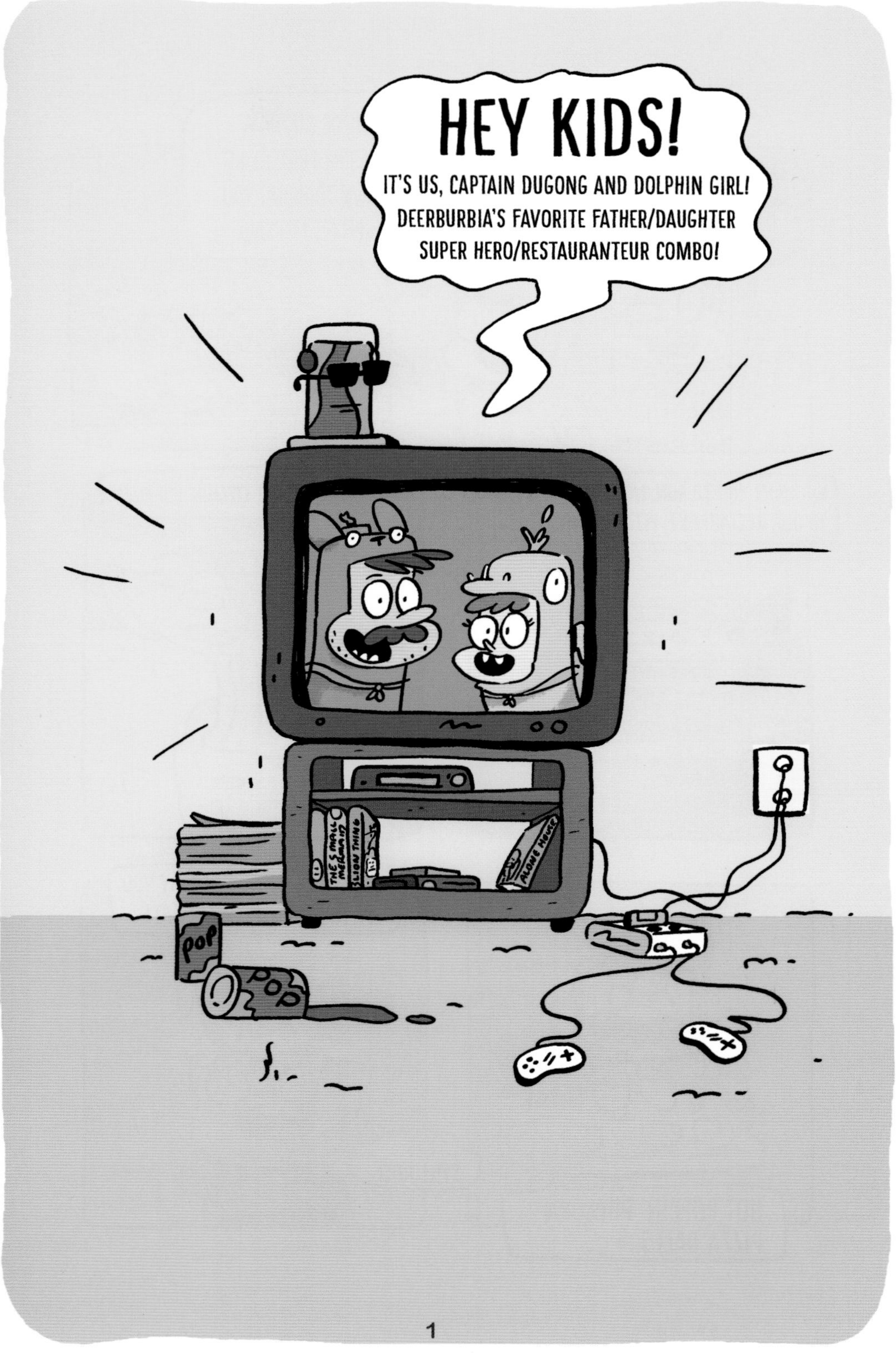
HEY KIDS!
IT'S US, CAPTAIN DUGONG AND DOLPHIN GIRL!
DEERBURBIA'S FAVORITE FATHER/DAUGHTER
SUPER HERO/RESTAURANTEUR COMBO!
ALONE HOUSE
POP
POP

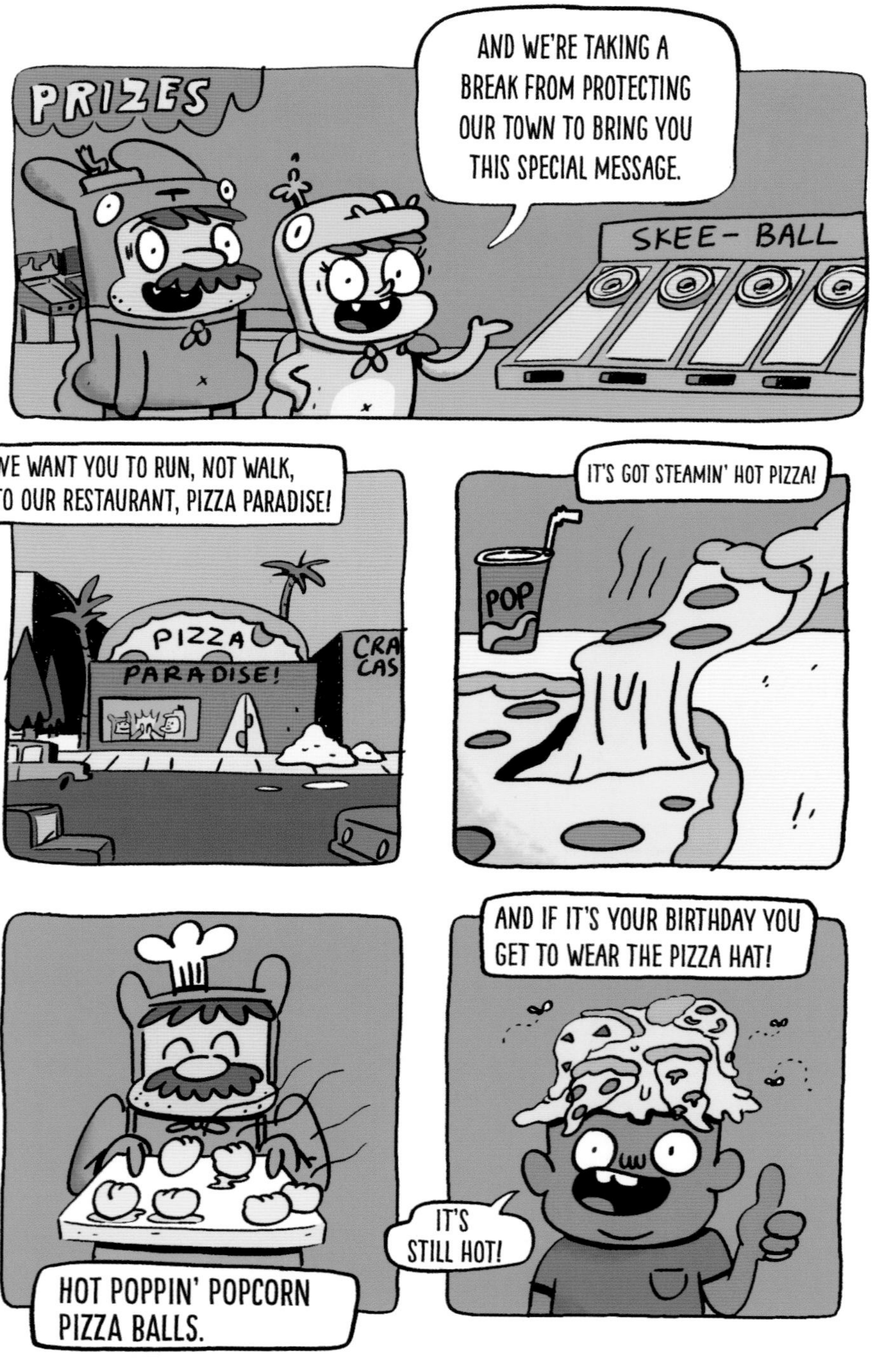
PRIZES
AND WE'RE TAKING A BREAK FROM PROTECTING OUR TOWN TO BRING YOU THIS SPECIAL MESSAGE.
SKEE- BALL
WE WANT YOU TO RUN, NOT WALK, TO OUR RESTAURANT, PIZZA PARADISE!
PIZZA
PARADISE!
IT'S GOT STEAMIN' HOT PIZZA!
POP
HOT POPPIN' POPCORN PIZZA BALLS.
AND IF IT'S YOUR BIRTHDAY YOU GET TO WEAR THE PIZZA HAT!
IT'S STILL HOT!

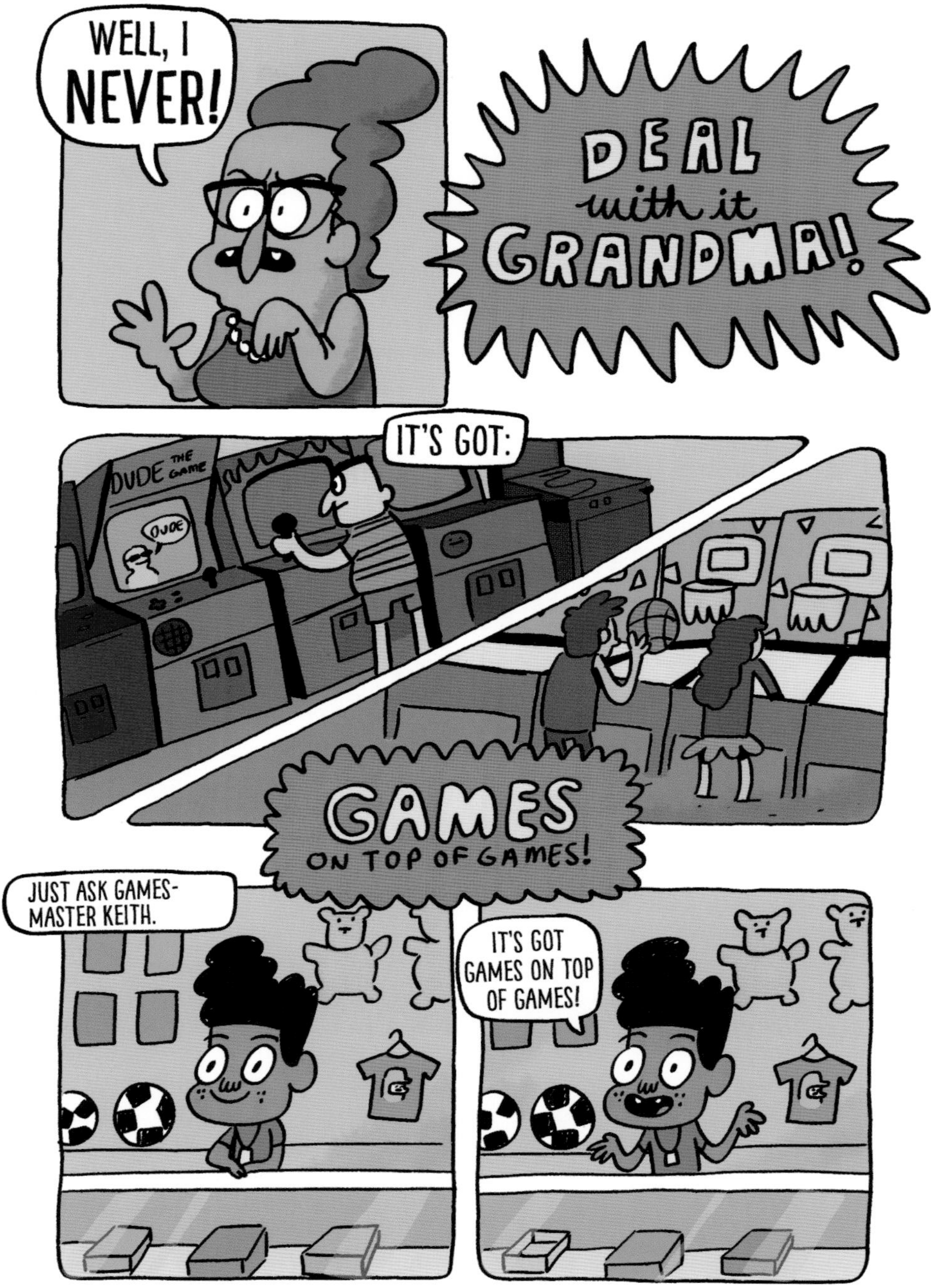
WELL, I NEVER!
DEAL with it GRANDMA!
IT'S GOT:
DUDE THE GAME
DUDE
GAMES ON TOP OF GAMES!
JUST ASK GAMES-MASTER KEITH.
IT'S GOT GAMES ON TOP OF GAMES!

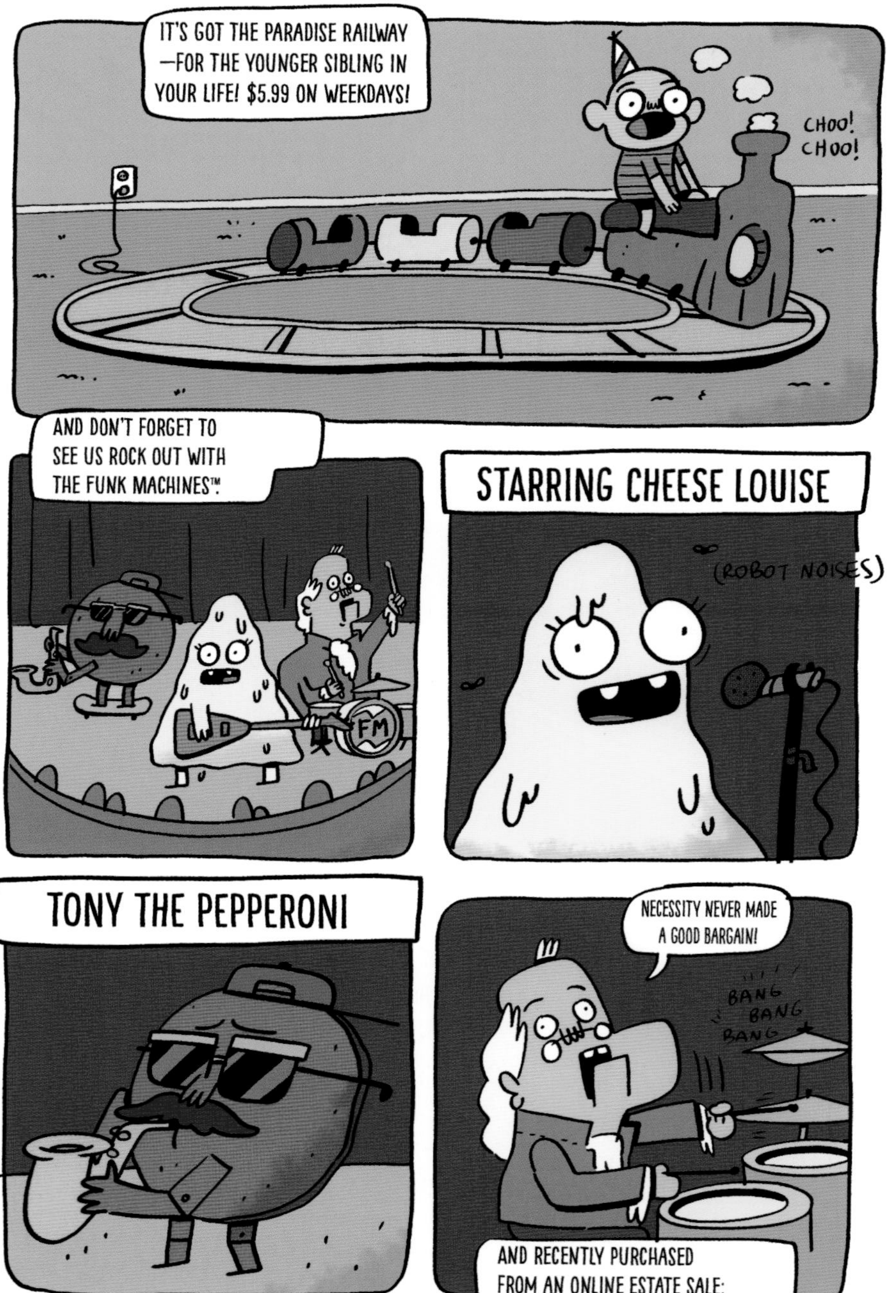
IT'S GOT THE PARADISE RAILWAY —FOR THE YOUNGER SIBLING IN YOUR LIFE! $5.99 ON WEEKDAYS!
CHOO! CHOO!
AND DON'T FORGET TO SEE US ROCK OUT WITH THE FUNK MACHINES™.
FM
STARRING CHEESE LOUISE
(ROBOT NOISES)
TONY THE PEPPERONI
NECESSITY NEVER MADE A GOOD BARGAIN!
BANG BANG BANG
AND RECENTLY PURCHASED FROM AN ONLINE ESTATE SALE:
ANIMATRONIC BEN FRANKLIN!

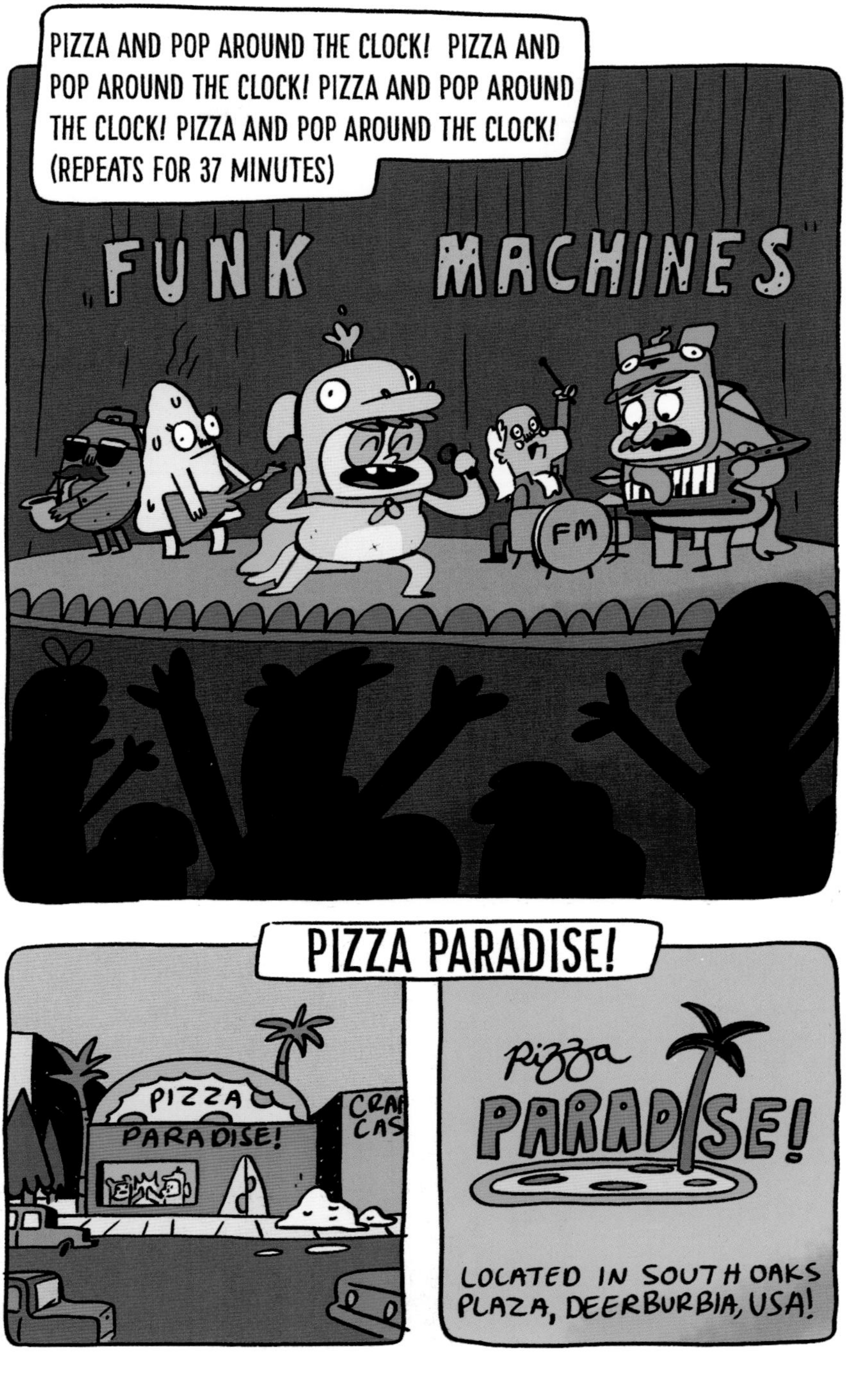
PIZZA AND POP AROUND THE CLOCK! PIZZA AND POP AROUND THE CLOCK! PIZZA AND POP AROUND THE CLOCK! PIZZA AND POP AROUND THE CLOCK! (REPEATS FOR 37 MINUTES)
FUNK MACHINES
FM
PIZZA PARADISE!
PIZZA
PARADISE!
Pizza
PARADISE!
LOCATED IN SOUTH OAKS PLAZA, DEERBURBIA, USA!

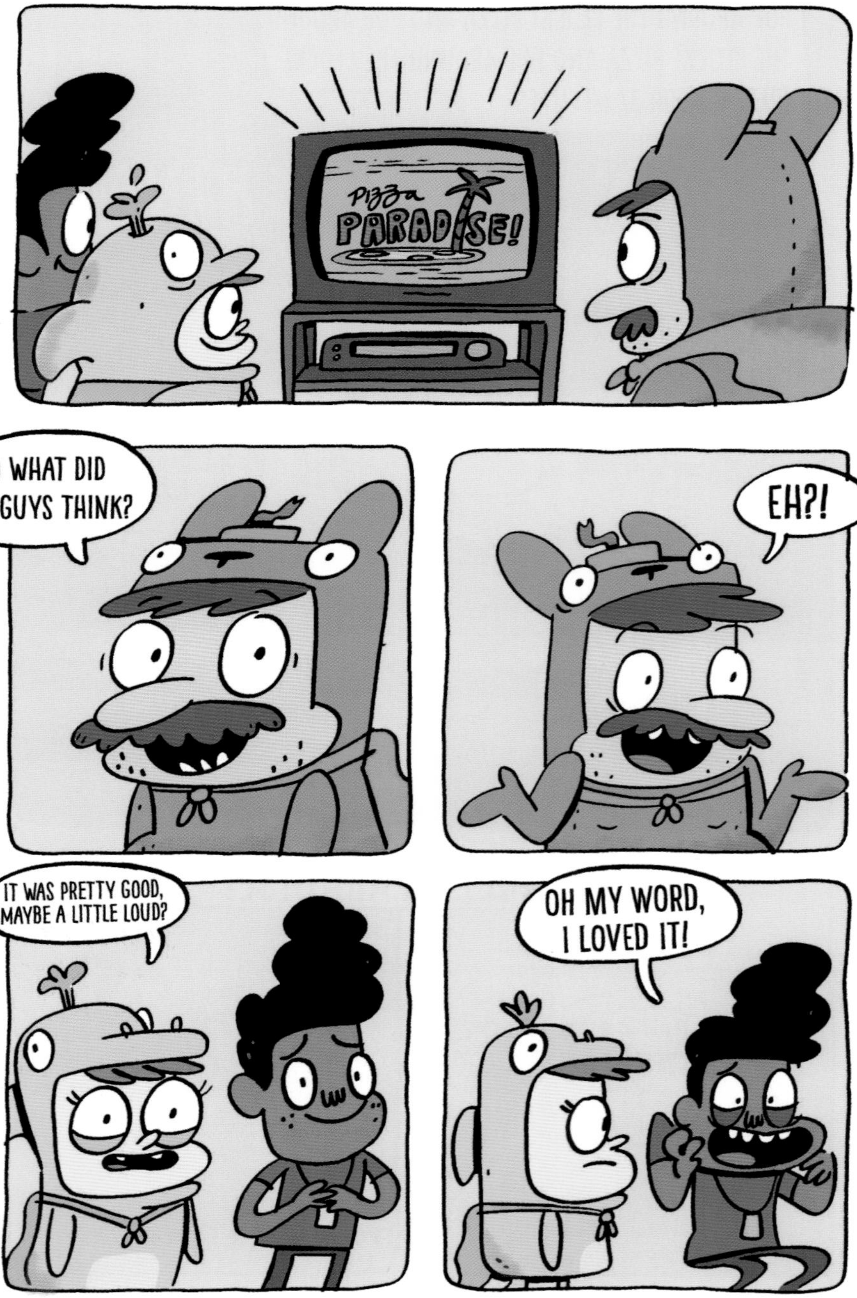
PIZZA PARADISE!
SO WHAT DID YOU GUYS THINK?
EH?!
IT WAS PRETTY GOOD, MAYBE A LITTLE LOUD?
OH MY WORD, I LOVED IT!

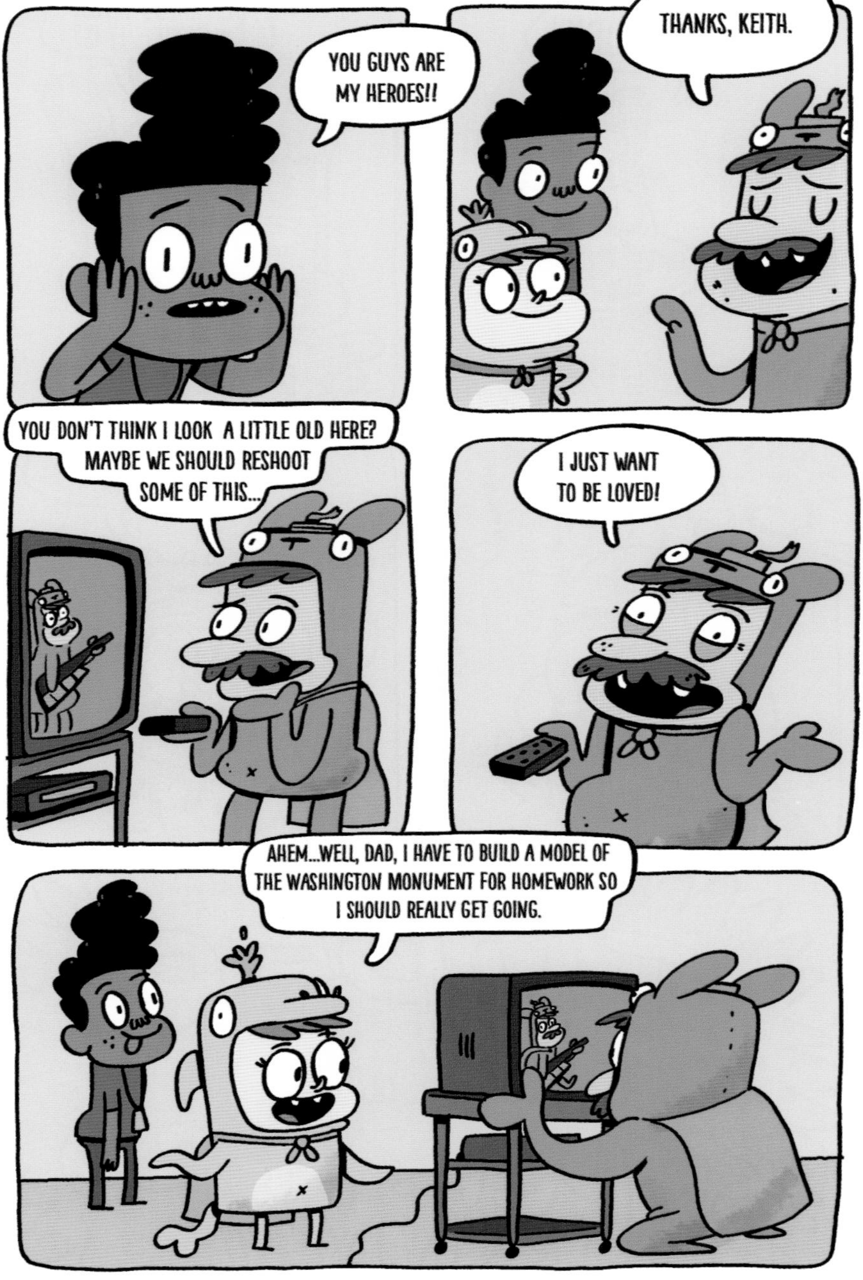
YOU GUYS ARE MY HEROES!!
THANKS, KEITH.
YOU DON'T THINK I LOOK A LITTLE OLD HERE? MAYBE WE SHOULD RESHOOT SOME OF THIS...
I JUST WANT TO BE LOVED!
AHEM...WELL, DAD, I HAVE TO BUILD A MODEL OF THE WASHINGTON MONUMENT FOR HOMEWORK SO I SHOULD REALLY GET GOING.

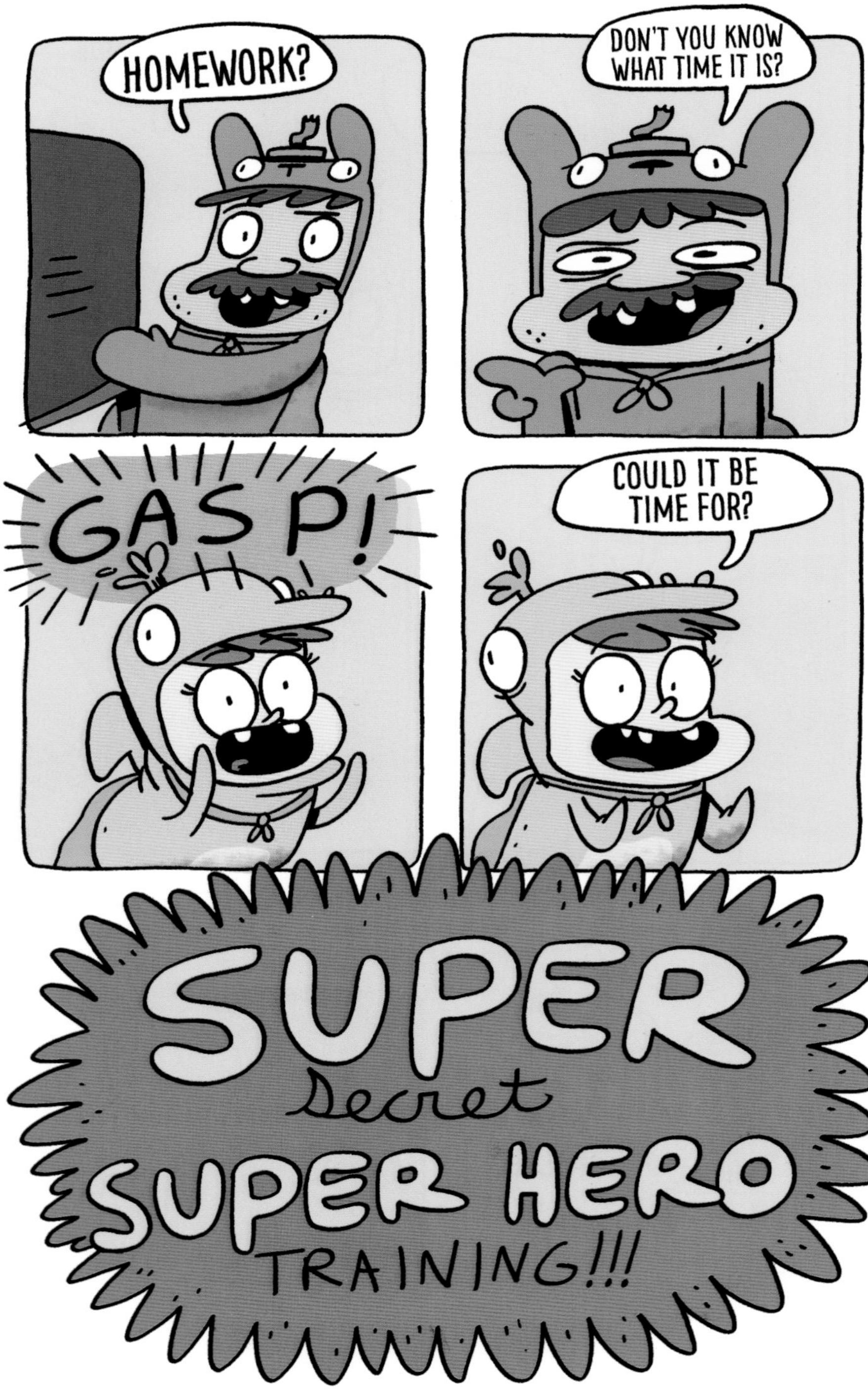
HOMEWORK?
DON'T YOU KNOW WHAT TIME IT IS?
GASP!
COULD IT BE TIME FOR?
SUPER Secret SUPER HERO TRAINING!!!

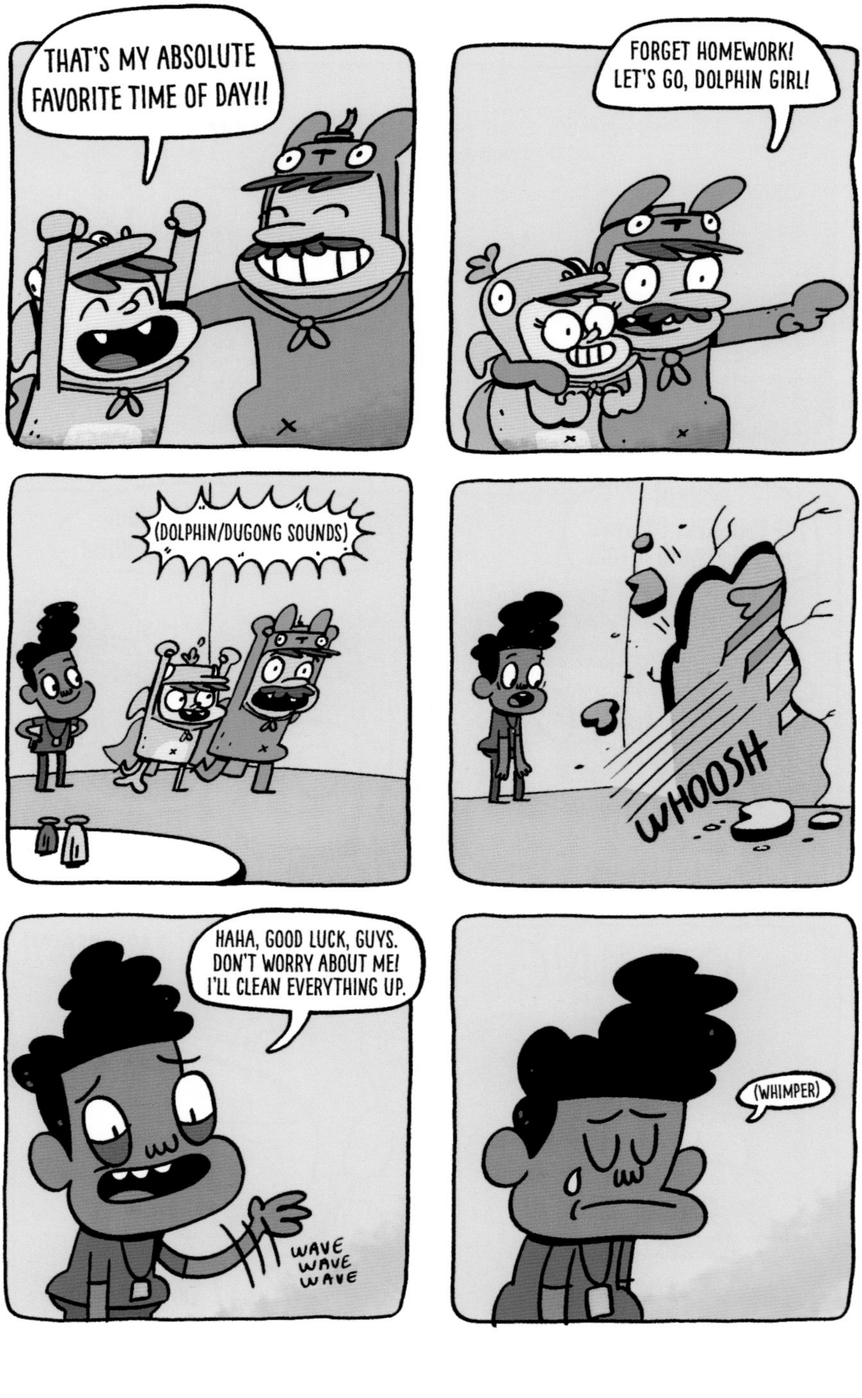
THAT'S MY ABSOLUTE FAVORITE TIME OF DAY!!
FORGET HOMEWORK! LET'S GO, DOLPHIN GIRL!
(DOLPHIN/DUGONG SOUNDS)
WHOOSH
HAHA, GOOD LUCK, GUYS. DON'T WORRY ABOUT ME! I'LL CLEAN EVERYTHING UP.
WAVE WAVE WAVE
(WHIMPER)

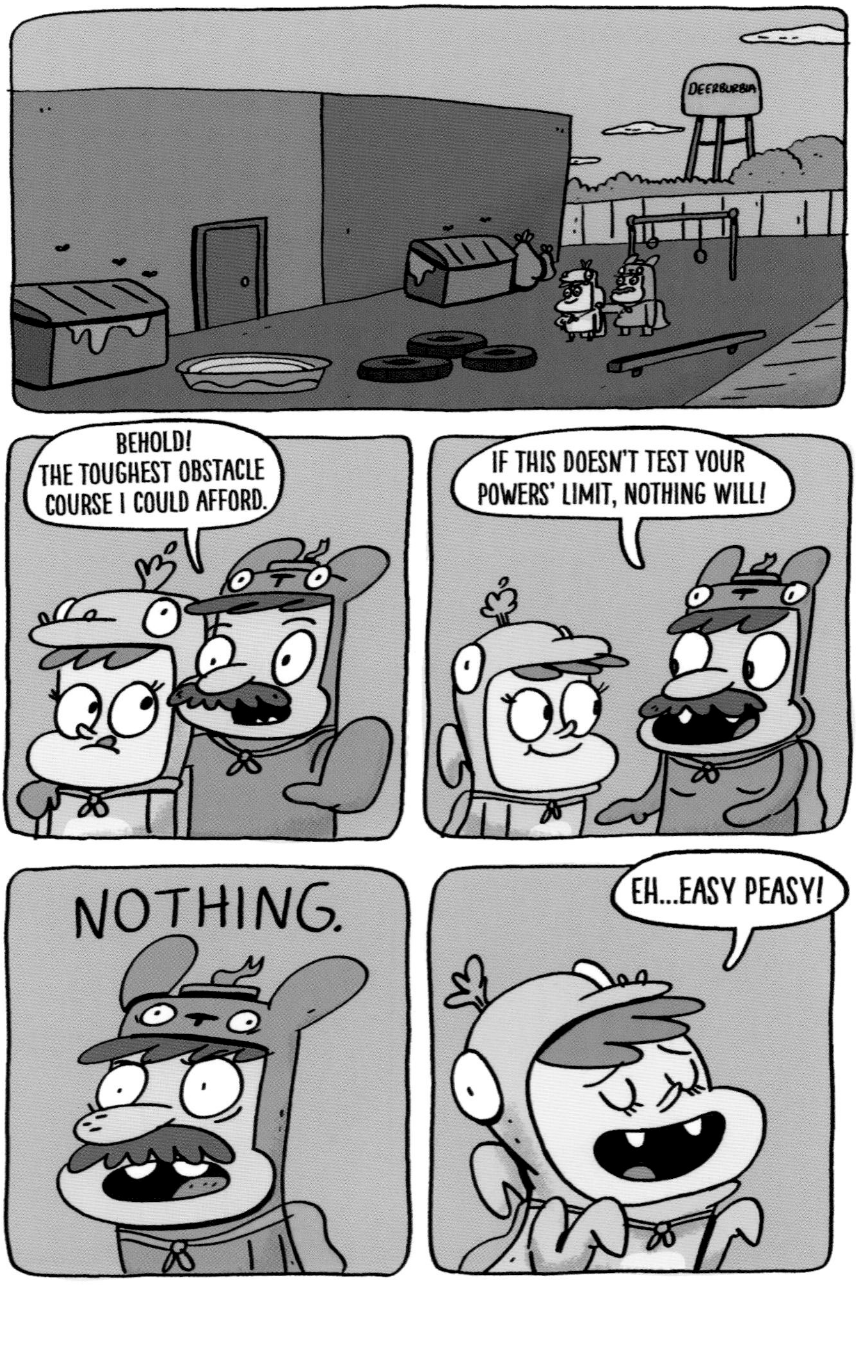

DEERBURBIA
BEHOLD! THE TOUGHEST OBSTACLE COURSE I COULD AFFORD.
IF THIS DOESN'T TEST YOUR POWERS' LIMIT, NOTHING WILL!
NOTHING.
EH...EASY PEASY!

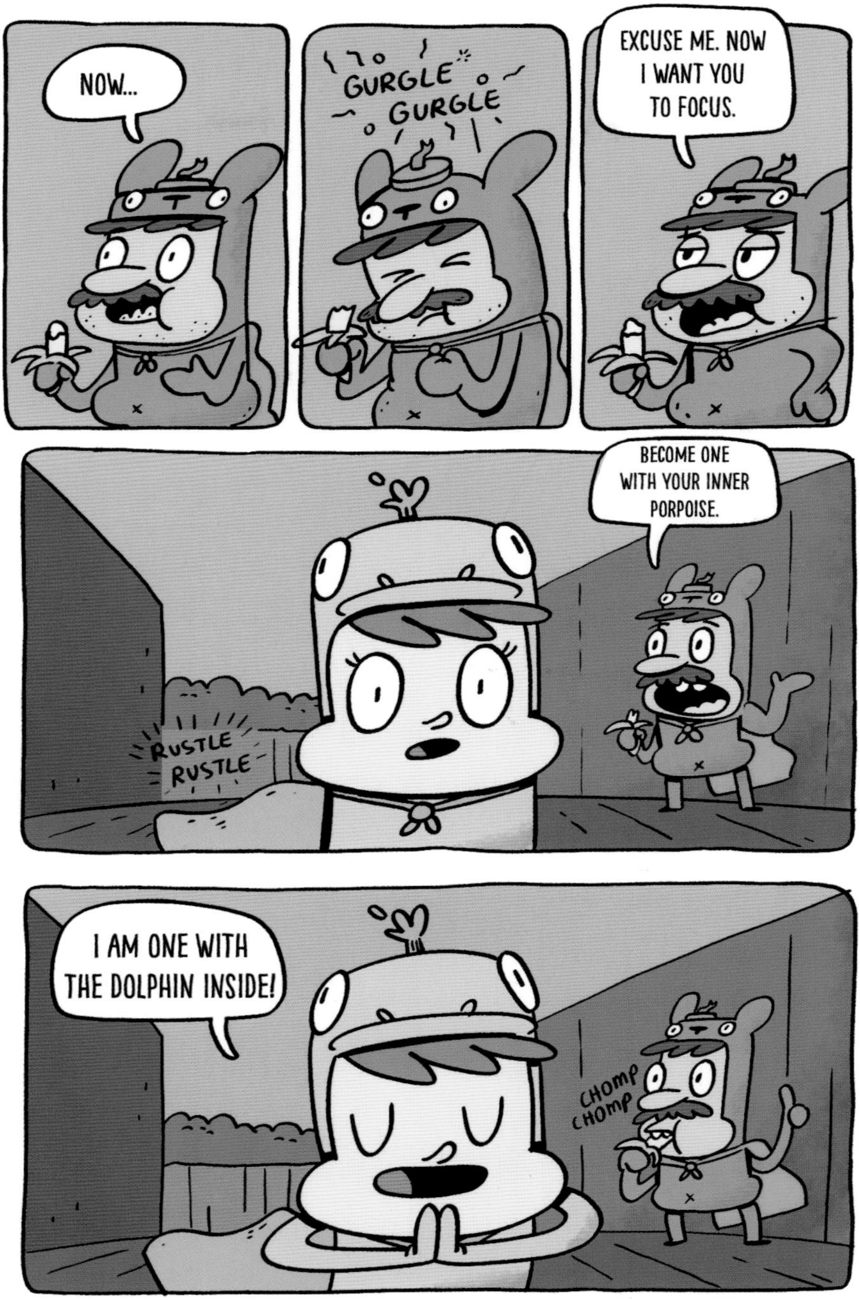
NOW...
GURGLE
GURGLE
EXCUSE ME. NOW I WANT YOU TO FOCUS.
RUSTLE
RUSTLE
BECOME ONE WITH YOUR INNER PORPOISE.
I AM ONE WITH THE DOLPHIN INSIDE!
CHOMP
CHOMP

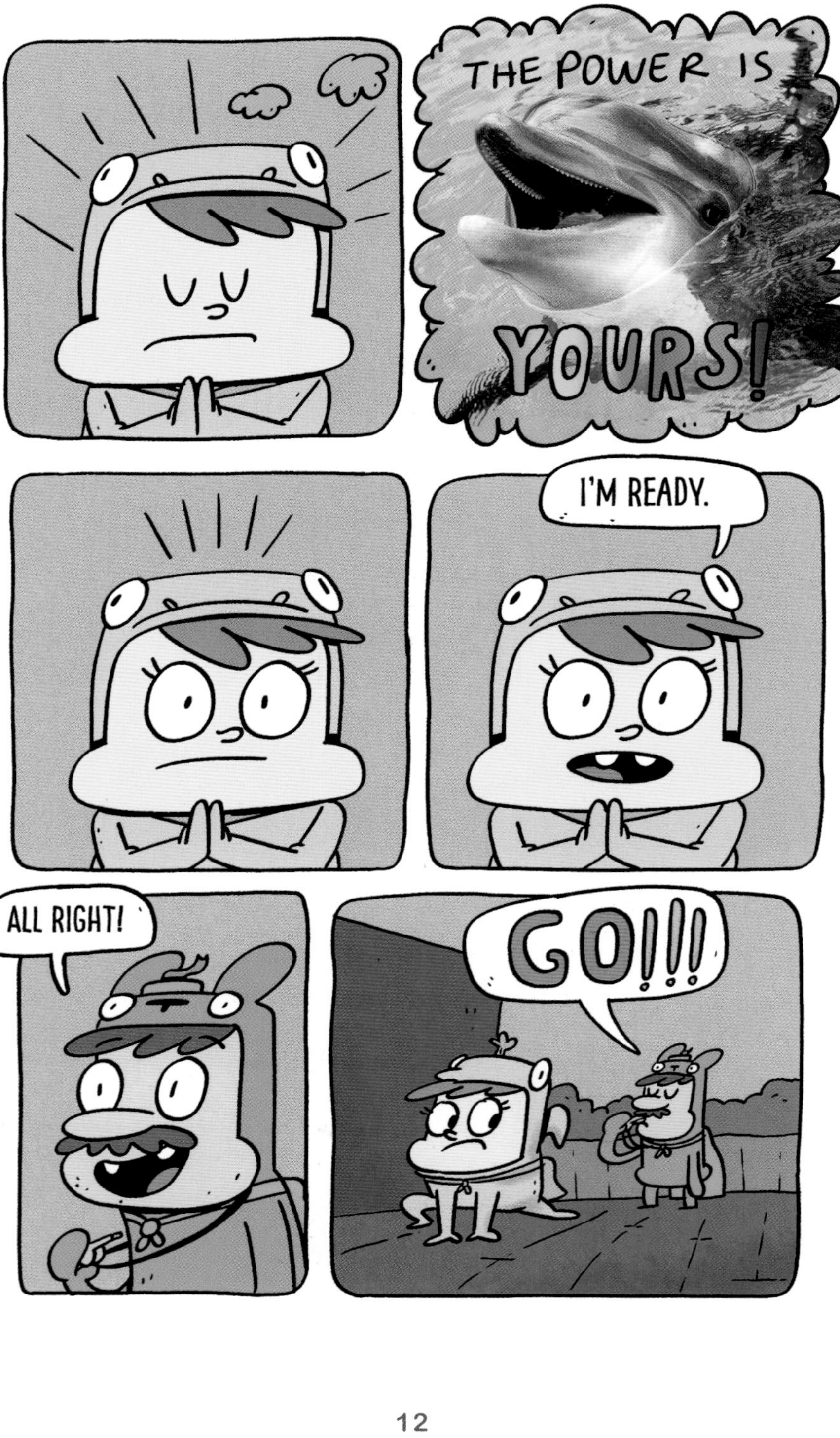
THE POWER IS
YOURS!
I'M READY.
ALL RIGHT!
GO!!!

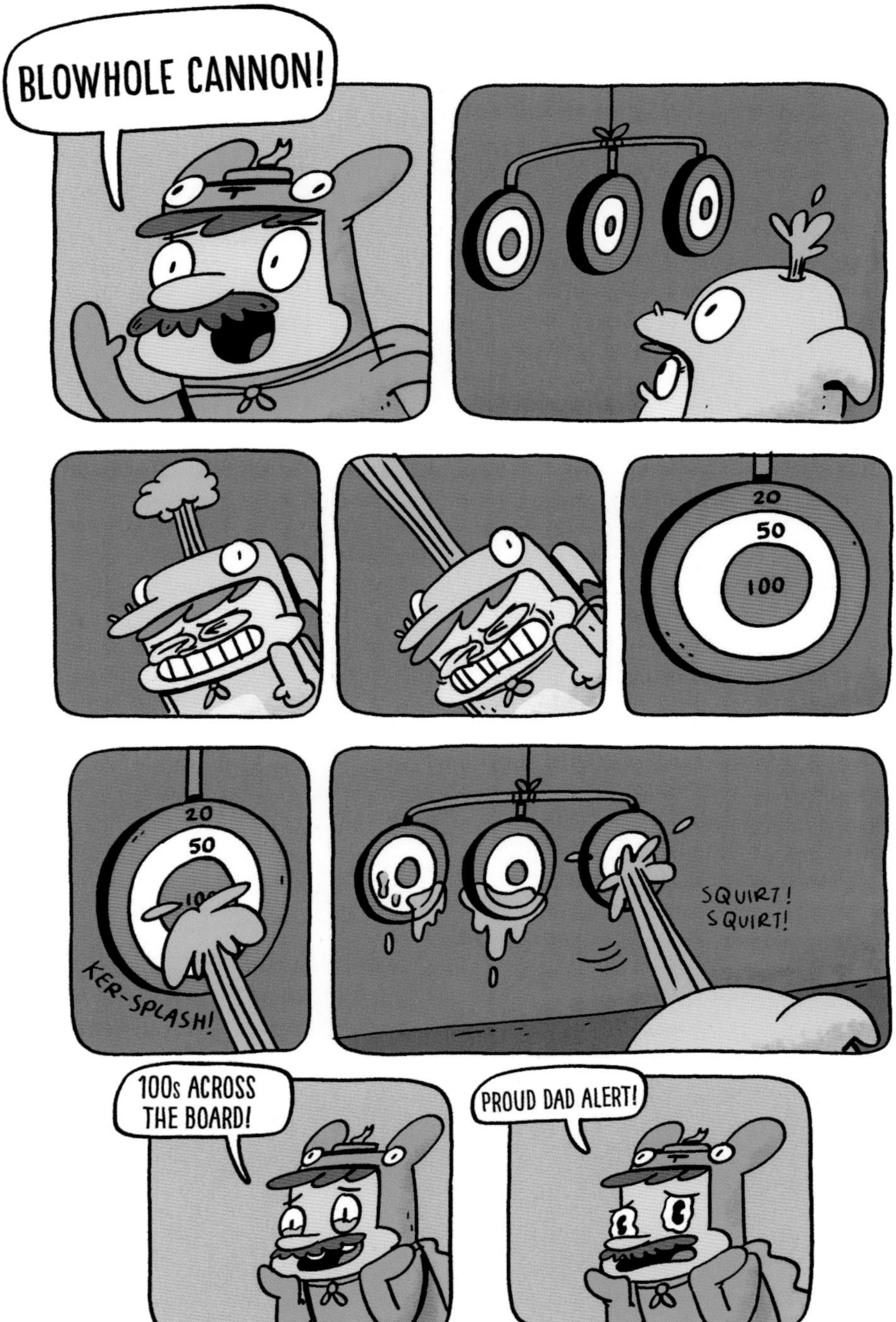
BLOWHOLE CANNON!
20
50
100
20
50
KER-SPLASH!
SQUIRT! SQUIRT!
100s ACROSS THE BOARD!
PROUD DAD ALERT!

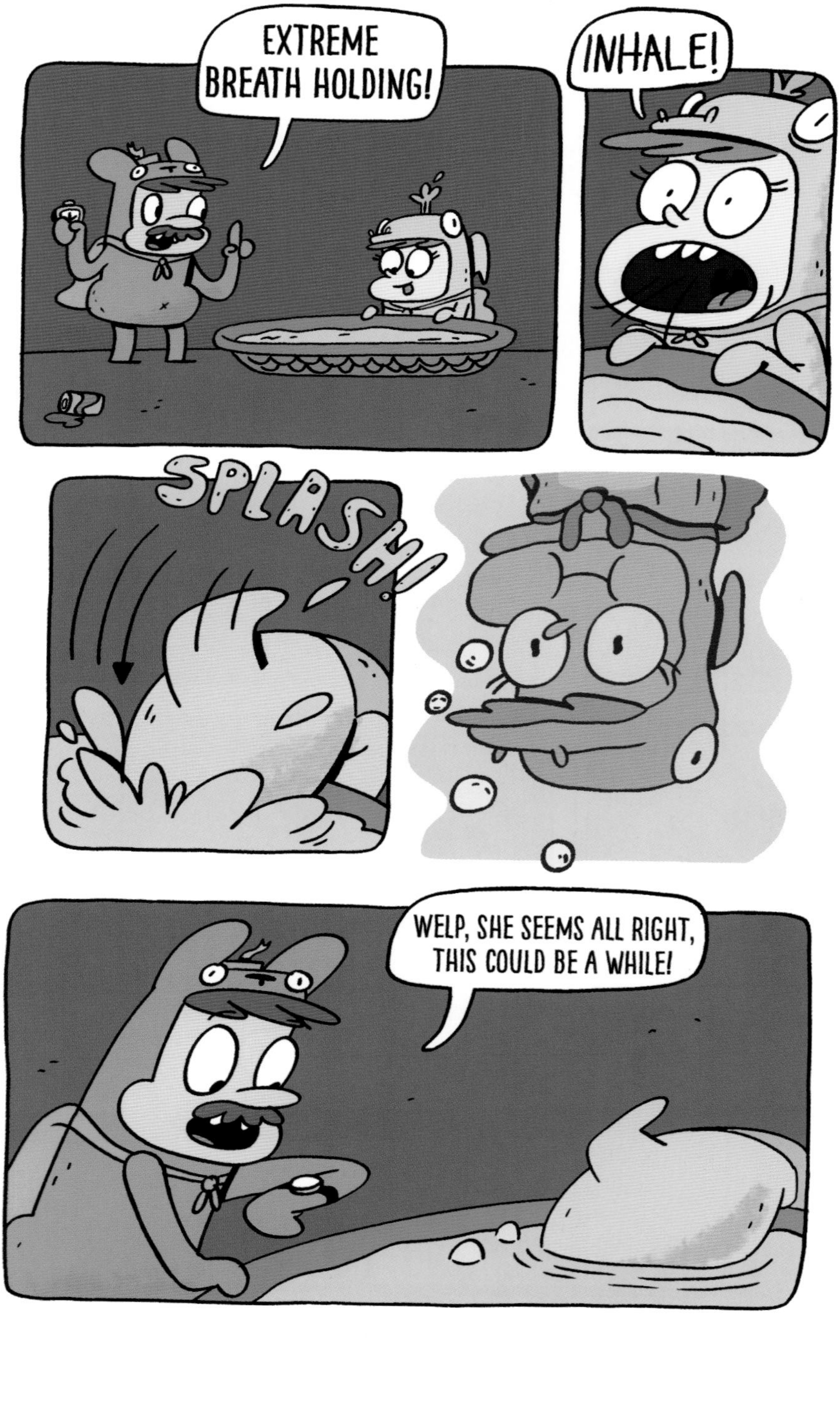
EXTREME BREATH HOLDING!
INHALE!
SPLASH!
WELP, SHE SEEMS ALL RIGHT, THIS COULD BE A WHILE!

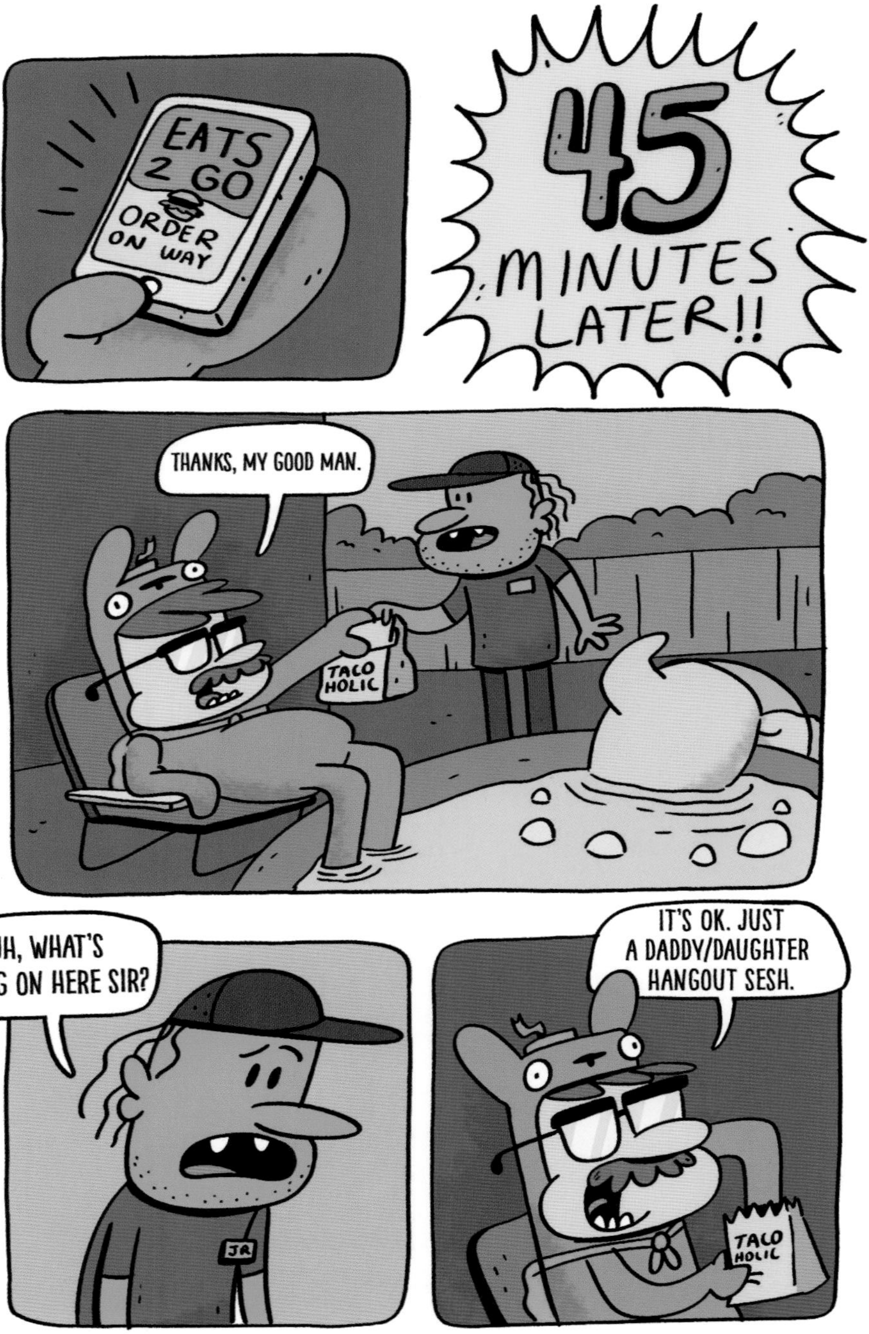
EATS 2 GO
ORDER ON WAY
45 MINUTES LATER!!
THANKS, MY GOOD MAN.
TACO HOLIC
UH, WHAT'S GOING ON HERE SIR?
JR
IT'S OK. JUST A DADDY/DAUGHTER HANGOUT SESH.
TACO HOLIC

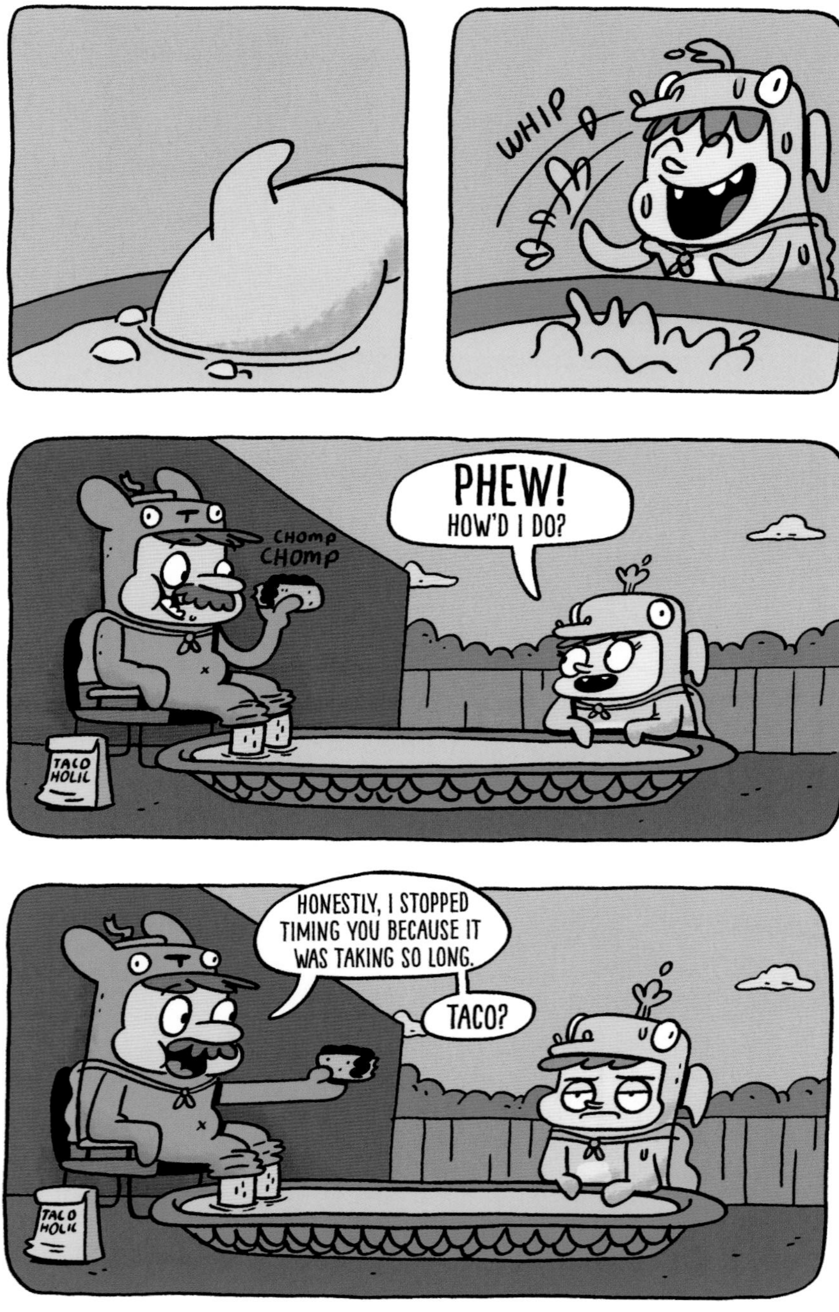
WHIP
PHEW!
HOW'D I DO?
CHOMP
CHOMP
TACO HOLIC
HONESTLY, I STOPPED TIMING YOU BECAUSE IT WAS TAKING SO LONG.
TACO?
TACO HOLIC

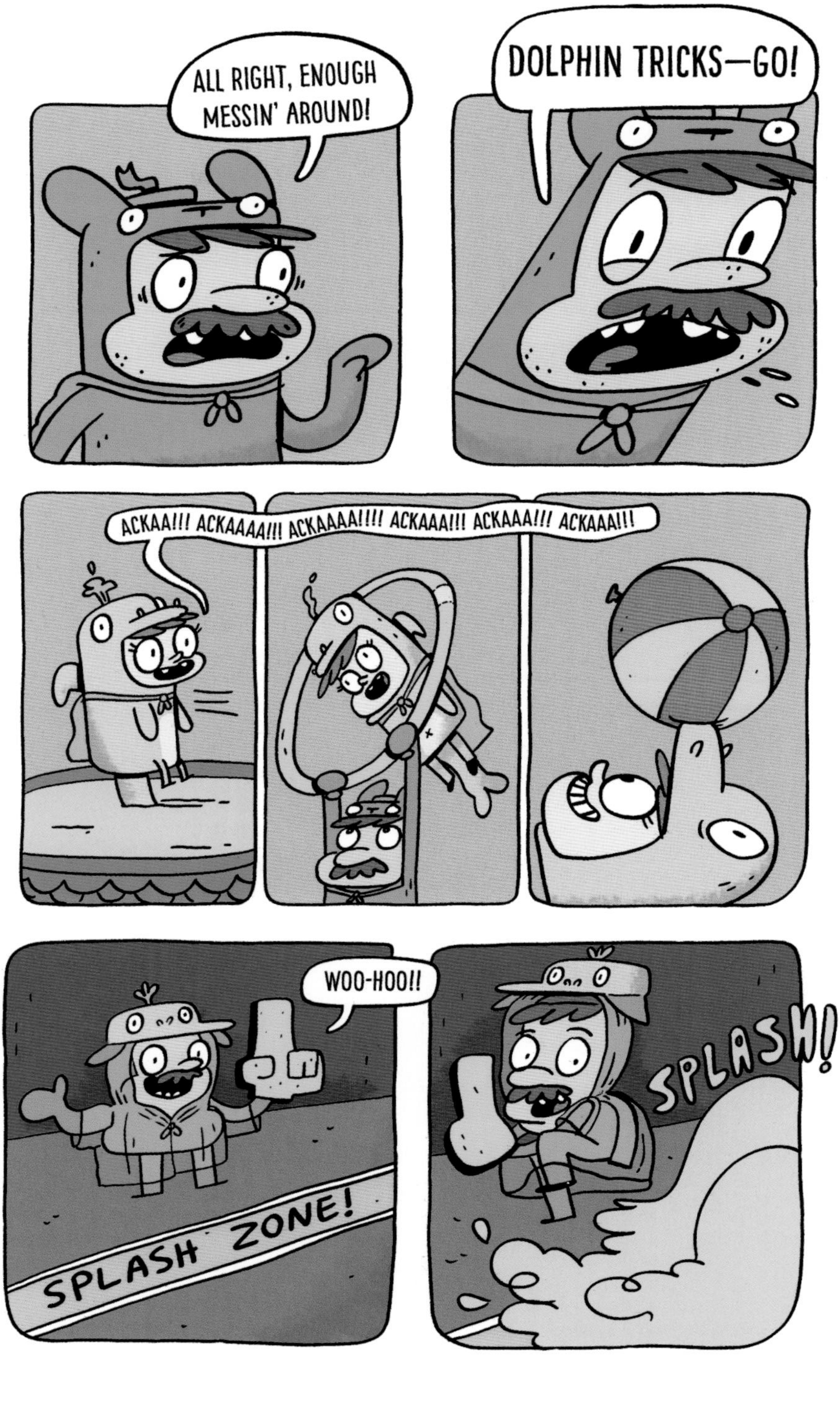
ALL RIGHT, ENOUGH MESSIN' AROUND!
DOLPHIN TRICKS—GO!
ACKAA!!! ACKAAAA!!! ACKAAAA!!!! ACKAAA!!! ACKAAA!!! ACKAAA!!!
WOO-HOO!!
SPLASH ZONE!
SPLASH!

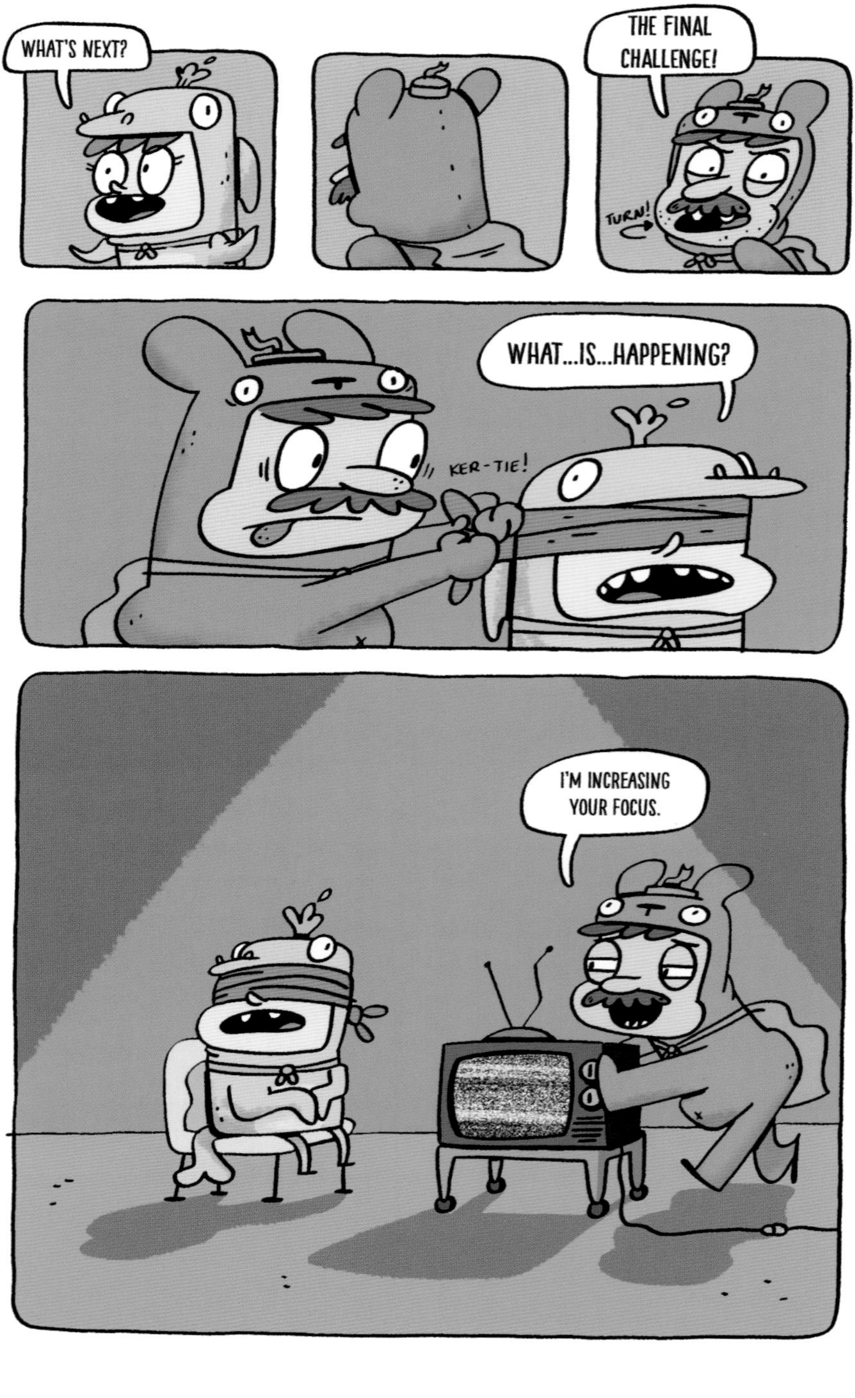
WHAT'S NEXT?
THE FINAL CHALLENGE!
TURN!
WHAT...IS...HAPPENING?
KER-TIE!
I'M INCREASING YOUR FOCUS.

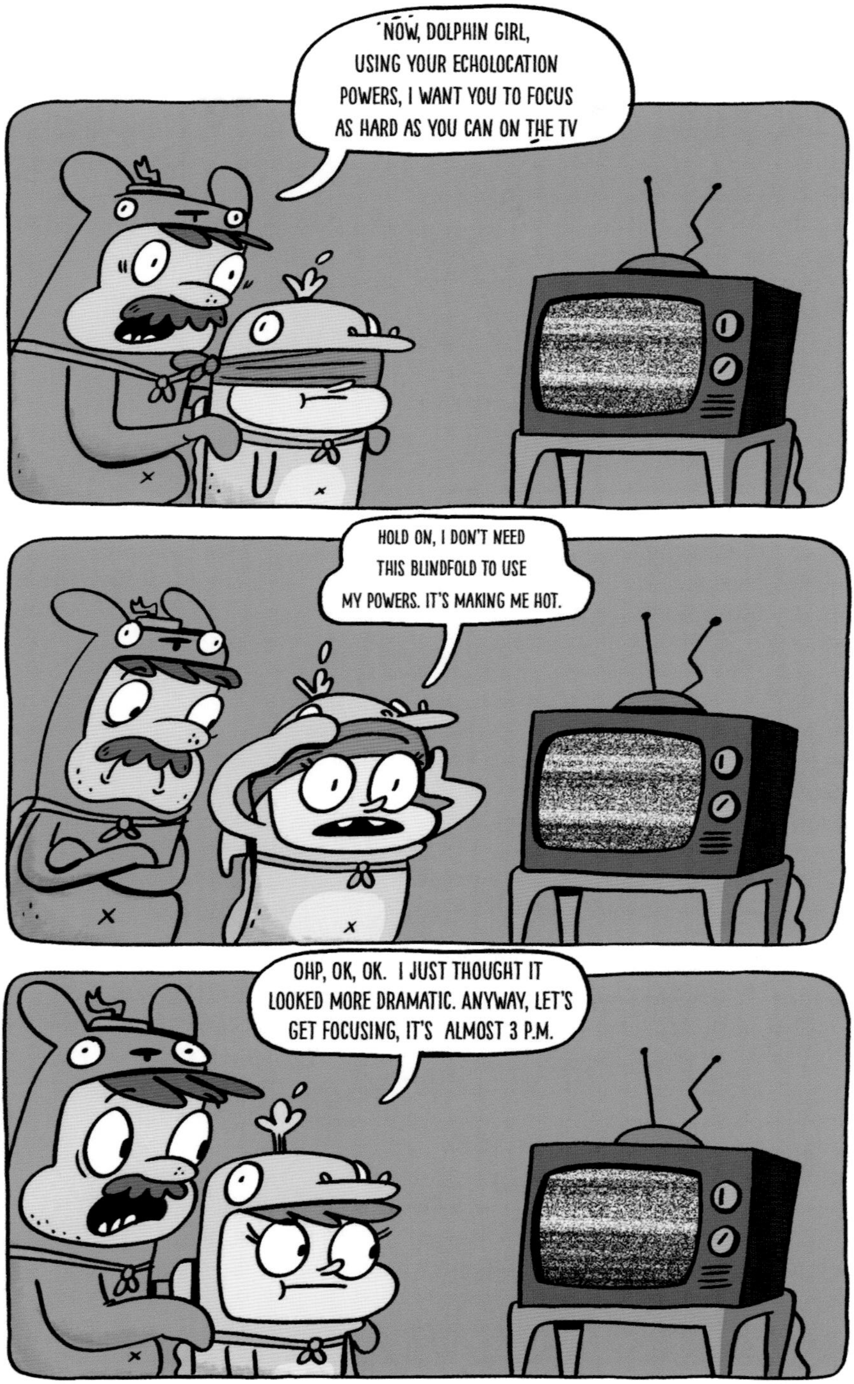
NOW, DOLPHIN GIRL, USING YOUR ECHOLOCATION POWERS, I WANT YOU TO FOCUS AS HARD AS YOU CAN ON THE TV
HOLD ON, I DON'T NEED THIS BLINDFOLD TO USE MY POWERS. IT'S MAKING ME HOT.
OHP, OK, OK. I JUST THOUGHT IT LOOKED MORE DRAMATIC. ANYWAY, LET'S GET FOCUSING, IT'S ALMOST 3 P.M.

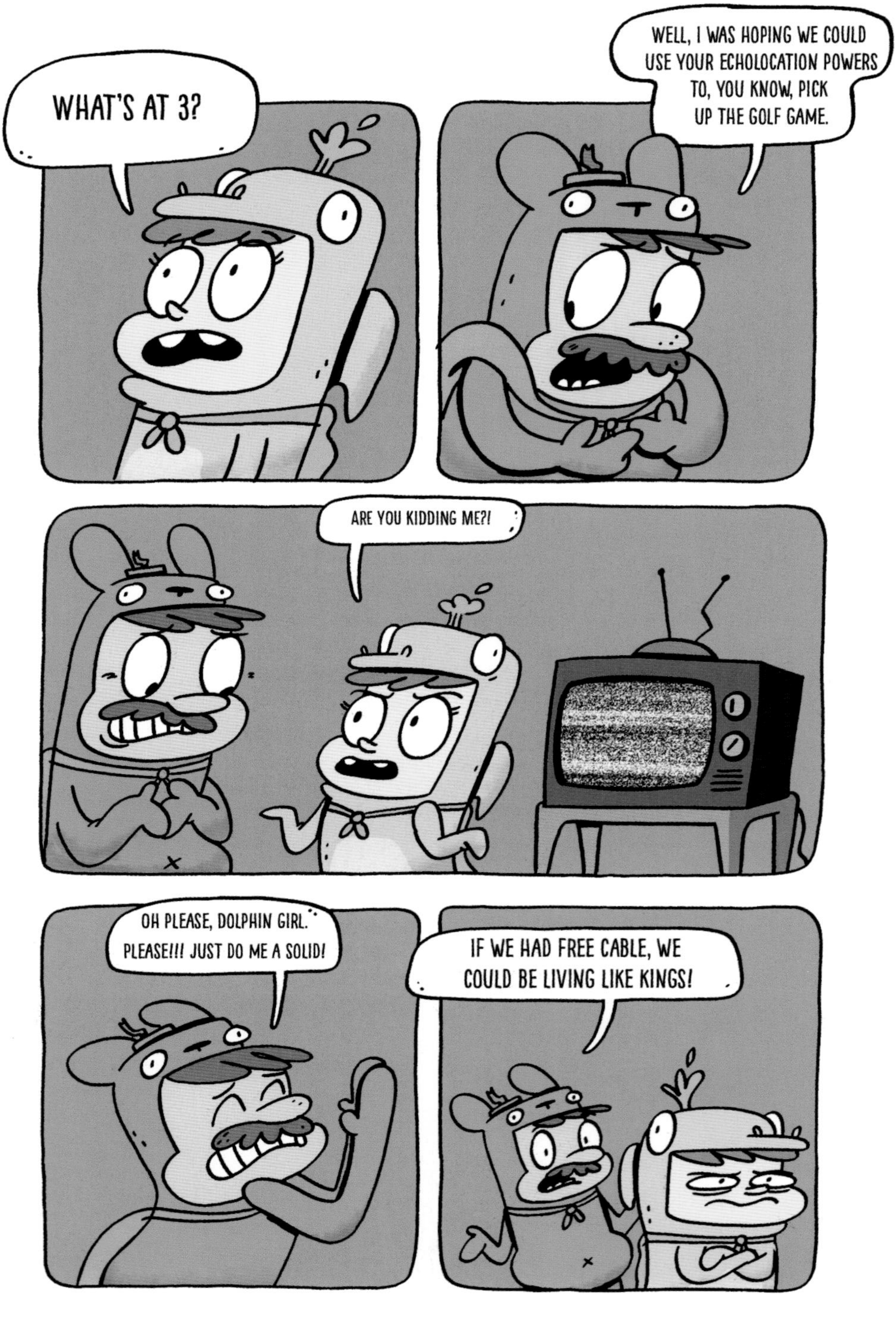
WHAT'S AT 3?
WELL, I WAS HOPING WE COULD USE YOUR ECHOLOCATION POWERS TO, YOU KNOW, PICK UP THE GOLF GAME.
ARE YOU KIDDING ME?!
OH PLEASE, DOLPHIN GIRL. PLEASE!!! JUST DO ME A SOLID!
IF WE HAD FREE CABLE, WE COULD BE LIVING LIKE KINGS!

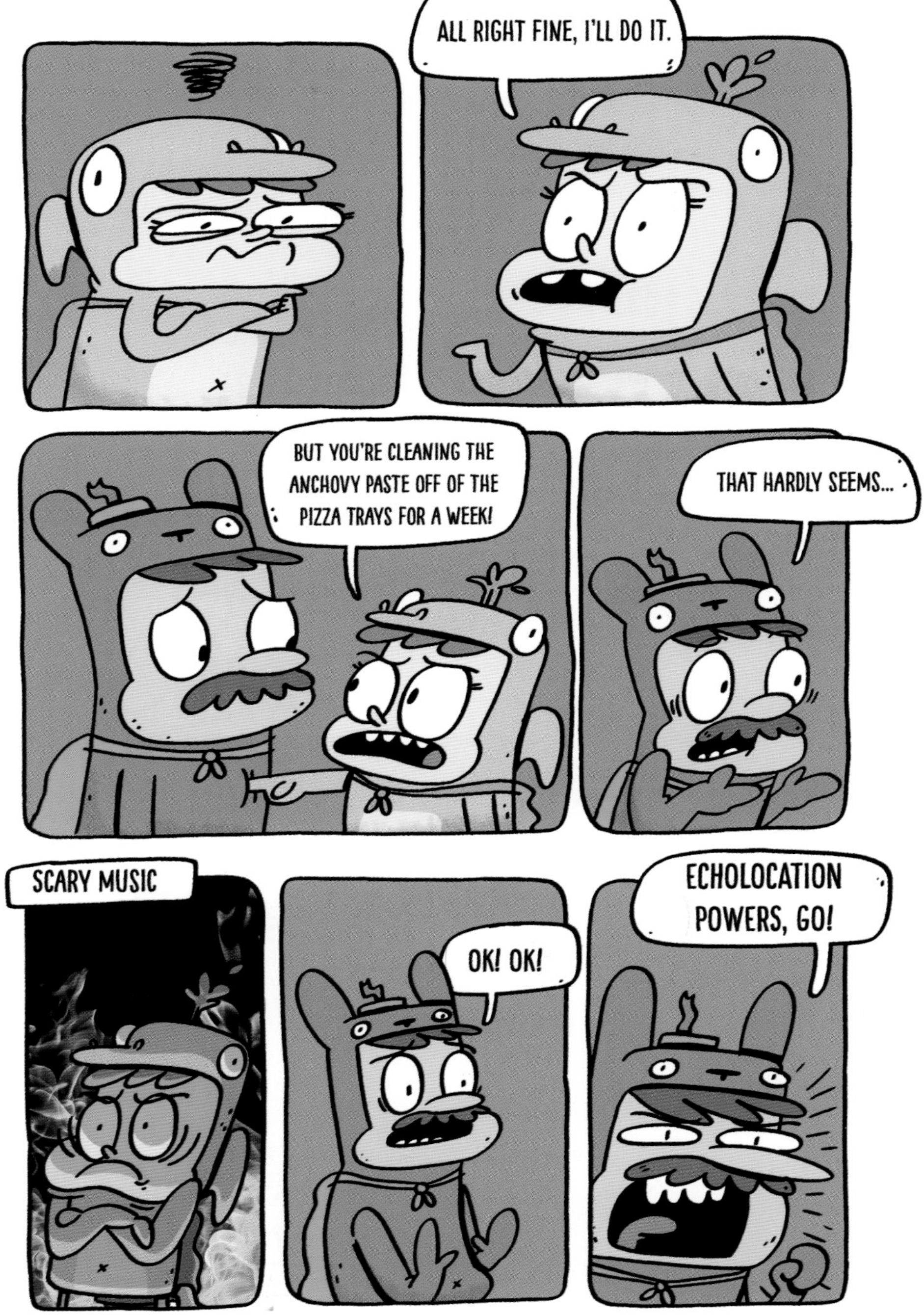
ALL RIGHT FINE, I'LL DO IT.
BUT YOU'RE CLEANING THE ANCHOVY PASTE OFF OF THE PIZZA TRAYS FOR A WEEK!
THAT HARDLY SEEMS...
SCARY MUSIC
OK! OK!
ECHOLOCATION POWERS, GO!

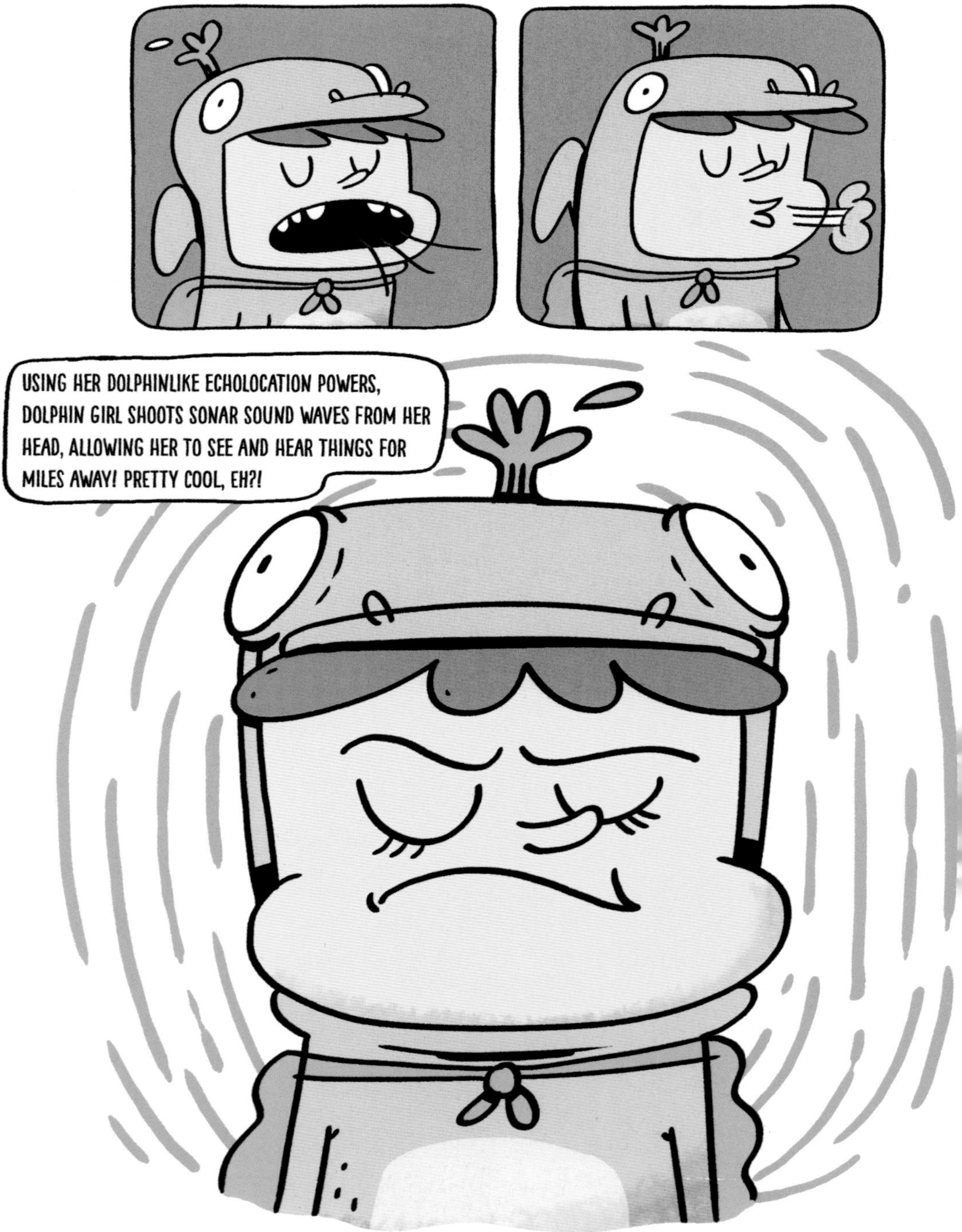
USING HER DOLPHINLIKE ECHOLOCATION POWERS, DOLPHIN GIRL SHOOTS SONAR SOUND WAVES FROM HER HEAD, ALLOWING HER TO SEE AND HEAR THINGS FOR MILES AWAY! PRETTY COOL, EH?!

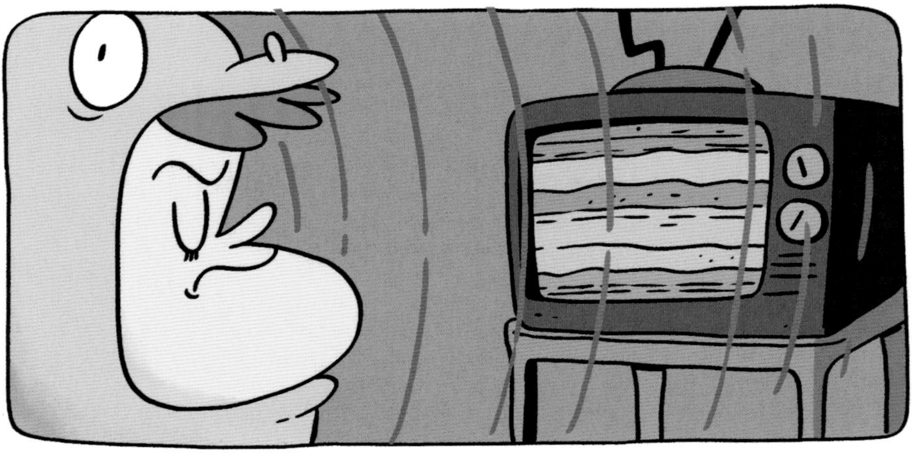

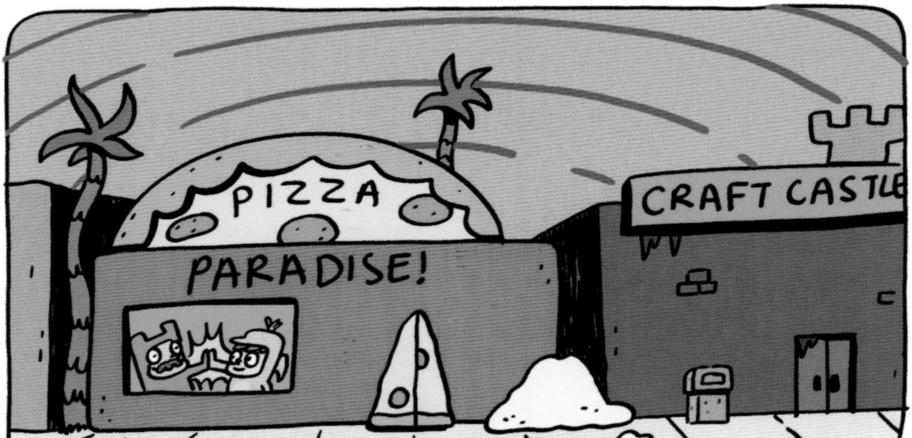
PIZZA
PARADISE!
CRAFT CASTLE

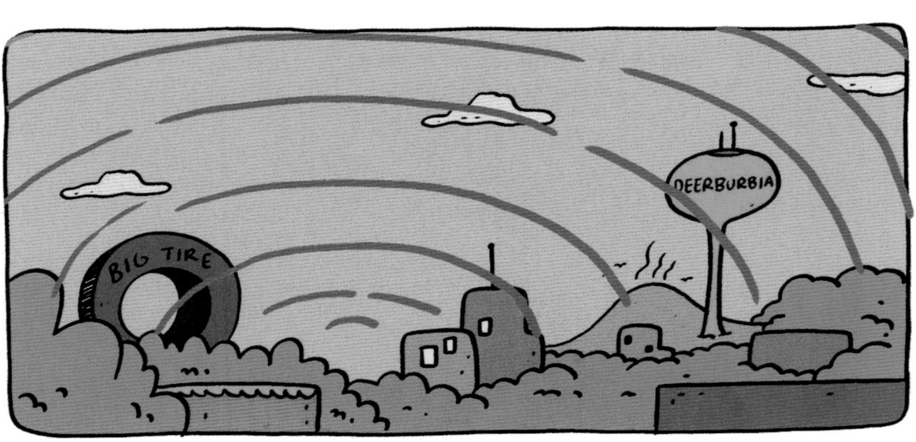
BIG TIRE
DEERBURBIA

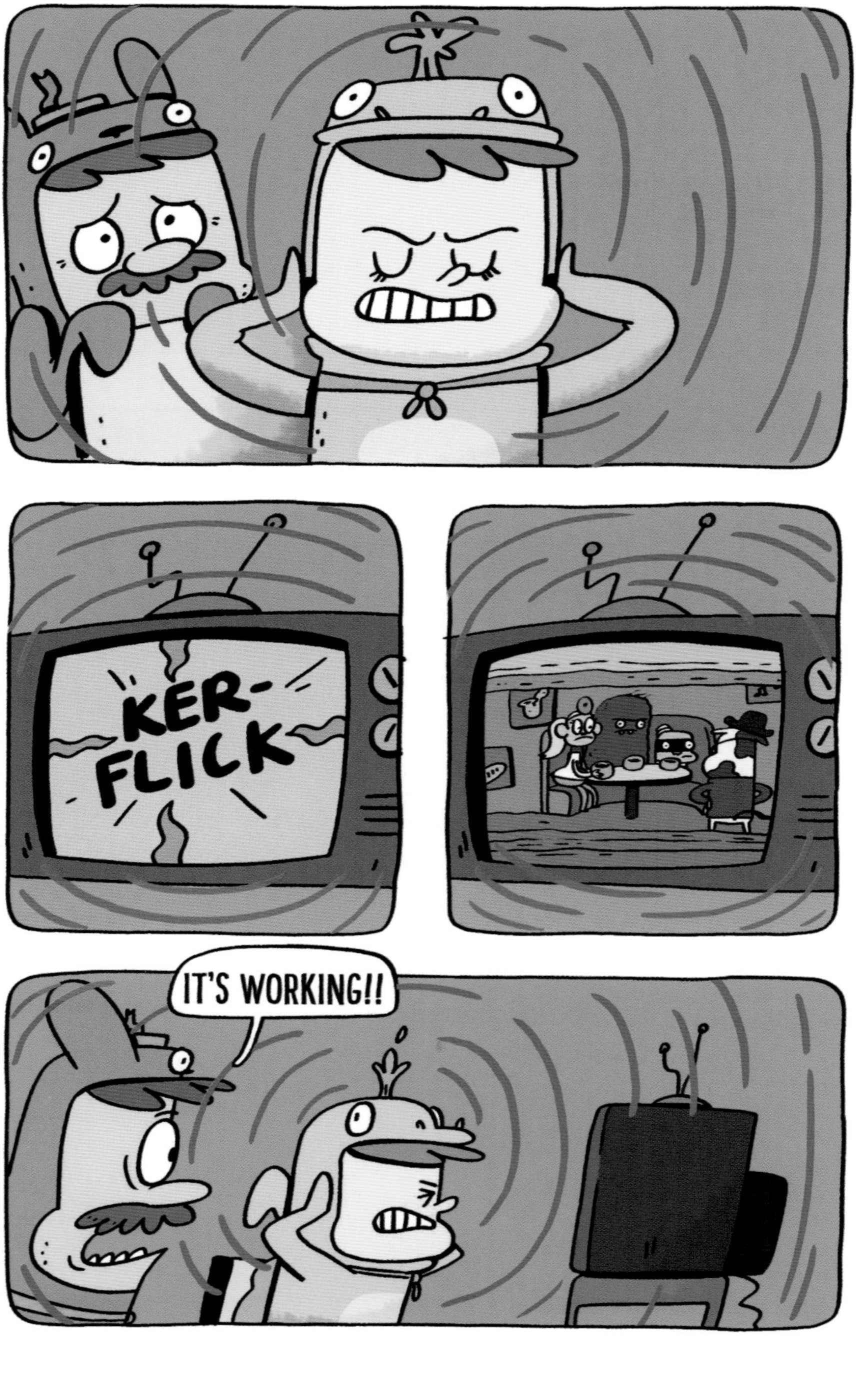
KER-
FLICK
IT'S WORKING!!

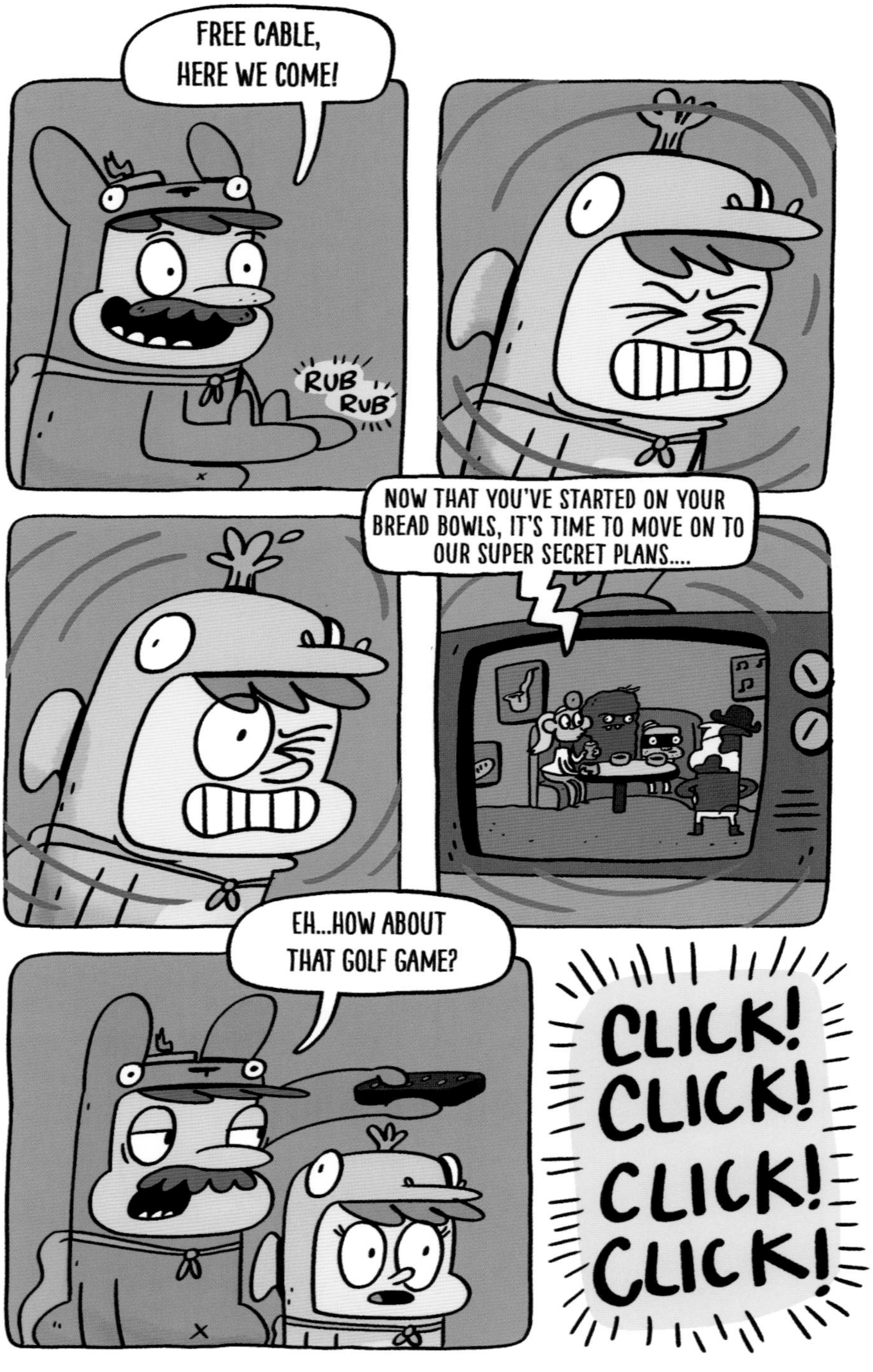
FREE CABLE, HERE WE COME!
RUB RUB
NOW THAT YOU'VE STARTED ON YOUR BREAD BOWLS, IT'S TIME TO MOVE ON TO OUR SUPER SECRET PLANS....
EH...HOW ABOUT THAT GOLF GAME?
CLICK! CLICK! CLICK! CLICK!

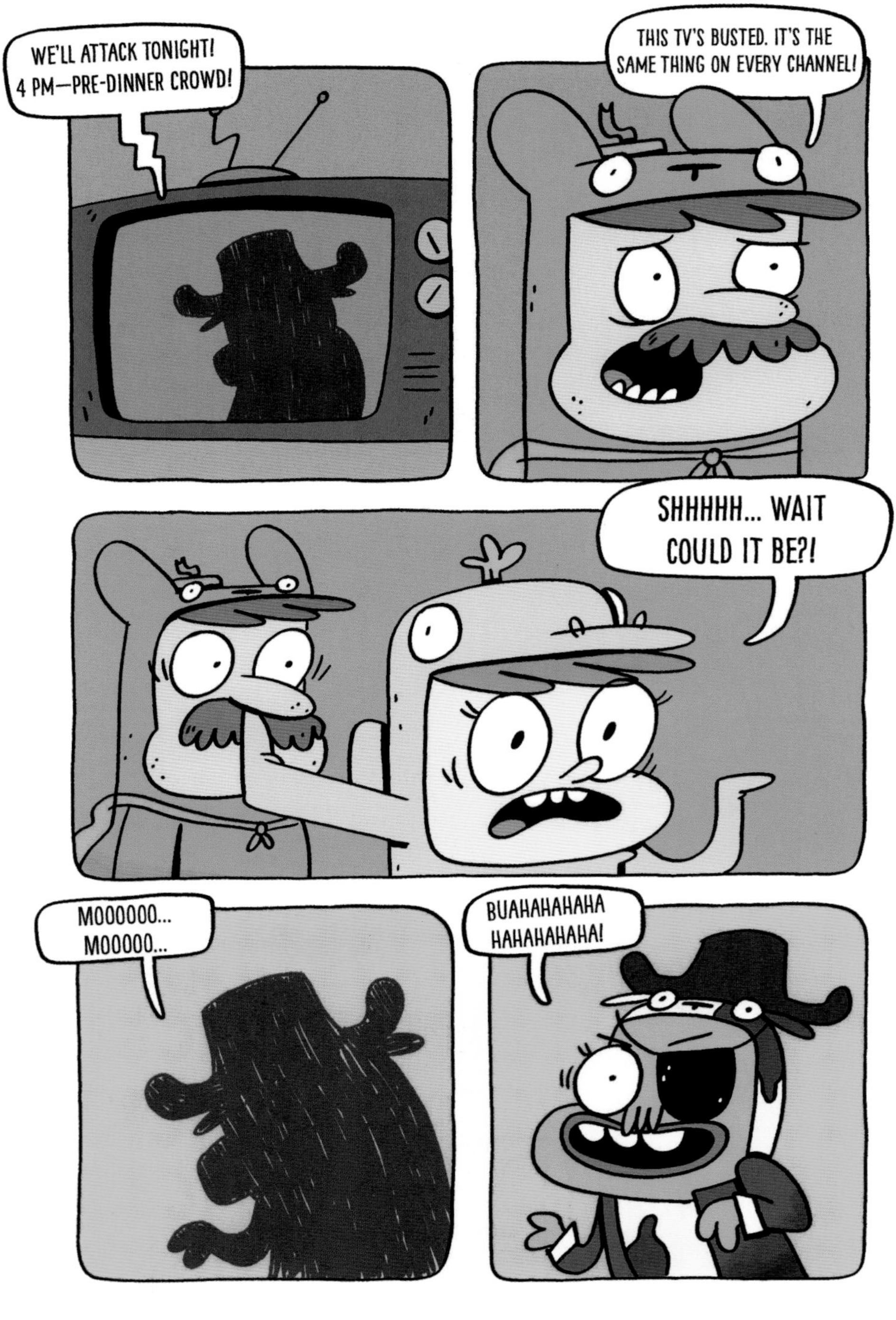
WE'LL ATTACK TONIGHT! 4 PM—PRE-DINNER CROWD!
THIS TV'S BUSTED. IT'S THE SAME THING ON EVERY CHANNEL!
SHHHHH... WAIT COULD IT BE?!
MOOOOOO... MOOOOO...
BUAHAHAHAHA HAHAHAHAHA!

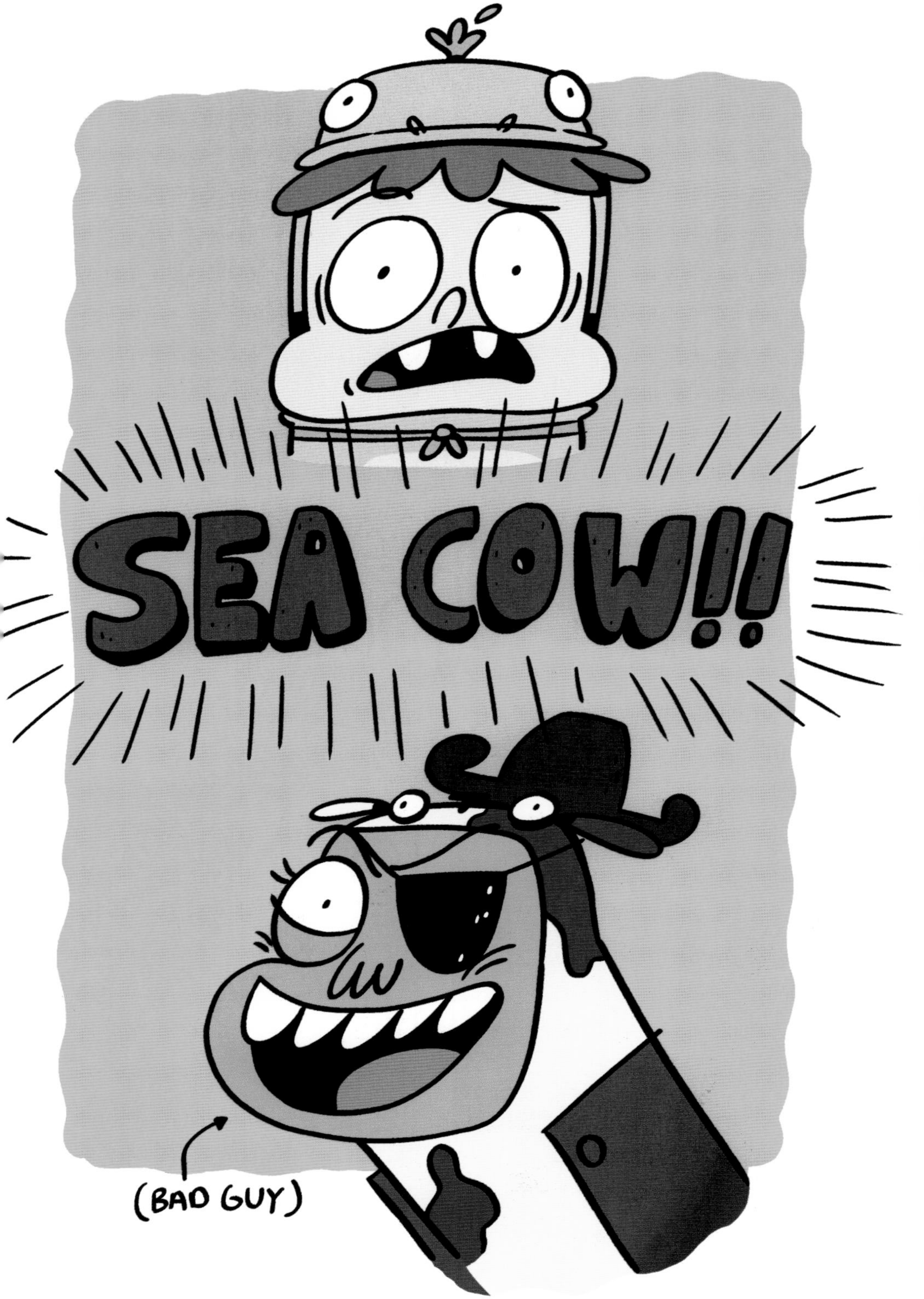
SEA COW!!
(BAD GUY)

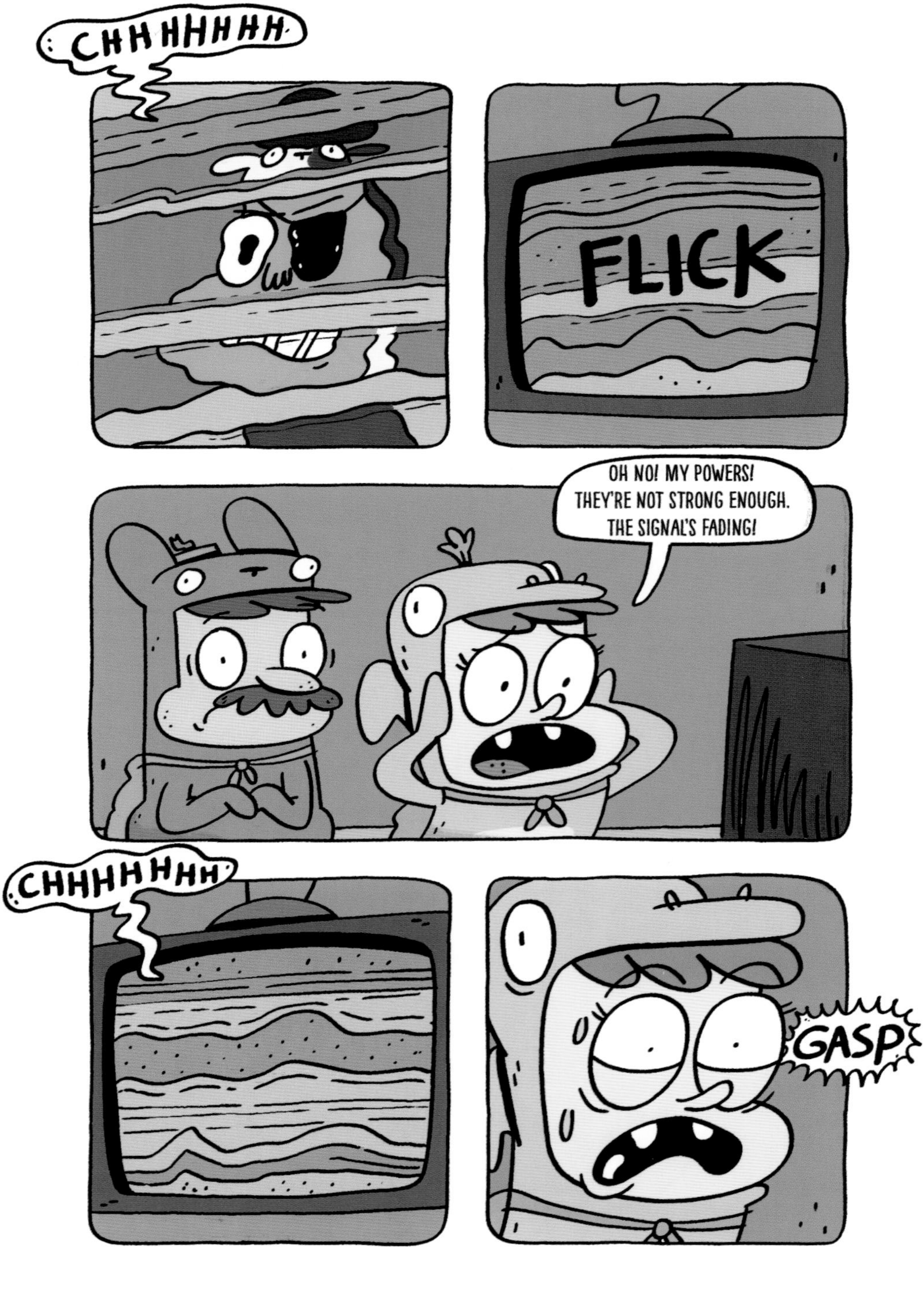
CHHHHHHH
FLICK
OH NO! MY POWERS! THEY'RE NOT STRONG ENOUGH. THE SIGNAL'S FADING!
CHHHHHHH
GASP

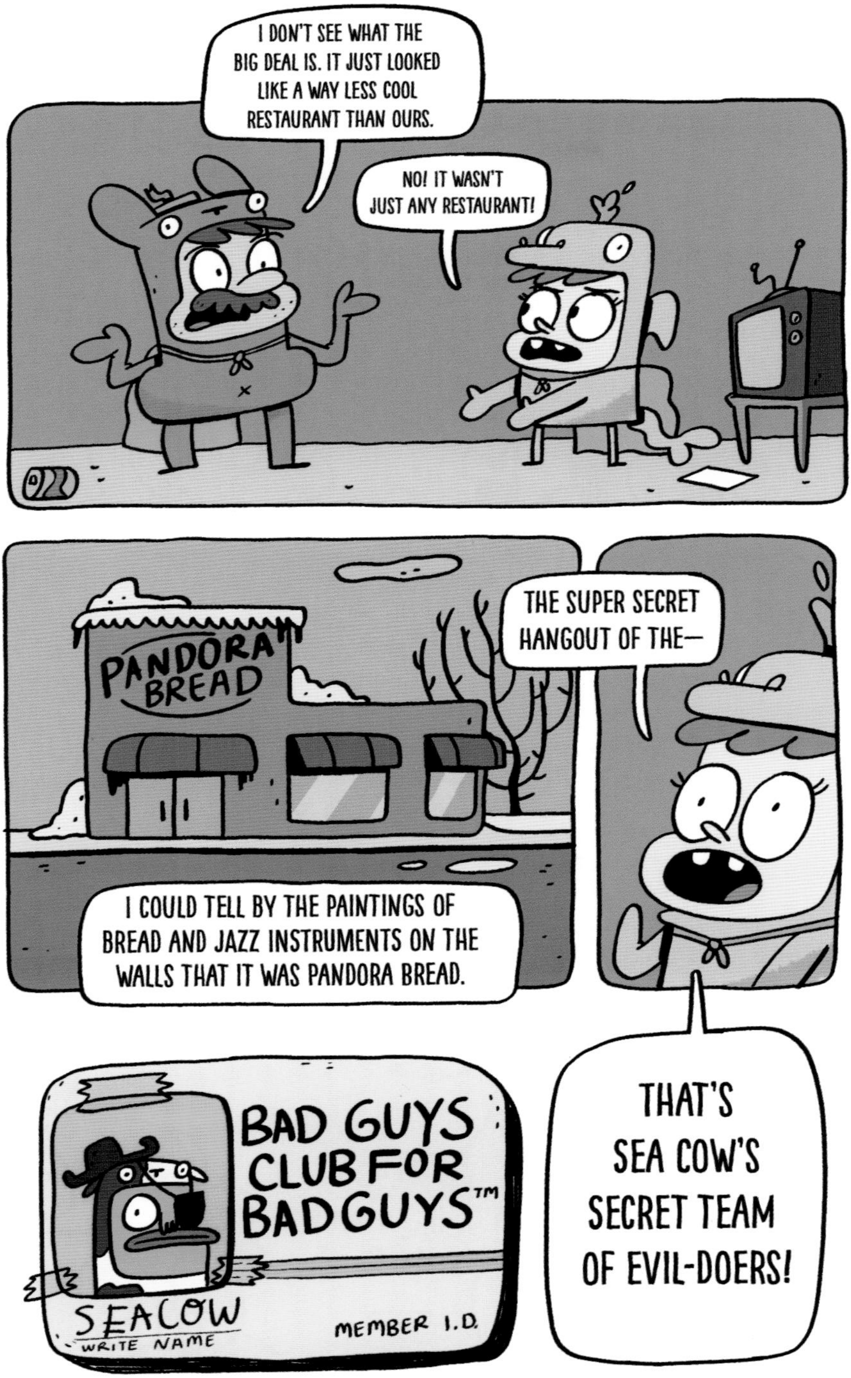
I DON'T SEE WHAT THE BIG DEAL IS. IT JUST LOOKED LIKE A WAY LESS COOL RESTAURANT THAN OURS.
NO! IT WASN'T JUST ANY RESTAURANT!
PANDORA BREAD
I COULD TELL BY THE PAINTINGS OF BREAD AND JAZZ INSTRUMENTS ON THE WALLS THAT IT WAS PANDORA BREAD.
THE SUPER SECRET HANGOUT OF THE—
BAD GUYS CLUB FOR BADGUYS™
SEACOW
WRITE NAME
MEMBER I.D.
THAT'S SEA COW'S SECRET TEAM OF EVIL-DOERS!

MEMBERS OF THE BAD GUYS CLUB FOR BAD GUYS™ OR T.B.G.C.F.B.G.™

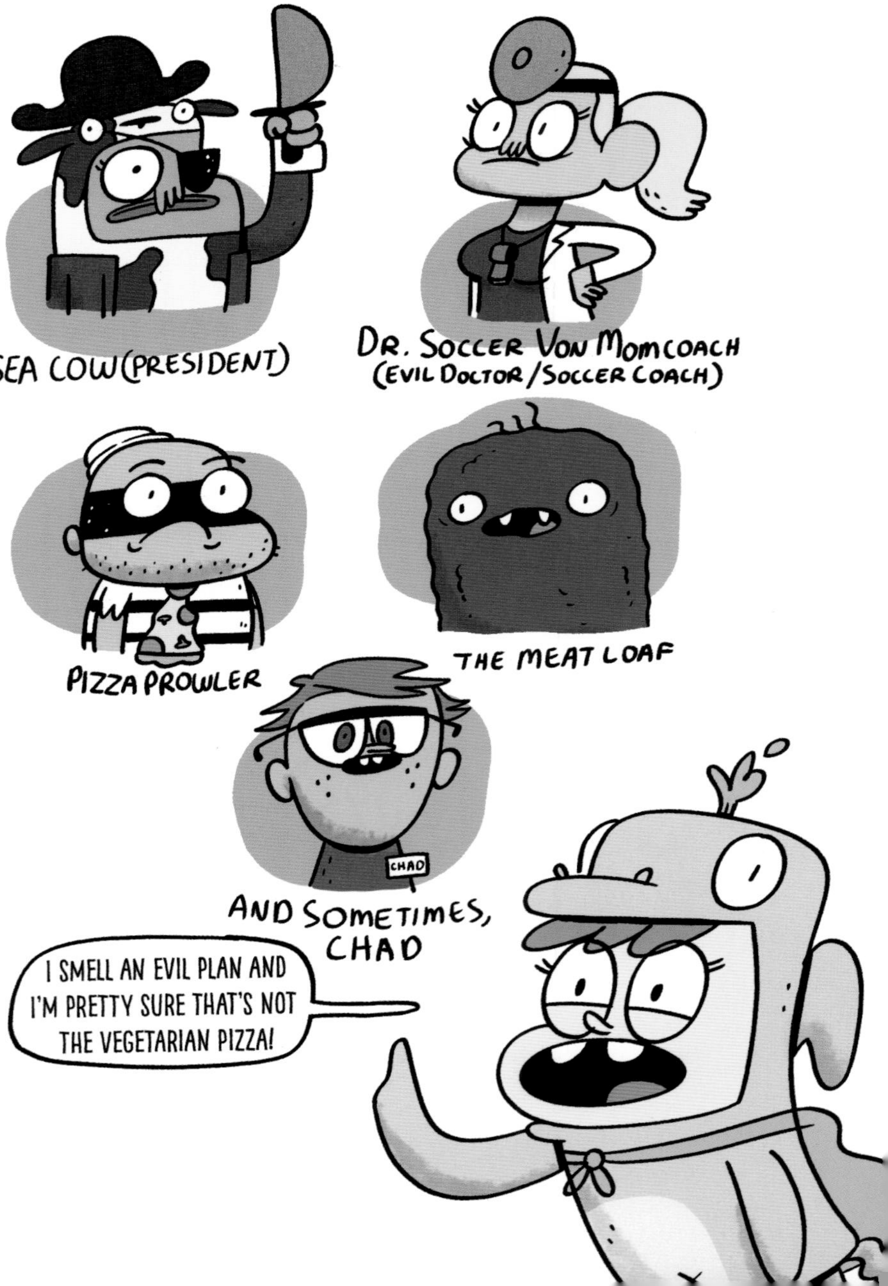
SEA COW (PRESIDENT)
DR. SOCCER VON MOMCOACH (EVIL DOCTOR / SOCCER COACH)
PIZZA PROWLER
THE MEAT LOAF
CHAD
AND SOMETIMES, CHAD
I SMELL AN EVIL PLAN AND I'M PRETTY SURE THAT'S NOT THE VEGETARIAN PIZZA!

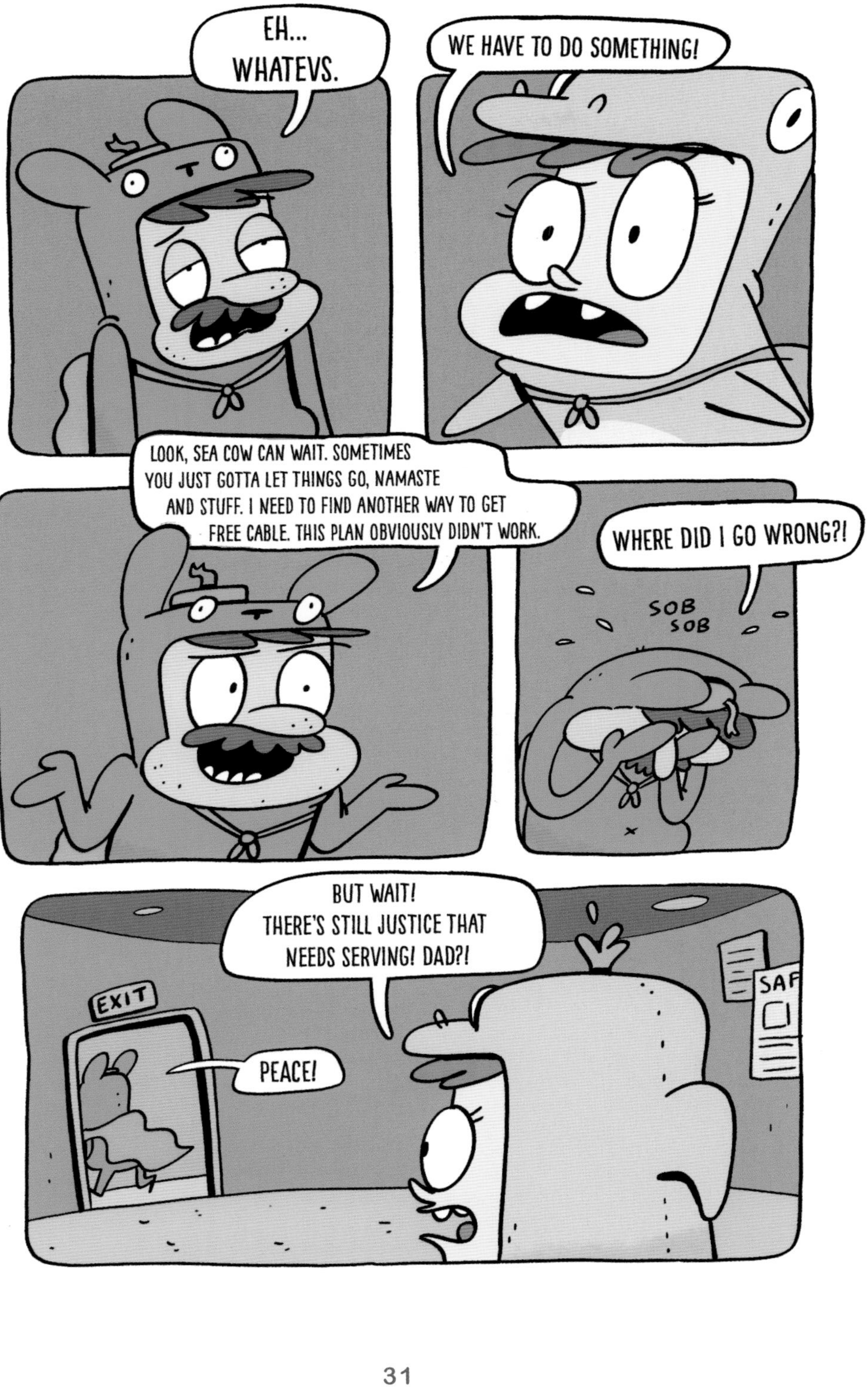
EH... WHATEVS.
WE HAVE TO DO SOMETHING!
LOOK, SEA COW CAN WAIT. SOMETIMES YOU JUST GOTTA LET THINGS GO, NAMASTE AND STUFF. I NEED TO FIND ANOTHER WAY TO GET FREE CABLE. THIS PLAN OBVIOUSLY DIDN'T WORK.
WHERE DID I GO WRONG?!
SOB SOB
BUT WAIT! THERE'S STILL JUSTICE THAT NEEDS SERVING! DAD?!
EXIT
PEACE!

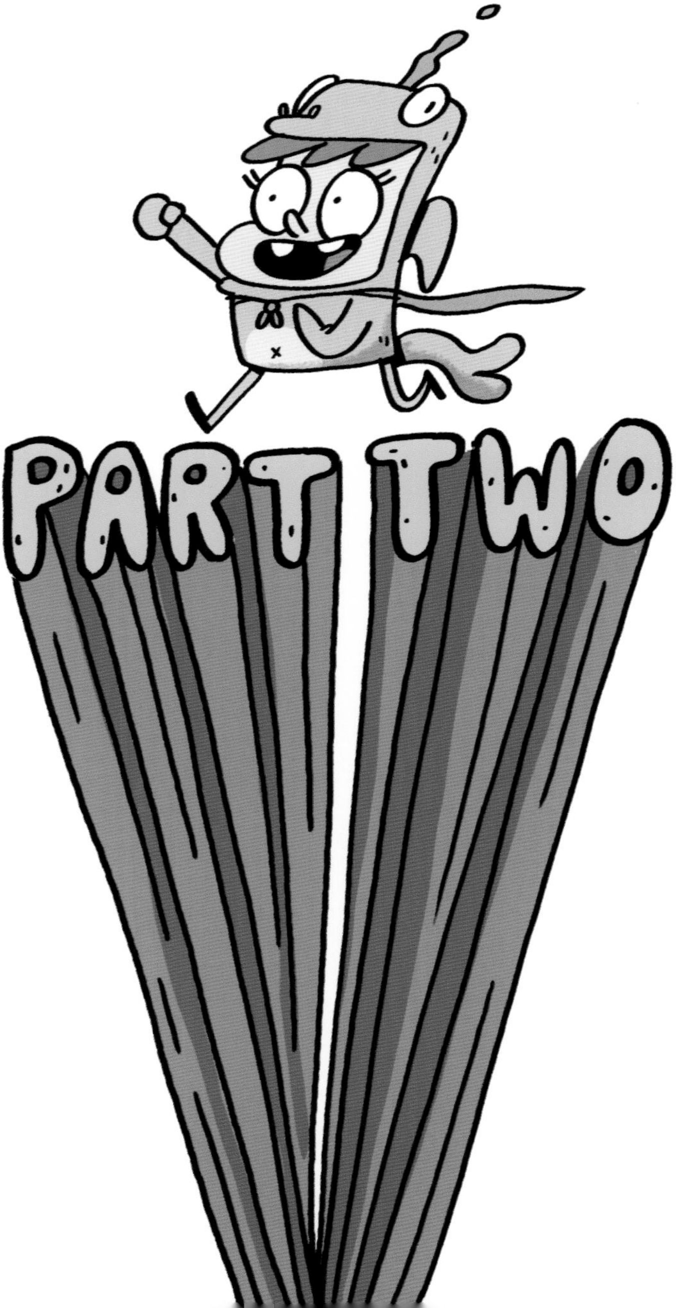
PART TWO

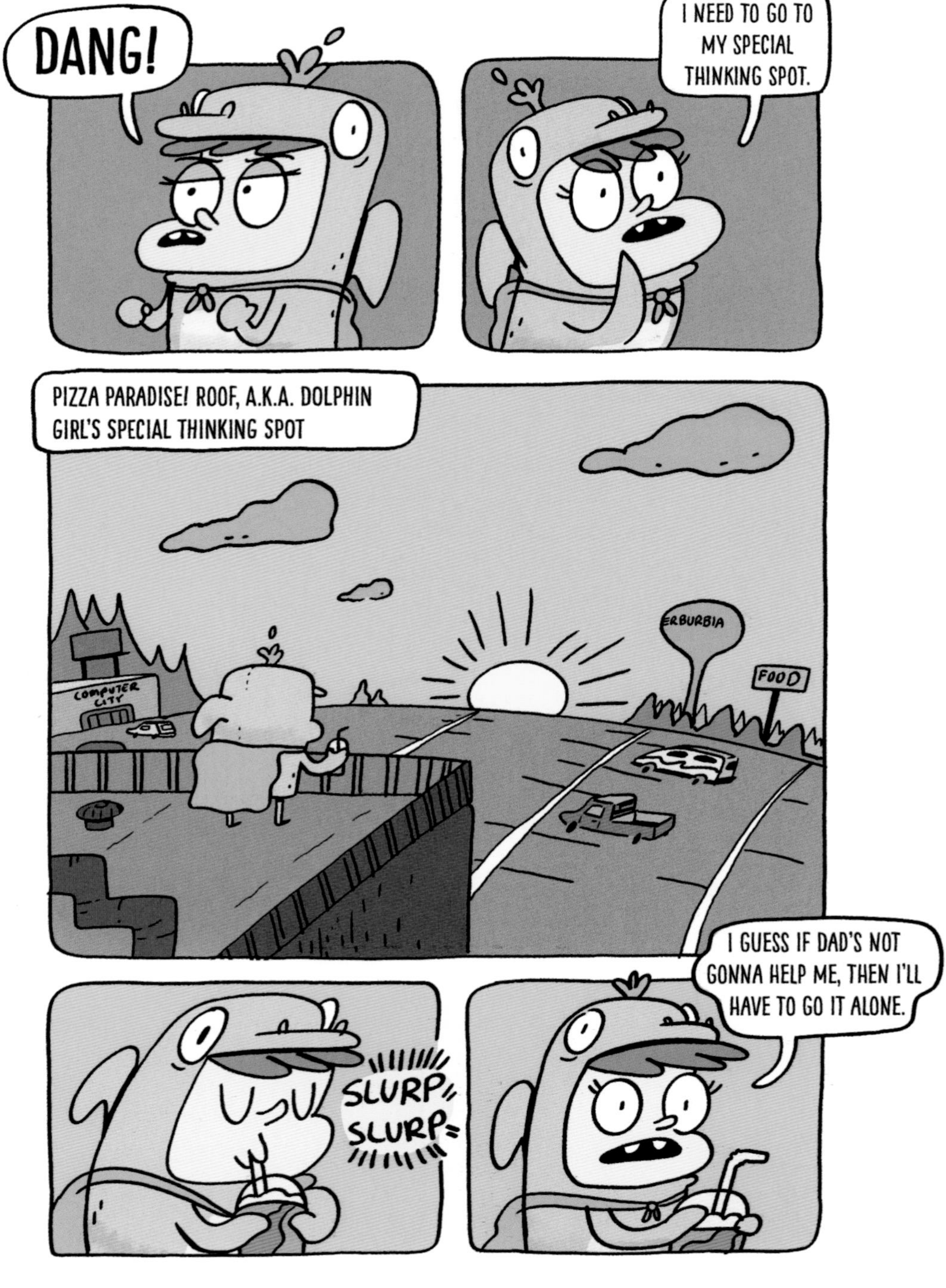
DANG!
I NEED TO GO TO MY SPECIAL THINKING SPOT.
PIZZA PARADISE! ROOF, A.K.A. DOLPHIN GIRL'S SPECIAL THINKING SPOT
COMPUTER CITY
ERBURBIA
FOOD
SLURP SLURP
I GUESS IF DAD'S NOT GONNA HELP ME, THEN I'LL HAVE TO GO IT ALONE.

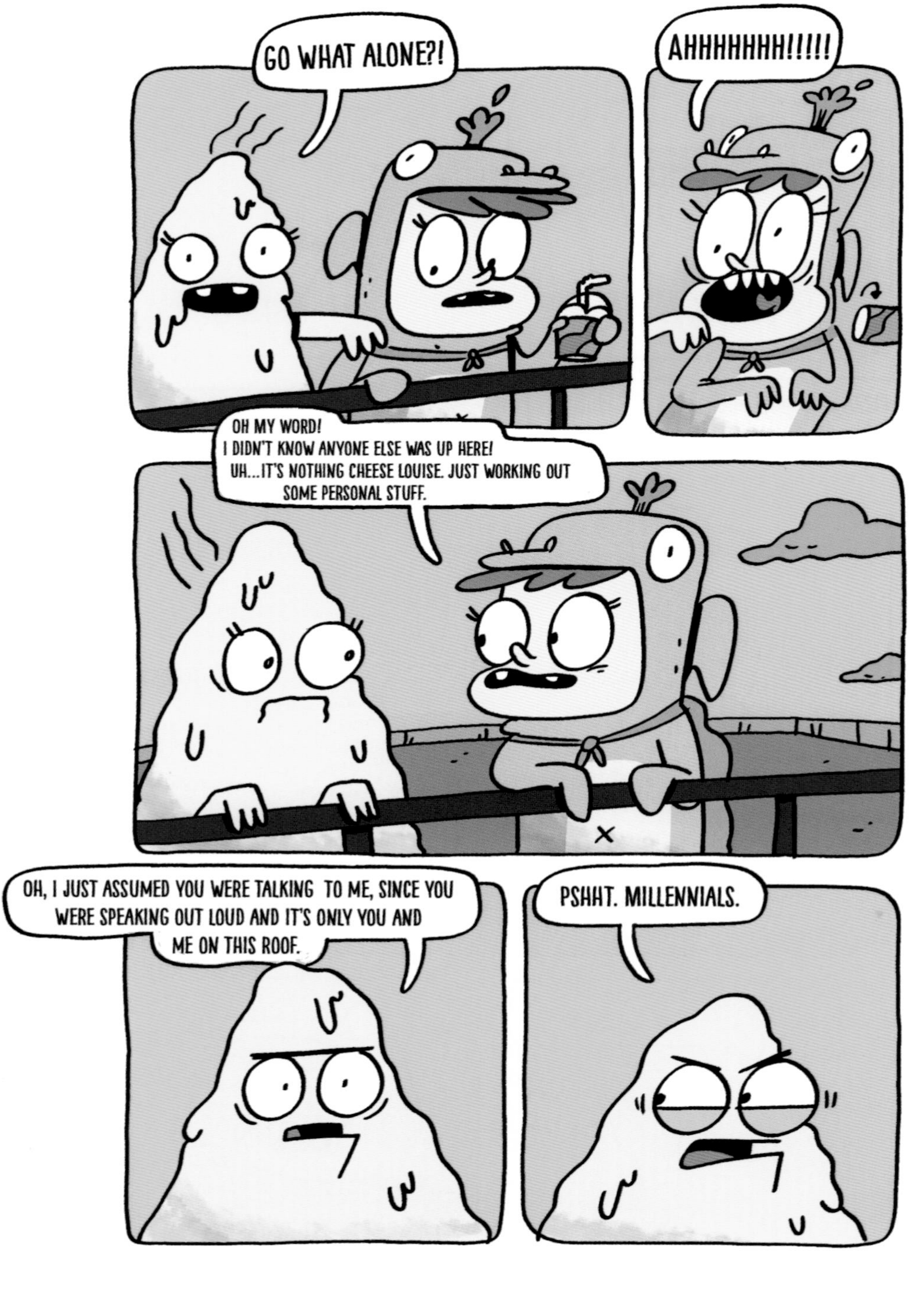
GO WHAT ALONE?!
AHHHHHHH!!!!!
OH MY WORD!
I DIDN'T KNOW ANYONE ELSE WAS UP HERE!
UH...IT'S NOTHING CHEESE LOUISE. JUST WORKING OUT SOME PERSONAL STUFF.
OH, I JUST ASSUMED YOU WERE TALKING TO ME, SINCE YOU WERE SPEAKING OUT LOUD AND IT'S ONLY YOU AND ME ON THIS ROOF.
PSHHT. MILLENNIALS.

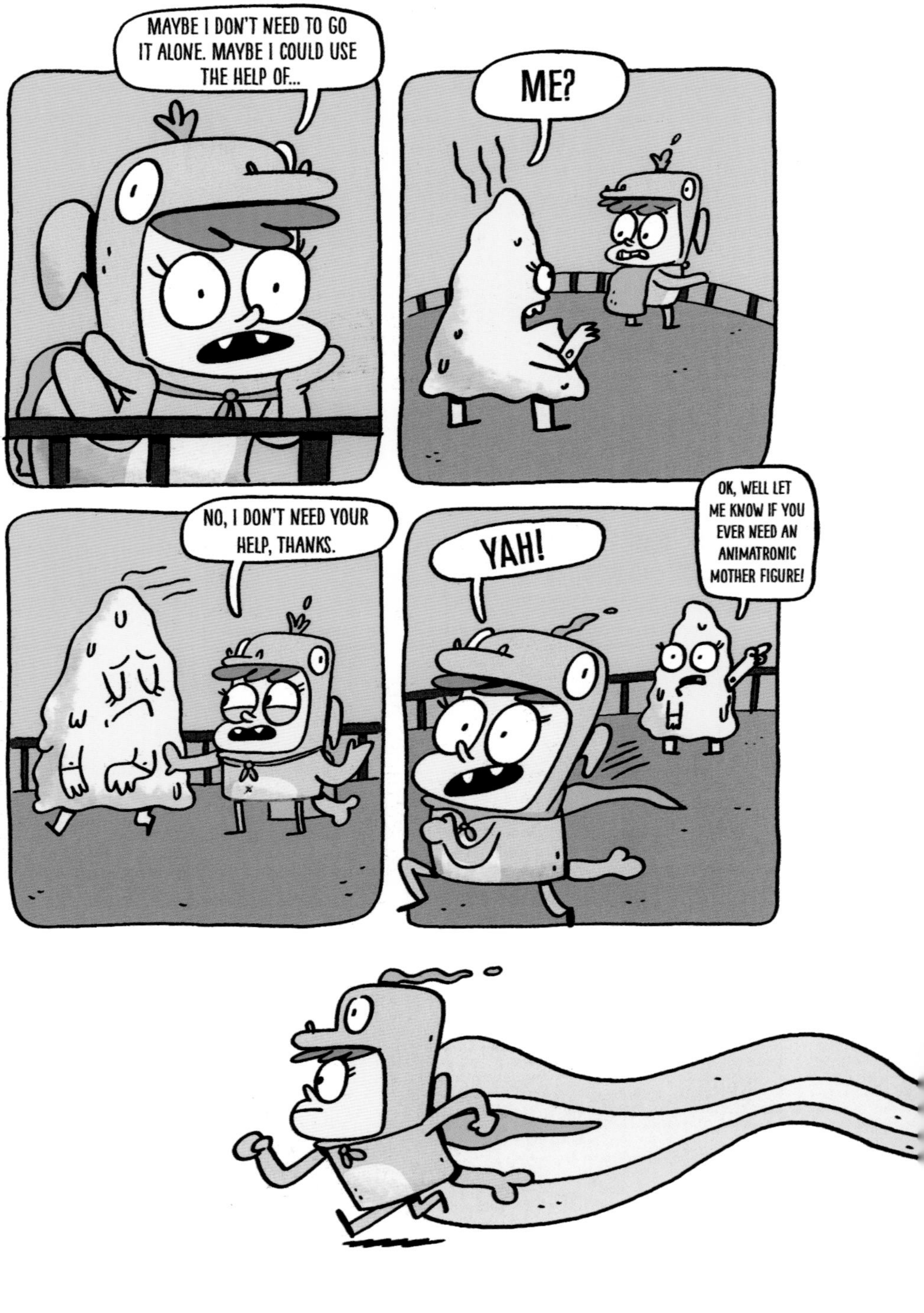
MAYBE I DON'T NEED TO GO IT ALONE. MAYBE I COULD USE THE HELP OF...
ME?
NO, I DON'T NEED YOUR HELP, THANKS.
YAH!
OK, WELL LET ME KNOW IF YOU EVER NEED AN ANIMATRONIC MOTHER FIGURE!

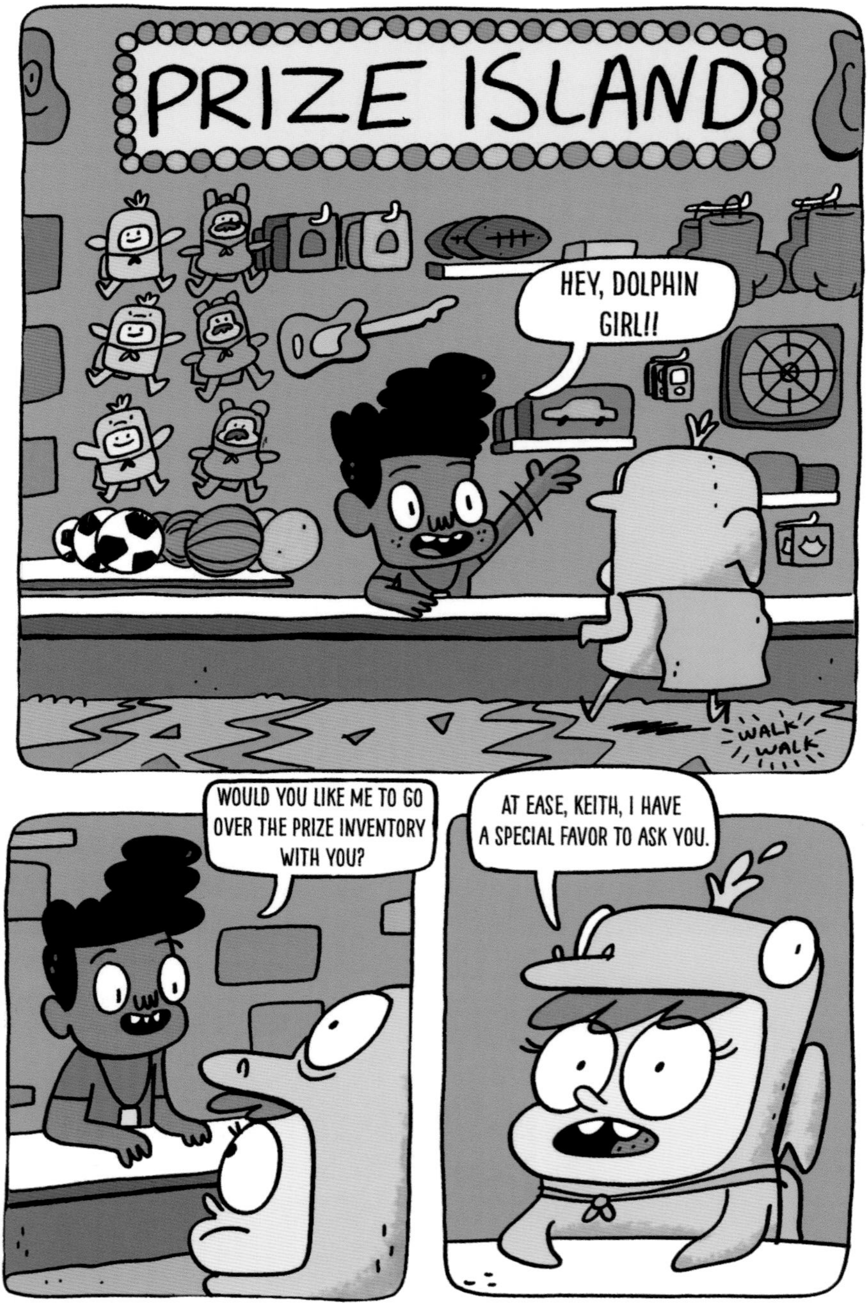
PRIZE ISLAND
HEY, DOLPHIN GIRL!!
WALK WALK
WOULD YOU LIKE ME TO GO OVER THE PRIZE INVENTORY WITH YOU?
AT EASE, KEITH, I HAVE A SPECIAL FAVOR TO ASK YOU.

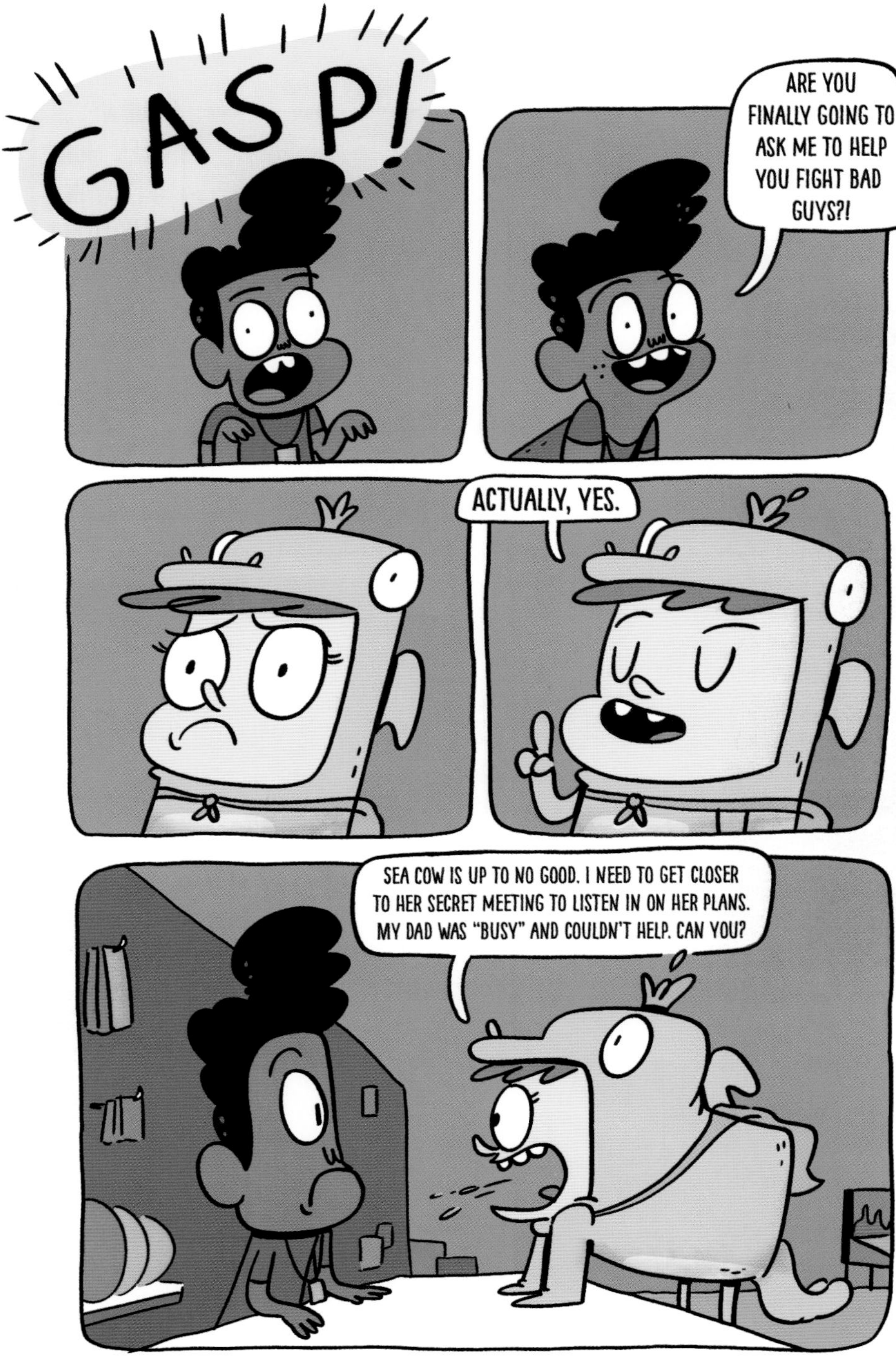
GASP!
ARE YOU FINALLY GOING TO ASK ME TO HELP YOU FIGHT BAD GUYS?!
ACTUALLY, YES.
SEA COW IS UP TO NO GOOD. I NEED TO GET CLOSER TO HER SECRET MEETING TO LISTEN IN ON HER PLANS. MY DAD WAS "BUSY" AND COULDN'T HELP. CAN YOU?

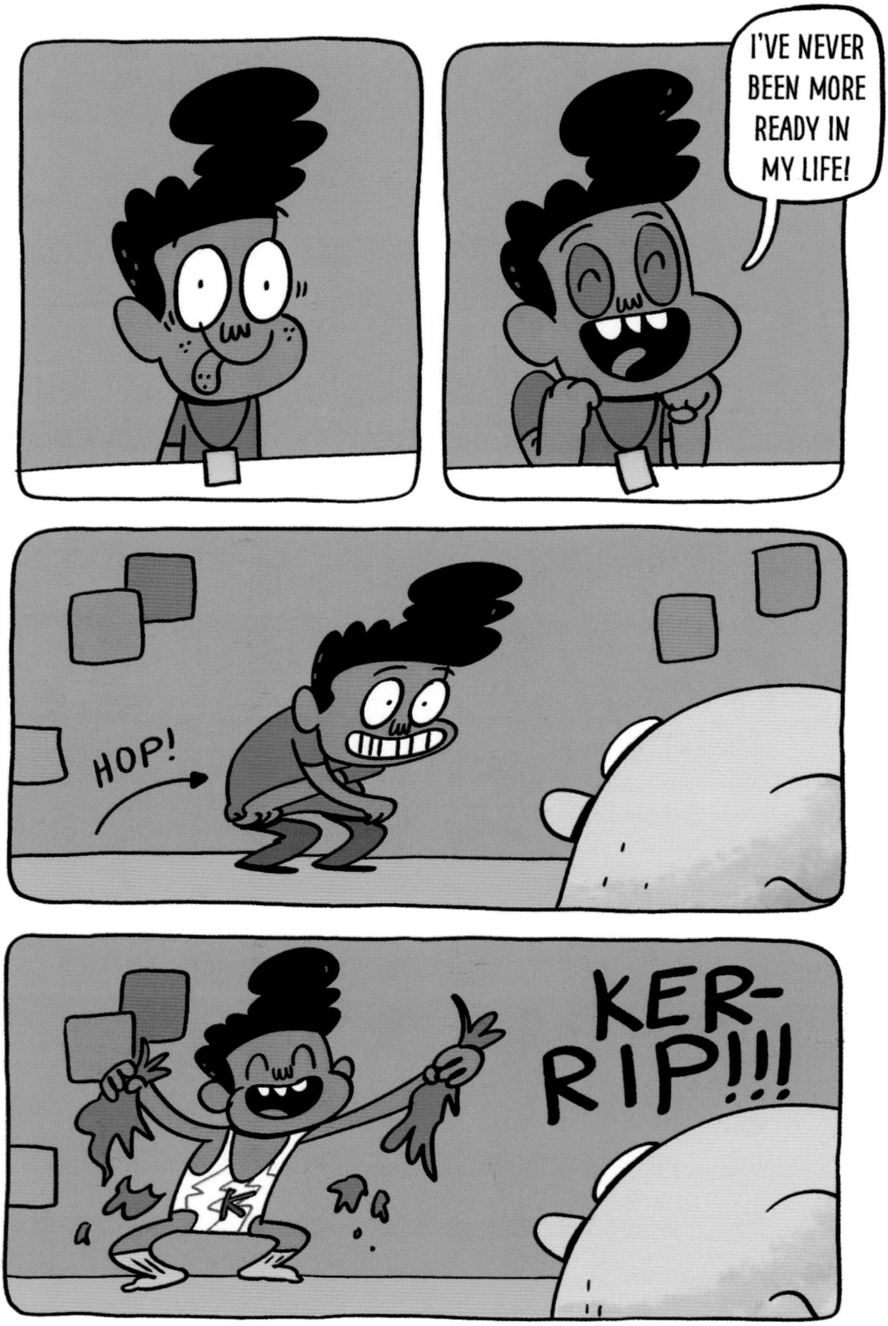
I'VE NEVER BEEN MORE READY IN MY LIFE!
HOP!
KER-RIP!!!

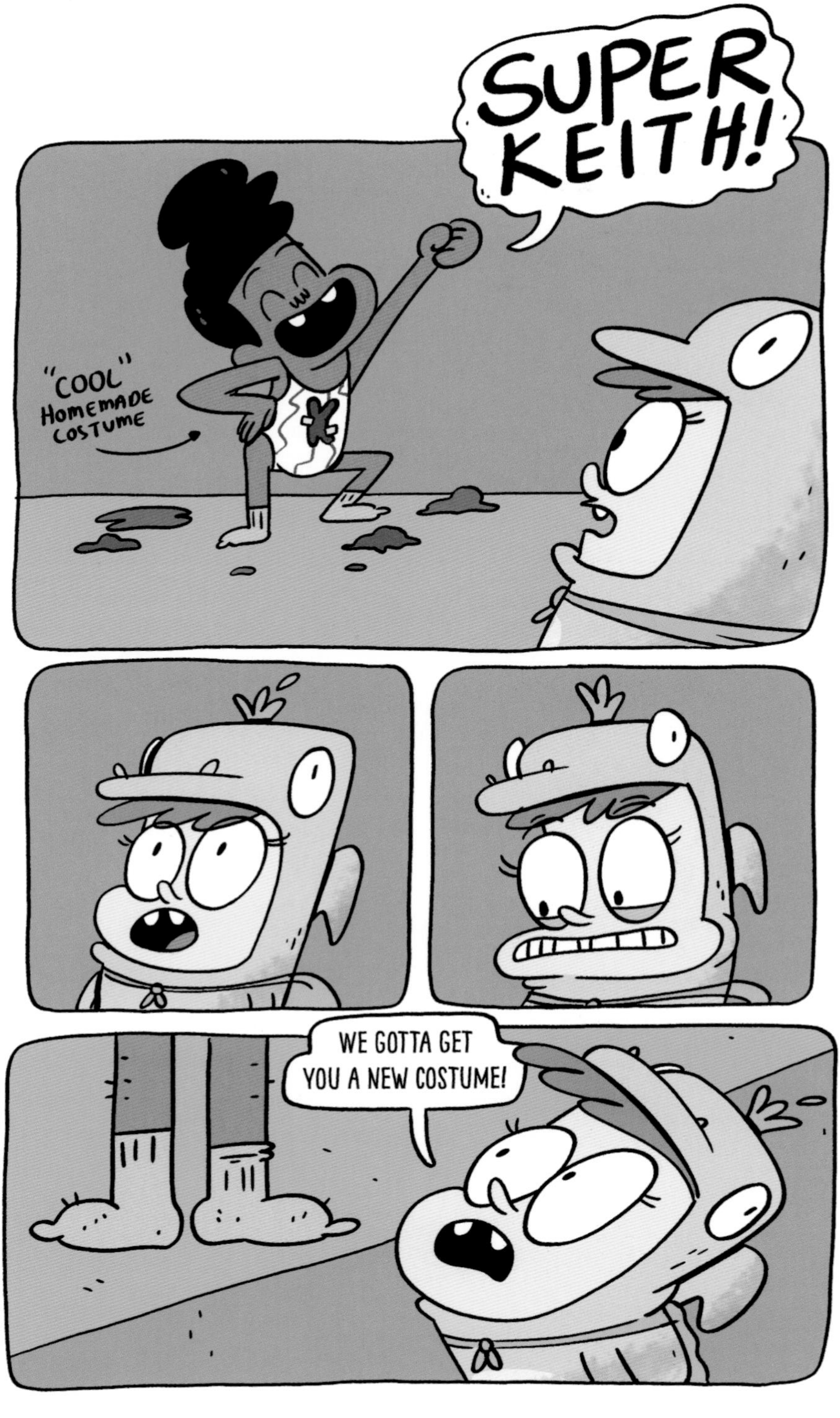
SUPER KEITH!
"COOL" HOMEMADE COSTUME
WE GOTTA GET YOU A NEW COSTUME!

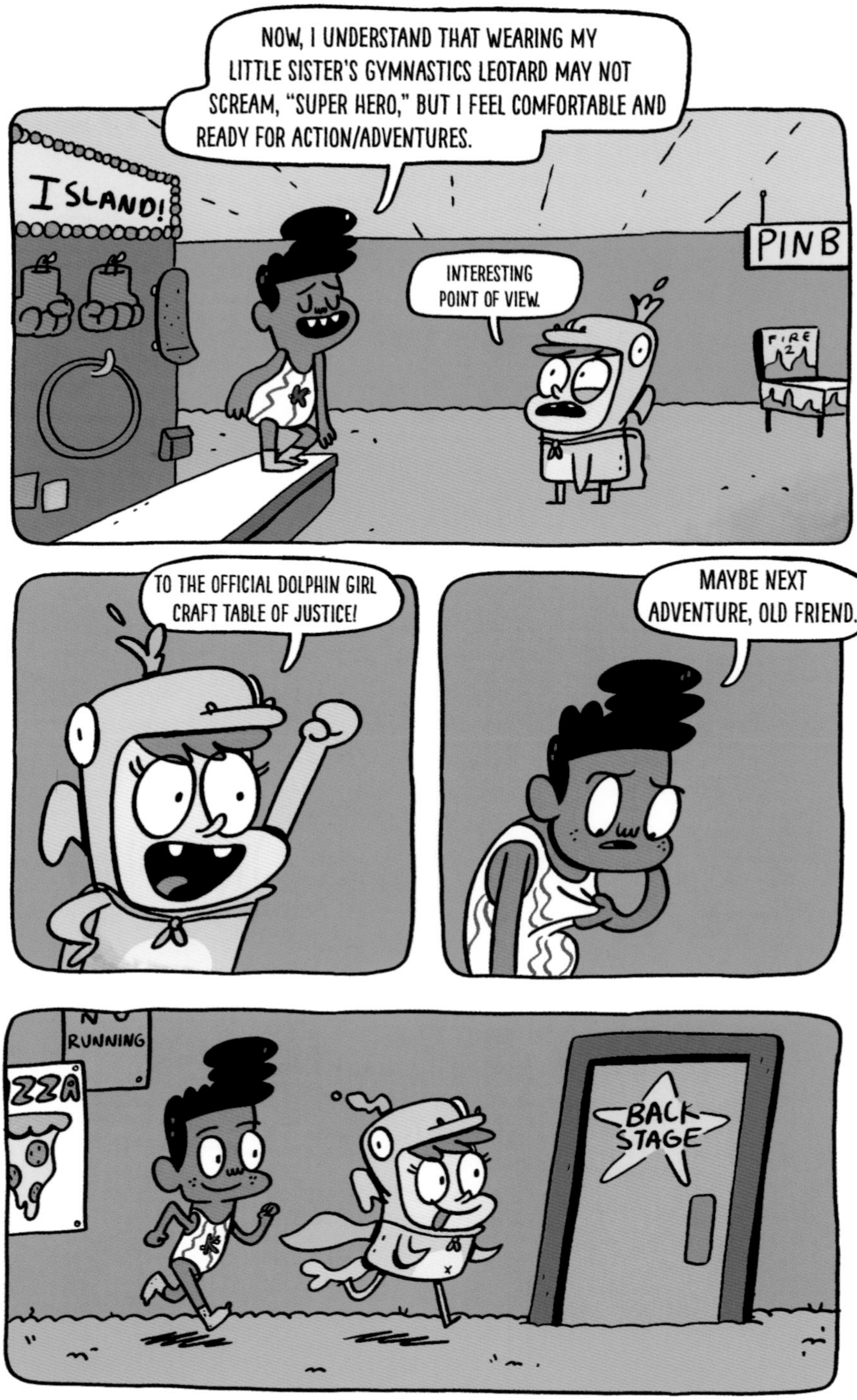
NOW, I UNDERSTAND THAT WEARING MY LITTLE SISTER'S GYMNASTICS LEOTARD MAY NOT SCREAM, "SUPER HERO," BUT I FEEL COMFORTABLE AND READY FOR ACTION/ADVENTURES.
ISLAND!
PINB
INTERESTING POINT OF VIEW.
TO THE OFFICIAL DOLPHIN GIRL CRAFT TABLE OF JUSTICE!
MAYBE NEXT ADVENTURE, OLD FRIEND.
RUNNING
ZZA
BACK STAGE

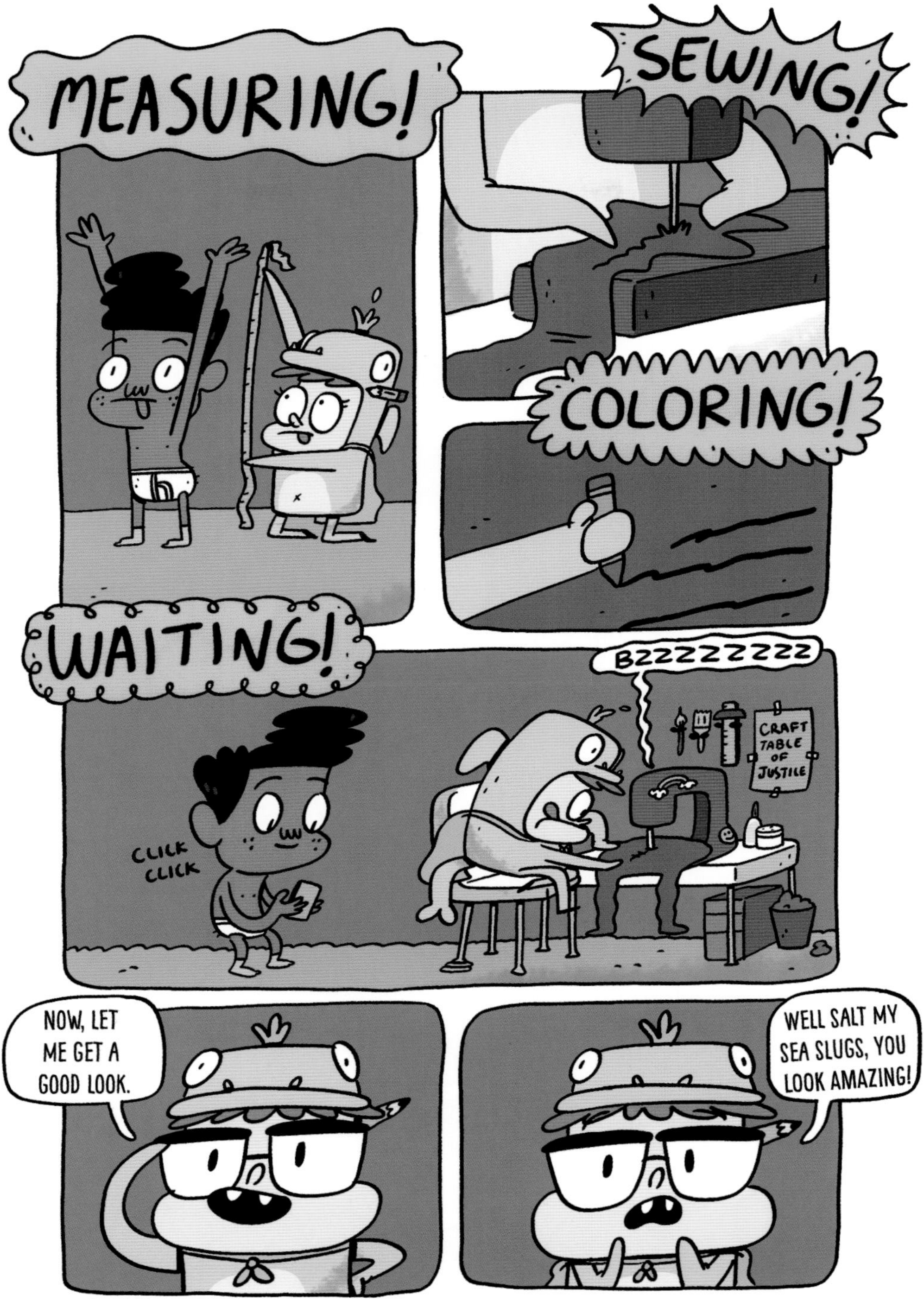
MEASURING!
SEWING!
COLORING!
WAITING!
BZZZZZZZZ
CLICK CLICK
CRAFT TABLE OF JUSTICE
NOW, LET ME GET A GOOD LOOK.
WELL SALT MY SEA SLUGS, YOU LOOK AMAZING!

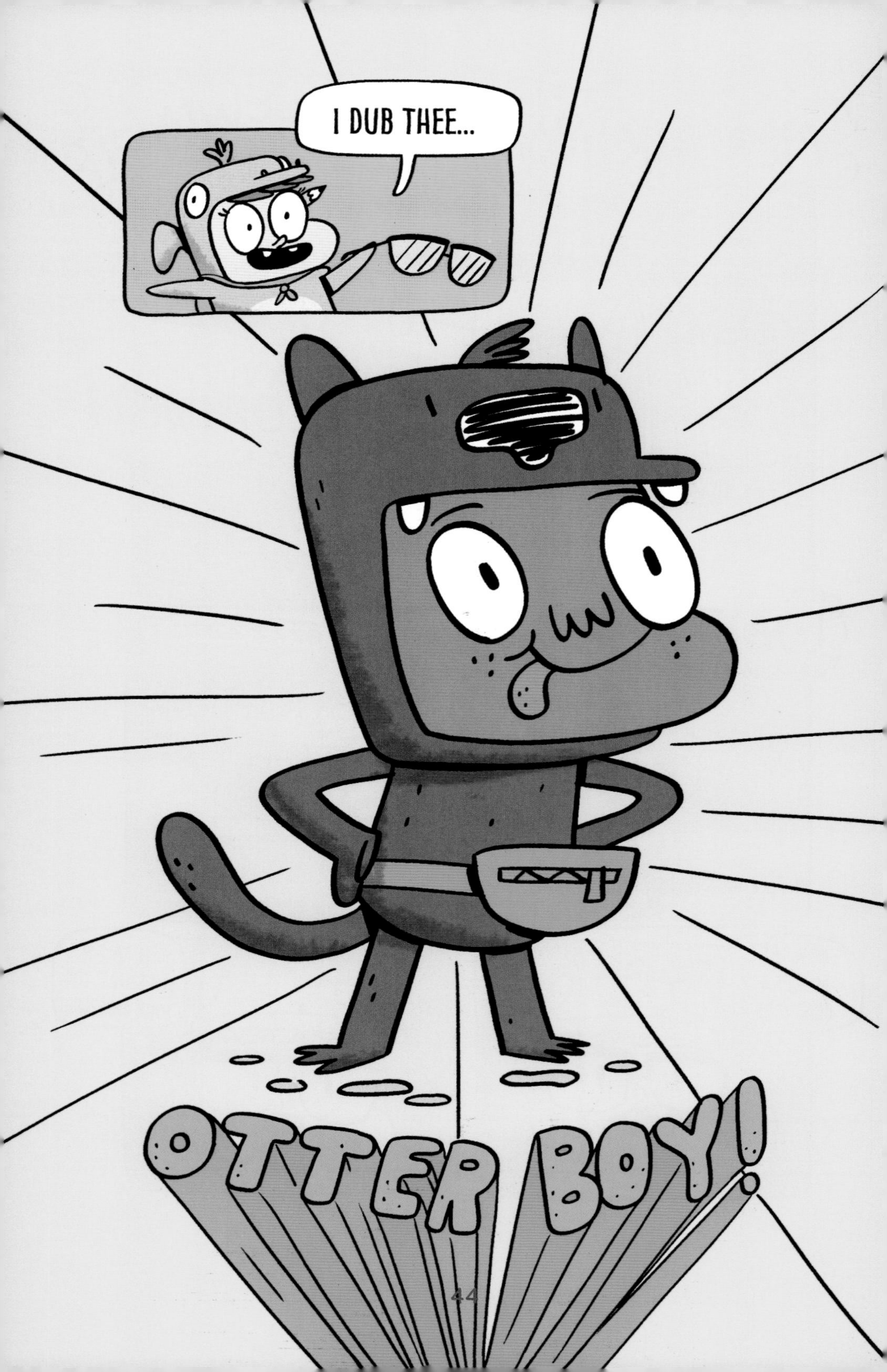
I DUB THEE...
OTTER BOY!

WITH THE OTTERFUL POWERS OF:

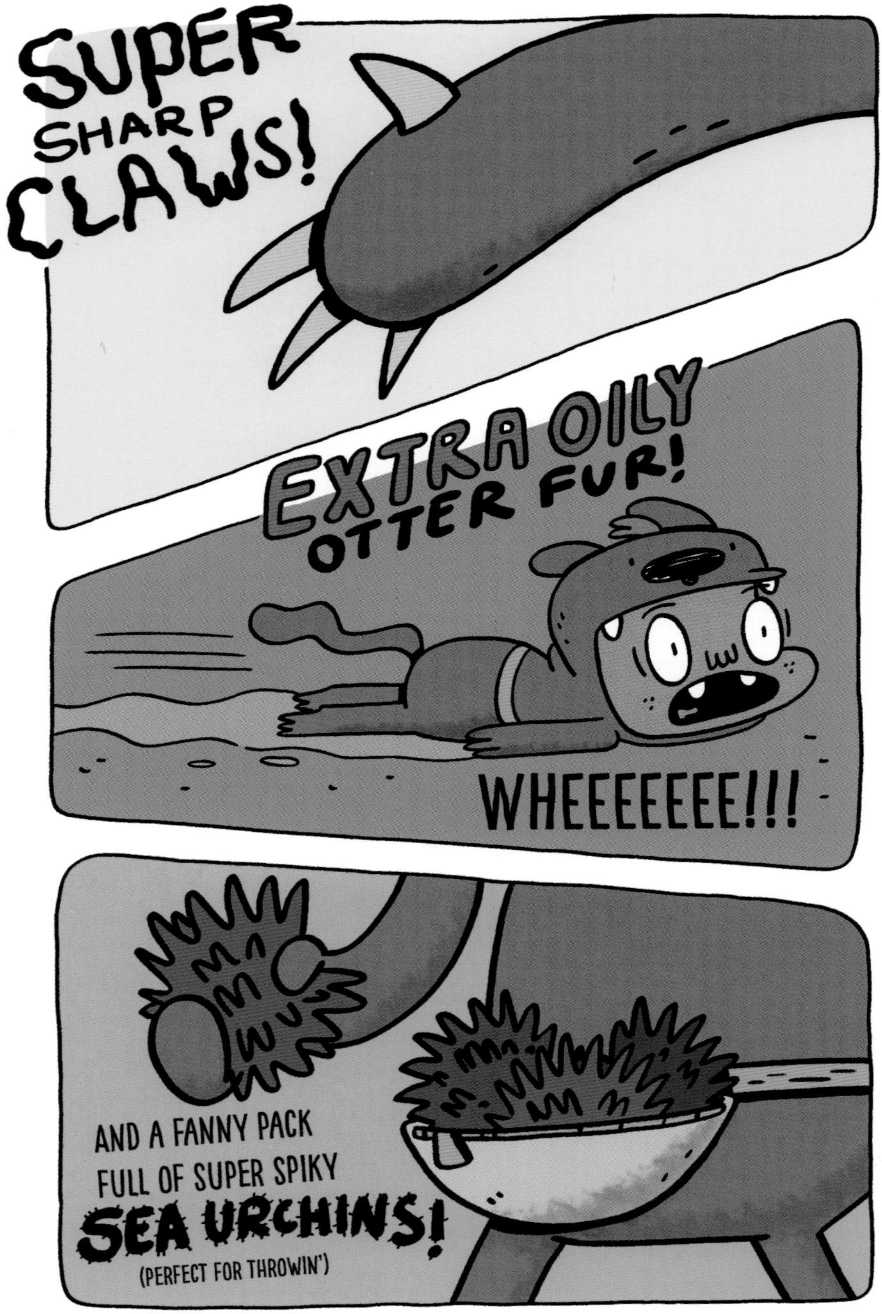
SUPER SHARP CLAWS!
EXTRA OILY OTTER FUR!
WHEEEEEEE!!!
AND A FANNY PACK FULL OF SUPER SPIKY SEA URCHINS!
(PERFECT FOR THROWIN')

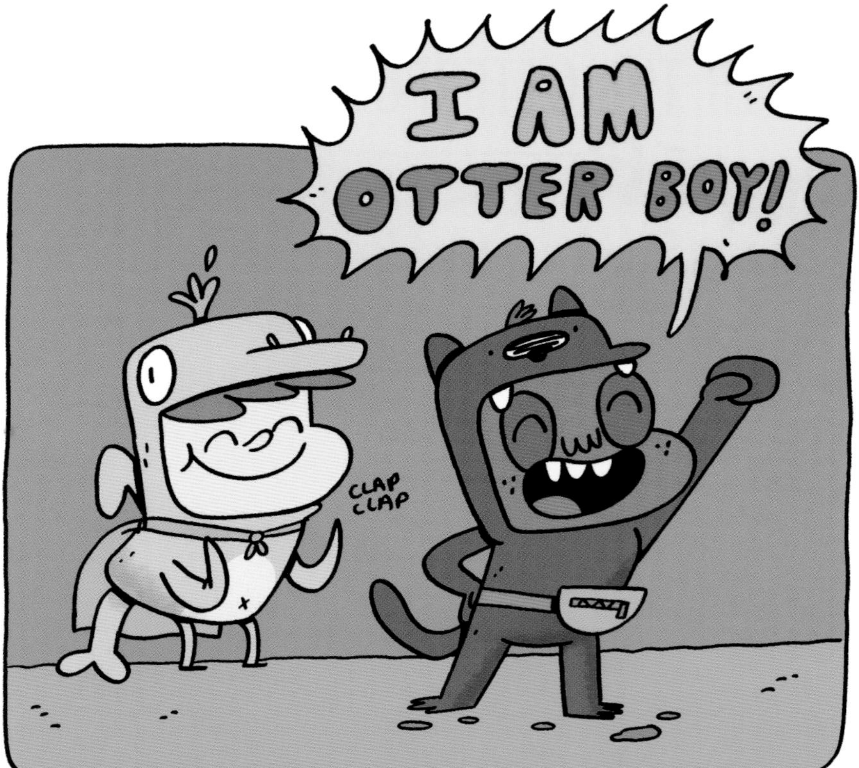
I AM OTTER BOY!
CLAP CLAP

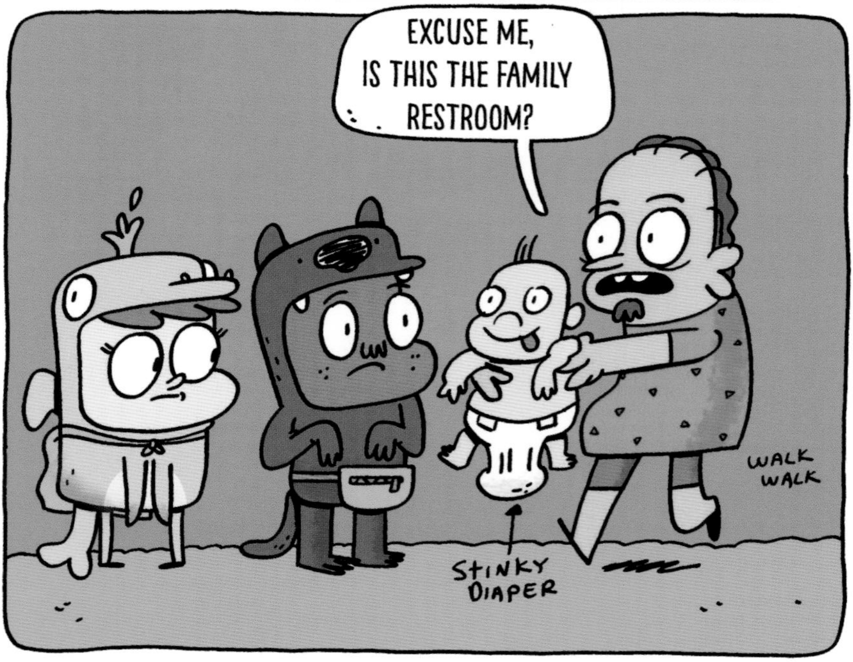
EXCUSE ME, IS THIS THE FAMILY RESTROOM?
WALK WALK
STINKY DIAPER

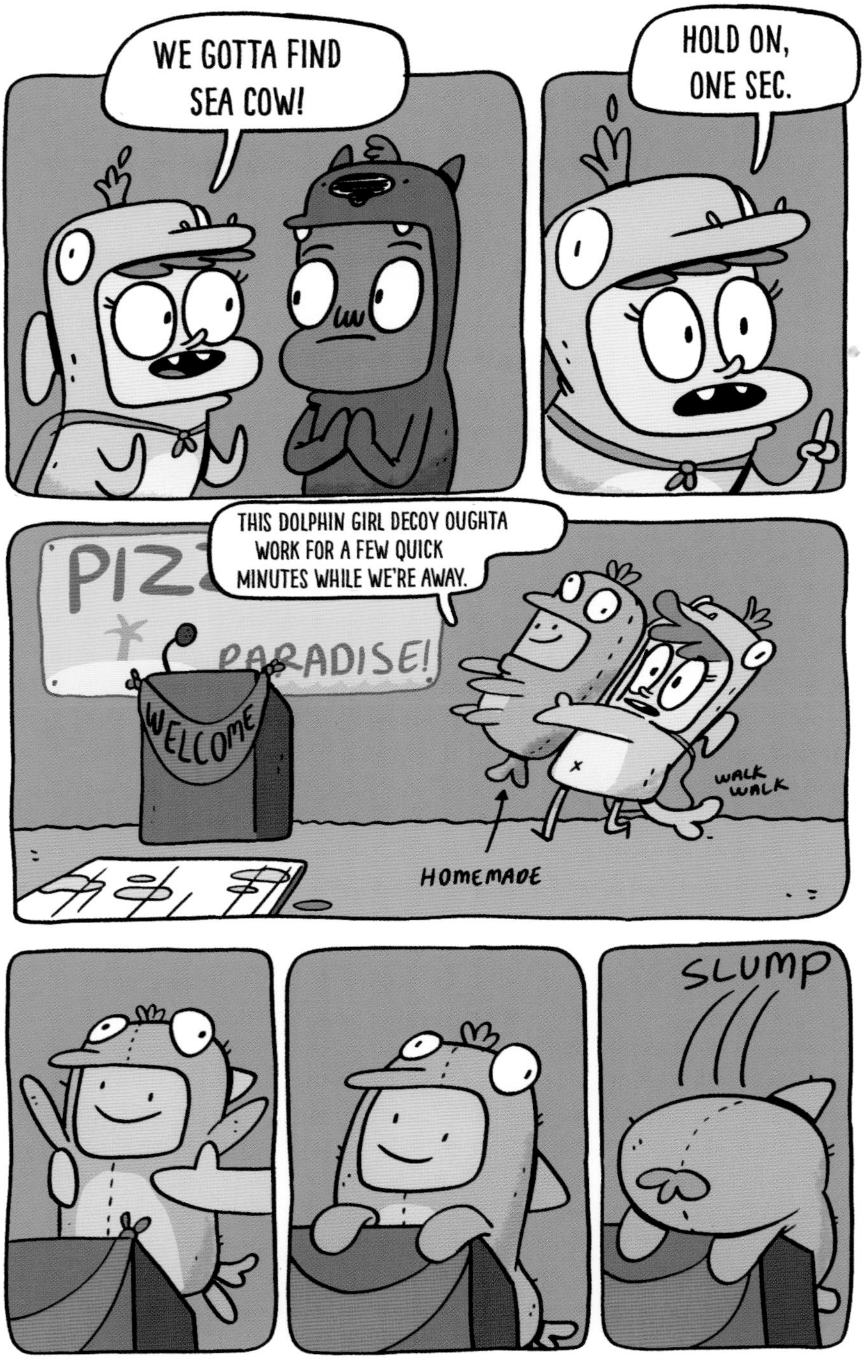
WE GOTTA FIND SEA COW!
HOLD ON, ONE SEC.
PIZZ
PARADISE!
THIS DOLPHIN GIRL DECOY OUGHTA WORK FOR A FEW QUICK MINUTES WHILE WE'RE AWAY.
WELCOME
WALK WALK
HOMEMADE
SLUMP

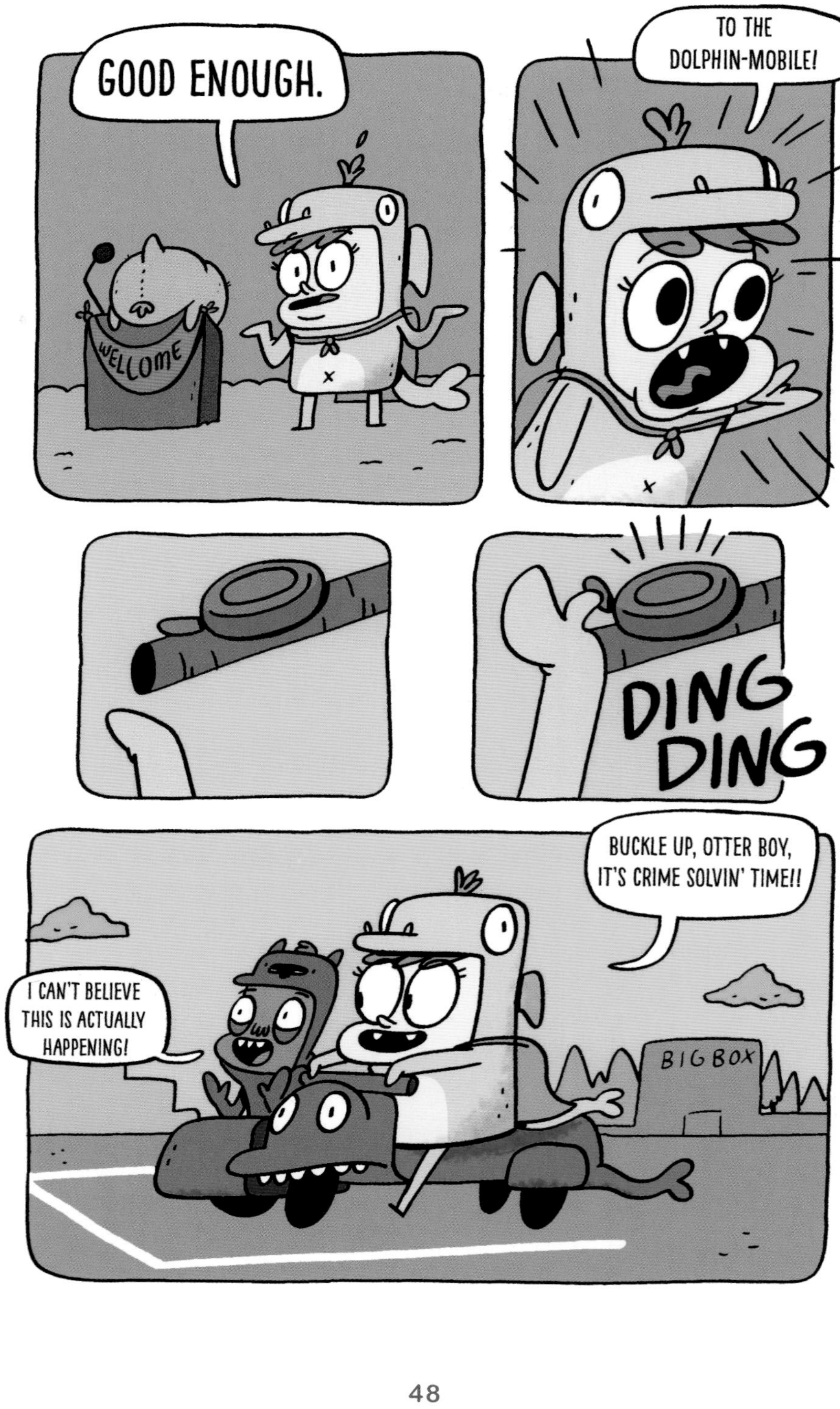
GOOD ENOUGH.
WELLOME
TO THE DOLPHIN-MOBILE!
DING DING
BUCKLE UP, OTTER BOY, IT'S CRIME SOLVIN' TIME!!
I CAN'T BELIEVE THIS IS ACTUALLY HAPPENING!
BIGBOX

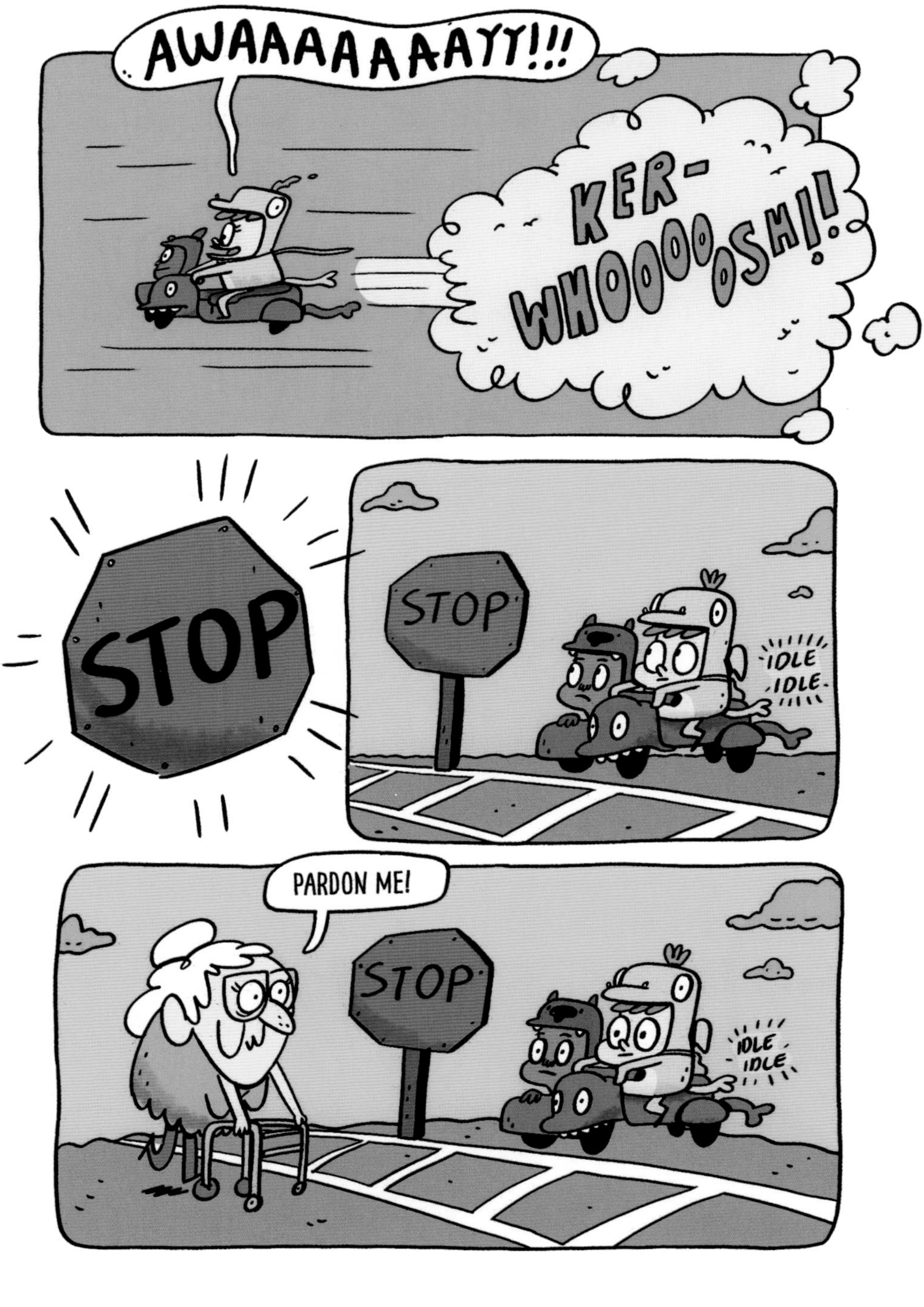
AWAAAAAAAYY!!!
KER-WHOOOOOSH!!
STOP
STOP
IDLE IDLE
PARDON ME!
STOP
IDLE IDLE

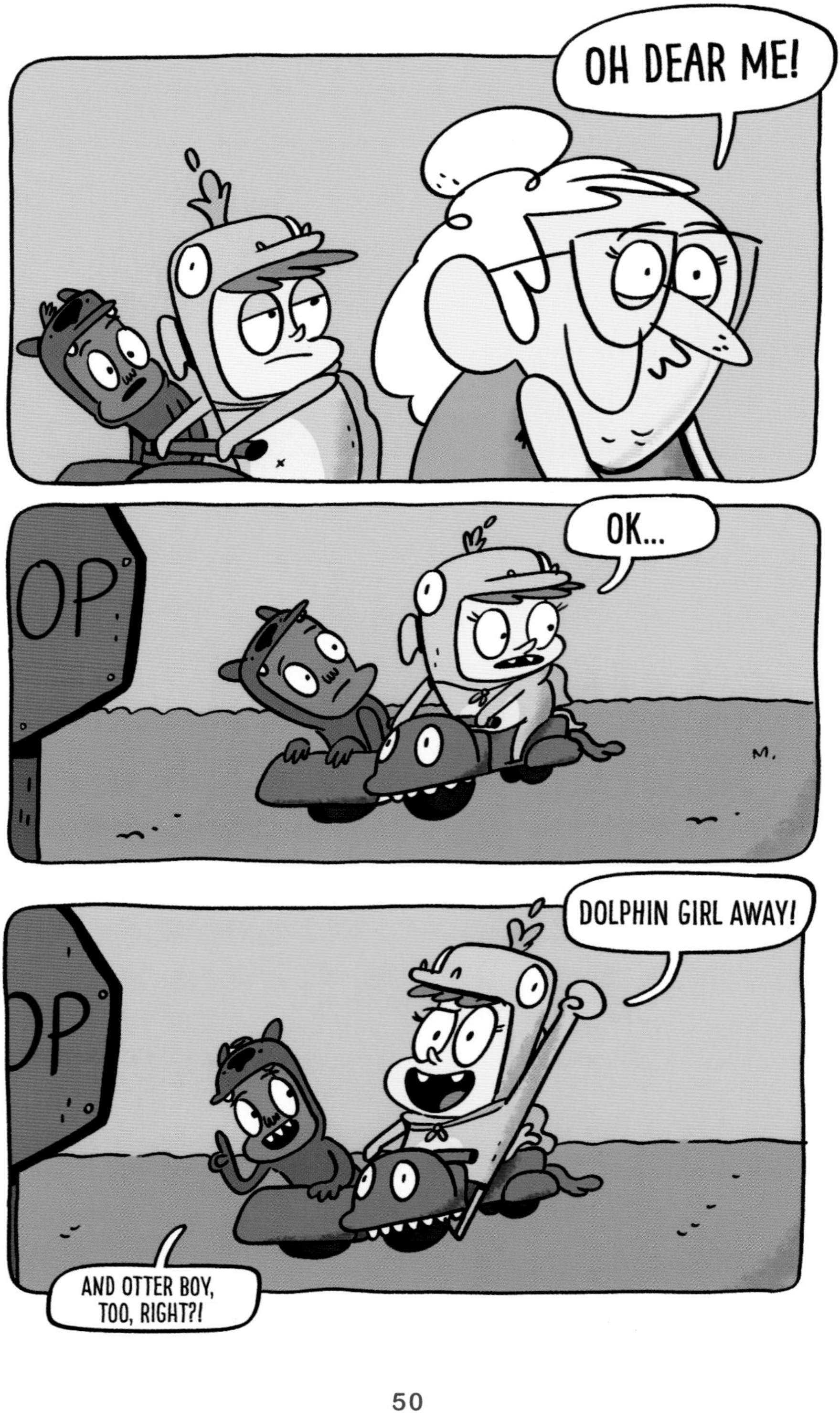
OH DEAR ME!
OK...
DOLPHIN GIRL AWAY!
AND OTTER BOY, TOO, RIGHT?!

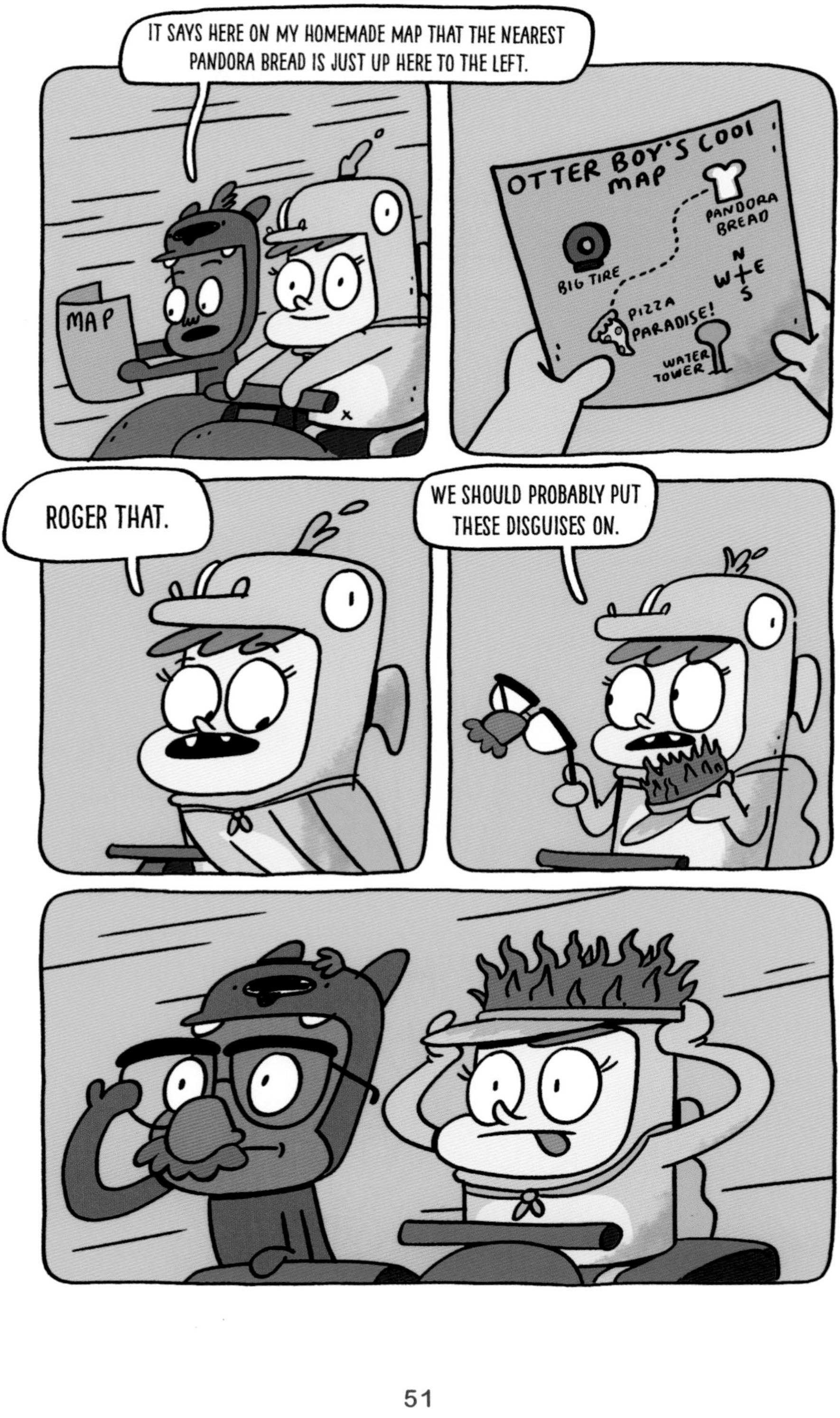
IT SAYS HERE ON MY HOMEMADE MAP THAT THE NEAREST PANDORA BREAD IS JUST UP HERE TO THE LEFT.
MAP
OTTER BOY'S COOl MAP
PANDORA BREAD
BIG TIRE
N W E S
PIZZA PARADISE!
WATER TOWER
ROGER THAT.
WE SHOULD PROBABLY PUT THESE DISGUISES ON.

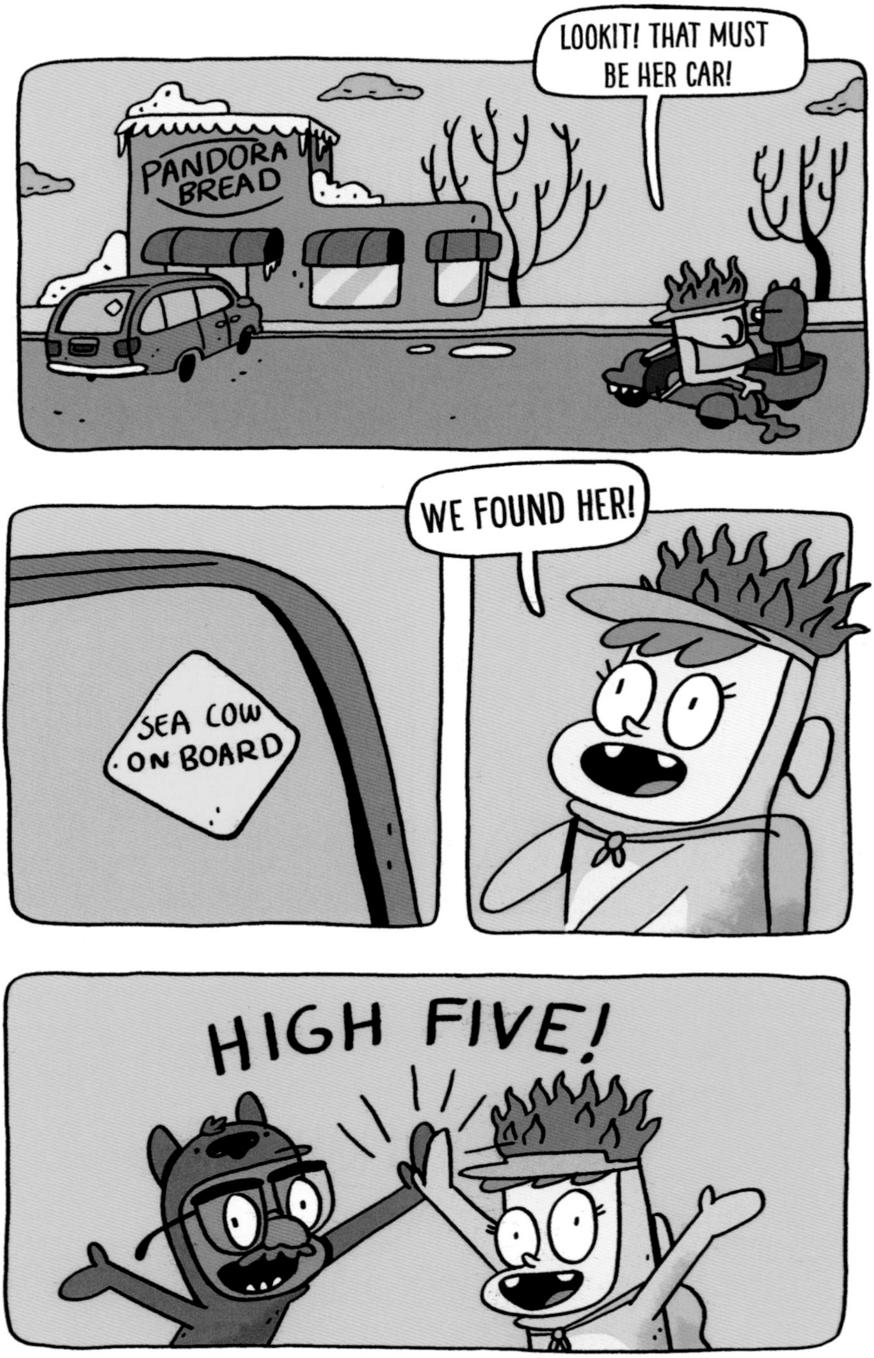
LOOKIT! THAT MUST BE HER CAR!
PANDORA BREAD
SEA COW ON BOARD
WE FOUND HER!
HIGH FIVE!

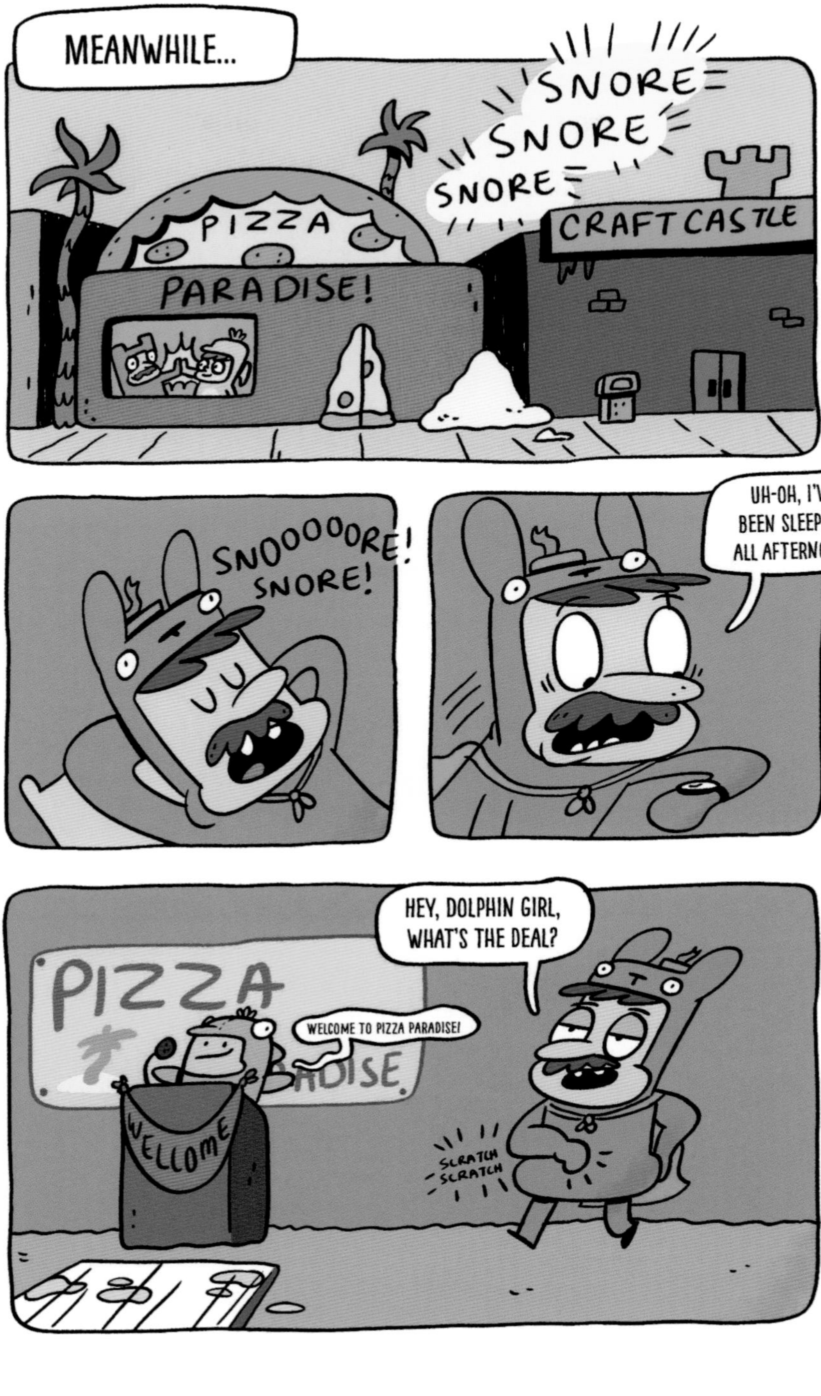
MEANWHILE...
SNORE
SNORE
SNORE
PIZZA
PARADISE!
CRAFT CASTLE
SNOOOOORE!
SNORE!
UH-OH, I'VE BEEN SLEEPING ALL AFTERNOON!
HEY, DOLPHIN GIRL, WHAT'S THE DEAL?
PIZZA
ADISE
WELCOME TO PIZZA PARADISE!
WELLOME
SCRATCH
SCRATCH

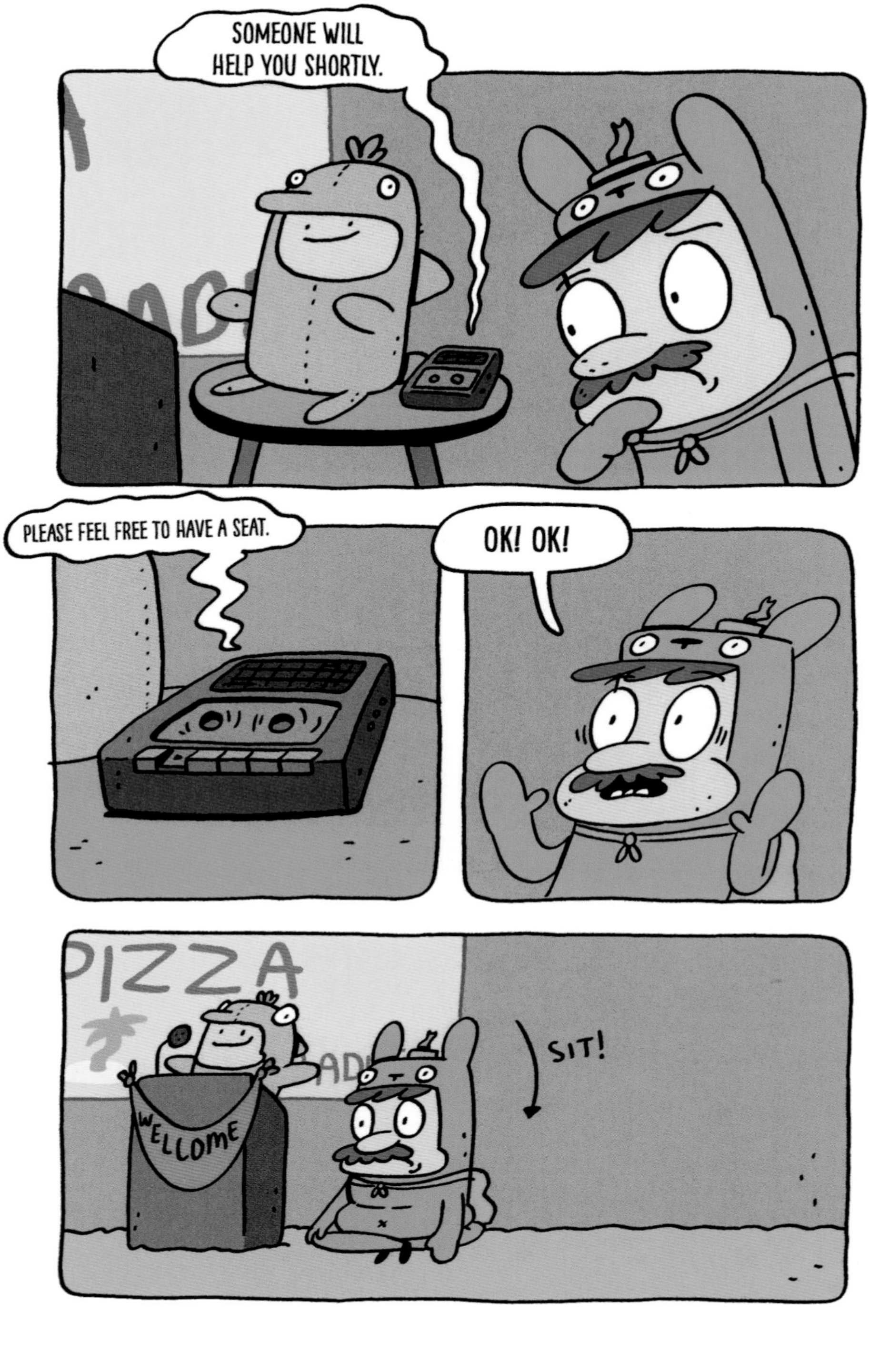
SOMEONE WILL HELP YOU SHORTLY.
PLEASE FEEL FREE TO HAVE A SEAT.
OK! OK!
PIZZA
WELLOME
SIT!

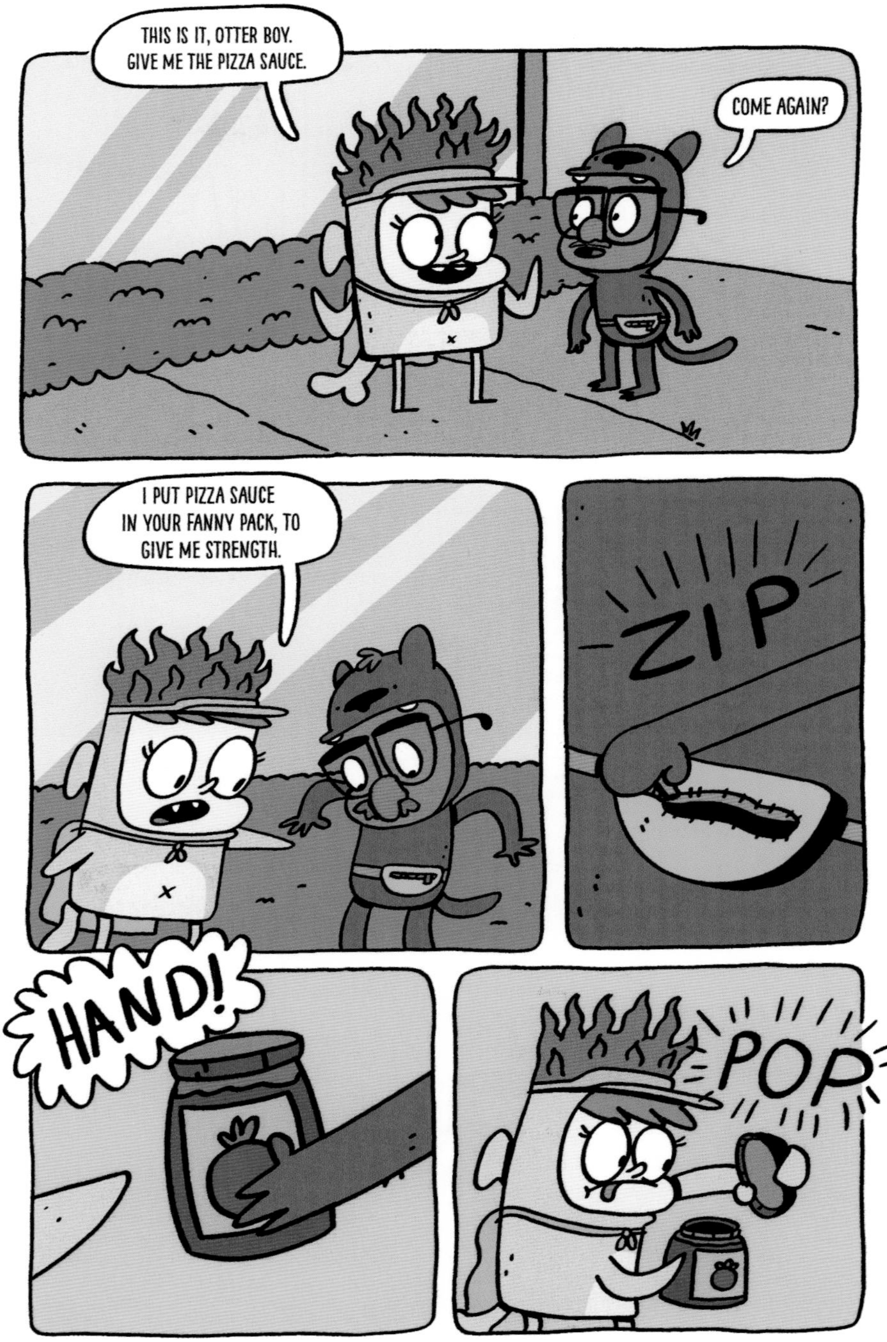

THIS IS IT, OTTER BOY. GIVE ME THE PIZZA SAUCE.
COME AGAIN?
I PUT PIZZA SAUCE IN YOUR FANNY PACK, TO GIVE ME STRENGTH.
ZIP
HAND!
POP

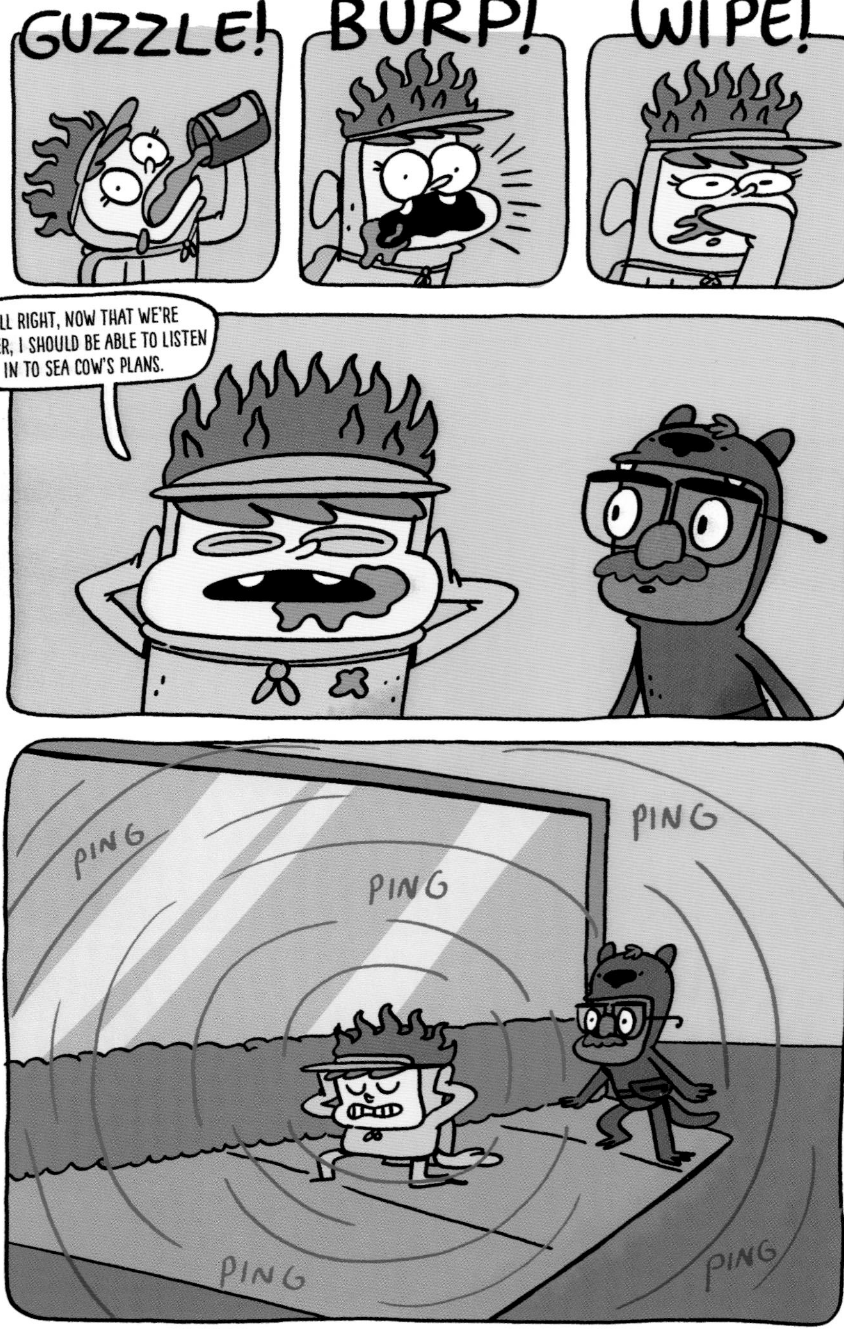
GUZZLE!
BURP!
WIPE!
ALL RIGHT, NOW THAT WE'RE CLOSER, I SHOULD BE ABLE TO LISTEN IN TO SEA COW'S PLANS.
PING
PING
PING
PING
PING

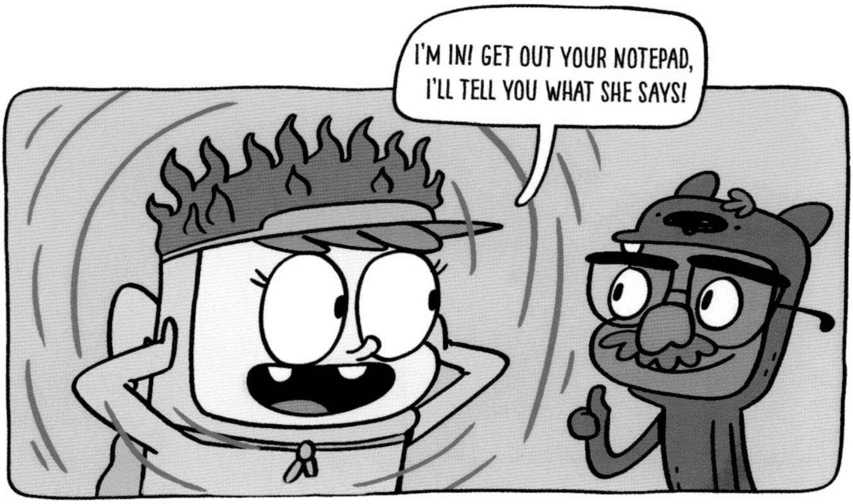
I'M IN! GET OUT YOUR NOTEPAD, I'LL TELL YOU WHAT SHE SAYS!

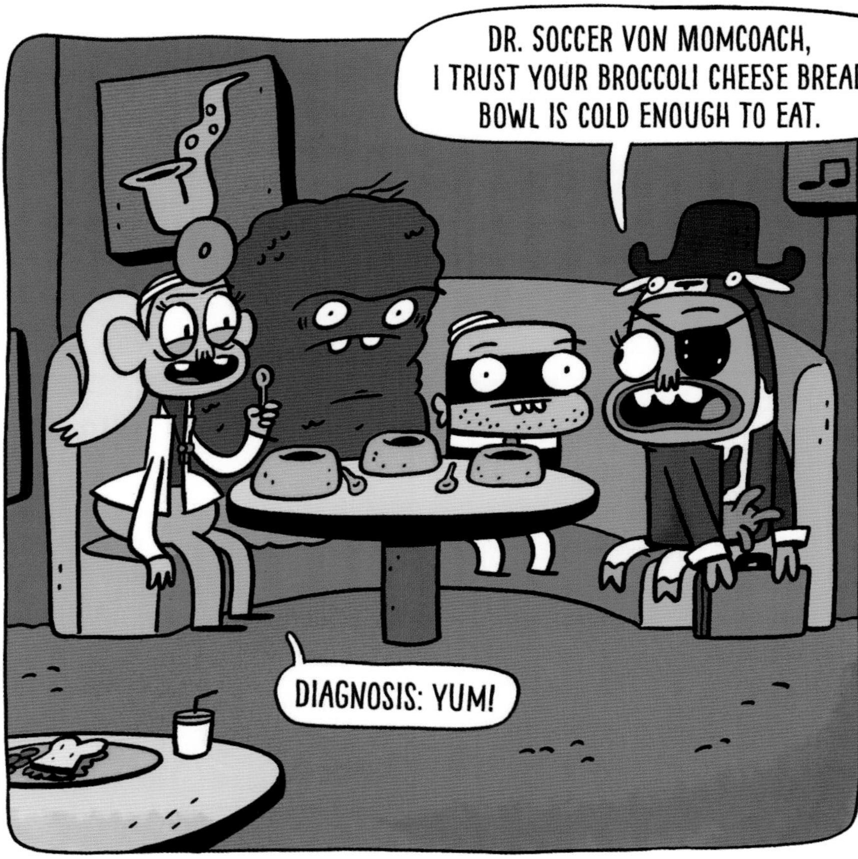
DR. SOCCER VON MOMCOACH, I TRUST YOUR BROCCOLI CHEESE BREAD BOWL IS COLD ENOUGH TO EAT.
DIAGNOSIS: YUM!

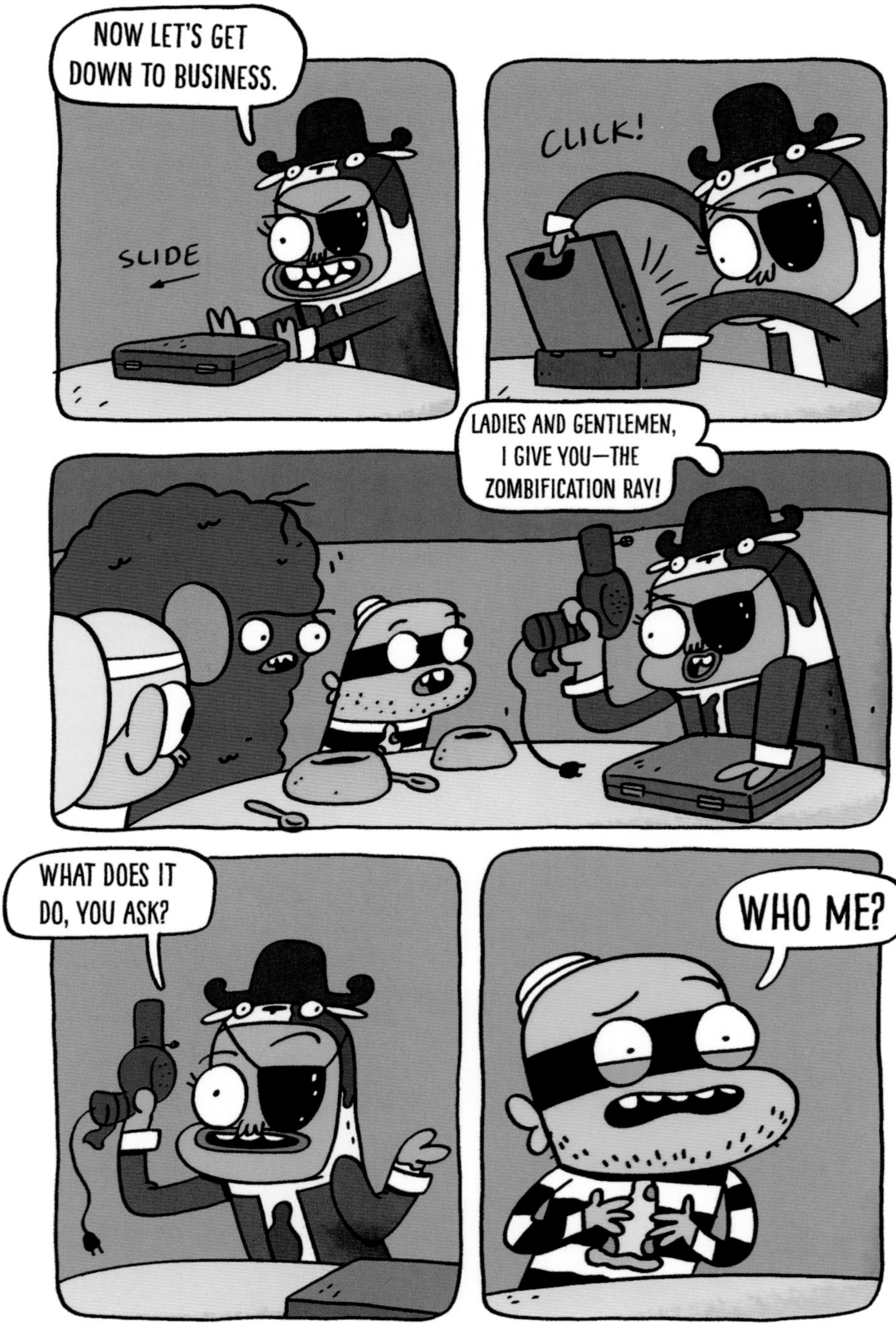
NOW LET'S GET DOWN TO BUSINESS.
SLIDE
CLICK!
LADIES AND GENTLEMEN, I GIVE YOU—THE ZOMBIFICATION RAY!
WHAT DOES IT DO, YOU ASK?
WHO ME?

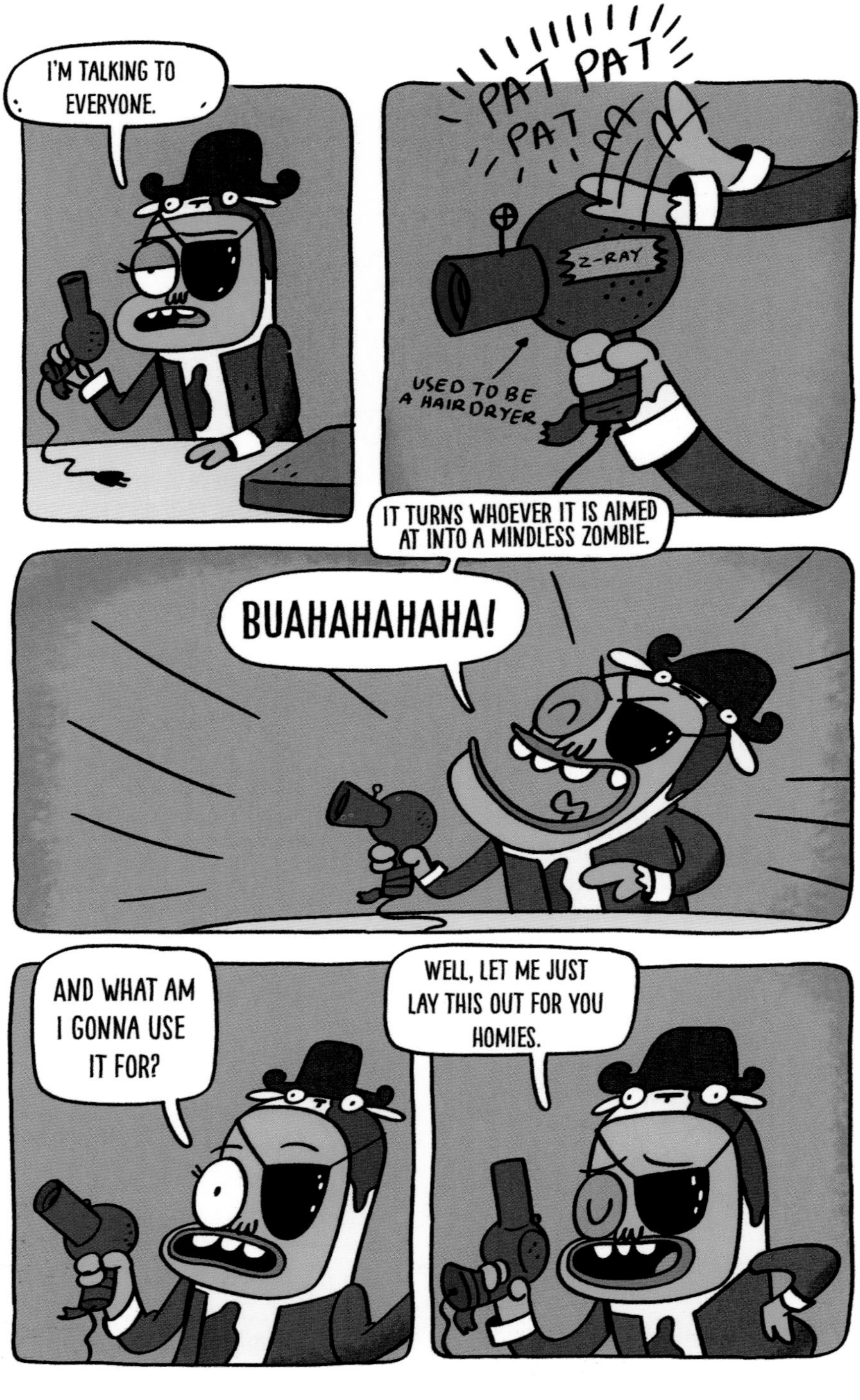
I'M TALKING TO EVERYONE.
PAT PAT PAT
Z-RAY
USED TO BE A HAIRDRYER
IT TURNS WHOEVER IT IS AIMED AT INTO A MINDLESS ZOMBIE.
BUAHAHAHAHA!
AND WHAT AM I GONNA USE IT FOR?
WELL, LET ME JUST LAY THIS OUT FOR YOU HOMIES.

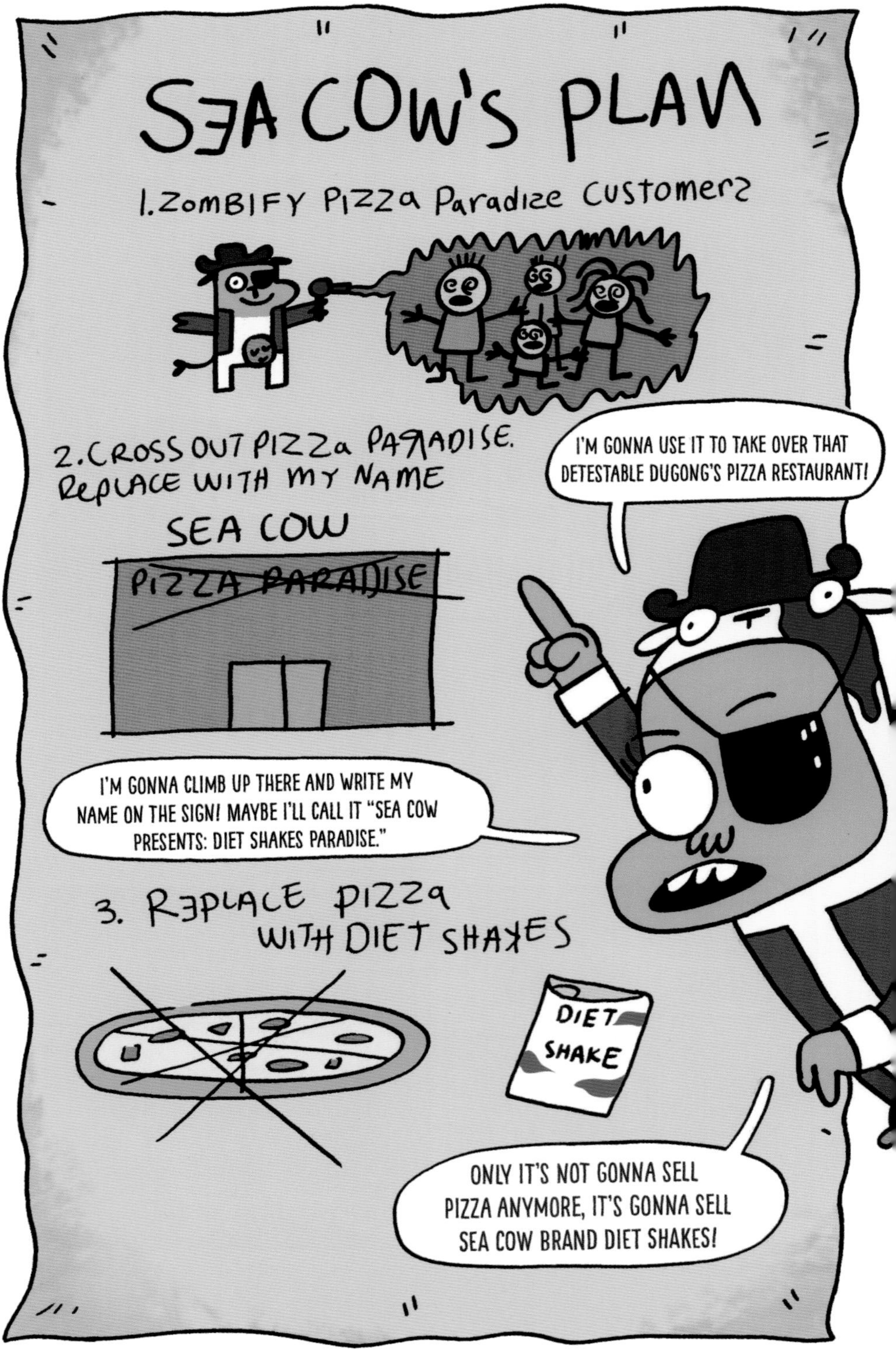
SEA COW'S PLAN
1. ZOMBIFY PIZZA Paradize Customerz
2. CROSS OUT PIZZA PARADISE. REPLACE WITH MY NAME
SEA COW
PIZZA PARADISE
I'M GONNA USE IT TO TAKE OVER THAT DETESTABLE DUGONG'S PIZZA RESTAURANT!
I'M GONNA CLIMB UP THERE AND WRITE MY NAME ON THE SIGN! MAYBE I'LL CALL IT "SEA COW PRESENTS: DIET SHAKES PARADISE."
3. REPLACE PIZZA WITH DIET SHAKES
DIET SHAKE
ONLY IT'S NOT GONNA SELL PIZZA ANYMORE, IT'S GONNA SELL SEA COW BRAND DIET SHAKES!

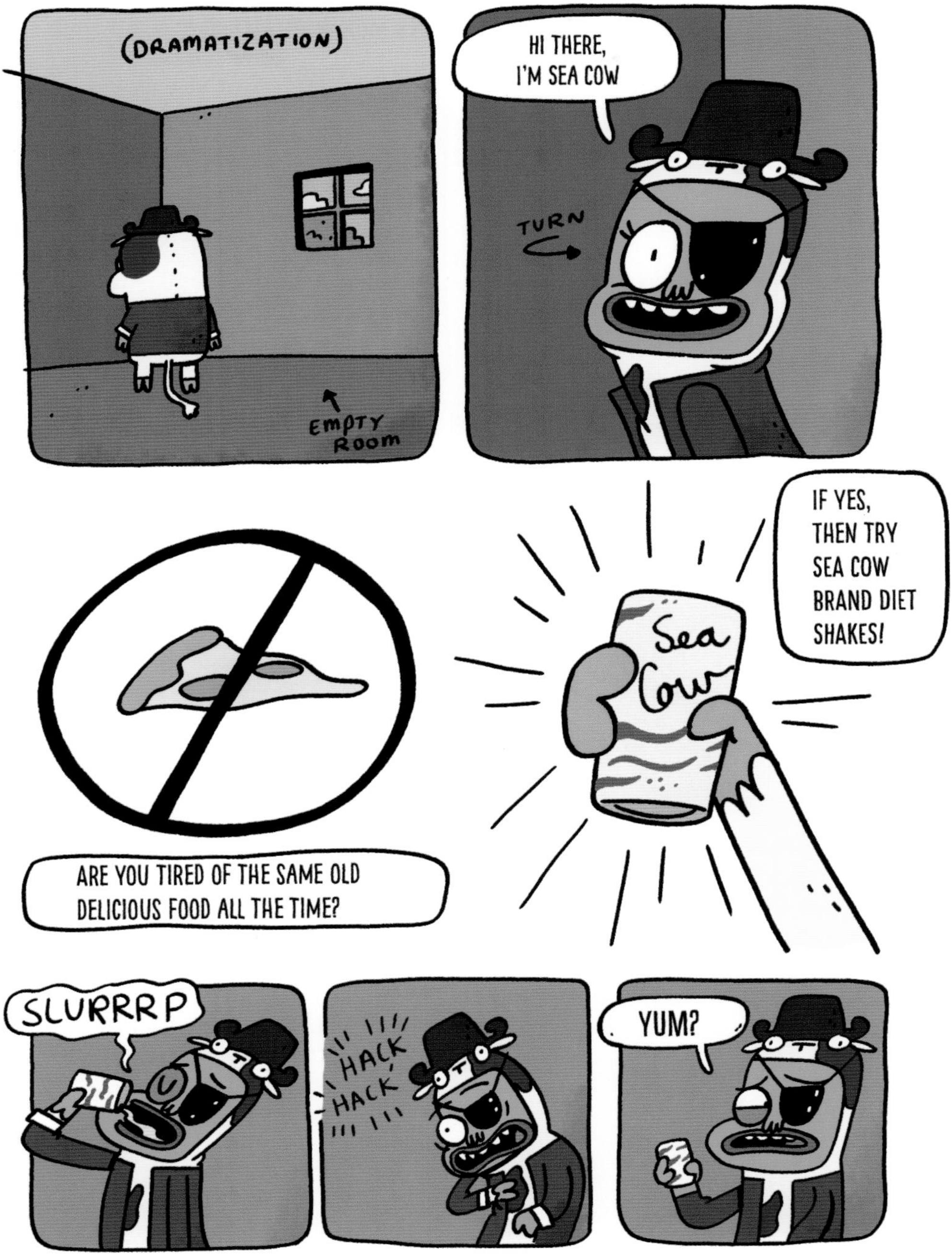
(DRAMATIZATION)
EMPTY ROOM
HI THERE, I'M SEA COW
TURN
ARE YOU TIRED OF THE SAME OLD DELICIOUS FOOD ALL THE TIME?
IF YES, THEN TRY SEA COW BRAND DIET SHAKES!
Sea Cow
SLURRRP
HACK HACK
YUM?

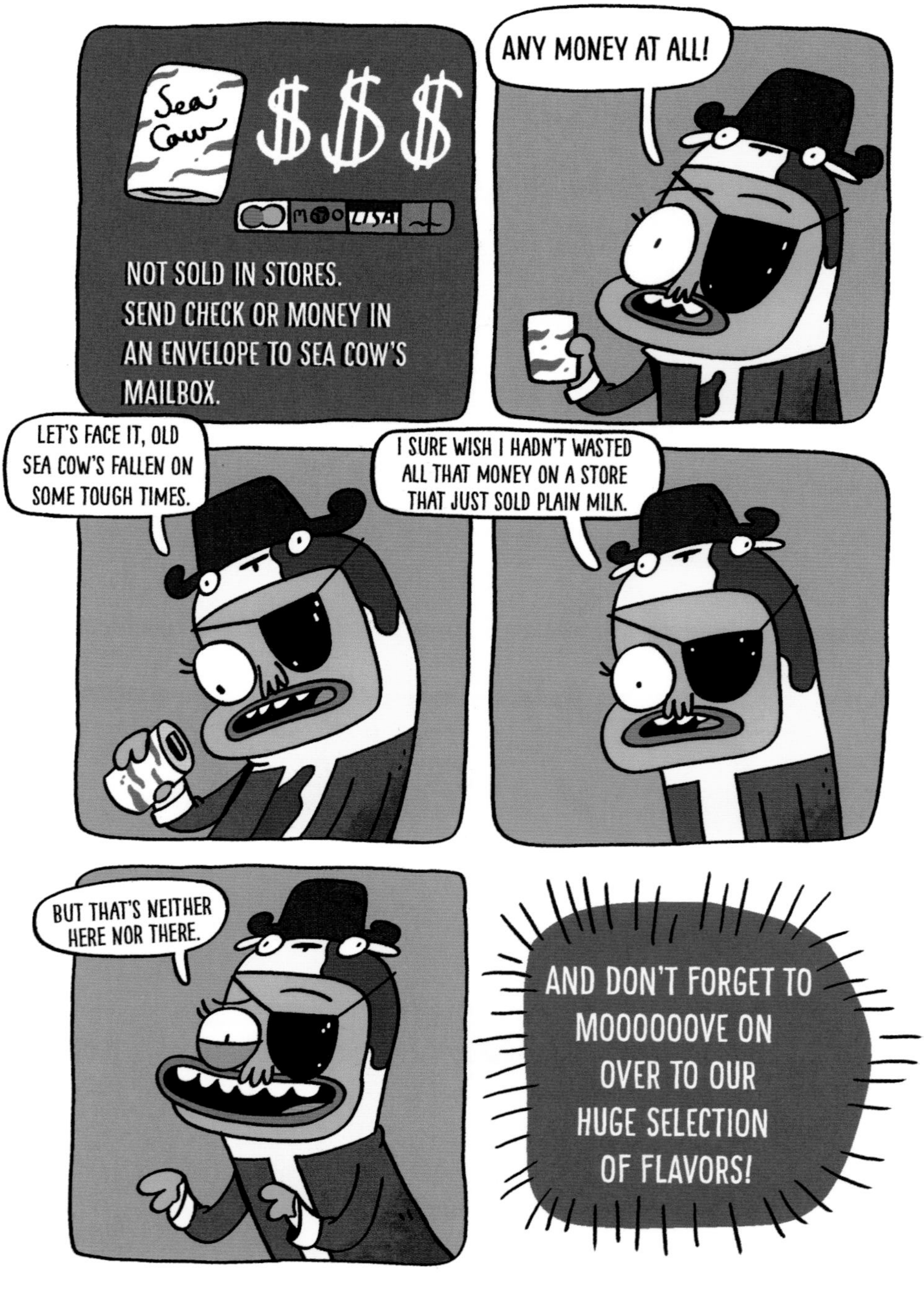
Sea Cow
$$$
NOT SOLD IN STORES.
SEND CHECK OR MONEY IN
AN ENVELOPE TO SEA COW'S
MAILBOX.
ANY MONEY AT ALL!
LET'S FACE IT, OLD SEA COW'S FALLEN ON SOME TOUGH TIMES.
I SURE WISH I HADN'T WASTED ALL THAT MONEY ON A STORE THAT JUST SOLD PLAIN MILK.
BUT THAT'S NEITHER HERE NOR THERE.
AND DON'T FORGET TO MOOOOOOVE ON OVER TO OUR HUGE SELECTION OF FLAVORS!

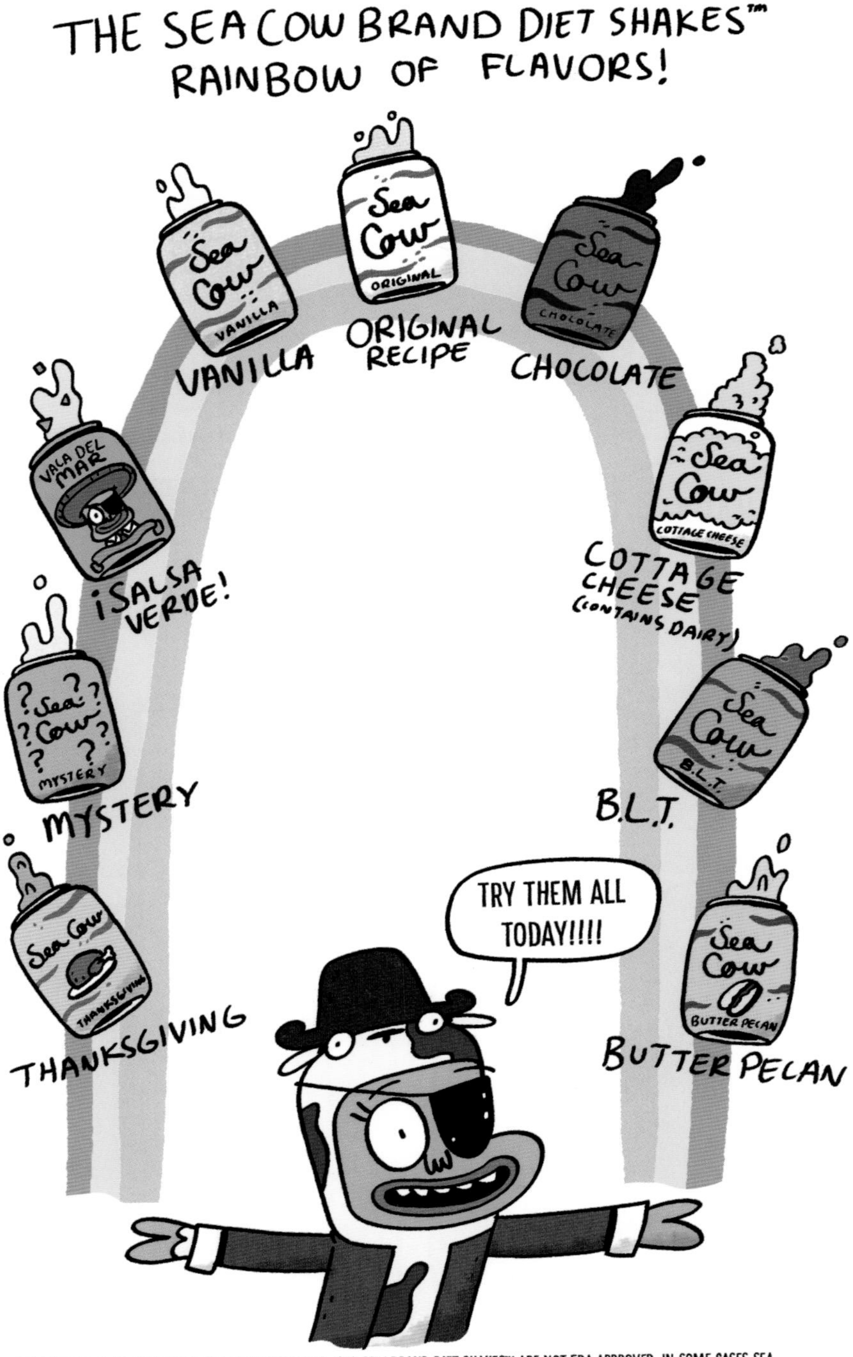
THE SEA COW BRAND DIET SHAKES™ RAINBOW OF FLAVORS!
Sea Cow VANILLA
VANILLA
Sea Cow ORIGINAL
ORIGINAL RECIPE
Sea Cow CHOCOLATE
CHOCOLATE
VACA DEL MAR
¡SALSA VERDE!
Sea Cow COTTAGE CHEESE
COTTAGE CHEESE (CONTAINS DAIRY)
Sea Cow MYSTERY
MYSTERY
Sea Cow B.L.T.
B.L.T.
Sea Cow THANKSGIVING
THANKSGIVING
Sea Cow BUTTER PECAN
BUTTER PECAN
TRY THEM ALL TODAY!!!!!

SEA COW BRAND DIET SHAKES™ MAY CAUSE THE TOOTS. SEA COW BRAND DIET SHAKES™ ARE NOT FDA APPROVED. IN SOME CASES SEA COW BRAND DIET SHAKES™ MAY CAUSE SWEATING, NIGHTMARES, OR RESTLESS LEG SYNDROME. SEA COW BRAND DIET SHAKES™ ARE PRODUCED IN A FACTORY THAT ALSO PRODUCES SEA COW BRAND DOG FOOD™.

BACK TO REALITY:

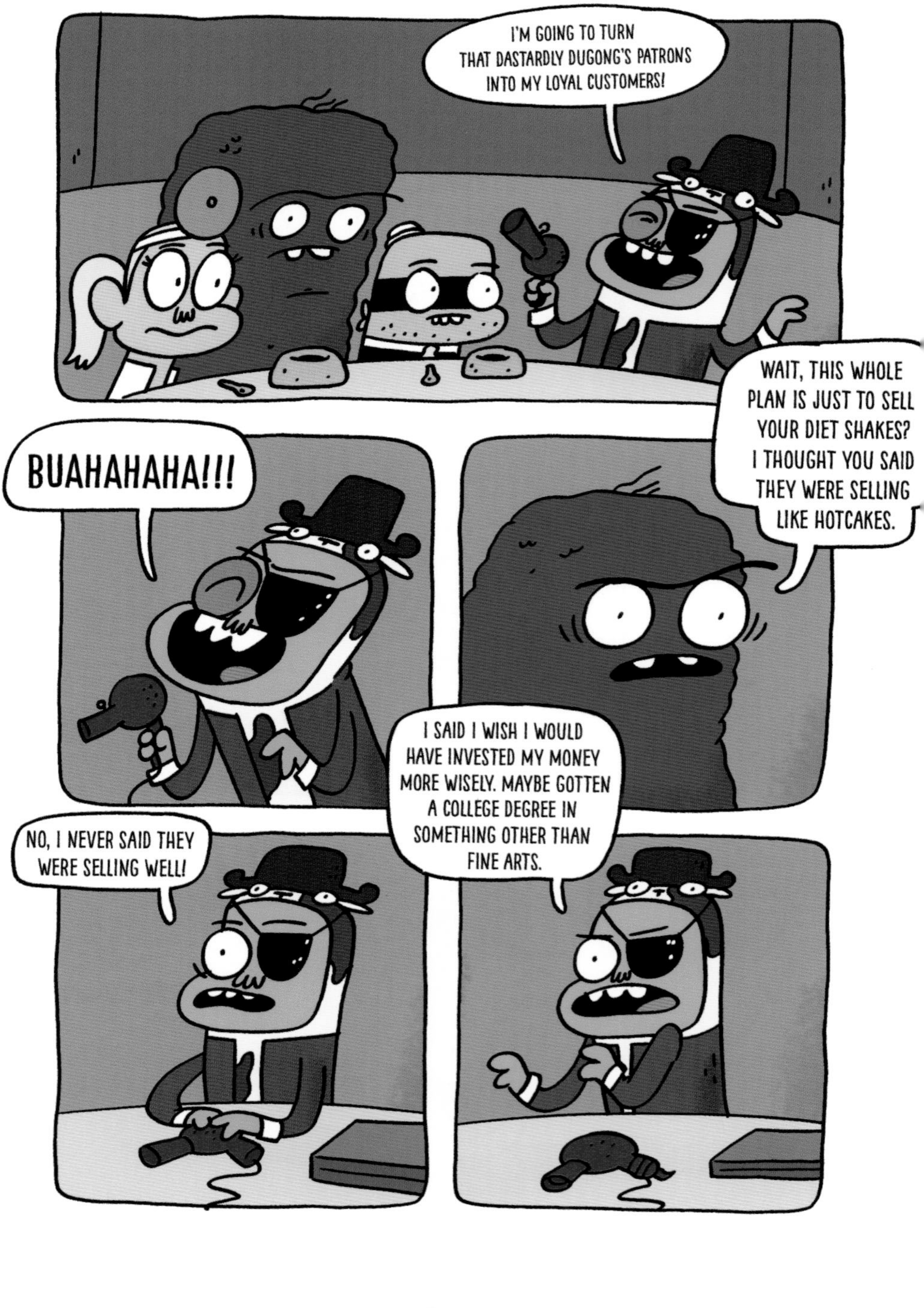
I'M GOING TO TURN THAT DASTARDLY DUGONG'S PATRONS INTO MY LOYAL CUSTOMERS!
BUAHAHAHA!!!
WAIT, THIS WHOLE PLAN IS JUST TO SELL YOUR DIET SHAKES? I THOUGHT YOU SAID THEY WERE SELLING LIKE HOTCAKES.
NO, I NEVER SAID THEY WERE SELLING WELL!
I SAID I WISH I WOULD HAVE INVESTED MY MONEY MORE WISELY. MAYBE GOTTEN A COLLEGE DEGREE IN SOMETHING OTHER THAN FINE ARTS.

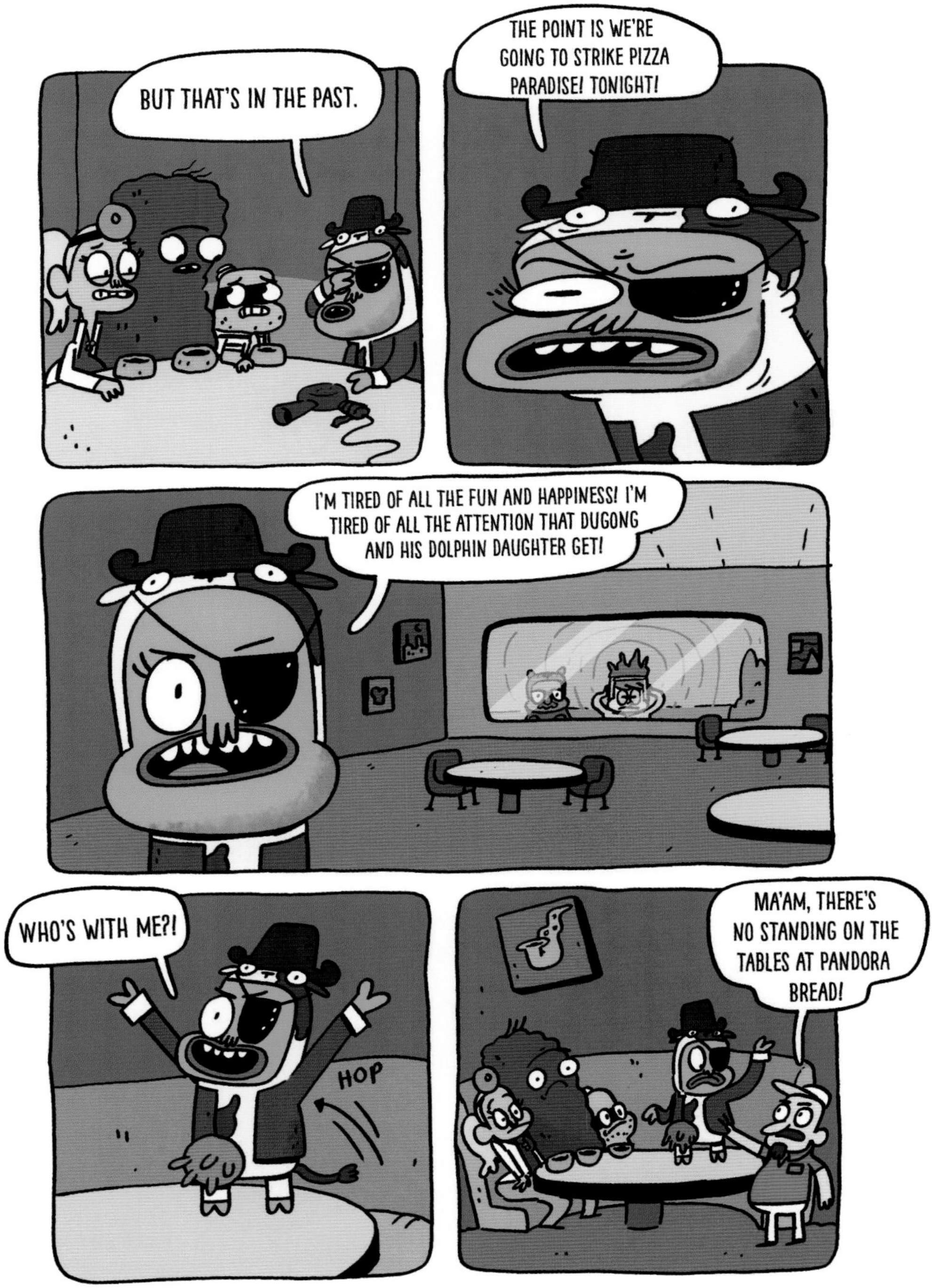
BUT THAT'S IN THE PAST.
THE POINT IS WE'RE GOING TO STRIKE PIZZA PARADISE! TONIGHT!
I'M TIRED OF ALL THE FUN AND HAPPINESS! I'M TIRED OF ALL THE ATTENTION THAT DUGONG AND HIS DOLPHIN DAUGHTER GET!
WHO'S WITH ME?!
HOP
MA'AM, THERE'S NO STANDING ON THE TABLES AT PANDORA BREAD!

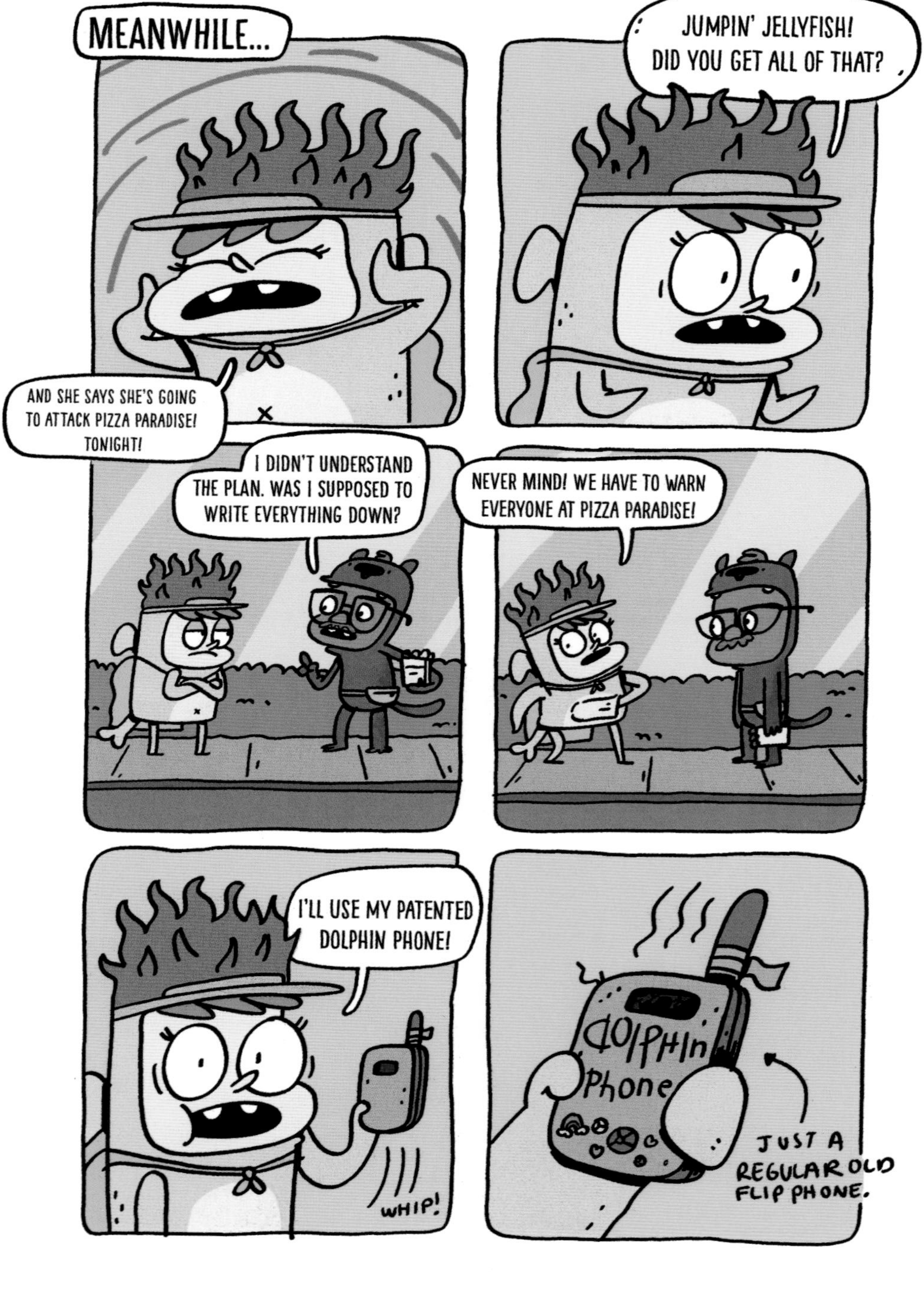
MEANWHILE...
AND SHE SAYS SHE'S GOING TO ATTACK PIZZA PARADISE! TONIGHT!
JUMPIN' JELLYFISH! DID YOU GET ALL OF THAT?
I DIDN'T UNDERSTAND THE PLAN. WAS I SUPPOSED TO WRITE EVERYTHING DOWN?
NEVER MIND! WE HAVE TO WARN EVERYONE AT PIZZA PARADISE!
I'LL USE MY PATENTED DOLPHIN PHONE!
WHIP!
DOLPHIN Phone
JUST A REGULAR OLD FLIP PHONE.

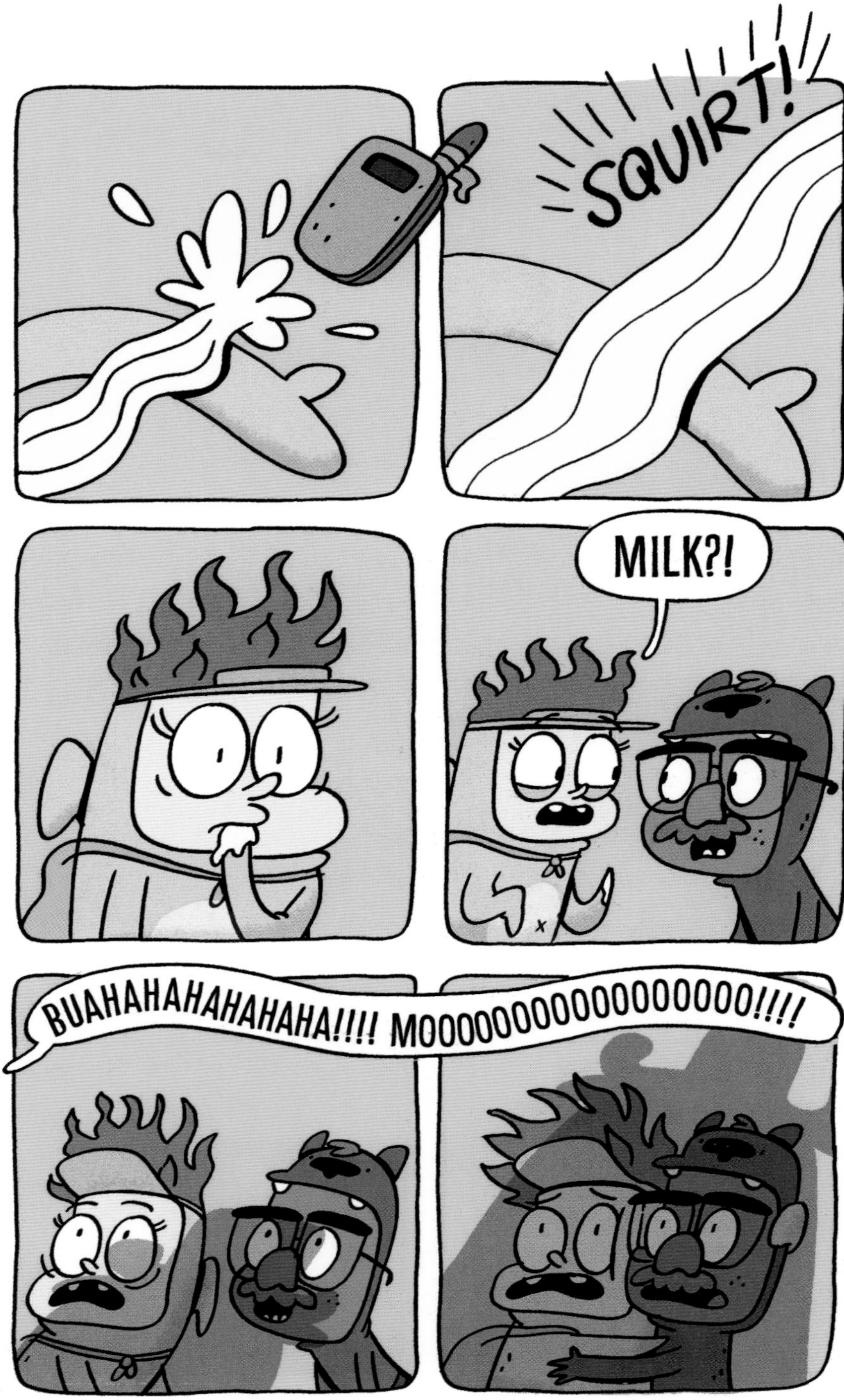
SQUIRT!
MILK?!
BUAHAHAHAHAHAHA!!!! MOOOOOOOOOOOOOOOOOO!!!!

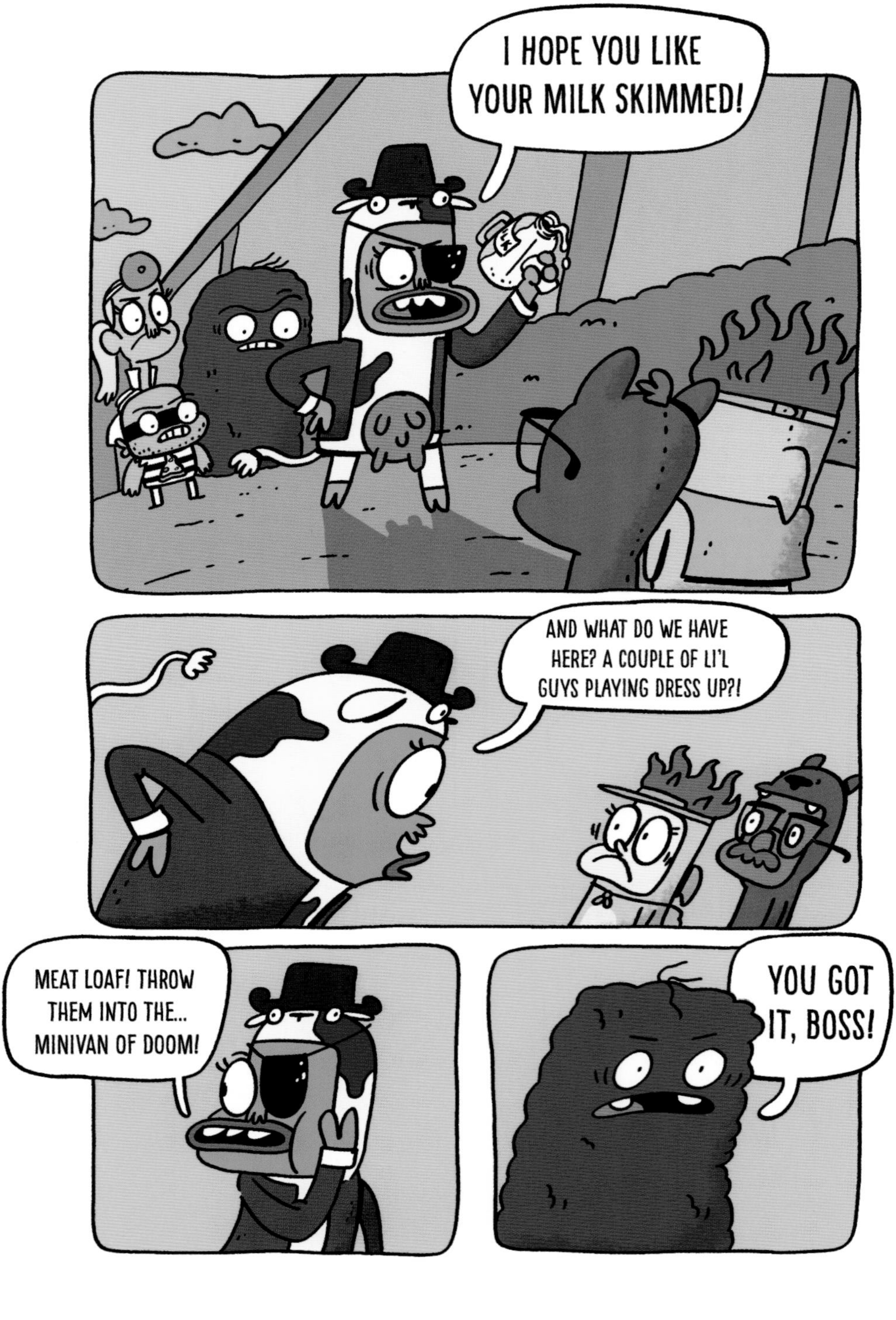
I HOPE YOU LIKE YOUR MILK SKIMMED!
MILK
AND WHAT DO WE HAVE HERE? A COUPLE OF LI'L GUYS PLAYING DRESS UP?!
MEAT LOAF! THROW THEM INTO THE... MINIVAN OF DOOM!
YOU GOT IT, BOSS!

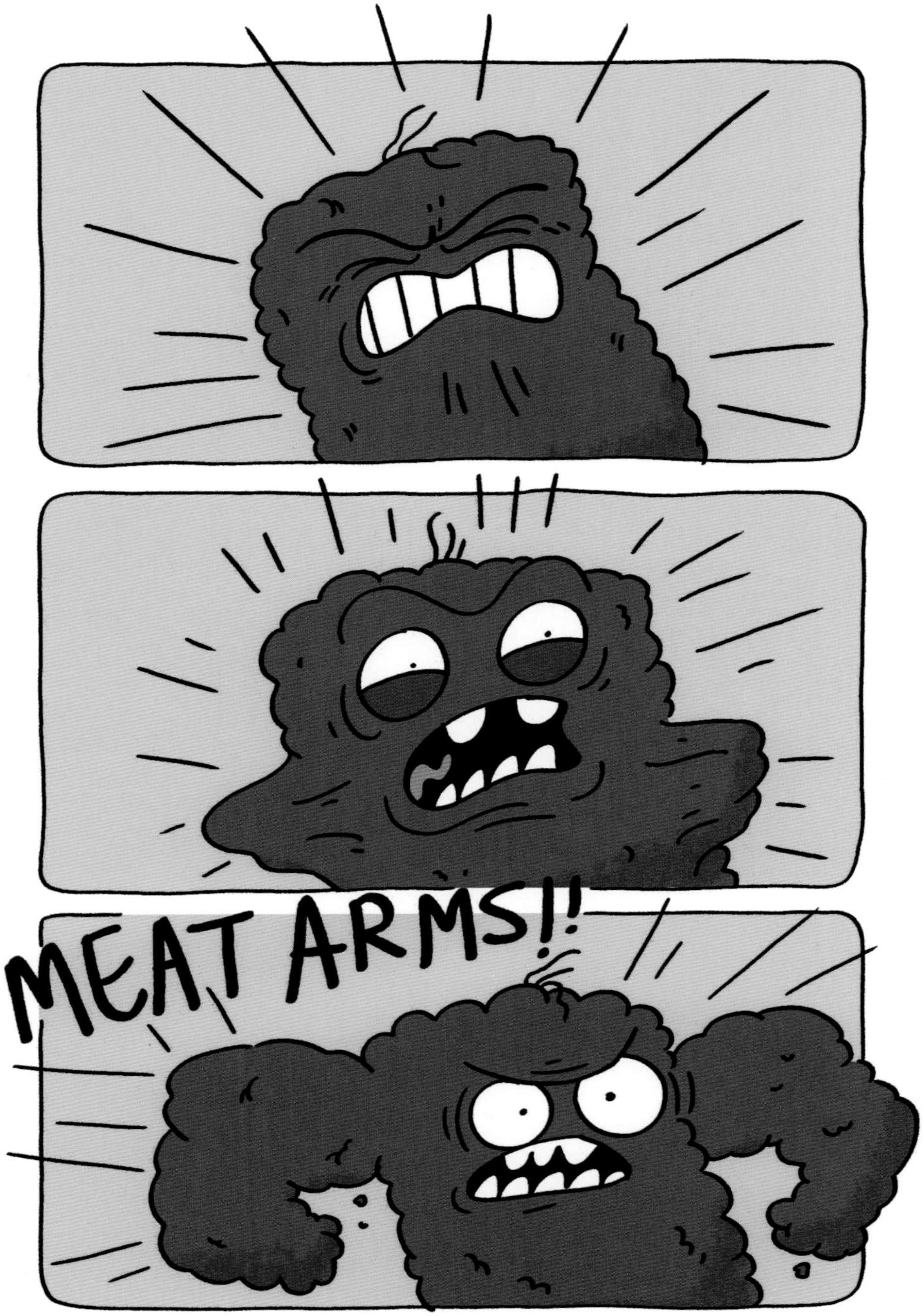
MEAT ARMS!!

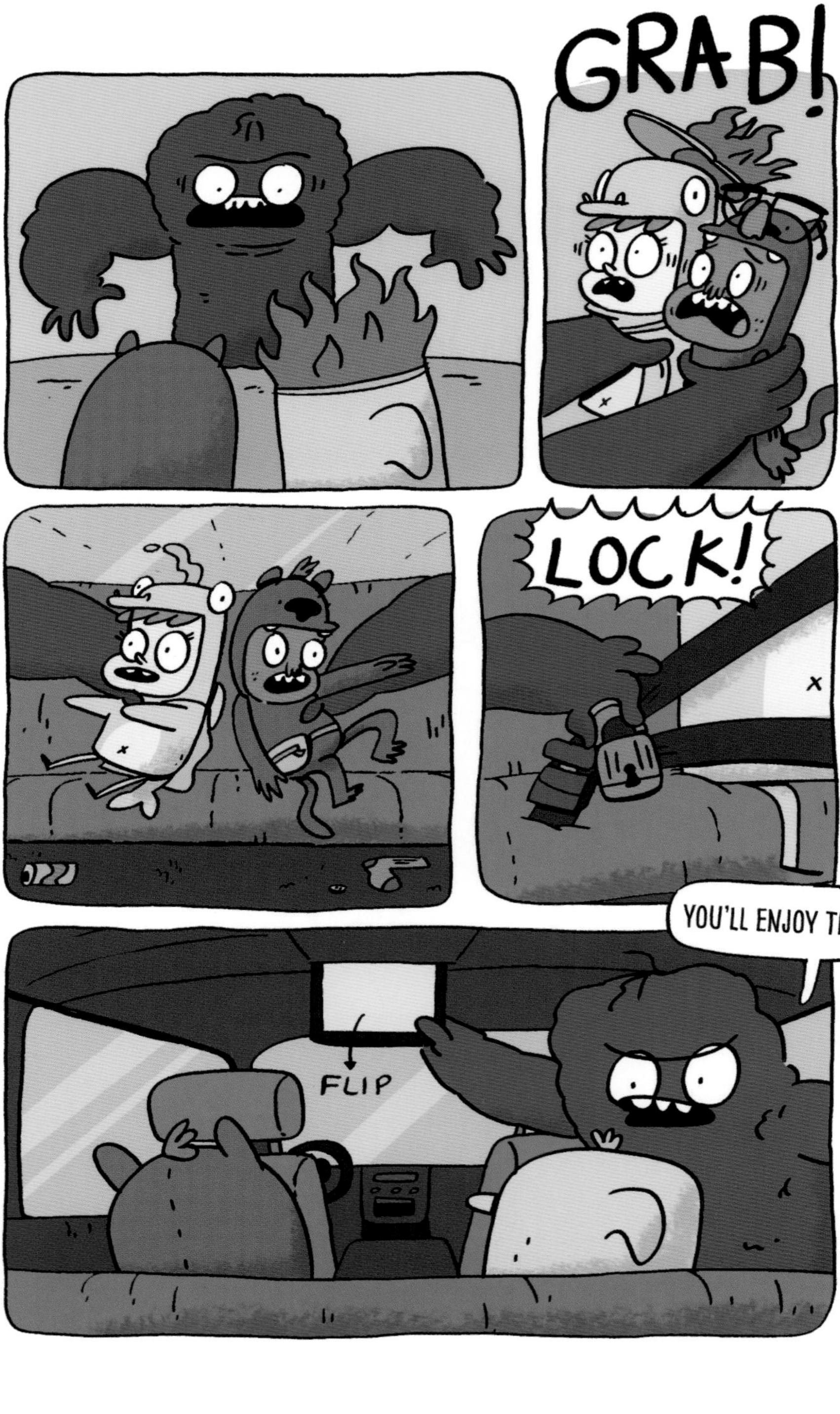
GRAB!
LOCK!
YOU'LL ENJOY THIS!
FLIP

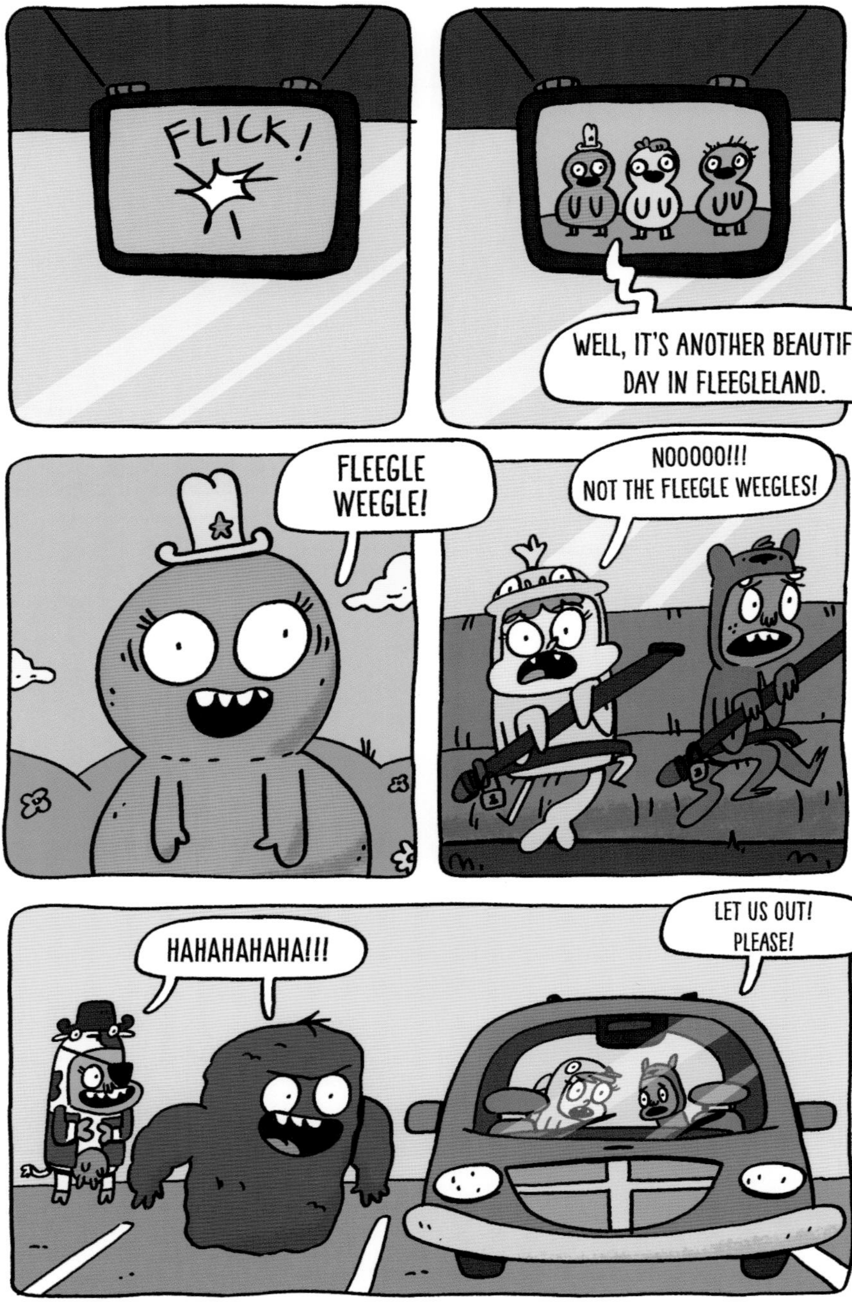
FLICK!
WELL, IT'S ANOTHER BEAUTIFUL DAY IN FLEEGLELAND.
FLEEGLE WEEGLE!
NOOOOO!!! NOT THE FLEEGLE WEEGLES!
HAHAHAHAHA!!!
LET US OUT! PLEASE!

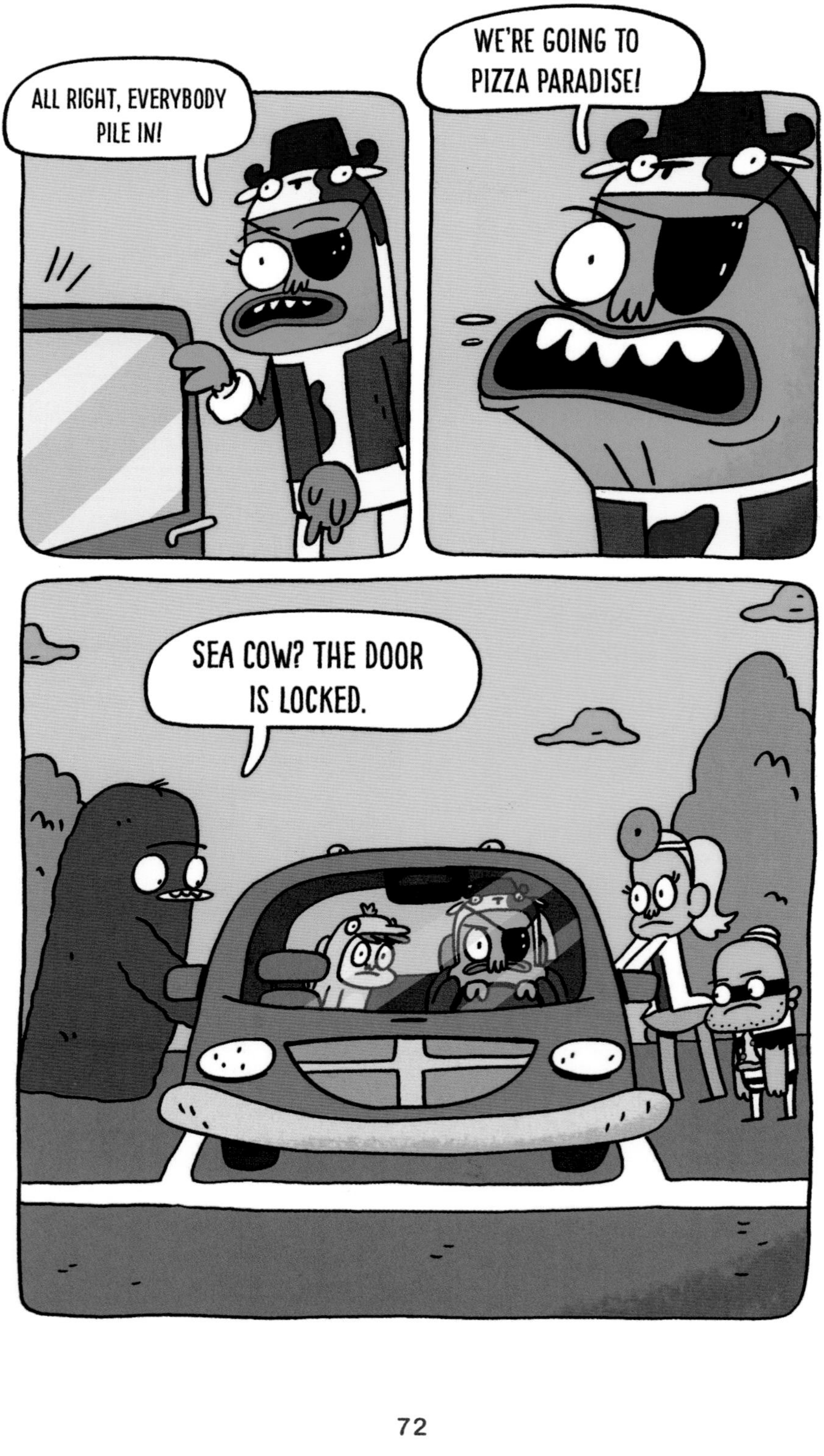
ALL RIGHT, EVERYBODY PILE IN!
WE'RE GOING TO PIZZA PARADISE!
SEA COW? THE DOOR IS LOCKED.

PART THREE

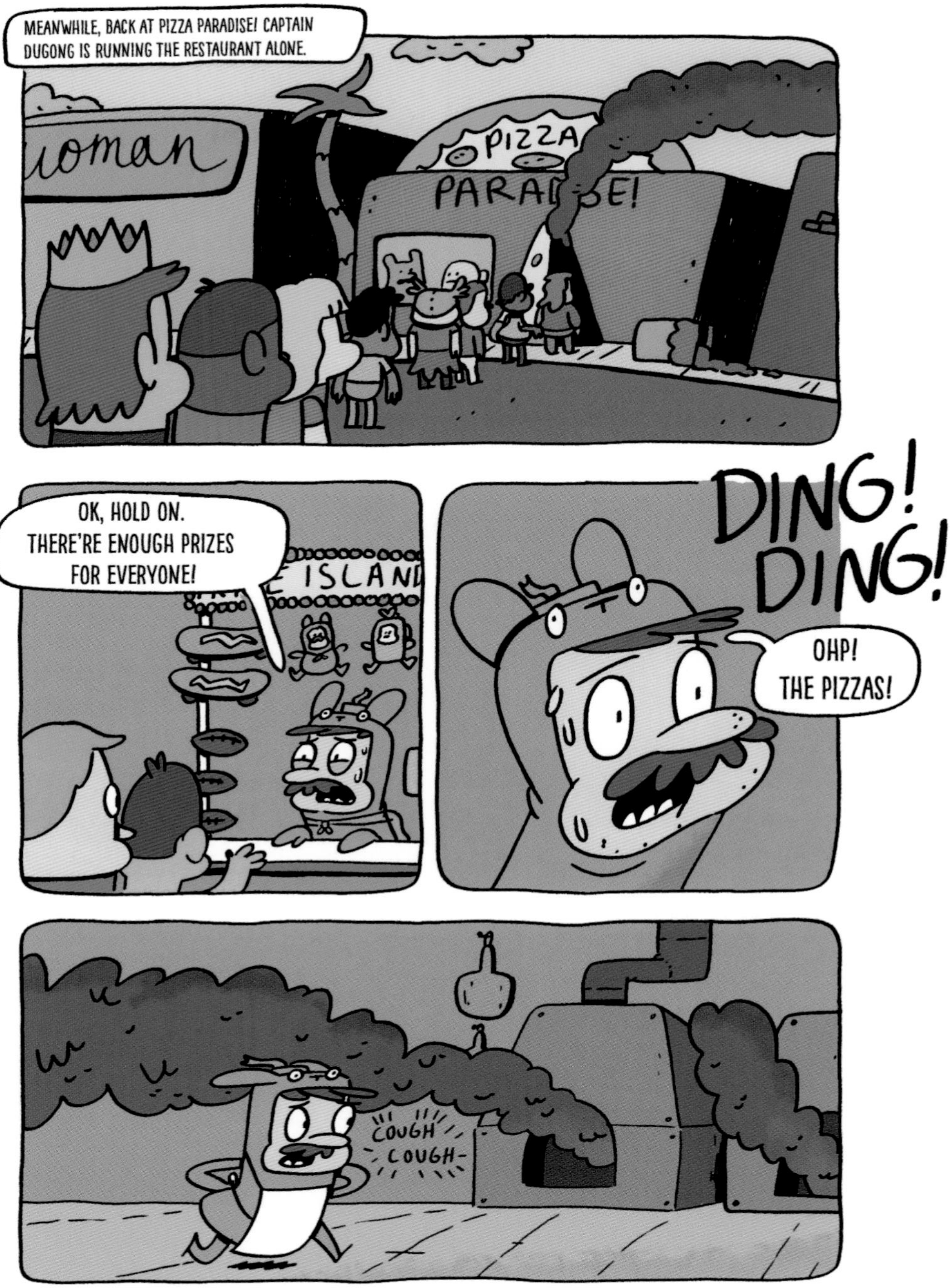
MEANWHILE, BACK AT PIZZA PARADISE! CAPTAIN DUGONG IS RUNNING THE RESTAURANT ALONE.
PIZZA
PARADISE!
OK, HOLD ON. THERE'RE ENOUGH PRIZES FOR EVERYONE!
ISLAND
DING! DING!
OHP! THE PIZZAS!
COUGH COUGH

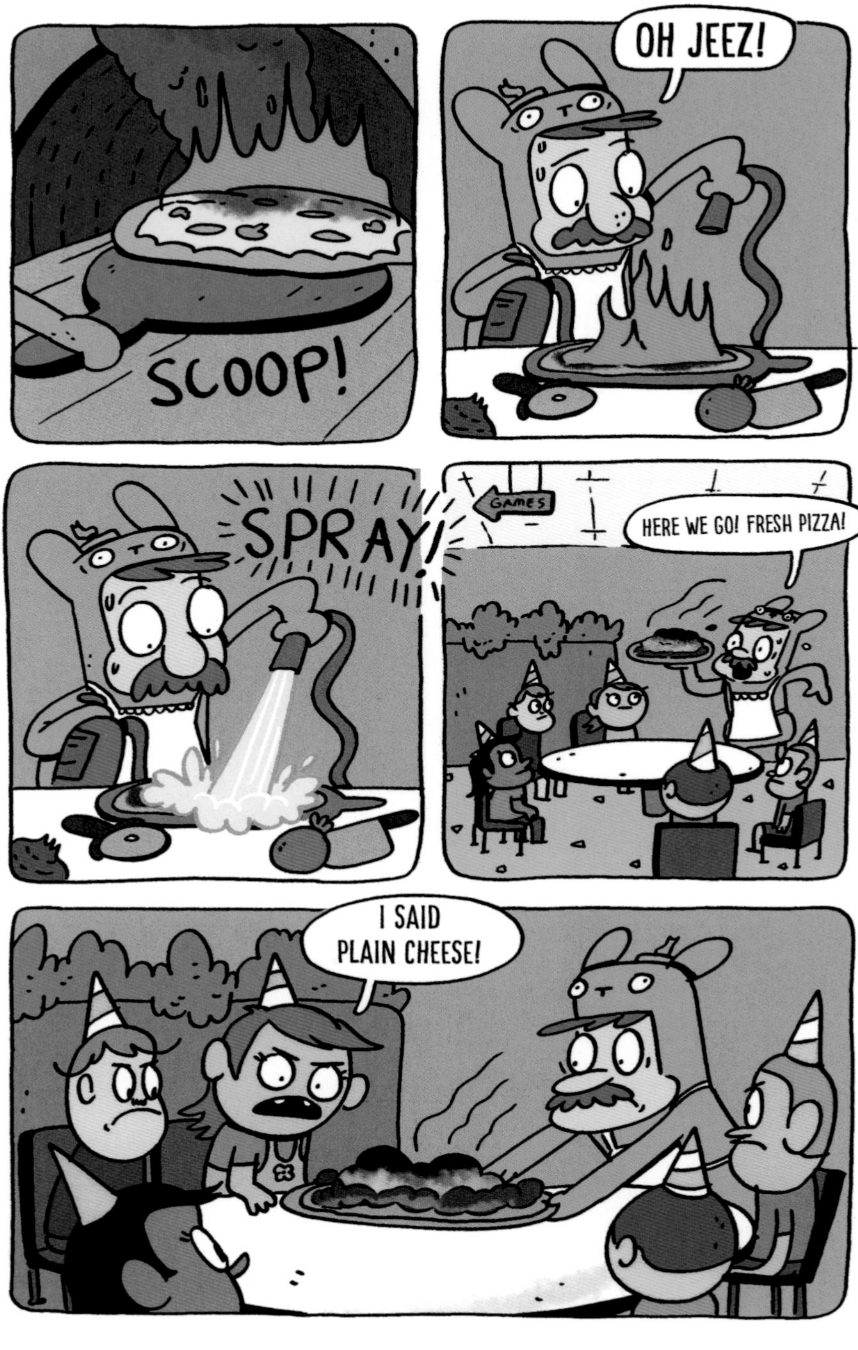
SCOOP!
OH JEEZ!
SPRAY!
GAMES
HERE WE GO! FRESH PIZZA!
I SAID
PLAIN CHEESE!

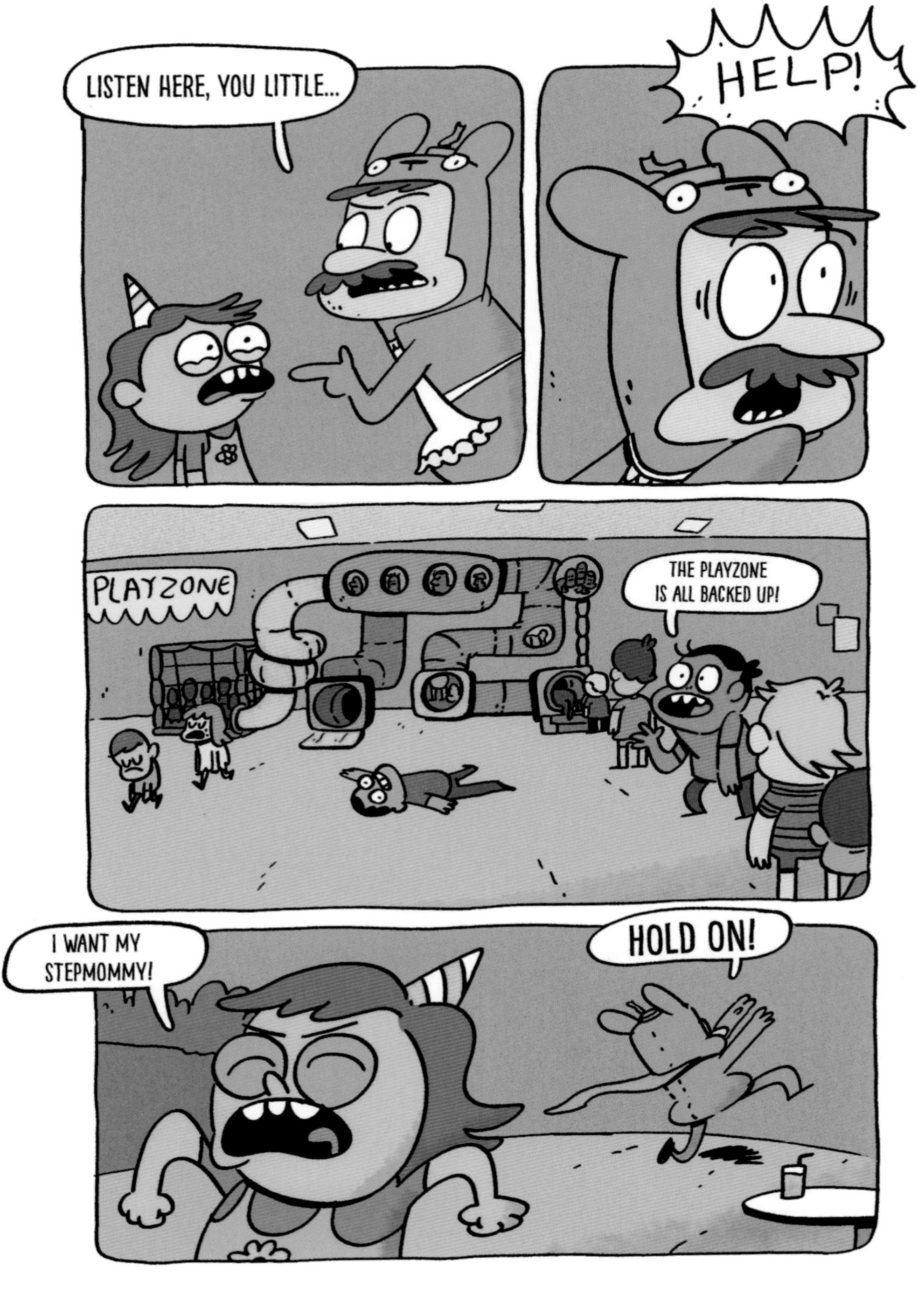
LISTEN HERE, YOU LITTLE...
HELP!
PLAYZONE
THE PLAYZONE IS ALL BACKED UP!
I WANT MY STEPMOMMY!
HOLD ON!

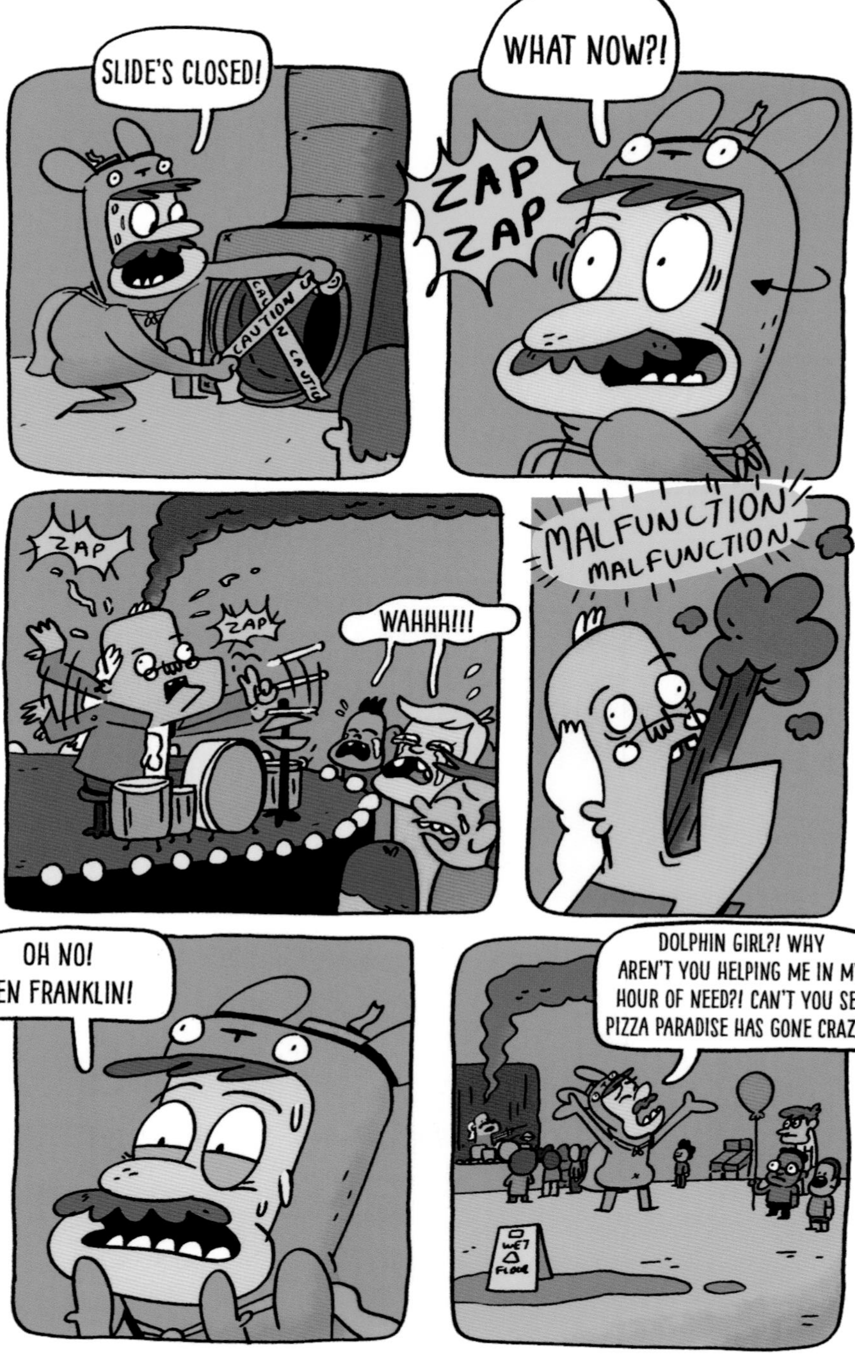
SLIDE'S CLOSED!
CAUTION
CAUTION
CAUTIO
WHAT NOW?!
ZAP ZAP
ZAP
ZAP
WAHHH!!!
MALFUNCTION MALFUNCTION
OH NO! BEN FRANKLIN!
DOLPHIN GIRL?! WHY AREN'T YOU HELPING ME IN MY HOUR OF NEED?! CAN'T YOU SEE PIZZA PARADISE HAS GONE CRAZY?!
WET FLOOR

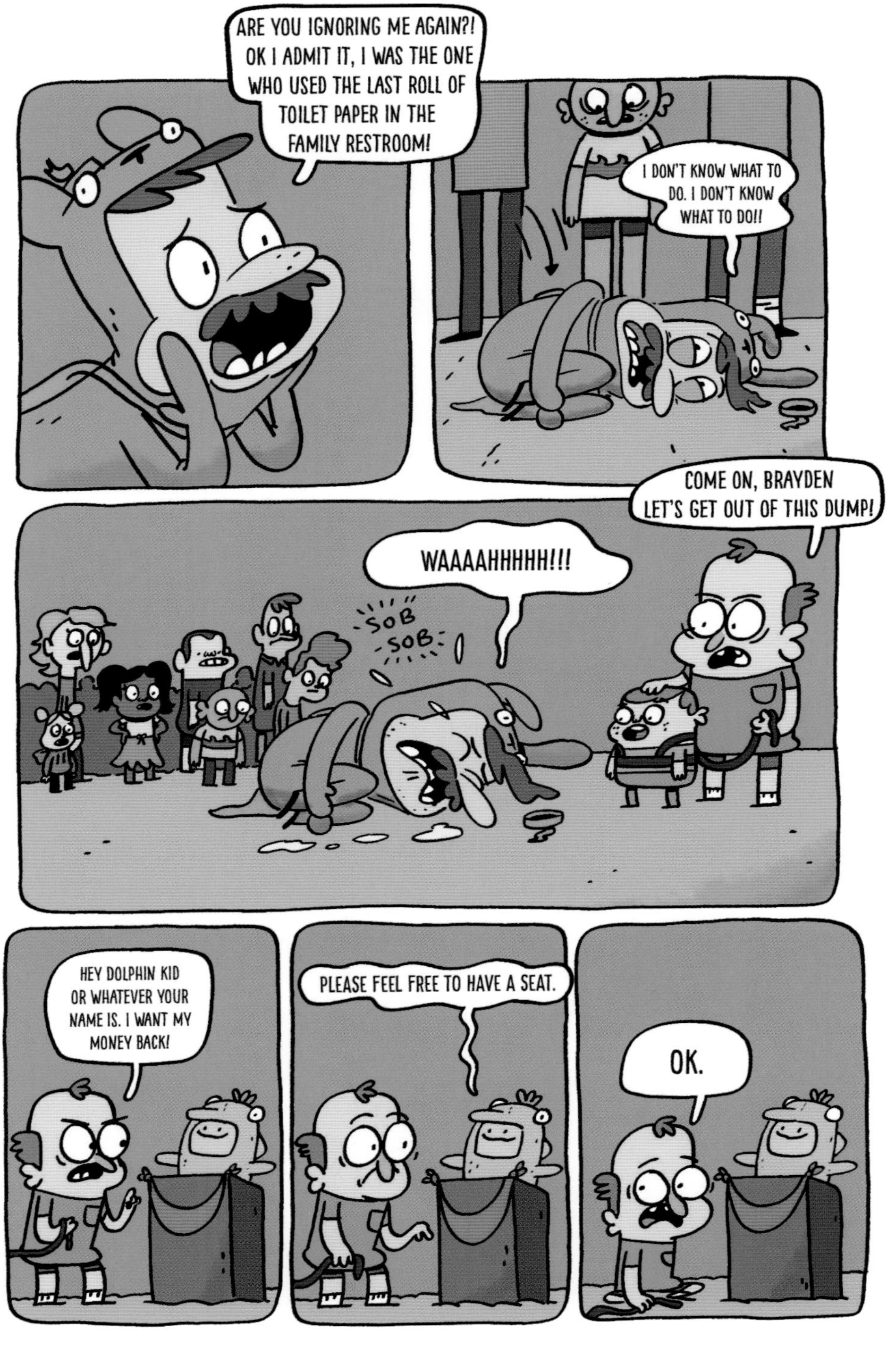
ARE YOU IGNORING ME AGAIN?! OK I ADMIT IT, I WAS THE ONE WHO USED THE LAST ROLL OF TOILET PAPER IN THE FAMILY RESTROOM!
I DON'T KNOW WHAT TO DO. I DON'T KNOW WHAT TO DO!!
COME ON, BRAYDEN LET'S GET OUT OF THIS DUMP!
WAAAAHHHHH!!!
SOB SOB
HEY DOLPHIN KID OR WHATEVER YOUR NAME IS. I WANT MY MONEY BACK!
PLEASE FEEL FREE TO HAVE A SEAT.
OK.

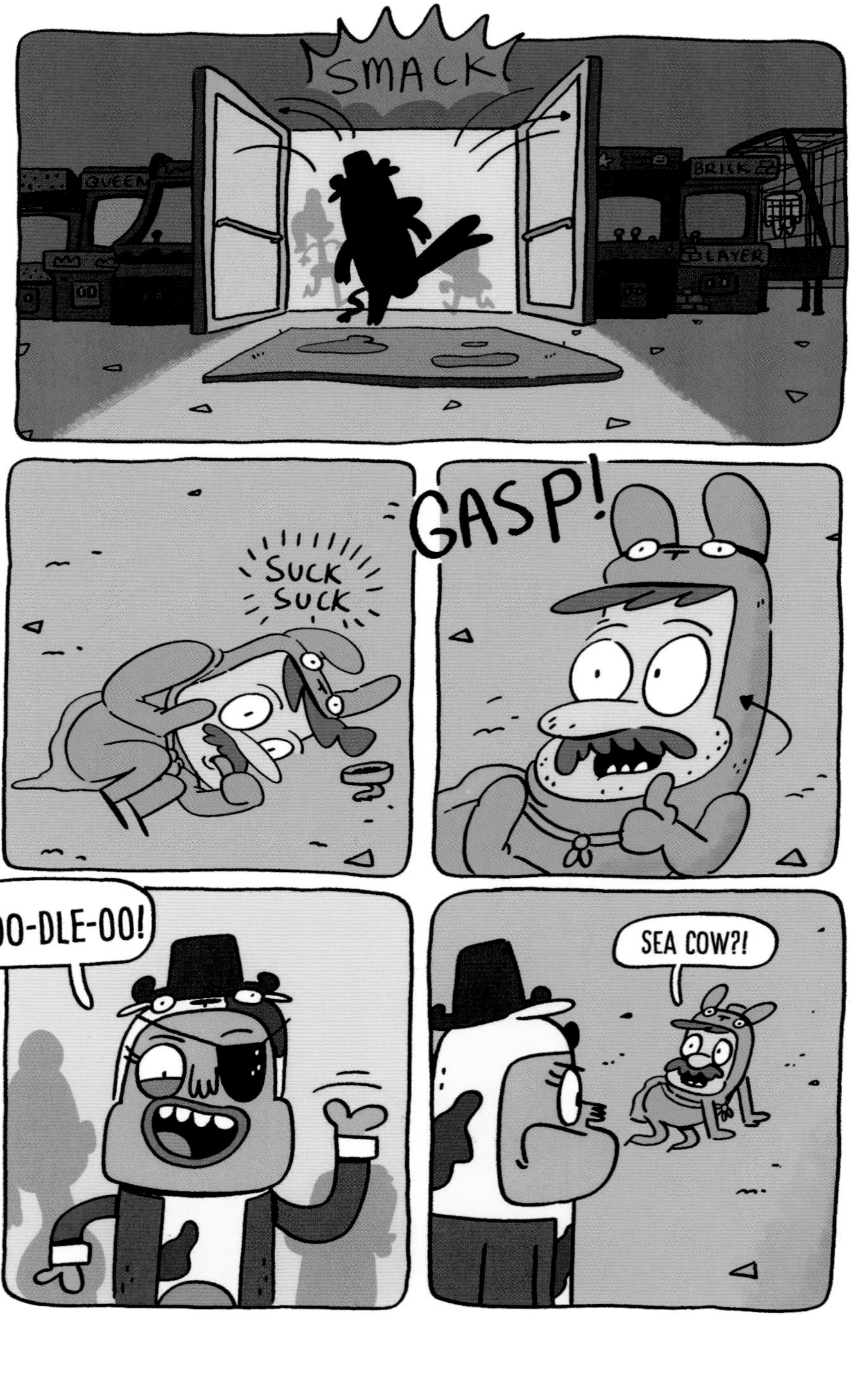
SMACK
QUEEN
BRICK
LAYER
SUCK SUCK
GASP!
MOO-DLE-OO!
SEA COW?!

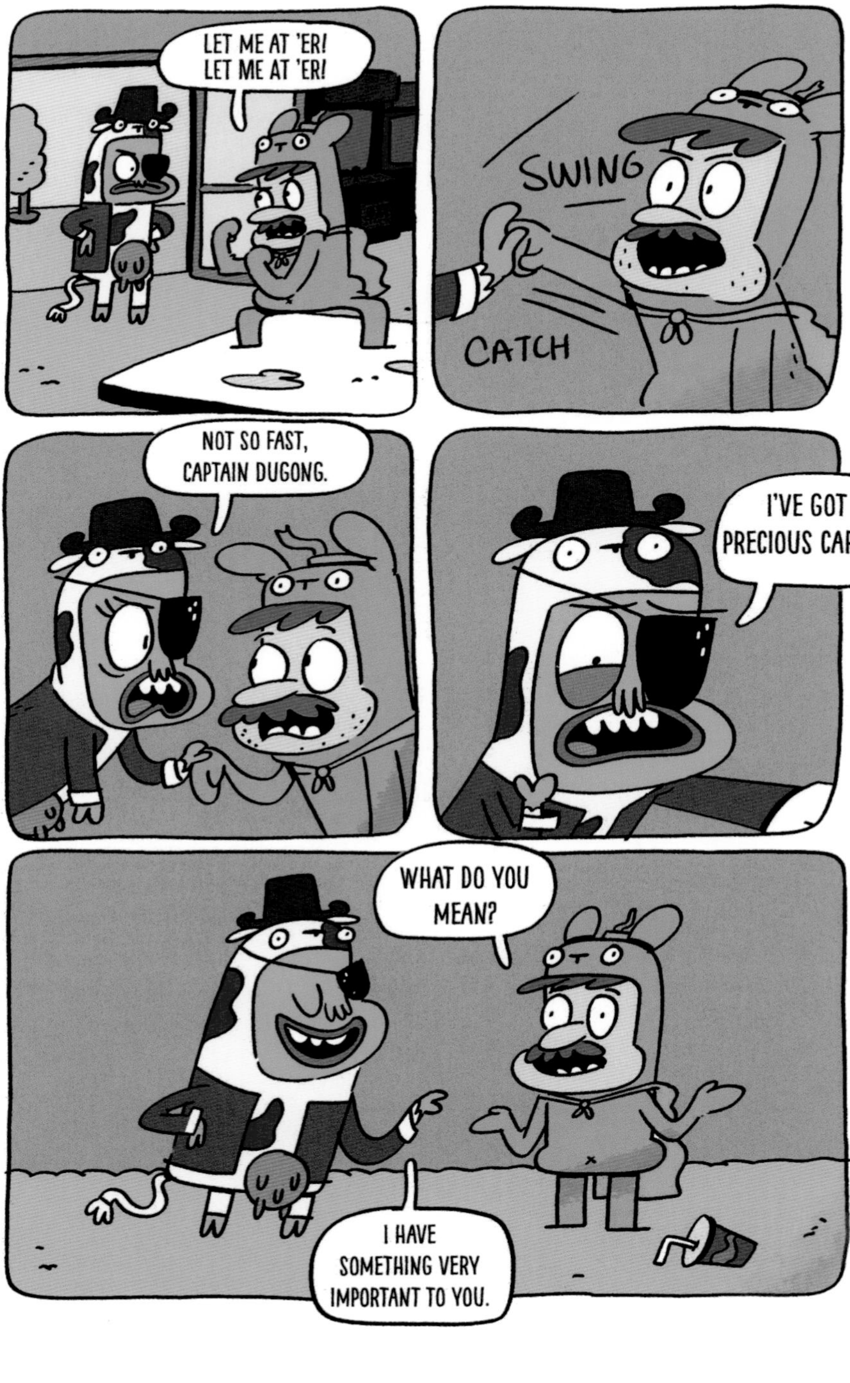
LET ME AT 'ER! LET ME AT 'ER!
SWING
CATCH
NOT SO FAST, CAPTAIN DUGONG.
I'VE GOT PRECIOUS CARGO!
WHAT DO YOU MEAN?
I HAVE SOMETHING VERY IMPORTANT TO YOU.

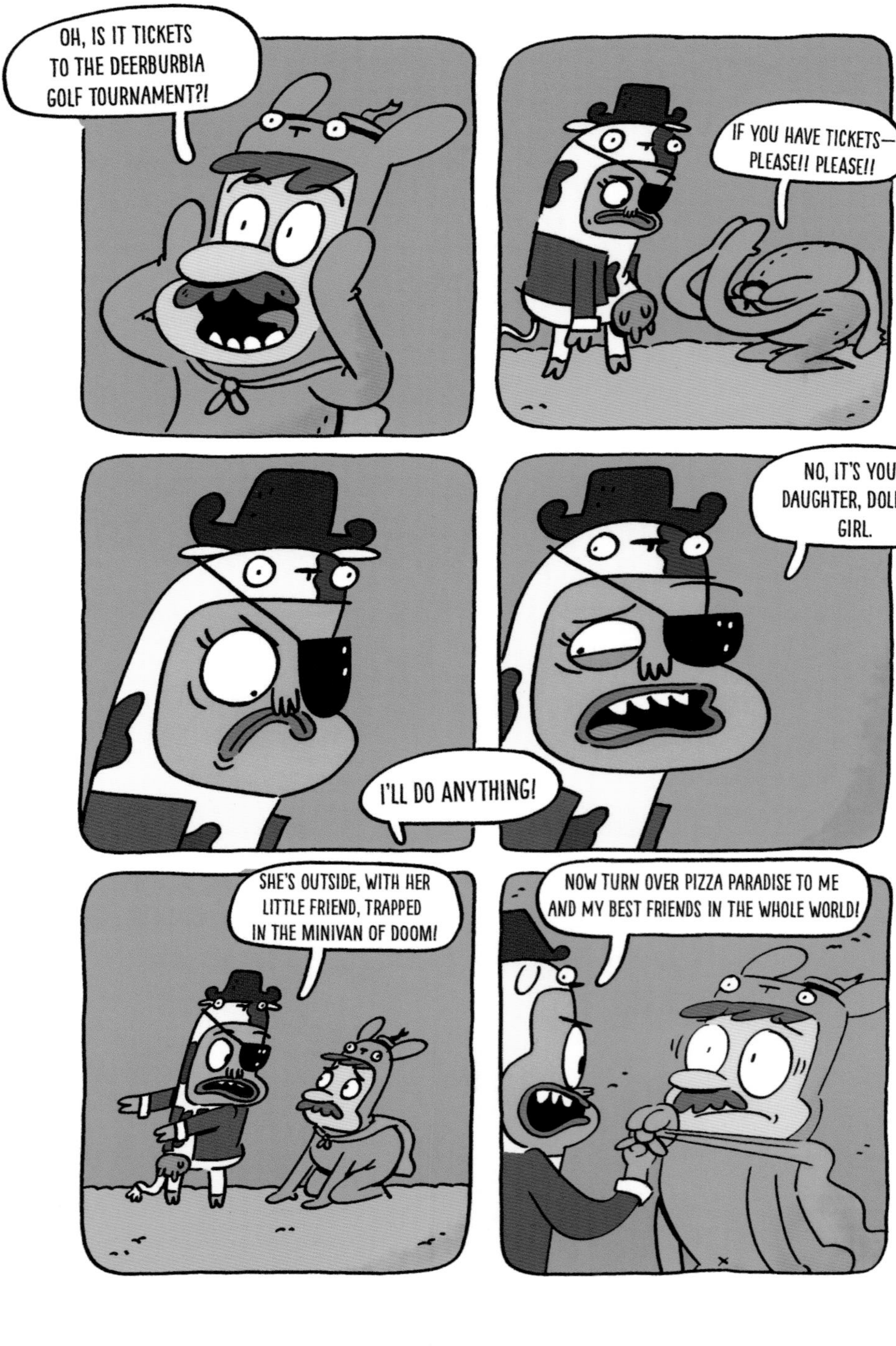
OH, IS IT TICKETS TO THE DEERBURBIA GOLF TOURNAMENT?!
IF YOU HAVE TICKETS— PLEASE!! PLEASE!!
I'LL DO ANYTHING!
NO, IT'S YOUR DAUGHTER, DOLPHIN GIRL.
SHE'S OUTSIDE, WITH HER LITTLE FRIEND, TRAPPED IN THE MINIVAN OF DOOM!
NOW TURN OVER PIZZA PARADISE TO ME AND MY BEST FRIENDS IN THE WHOLE WORLD!

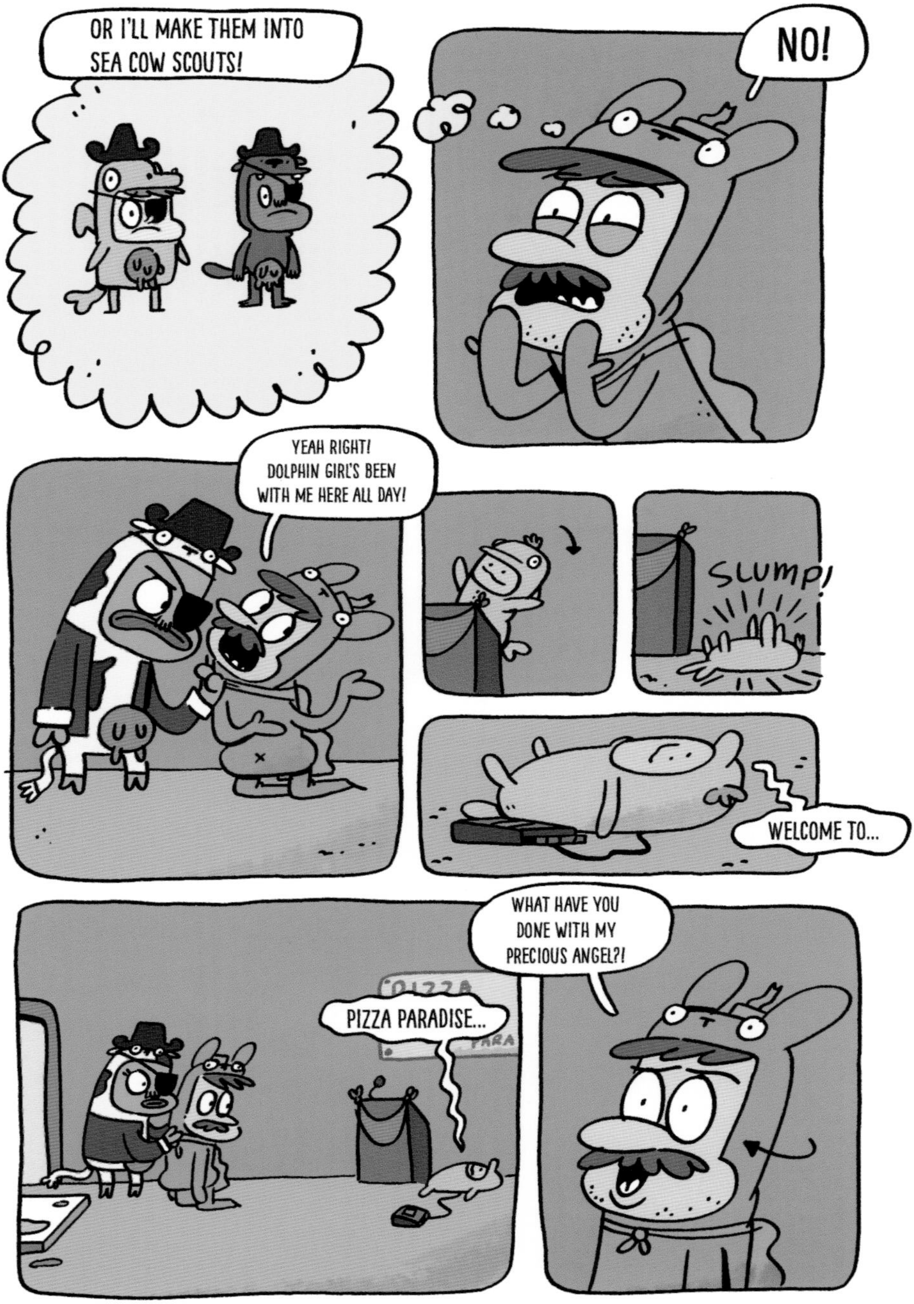

OR I'LL MAKE THEM INTO SEA COW SCOUTS!
NO!
YEAH RIGHT! DOLPHIN GIRL'S BEEN WITH ME HERE ALL DAY!
SLUMP!
WELCOME TO...
PIZZA PARADISE...
WHAT HAVE YOU DONE WITH MY PRECIOUS ANGEL?!

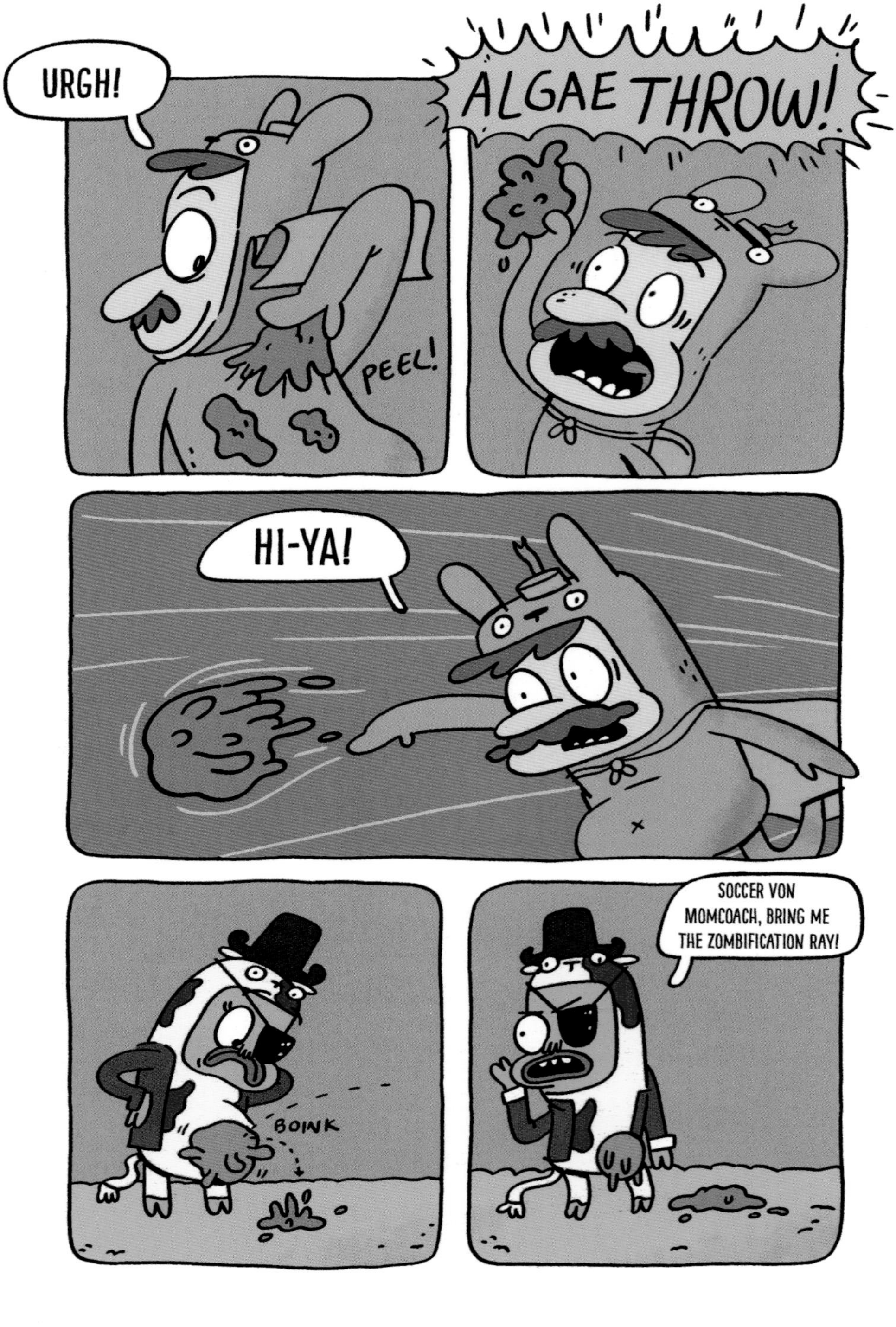
URGH!
PEEL!
ALGAE THROW!
HI-YA!
BOINK
SOCCER VON MOMCOACH, BRING ME THE ZOMBIFICATION RAY!

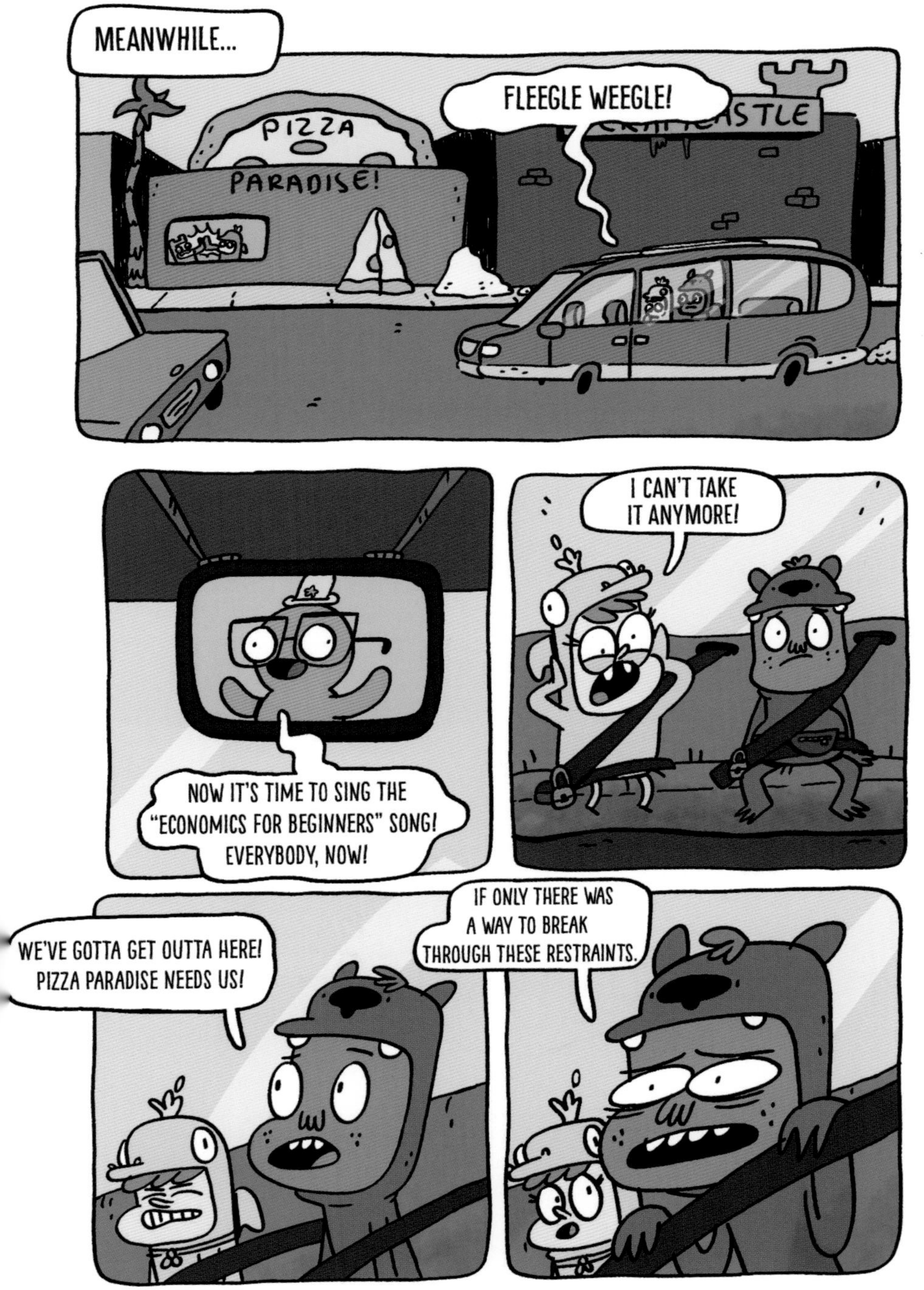
MEANWHILE...
FLEEGLE WEEGLE!
PIZZA
PARADISE!
NOW IT'S TIME TO SING THE "ECONOMICS FOR BEGINNERS" SONG! EVERYBODY, NOW!
I CAN'T TAKE IT ANYMORE!
WE'VE GOTTA GET OUTTA HERE! PIZZA PARADISE NEEDS US!
IF ONLY THERE WAS A WAY TO BREAK THROUGH THESE RESTRAINTS.

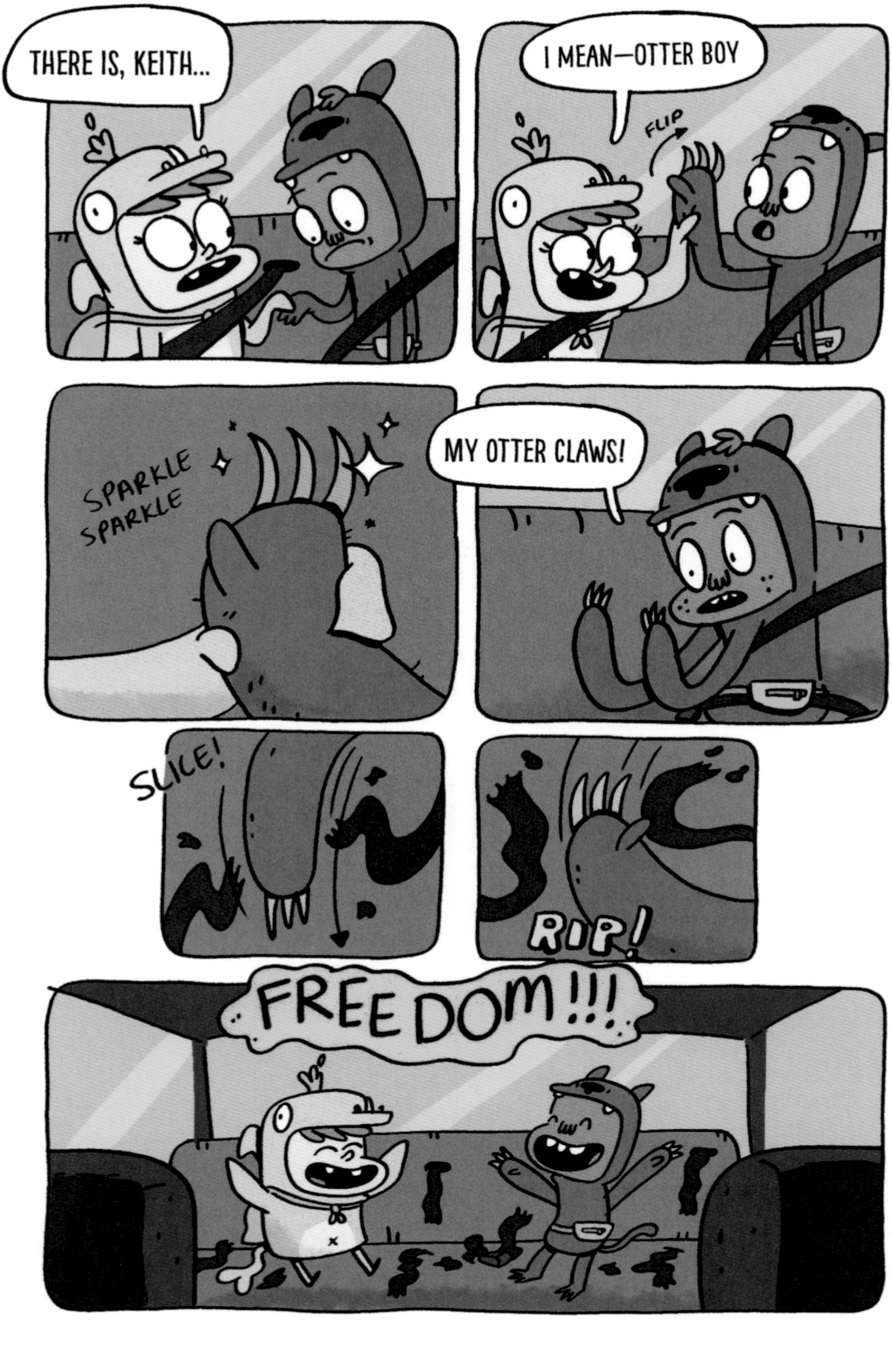
THERE IS, KEITH...
I MEAN—OTTER BOY
FLIP
SPARKLE
SPARKLE
MY OTTER CLAWS!
SLICE!
RIP!
FREEDOM!!!

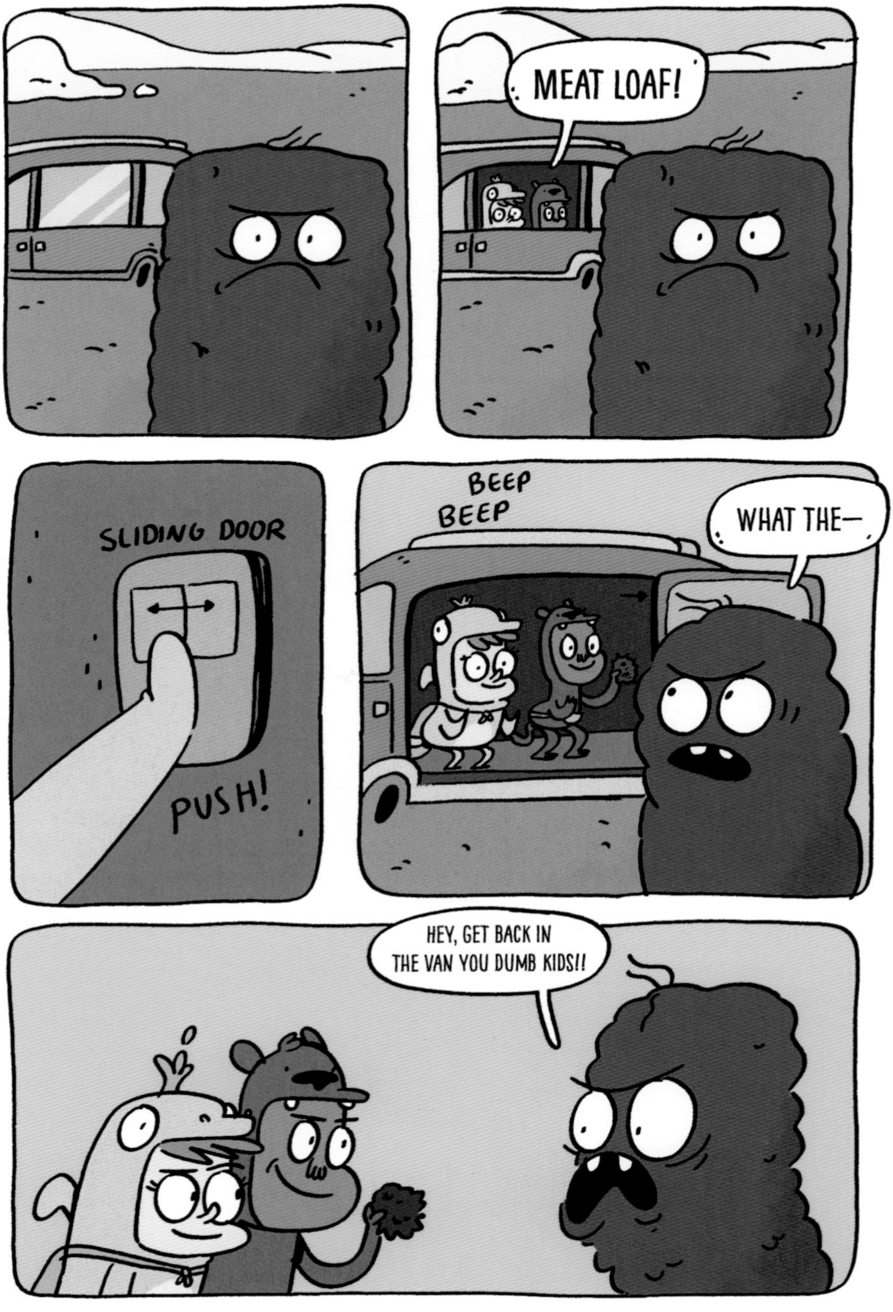
MEAT LOAF!
SLIDING DOOR
PUSH!
BEEP
BEEP
WHAT THE—
HEY, GET BACK IN THE VAN YOU DUMB KIDS!!

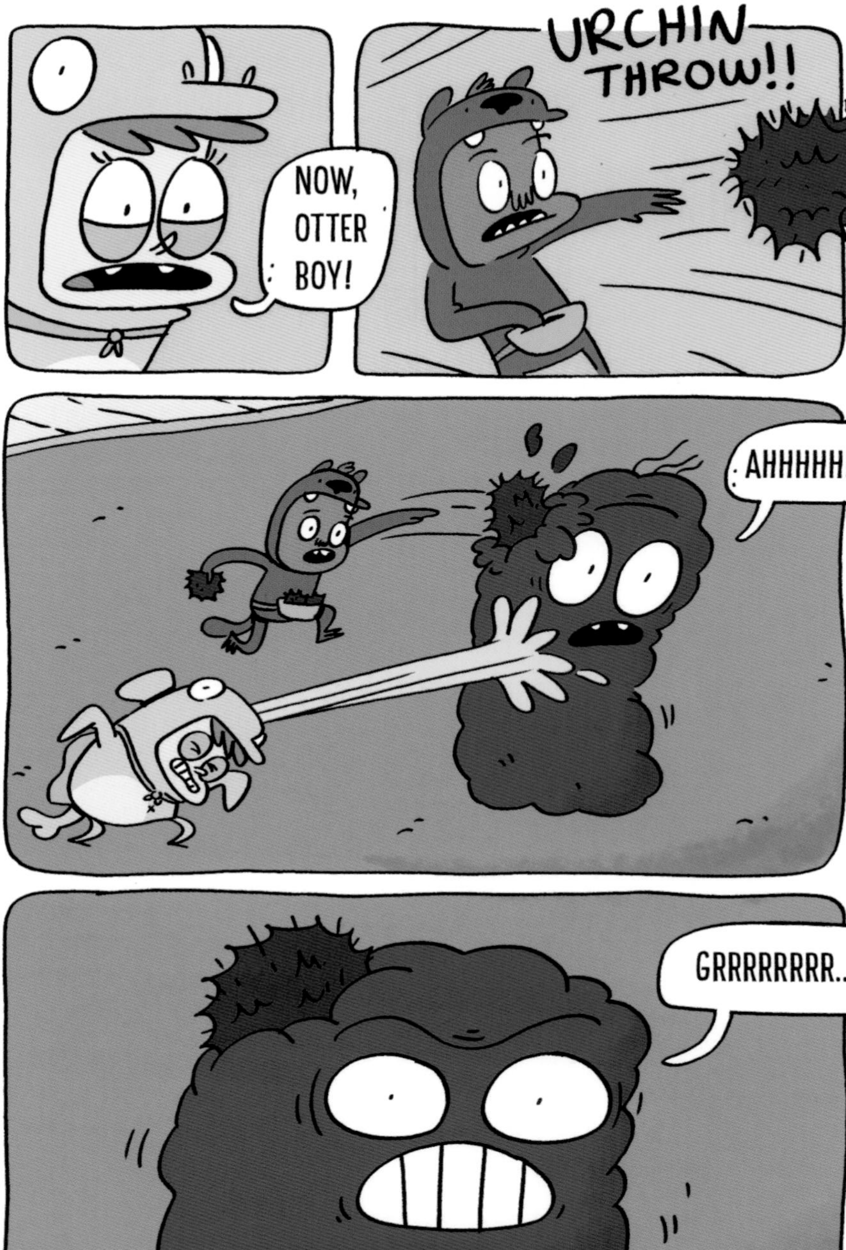
NOW, OTTER BOY!
URCHIN THROW!!
AHHHHH!!!
GRRRRRRRR...

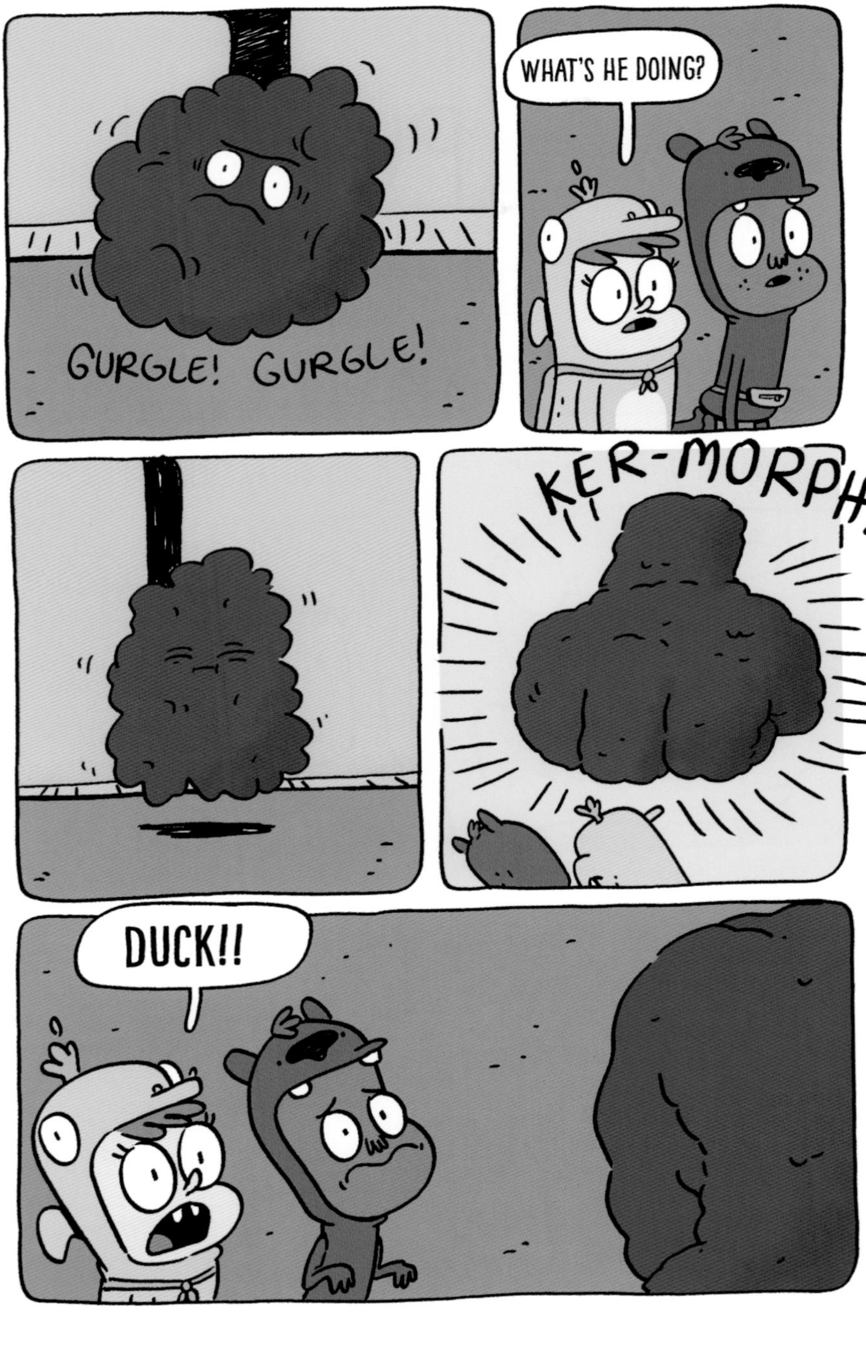
GURGLE! GURGLE!
WHAT'S HE DOING?
KER-MORPH!
DUCK!!

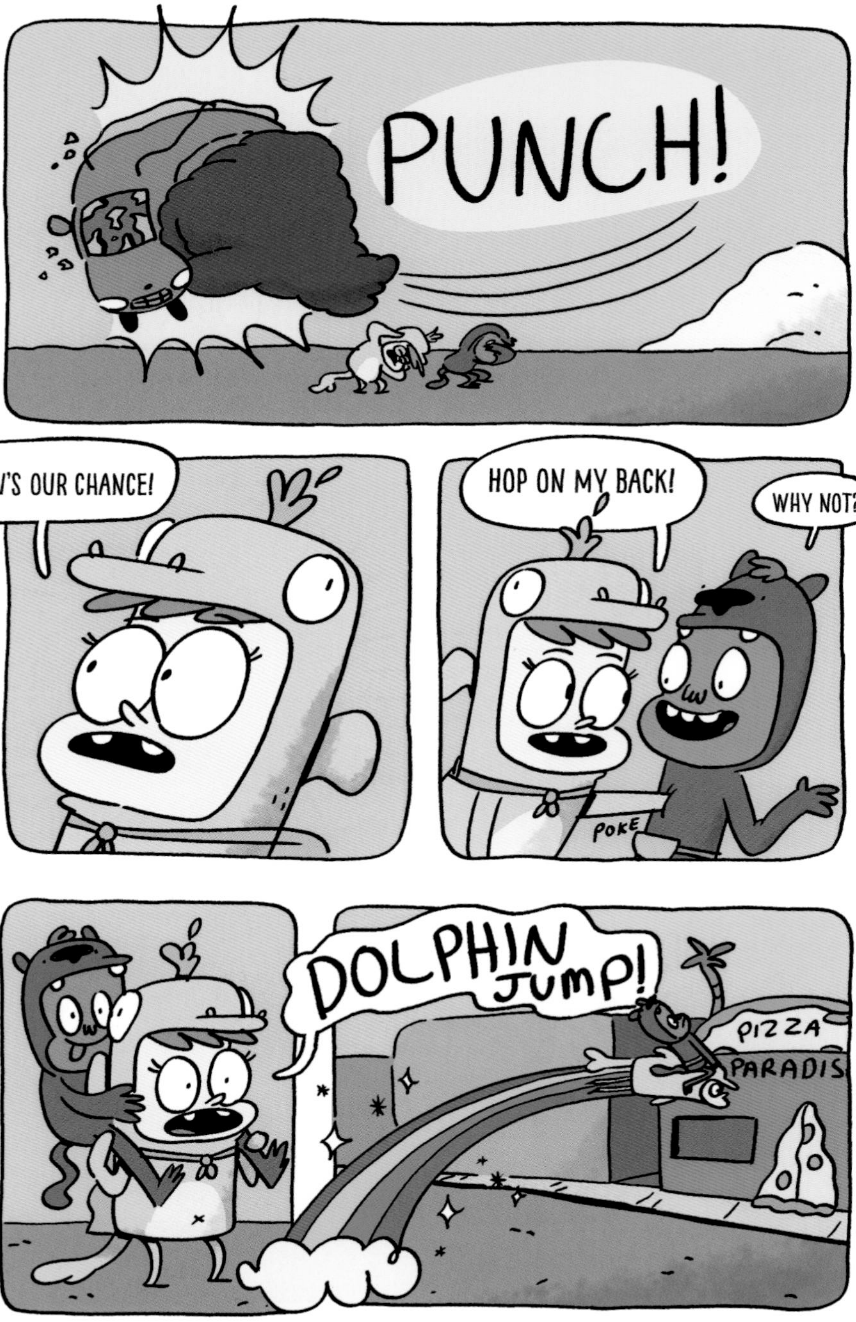
PUNCH!
NOW'S OUR CHANCE!
HOP ON MY BACK!
WHY NOT?
POKE
DOLPHIN JUMP!
PIZZA
PARADIS

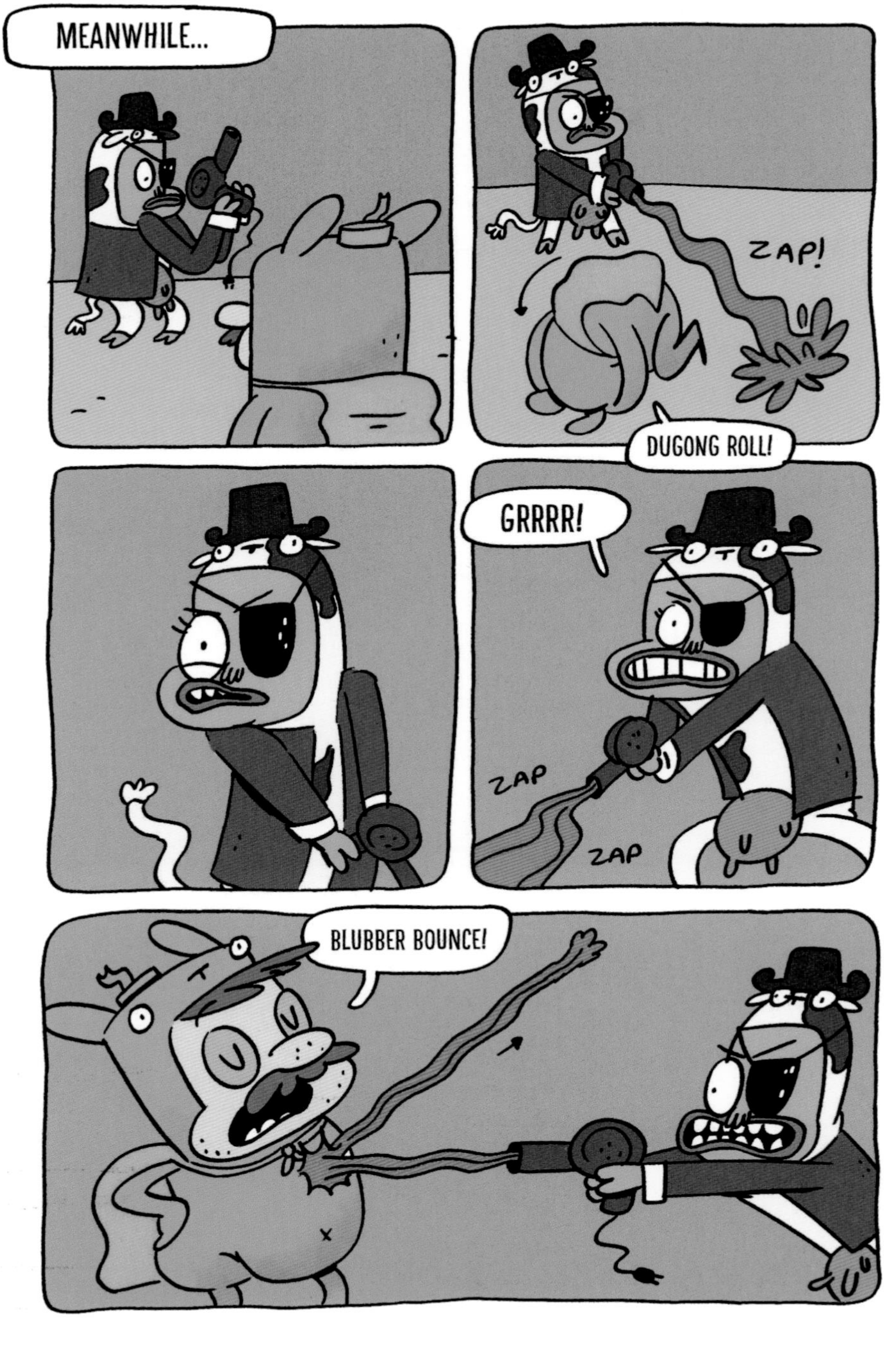
MEANWHILE...
ZAP!
DUGONG ROLL!
GRRRR!
ZAP
ZAP
BLUBBER BOUNCE!

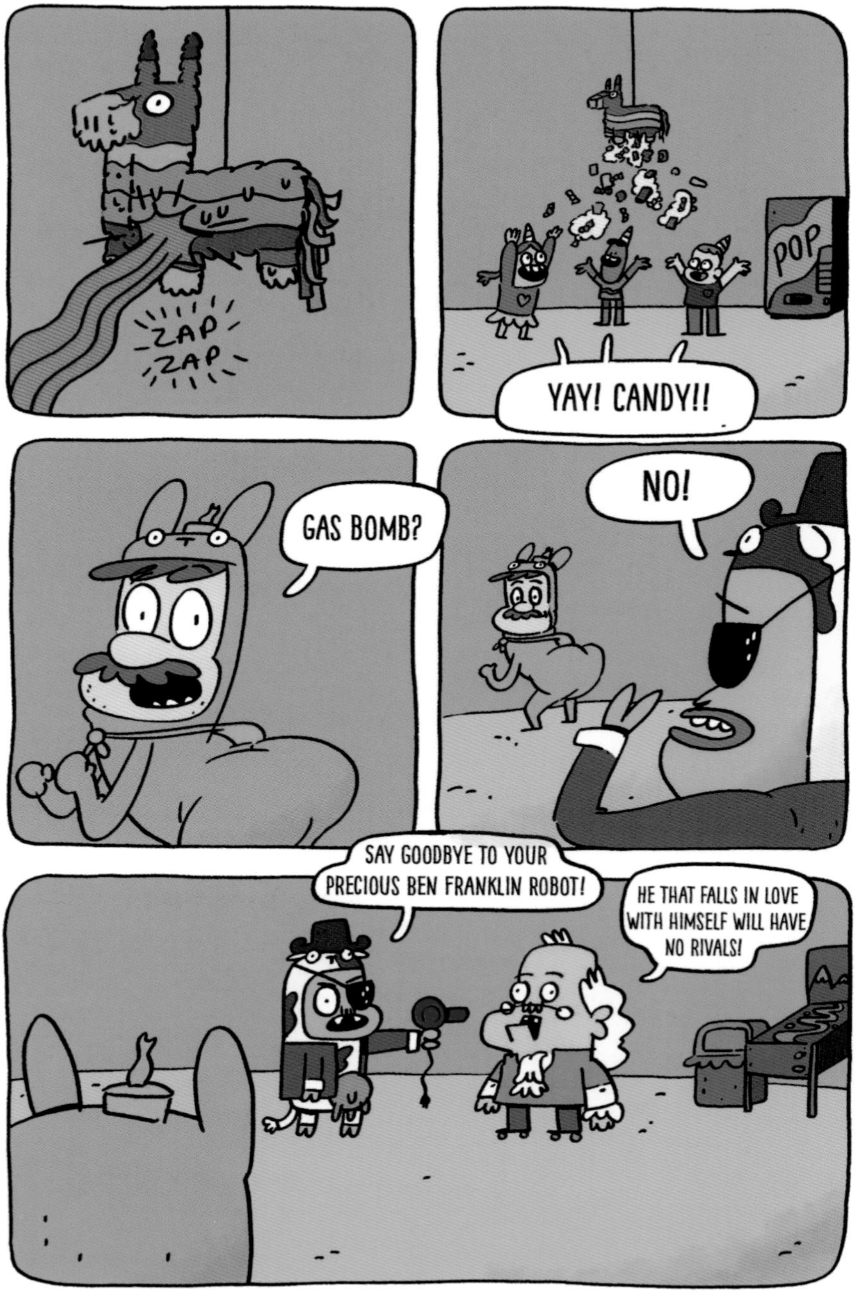
ZAP
ZAP
POP
YAY! CANDY!!
GAS BOMB?
NO!
SAY GOODBYE TO YOUR PRECIOUS BEN FRANKLIN ROBOT!
HE THAT FALLS IN LOVE WITH HIMSELF WILL HAVE NO RIVALS!

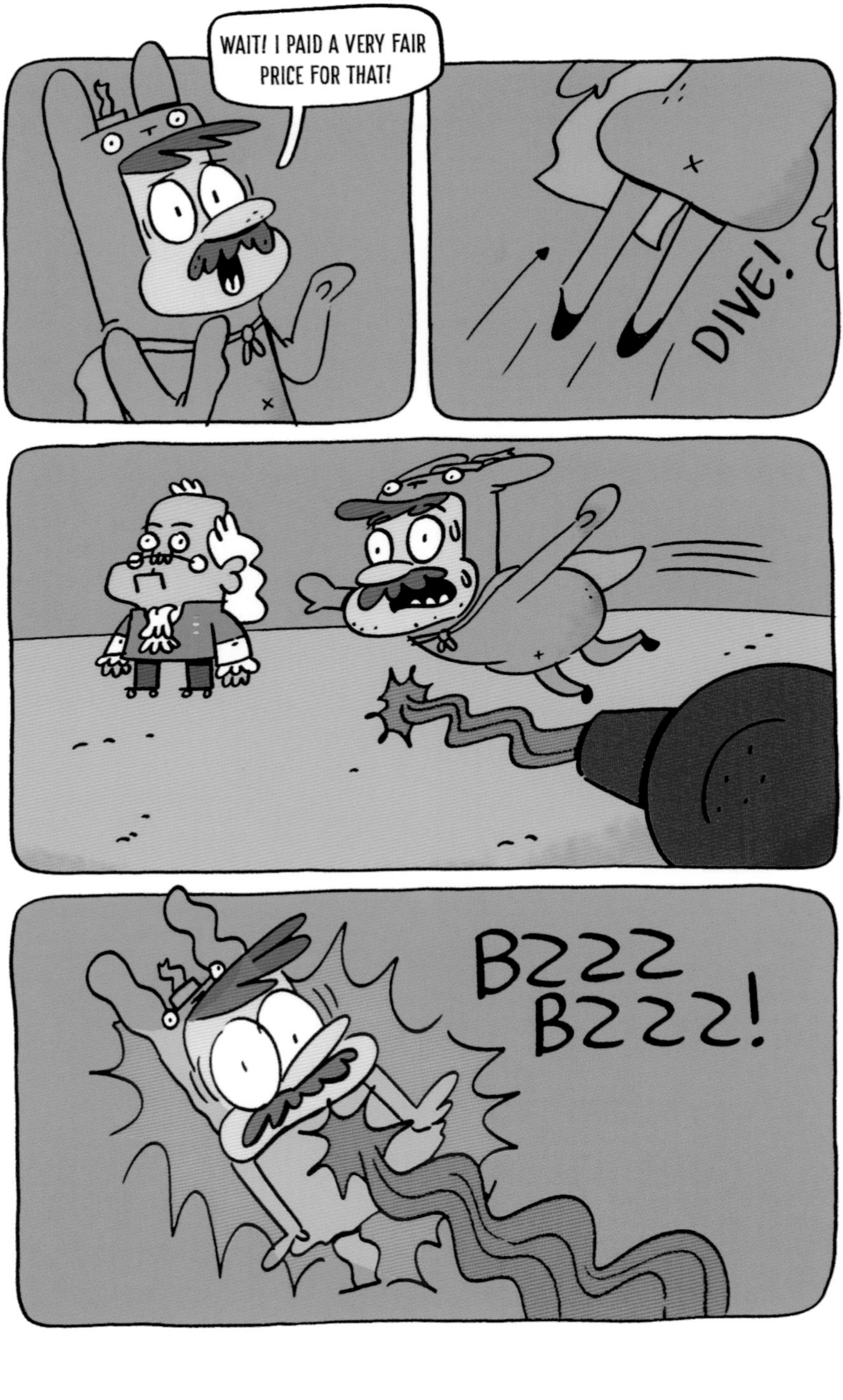
WAIT! I PAID A VERY FAIR PRICE FOR THAT!
DIVE!
BZZZ BZZZ!

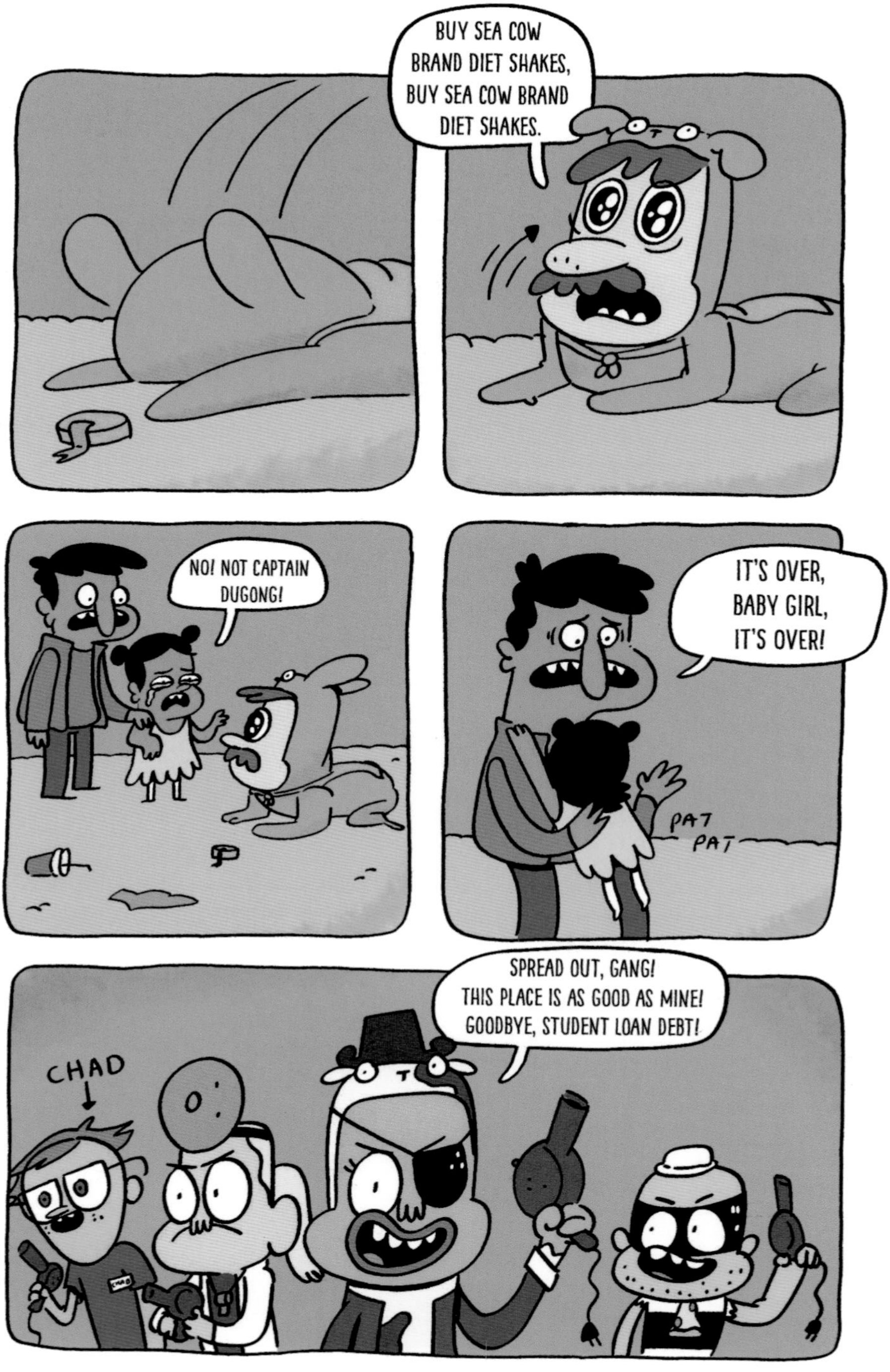

BUY SEA COW BRAND DIET SHAKES, BUY SEA COW BRAND DIET SHAKES.
NO! NOT CAPTAIN DUGONG!
IT'S OVER, BABY GIRL, IT'S OVER!
PAT PAT
SPREAD OUT, GANG! THIS PLACE IS AS GOOD AS MINE! GOODBYE, STUDENT LOAN DEBT!
CHAD

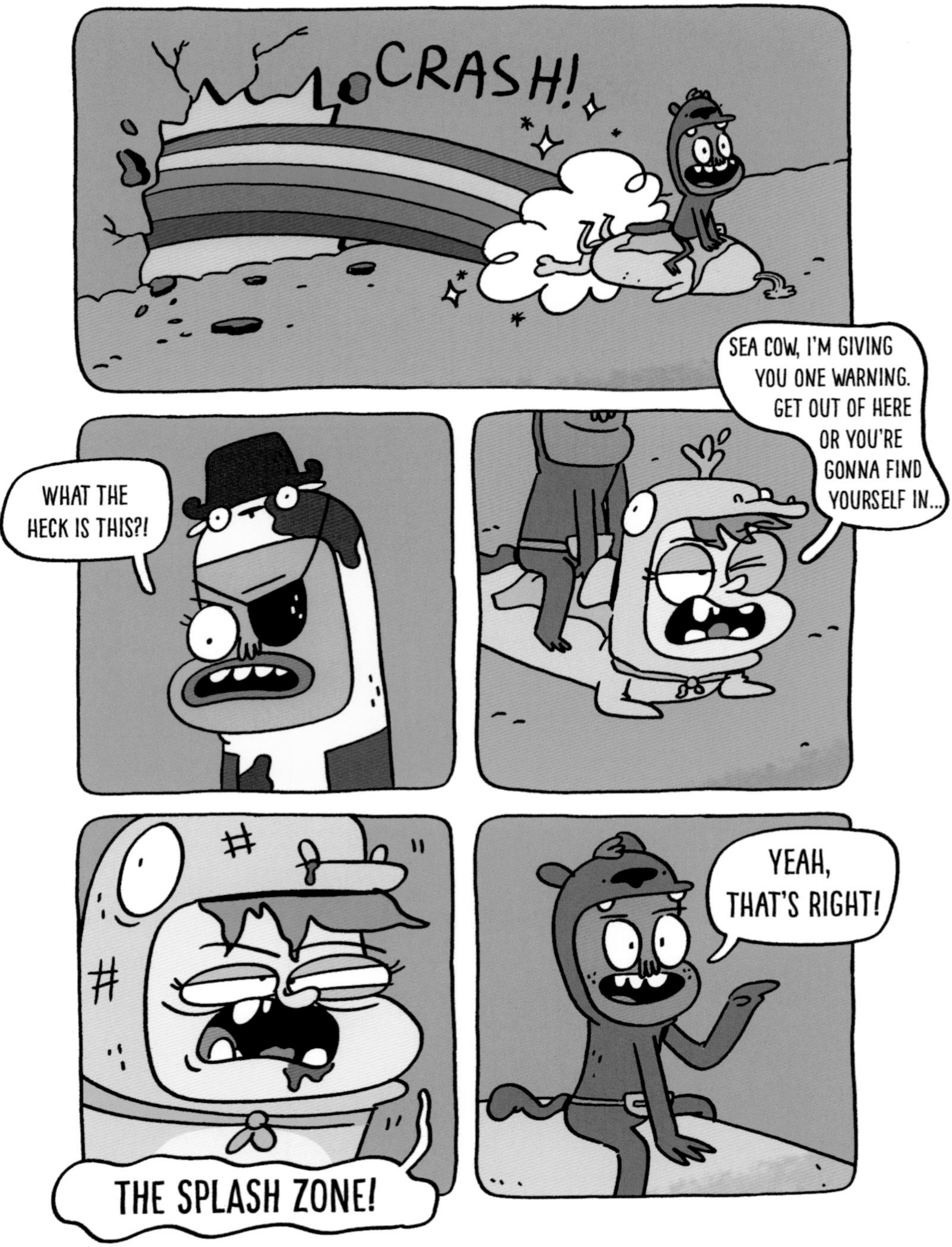
CRASH!
WHAT THE HECK IS THIS?!
SEA COW, I'M GIVING YOU ONE WARNING. GET OUT OF HERE OR YOU'RE GONNA FIND YOURSELF IN...
THE SPLASH ZONE!
YEAH, THAT'S RIGHT!

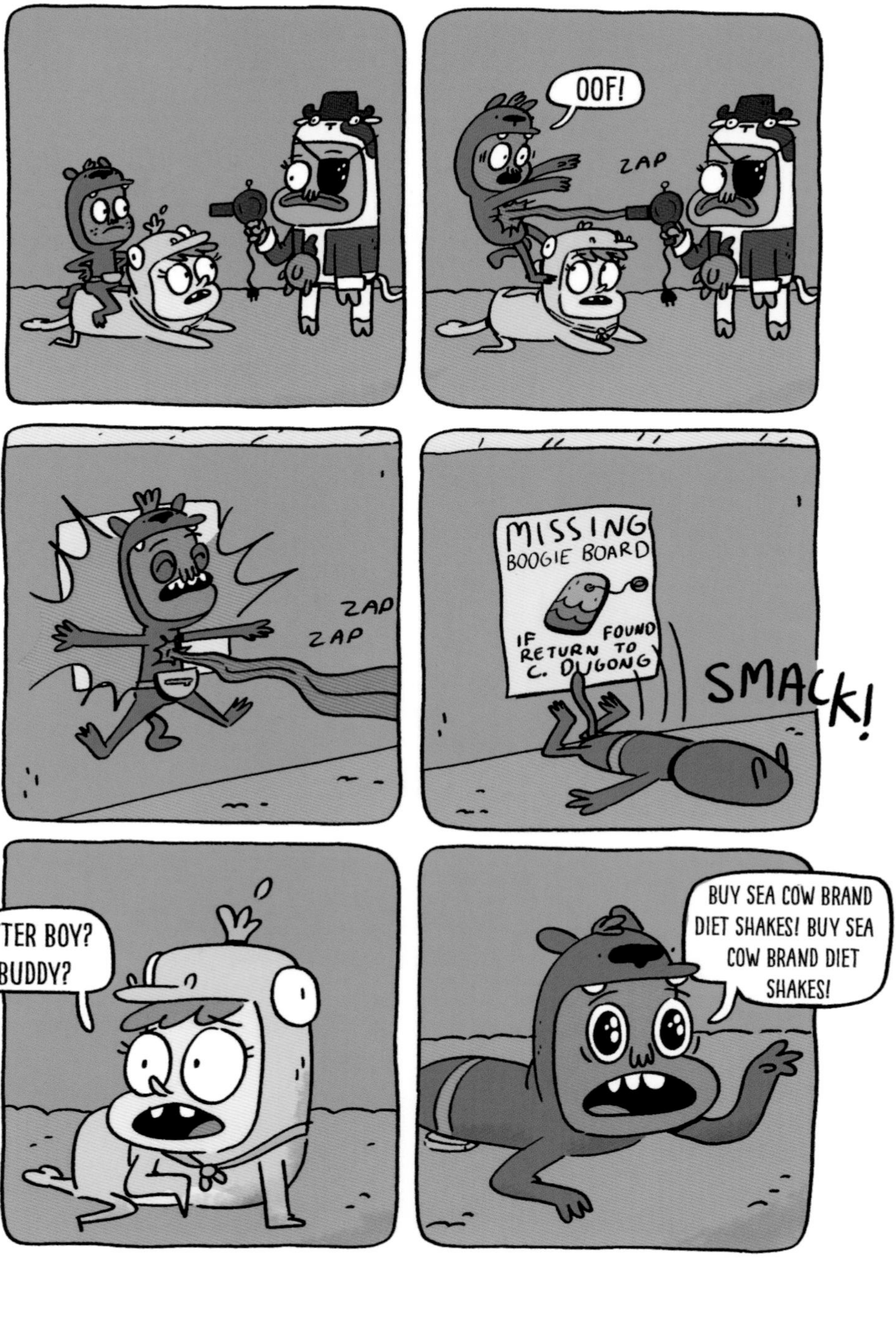
OOF!
ZAP
ZAP
ZAP
MISSING
BOOGIE BOARD
IF FOUND
RETURN TO
C. DUGONG
SMACK!
OTTER BOY?
BUDDY?
BUY SEA COW BRAND DIET SHAKES! BUY SEA COW BRAND DIET SHAKES!

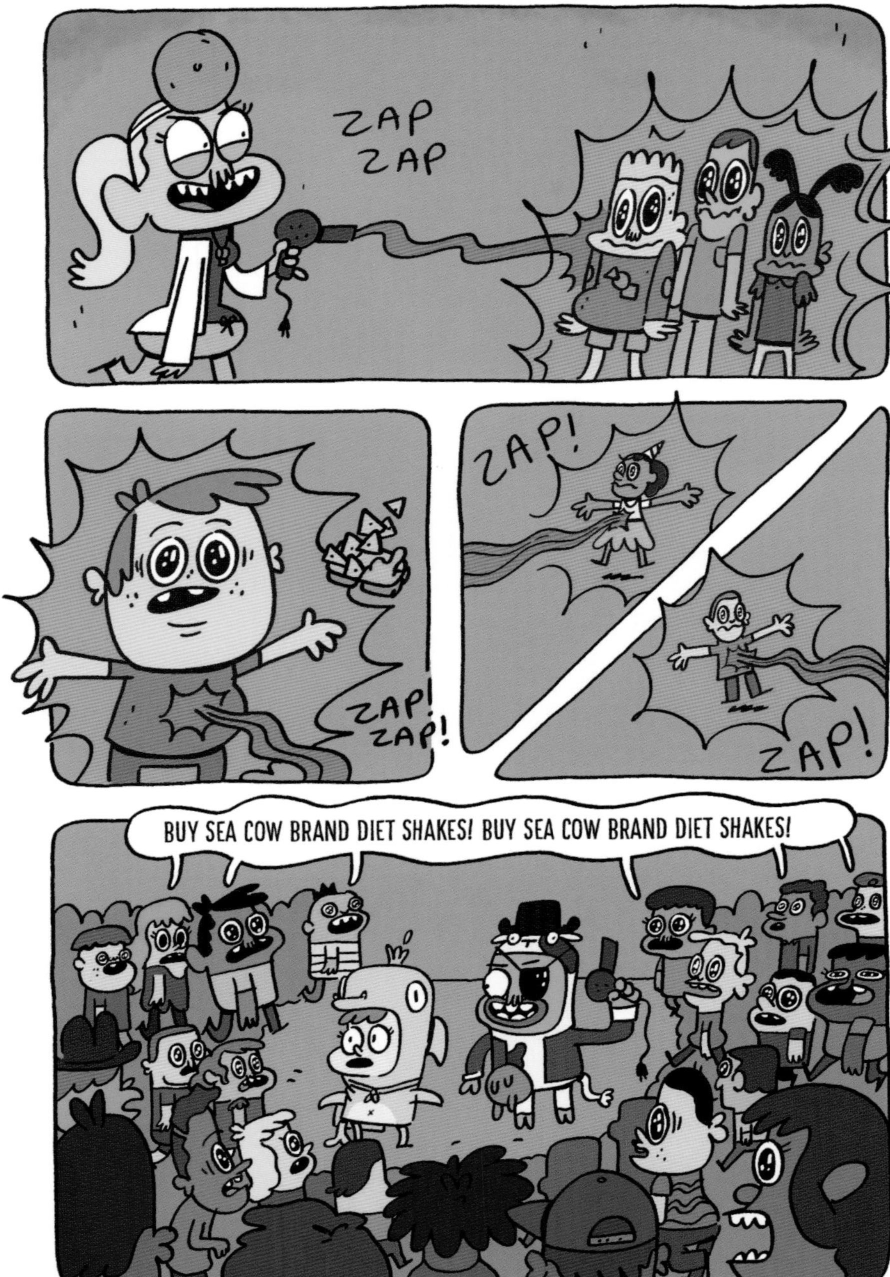
ZAP
ZAP
ZAP!
ZAP!
ZAP!
ZAP!
ZAP!
BUY SEA COW BRAND DIET SHAKES! BUY SEA COW BRAND DIET SHAKES!

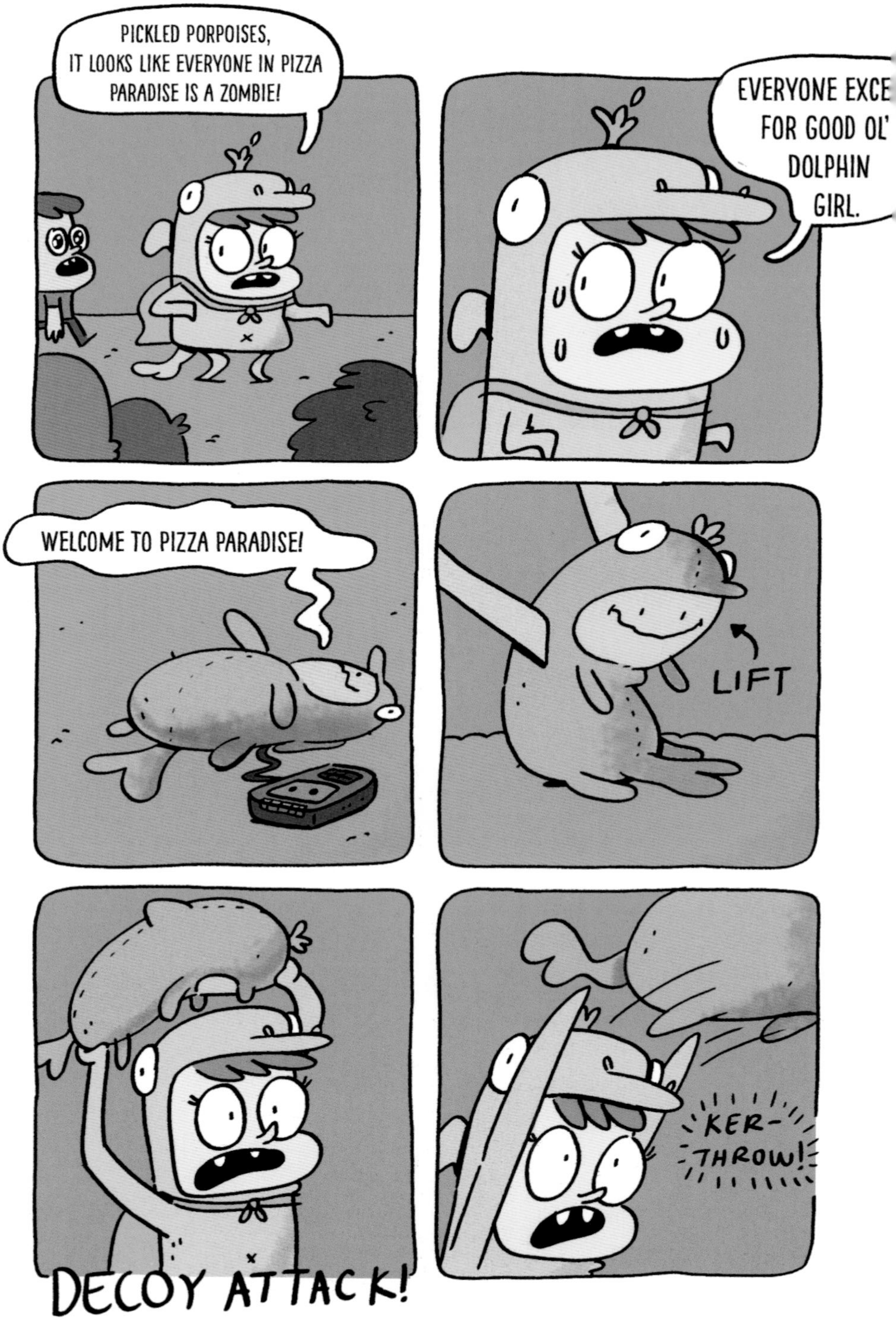
PICKLED PORPOISES, IT LOOKS LIKE EVERYONE IN PIZZA PARADISE IS A ZOMBIE!
EVERYONE EXCE FOR GOOD OL' DOLPHIN GIRL.
WELCOME TO PIZZA PARADISE!
LIFT
DECOY ATTACK!
KER-THROW!

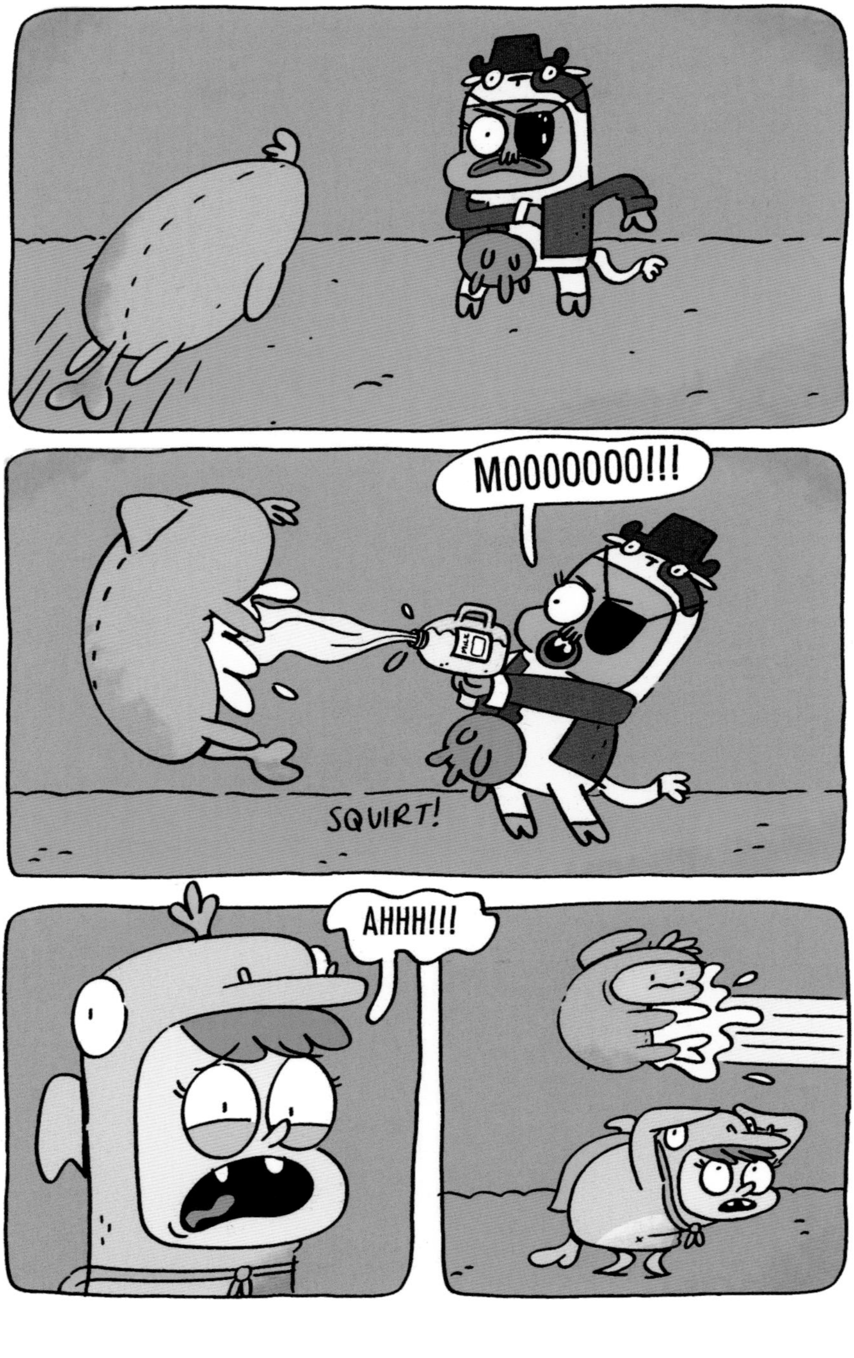
MOOOOOOO!!!
MILK
SQUIRT!
AHHH!!!

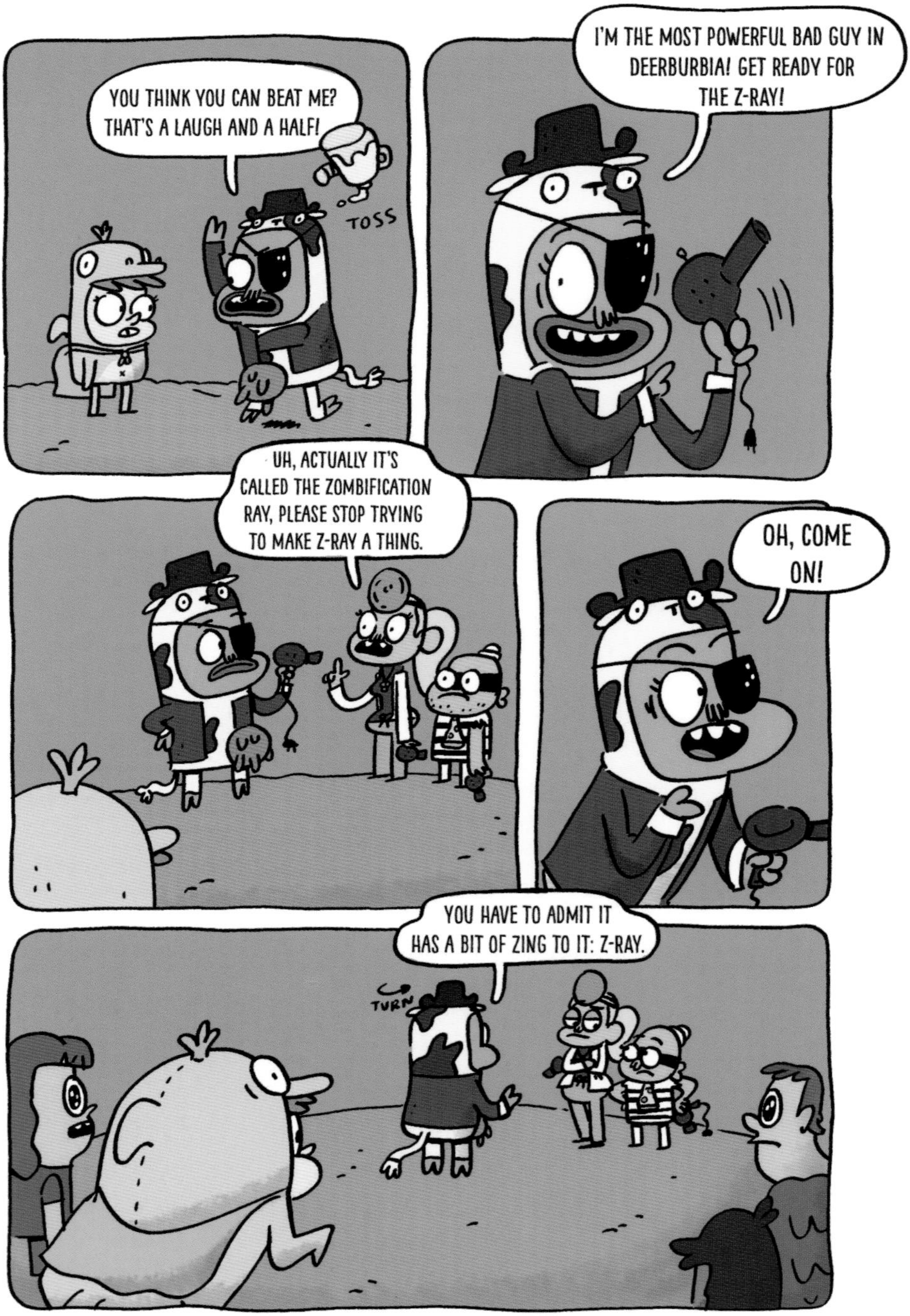
YOU THINK YOU CAN BEAT ME? THAT'S A LAUGH AND A HALF!
TOSS
I'M THE MOST POWERFUL BAD GUY IN DEERBURBIA! GET READY FOR THE Z-RAY!
UH, ACTUALLY IT'S CALLED THE ZOMBIFICATION RAY, PLEASE STOP TRYING TO MAKE Z-RAY A THING.
OH, COME ON!
YOU HAVE TO ADMIT IT HAS A BIT OF ZING TO IT: Z-RAY.
TURN

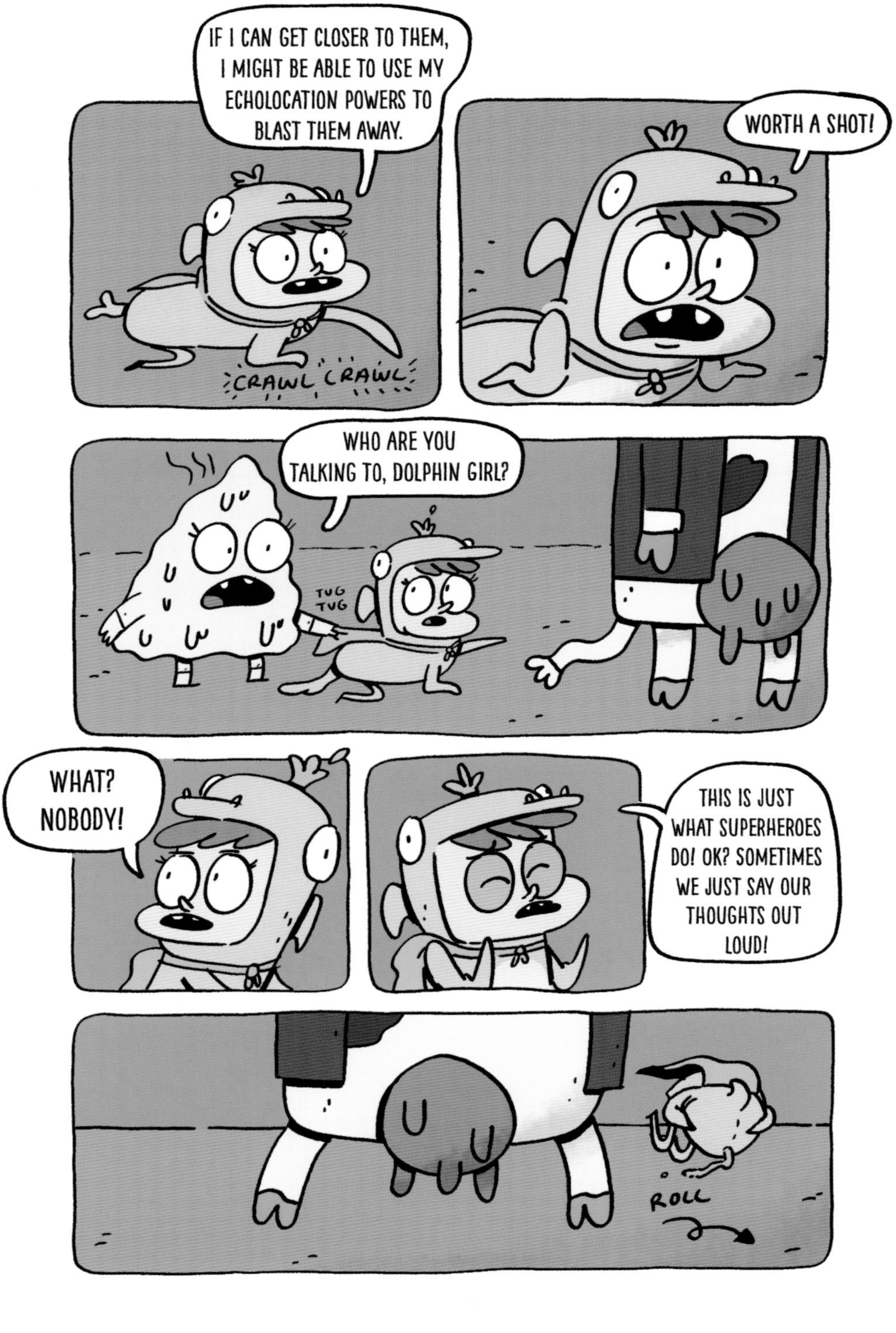
IF I CAN GET CLOSER TO THEM, I MIGHT BE ABLE TO USE MY ECHOLOCATION POWERS TO BLAST THEM AWAY.
CRAWL CRAWL
WORTH A SHOT!
WHO ARE YOU TALKING TO, DOLPHIN GIRL?
TUG TUG
WHAT? NOBODY!
THIS IS JUST WHAT SUPERHEROES DO! OK? SOMETIMES WE JUST SAY OUR THOUGHTS OUT LOUD!
ROLL

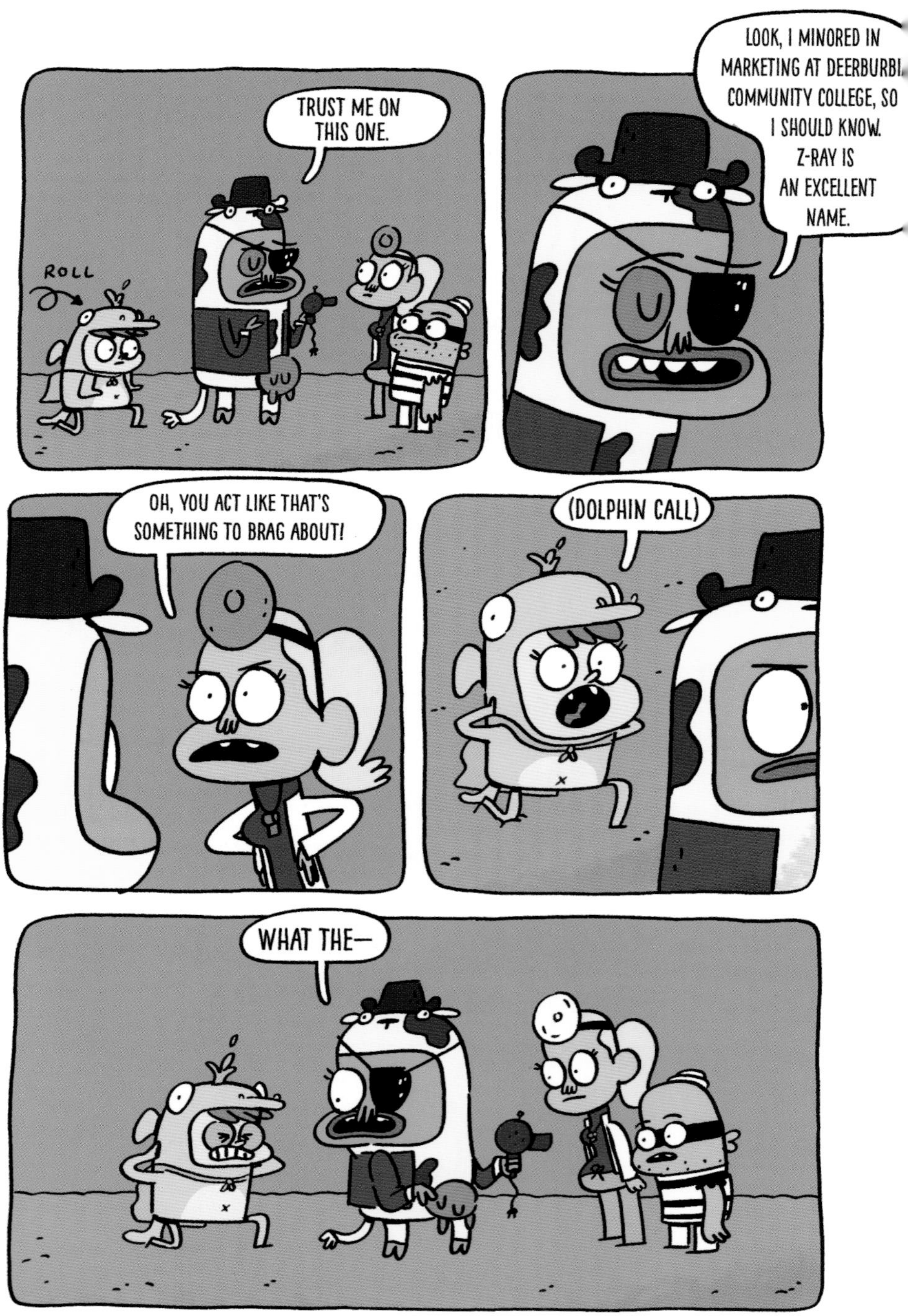
TRUST ME ON THIS ONE.
ROLL
LOOK, I MINORED IN MARKETING AT DEERBURBI COMMUNITY COLLEGE, SO I SHOULD KNOW. Z-RAY IS AN EXCELLENT NAME.
OH, YOU ACT LIKE THAT'S SOMETHING TO BRAG ABOUT!
(DOLPHIN CALL)
WHAT THE—

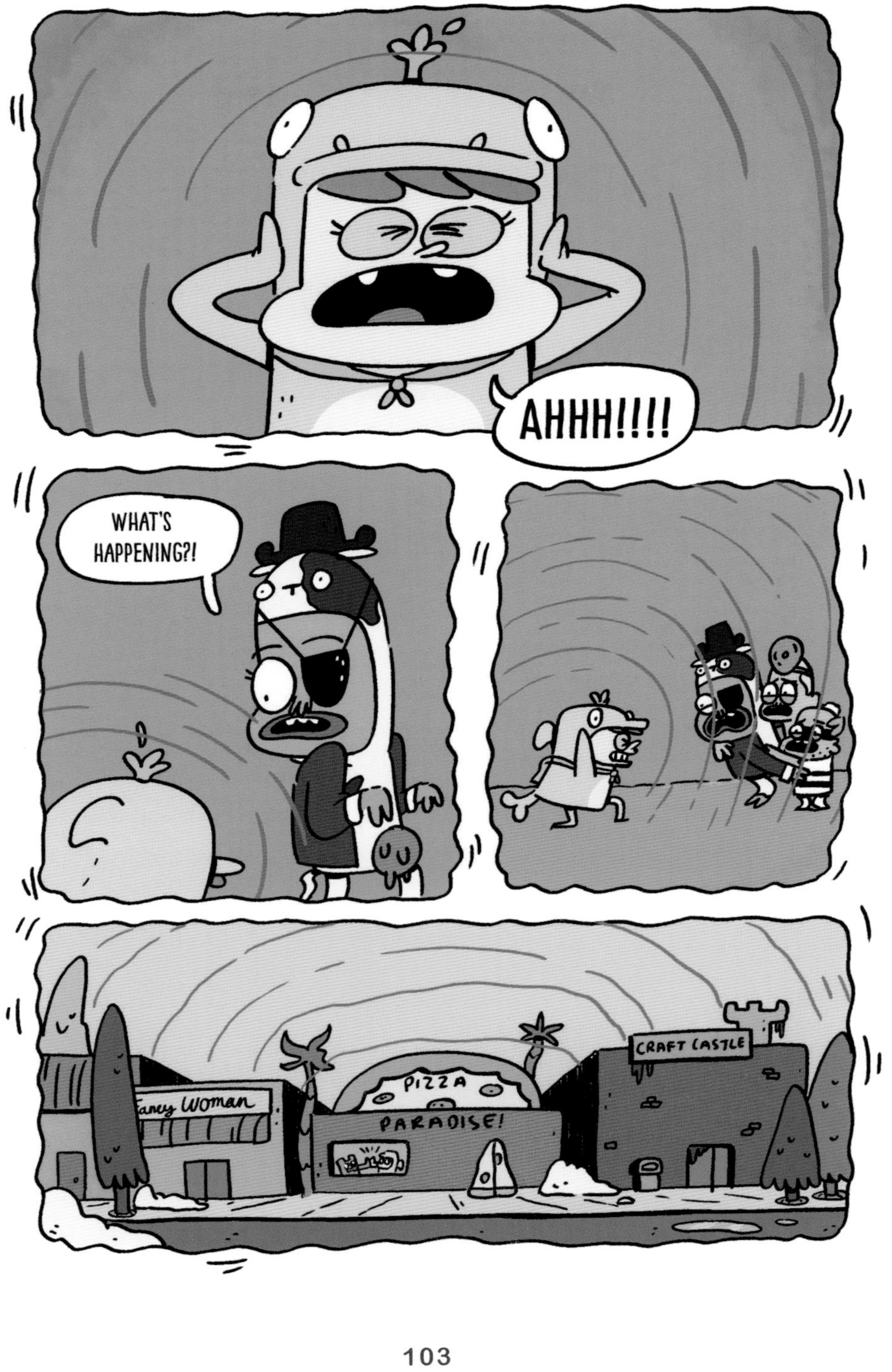
AHHH!!!!
WHAT'S HAPPENING?!
Fancy Woman
PIZZA
PARADISE!
CRAFT CASTLE

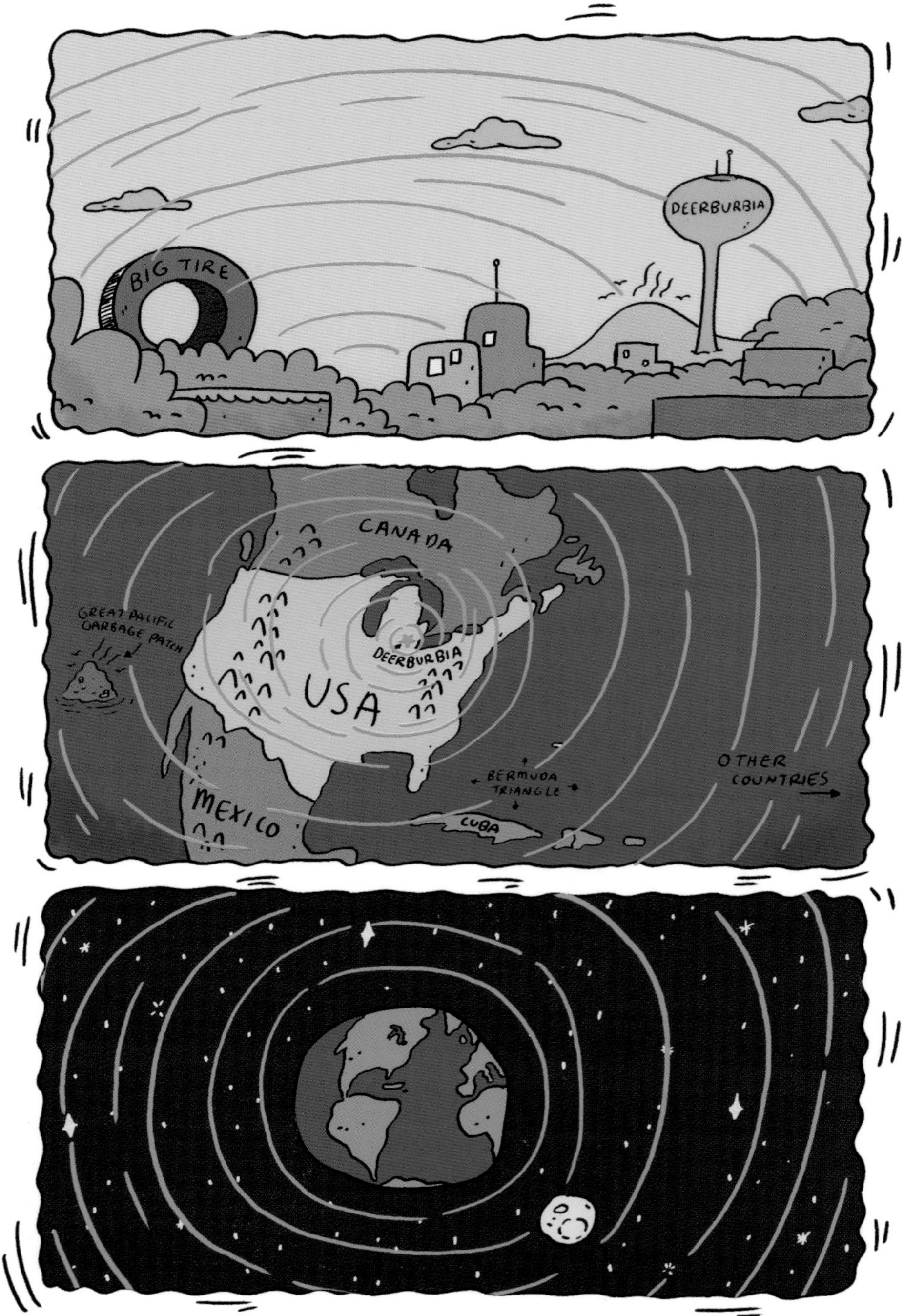
BIG TIRE
DEERBURBIA
CANADA
GREAT PACIFIC GARBAGE PATCH
DEERBURBIA
USA
MEXICO
BERMUDA TRIANGLE
CUBA
OTHER COUNTRIES

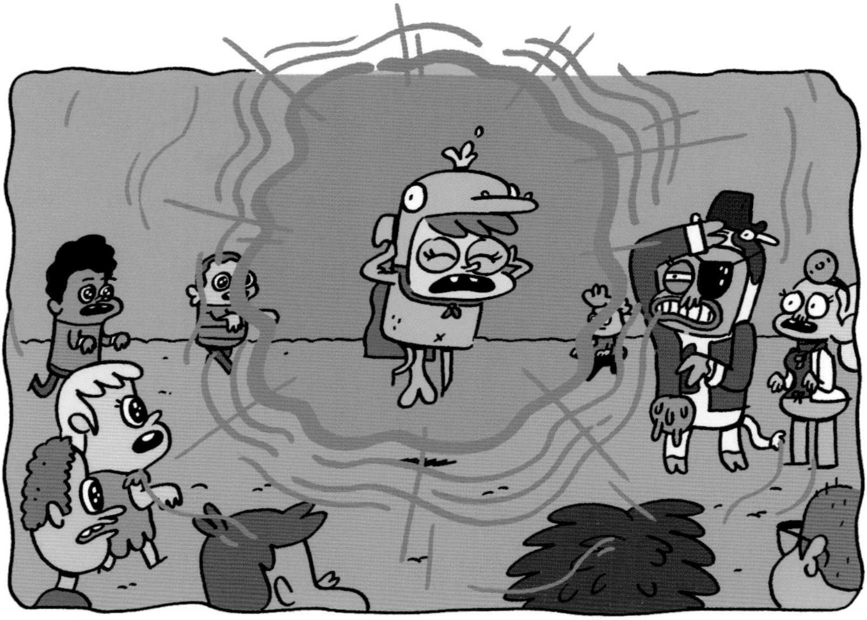

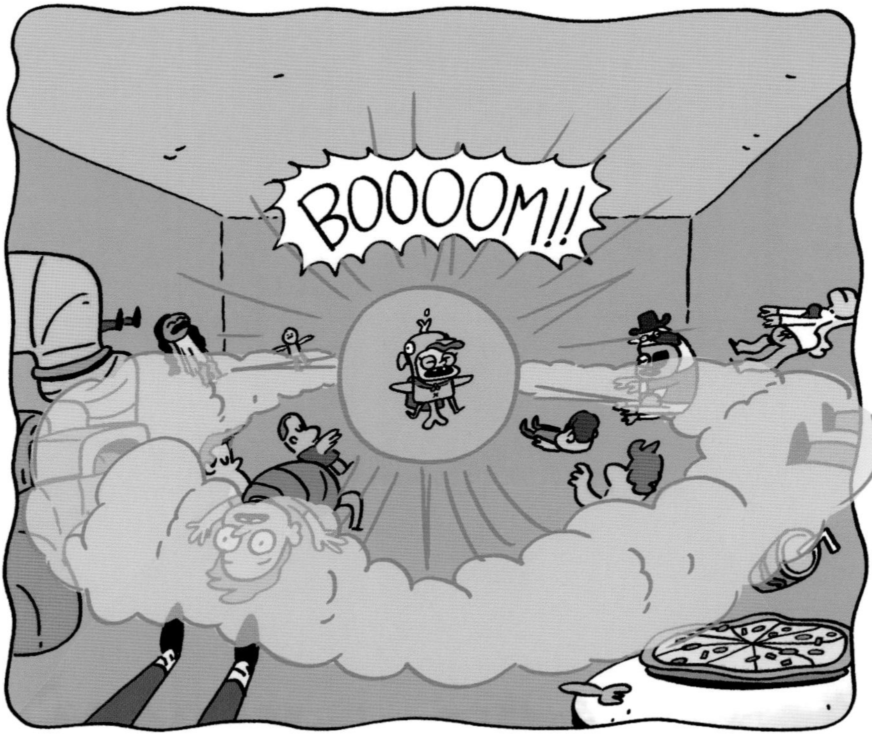
BOOOOM!!

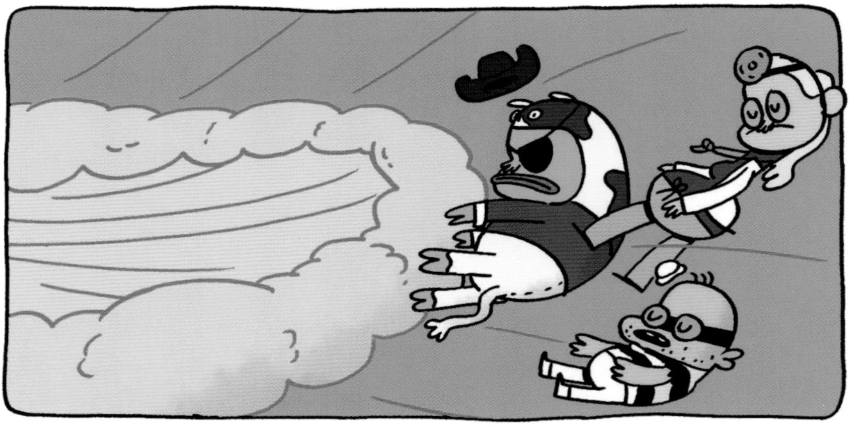

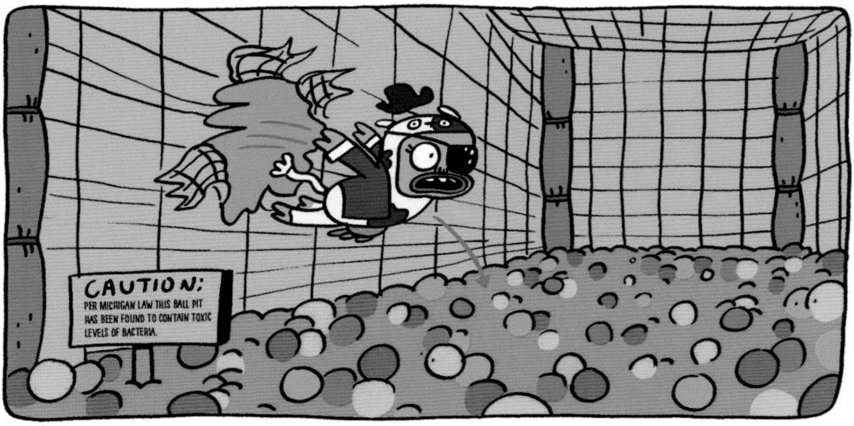
CAUTION:
PER MICHIGAN LAW THIS BALL PIT HAS BEEN FOUND TO CONTAIN TOXIC LEVELS OF BACTERIA.

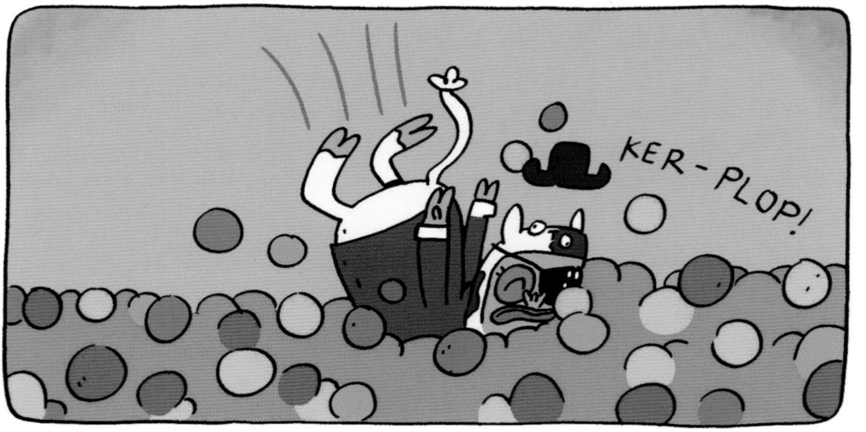
KER-PLOP!

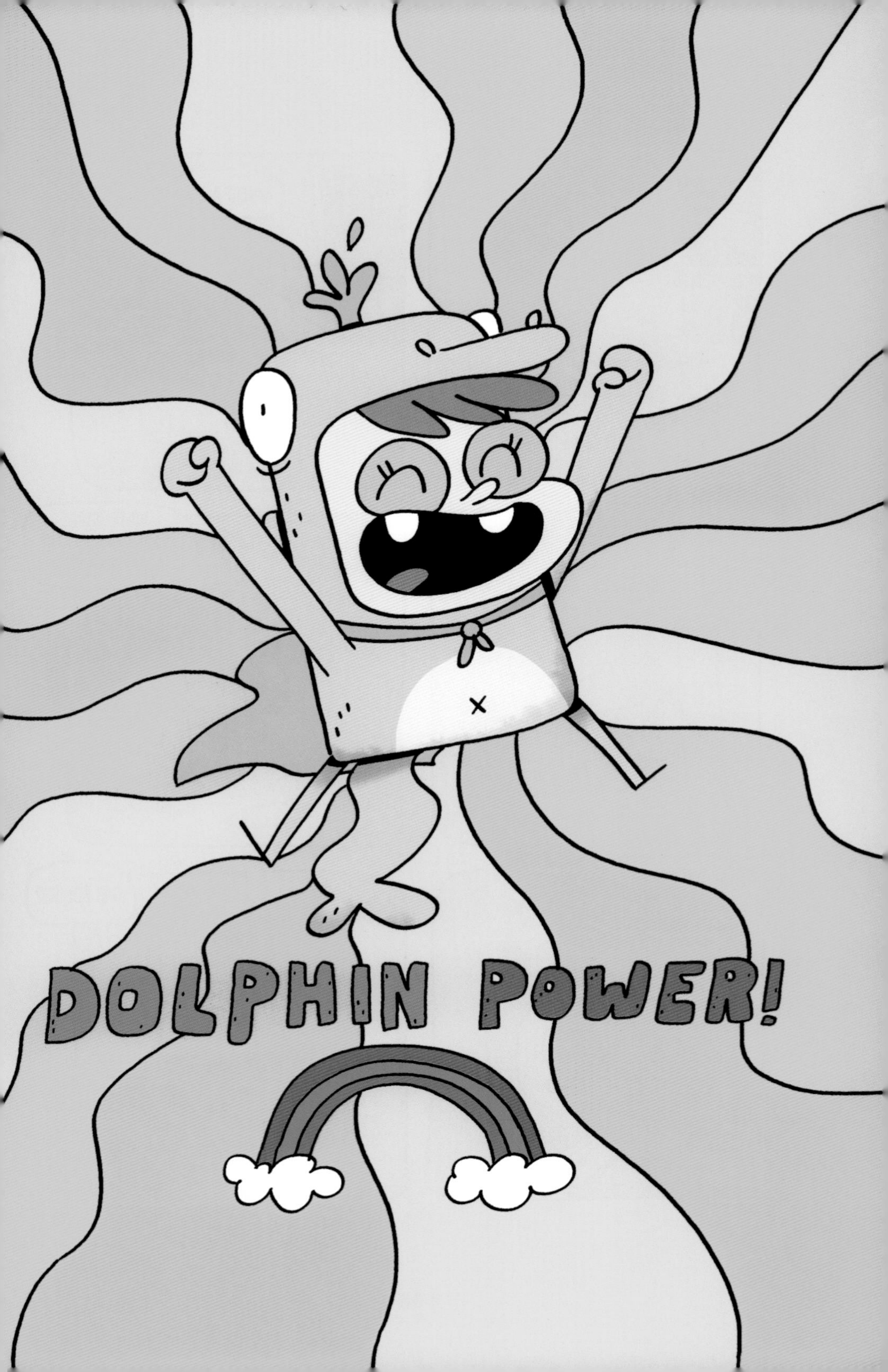
DOLPHIN POWER!

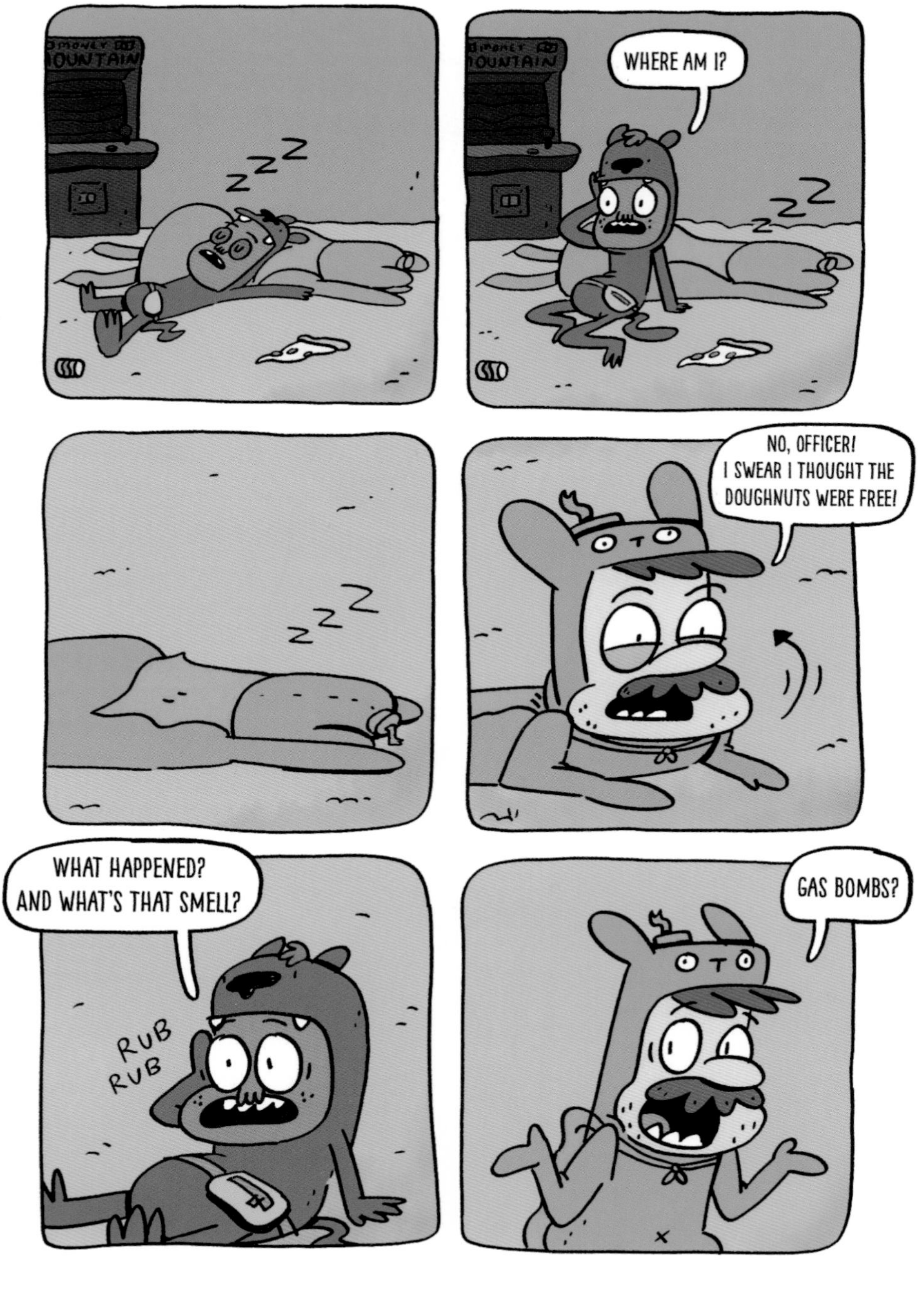
MONEY
MOUNTAIN
ZZZ
MONEY
MOUNTAIN
WHERE AM I?
ZZZ
ZZZ
NO, OFFICER!
I SWEAR I THOUGHT THE
DOUGHNUTS WERE FREE!
WHAT HAPPENED?
AND WHAT'S THAT SMELL?
RUB
RUB
GAS BOMBS?

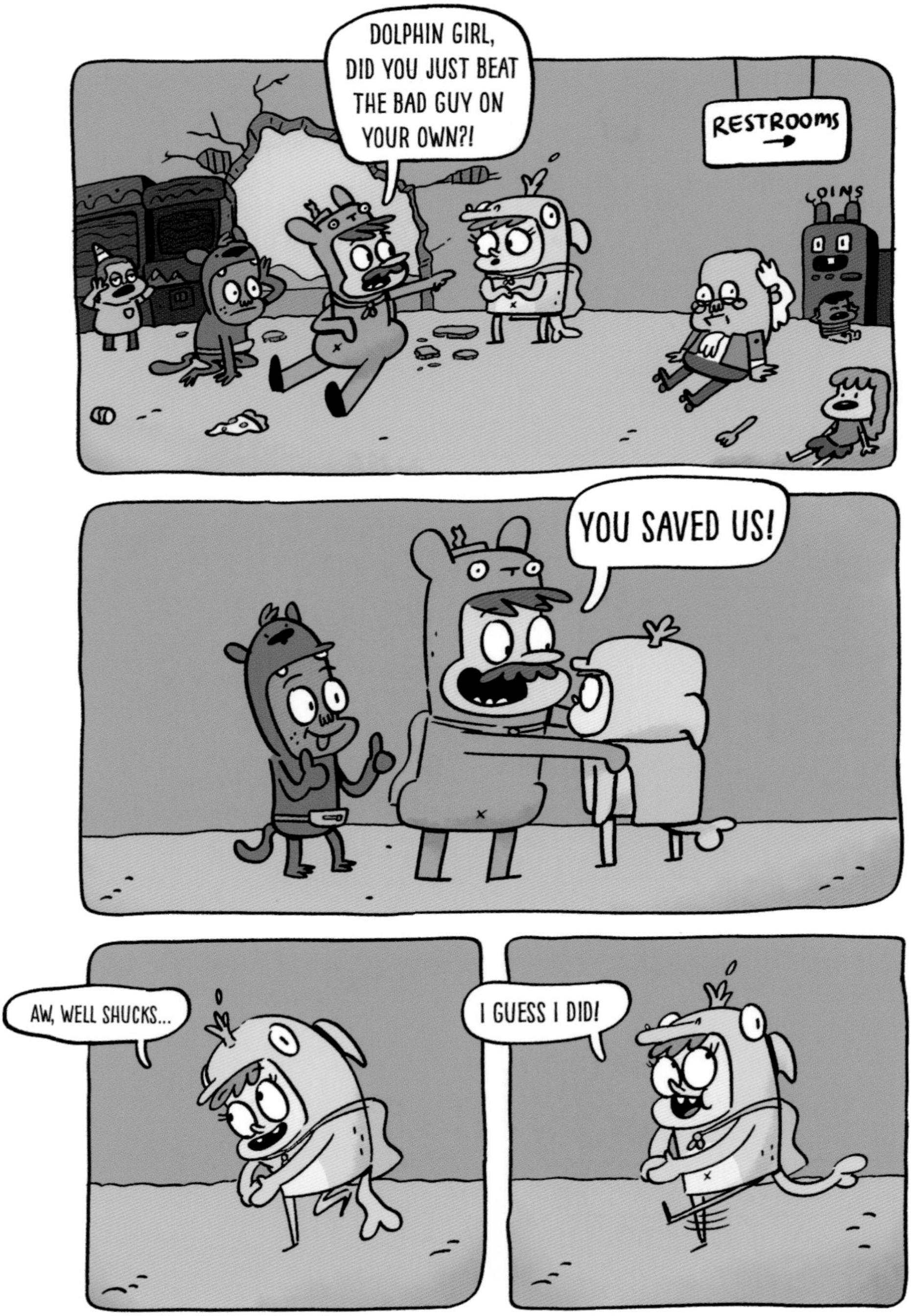
DOLPHIN GIRL, DID YOU JUST BEAT THE BAD GUY ON YOUR OWN?!
RESTROOMS
COINS
YOU SAVED US!
AW, WELL SHUCKS...
I GUESS I DID!

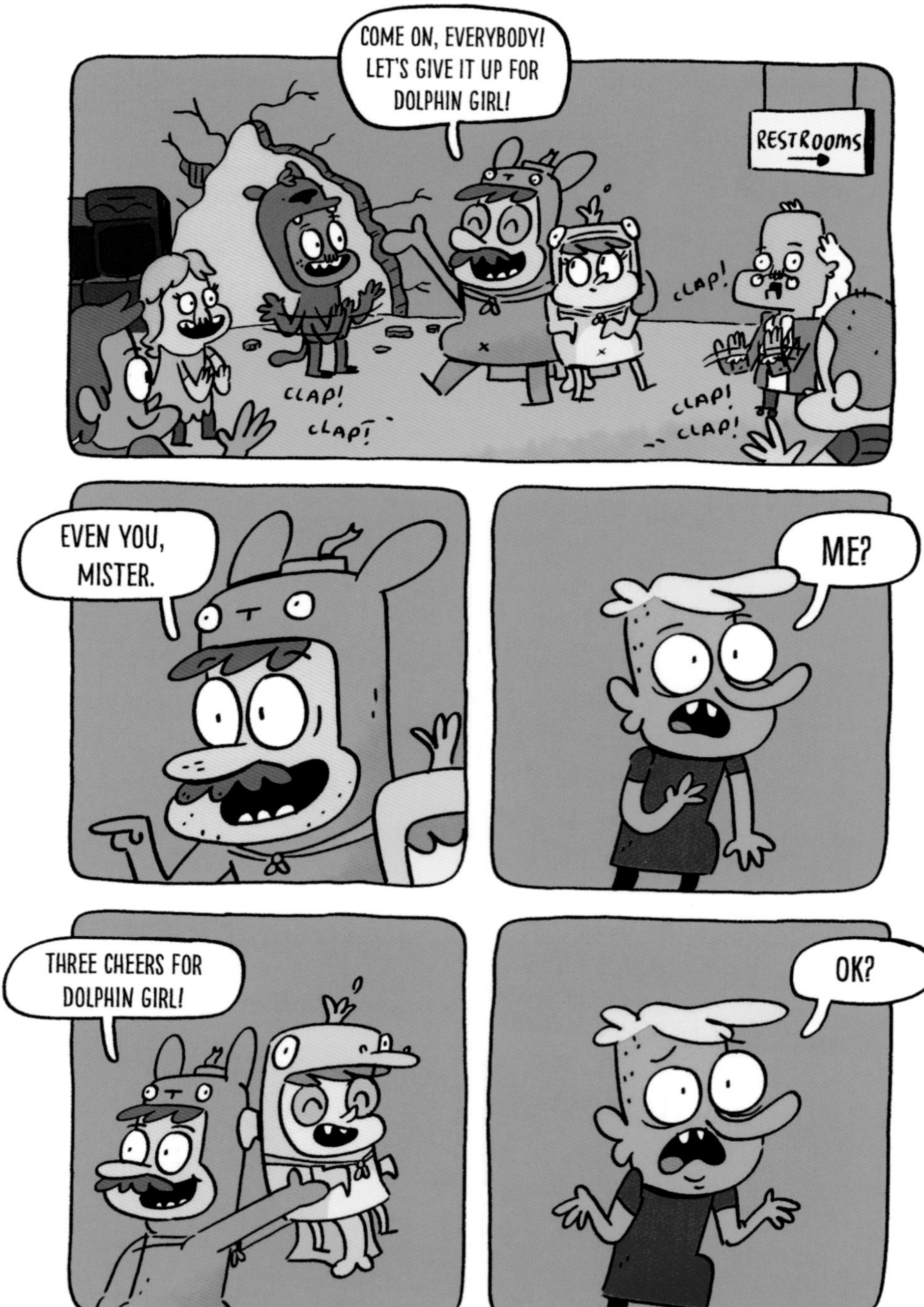
COME ON, EVERYBODY! LET'S GIVE IT UP FOR DOLPHIN GIRL!
RESTROOMS
CLAP!
CLAP!
CLAP!
CLAP!
CLAP!
EVEN YOU, MISTER.
ME?
THREE CHEERS FOR DOLPHIN GIRL!
OK?

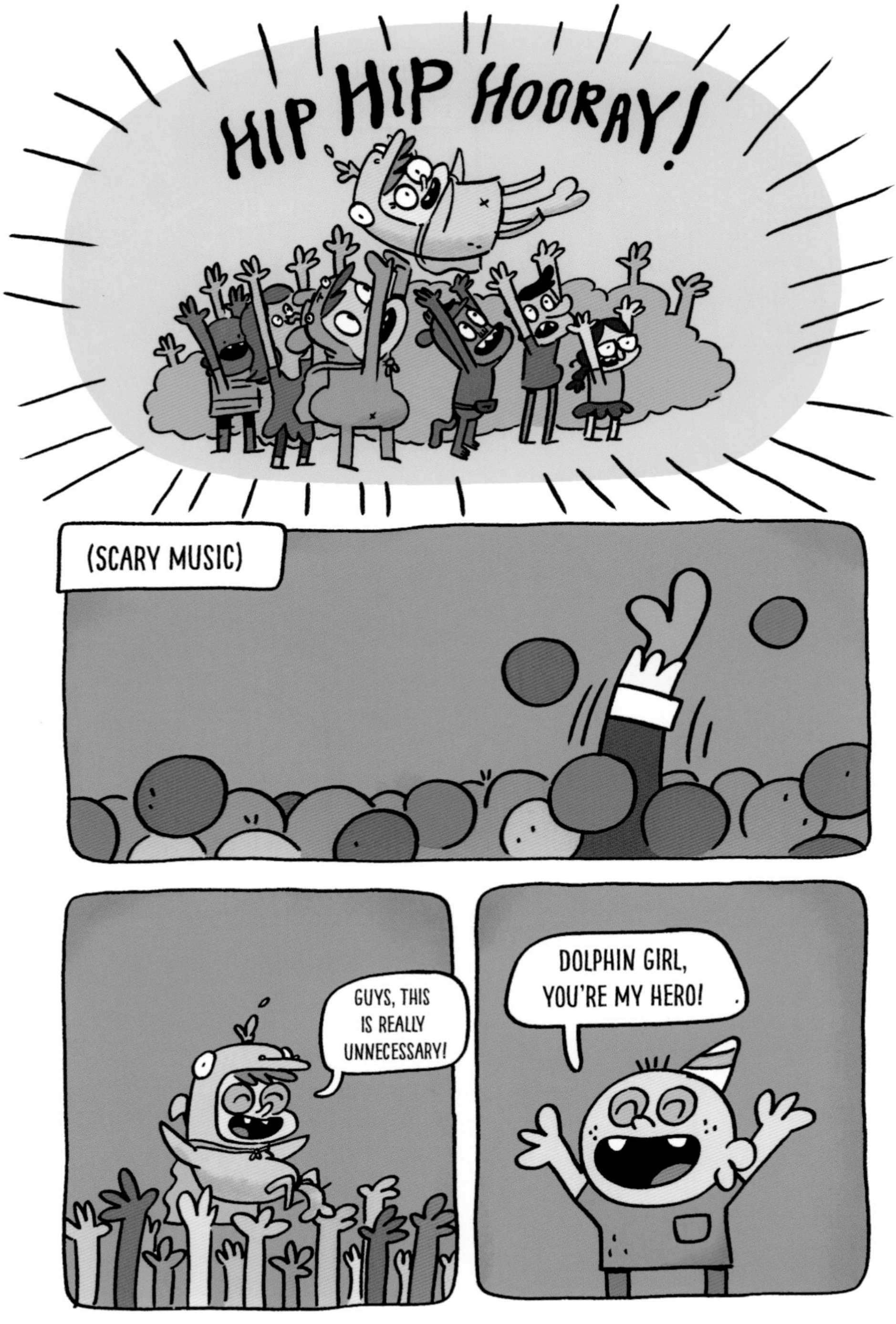
HIP HIP HOORAY!
(SCARY MUSIC)
GUYS, THIS IS REALLY UNNECESSARY!
DOLPHIN GIRL, YOU'RE MY HERO!

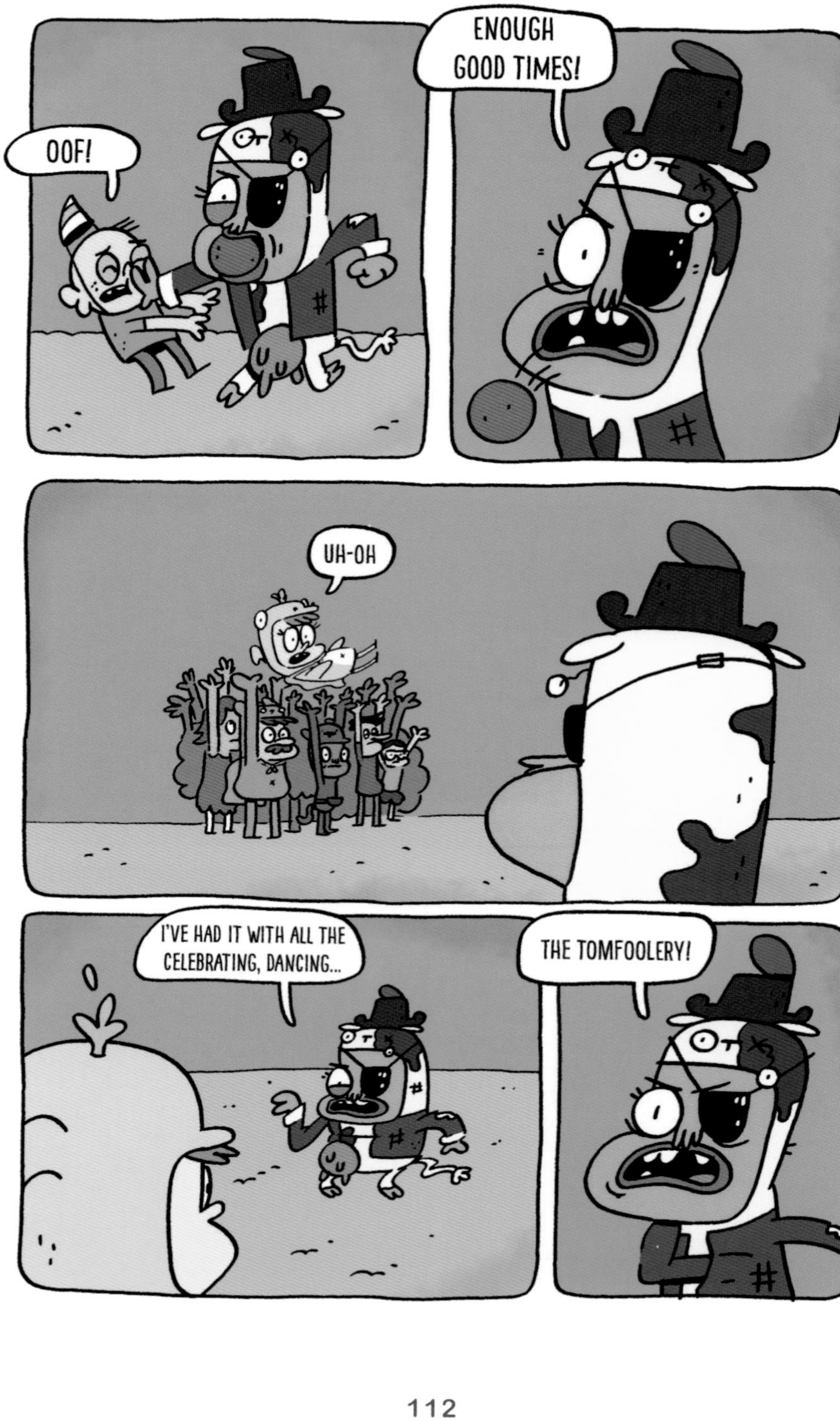
OOF!
ENOUGH GOOD TIMES!
UH-OH
I'VE HAD IT WITH ALL THE CELEBRATING, DANCING...
THE TOMFOOLERY!

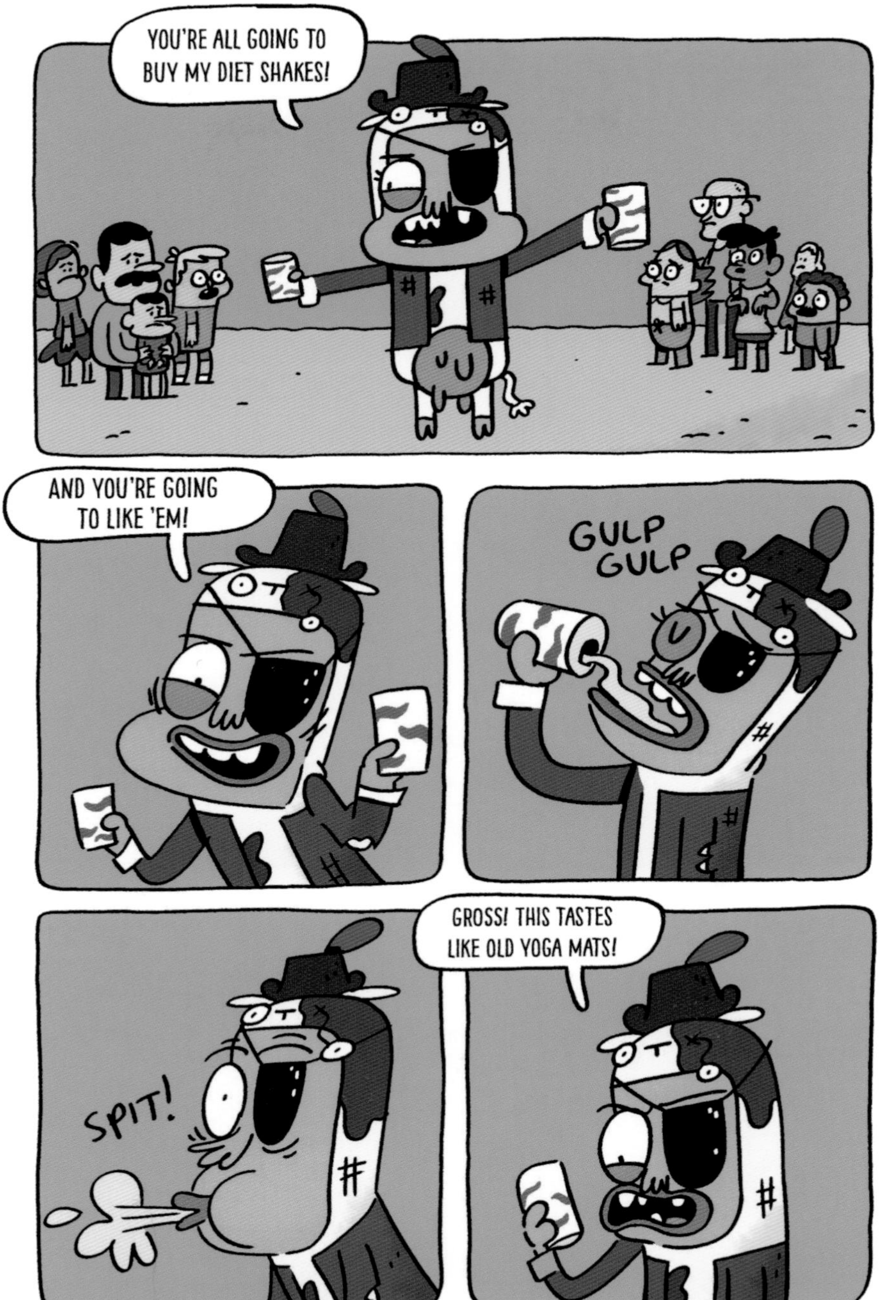
YOU'RE ALL GOING TO BUY MY DIET SHAKES!
AND YOU'RE GOING TO LIKE 'EM!
GULP GULP
SPIT!
GROSS! THIS TASTES LIKE OLD YOGA MATS!

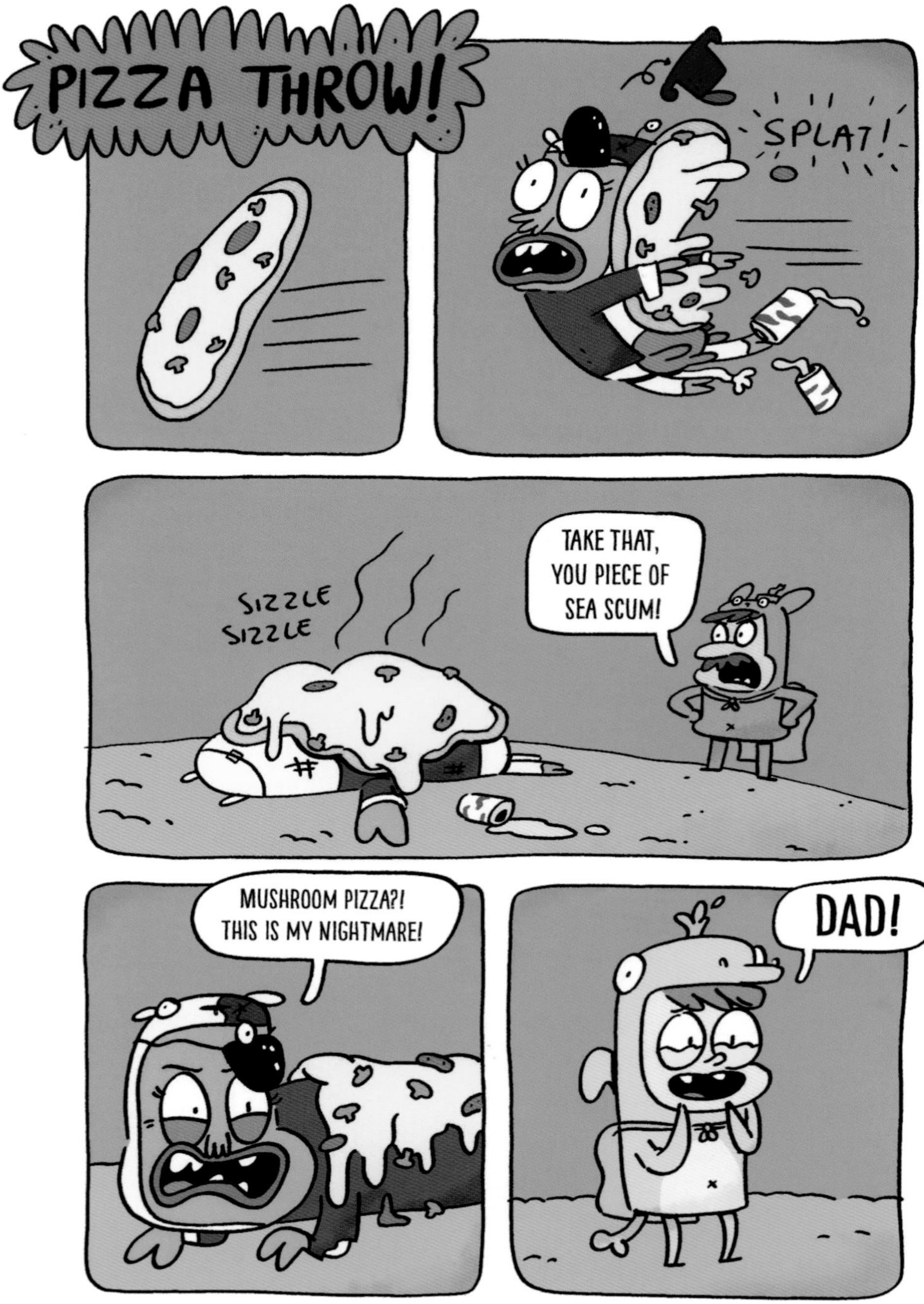
PIZZA THROW!
SPLAT!
SIZZLE SIZZLE
TAKE THAT, YOU PIECE OF SEA SCUM!
MUSHROOM PIZZA?! THIS IS MY NIGHTMARE!
DAD!

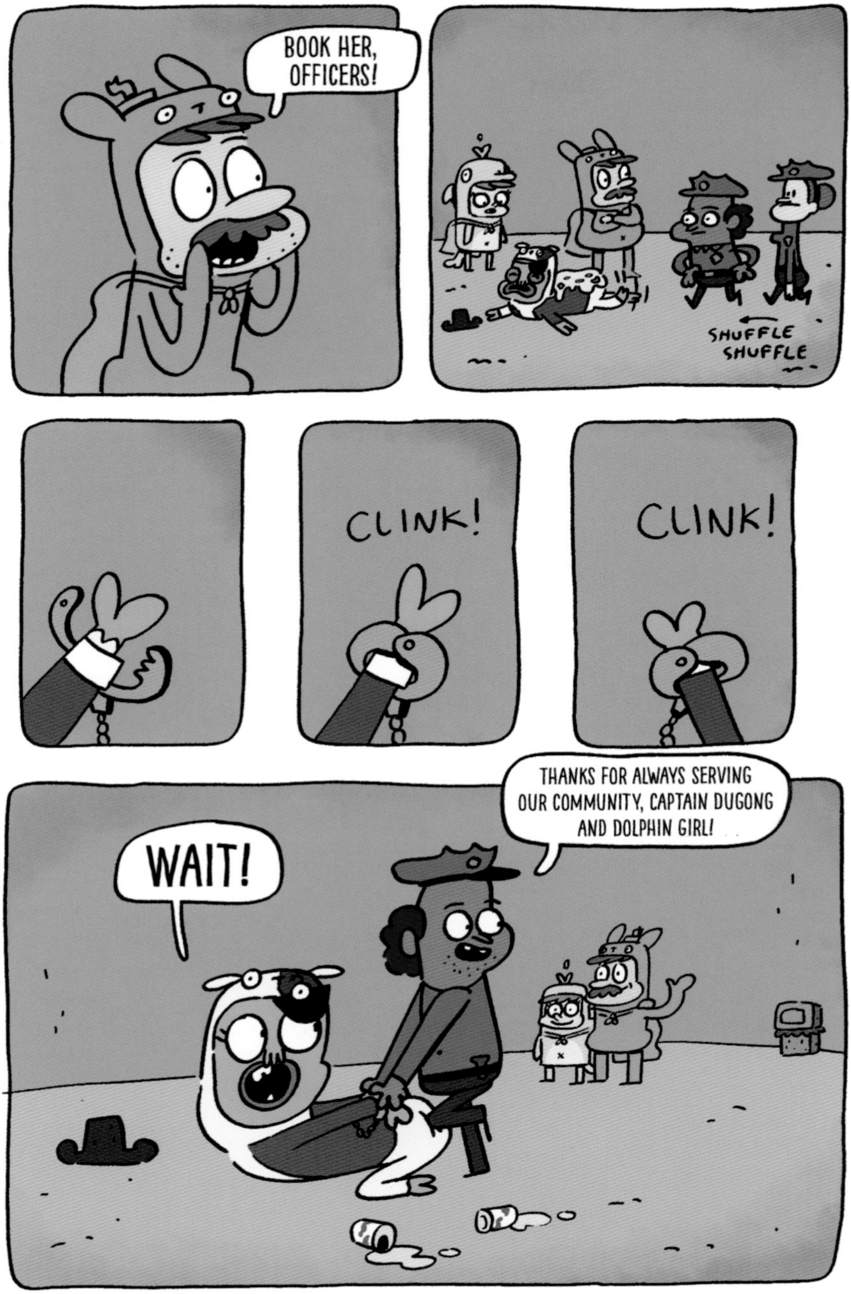
BOOK HER, OFFICERS!
SHUFFLE SHUFFLE
CLINK!
CLINK!
THANKS FOR ALWAYS SERVING OUR COMMUNITY, CAPTAIN DUGONG AND DOLPHIN GIRL!
WAIT!

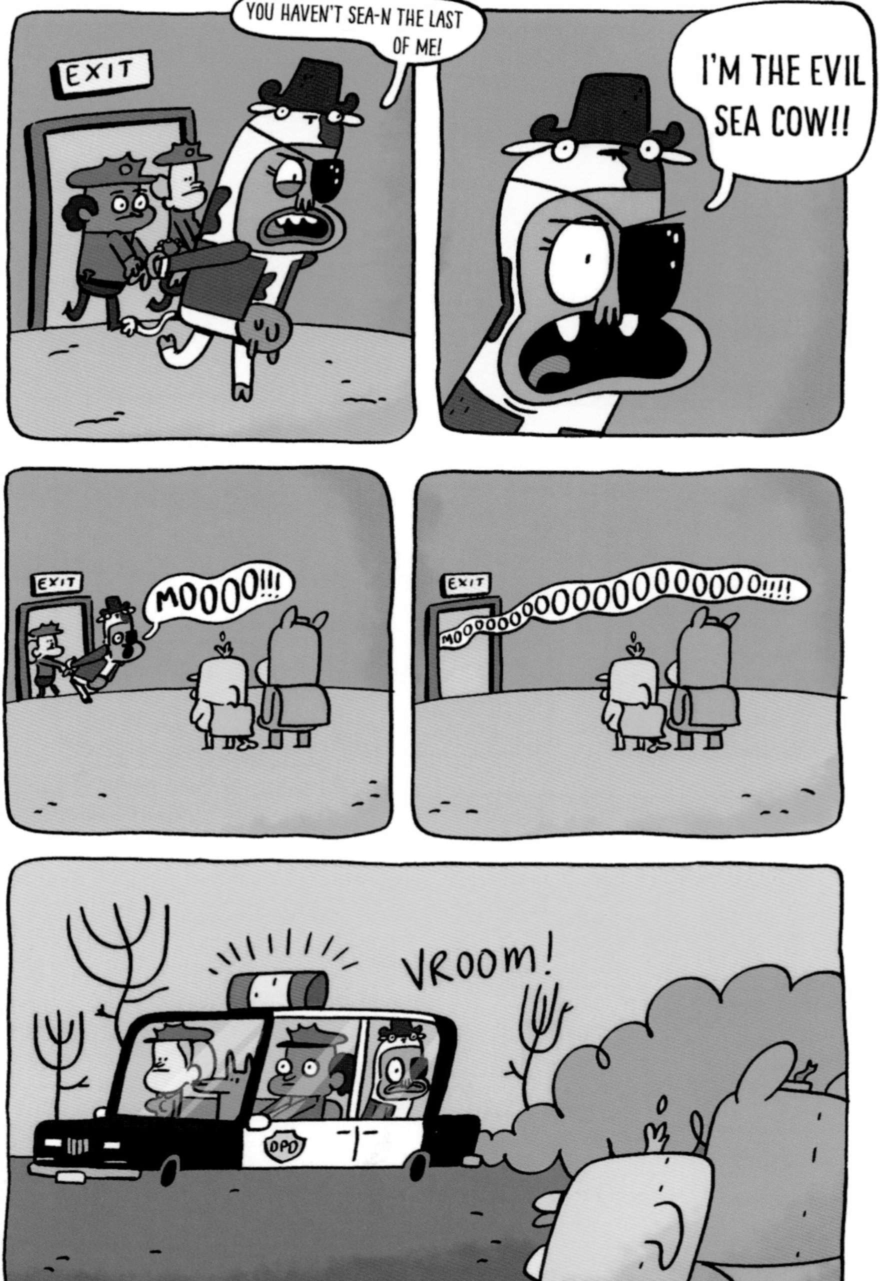
EXIT
YOU HAVEN'T SEA-N THE LAST OF ME!
I'M THE EVIL SEA COW!!
EXIT
MOOOO!!!
EXIT
MOOOOOOOOOOOOOOOOOOOOOOOOO!!!!
VROOM!
OPD

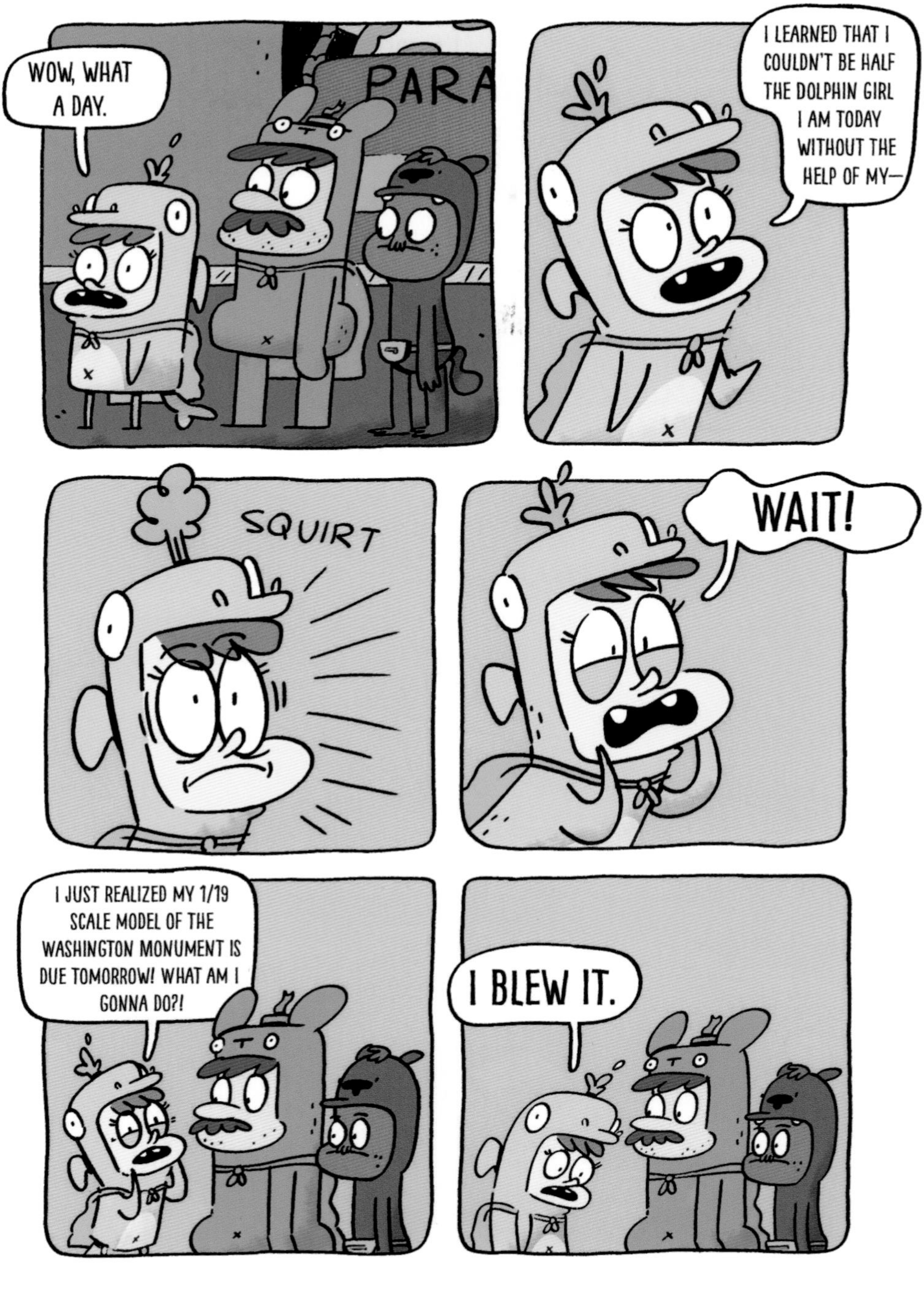
PARA
WOW, WHAT A DAY.
I LEARNED THAT I COULDN'T BE HALF THE DOLPHIN GIRL I AM TODAY WITHOUT THE HELP OF MY—
SQUIRT
WAIT!
I JUST REALIZED MY 1/19 SCALE MODEL OF THE WASHINGTON MONUMENT IS DUE TOMORROW! WHAT AM I GONNA DO?!
I BLEW IT.

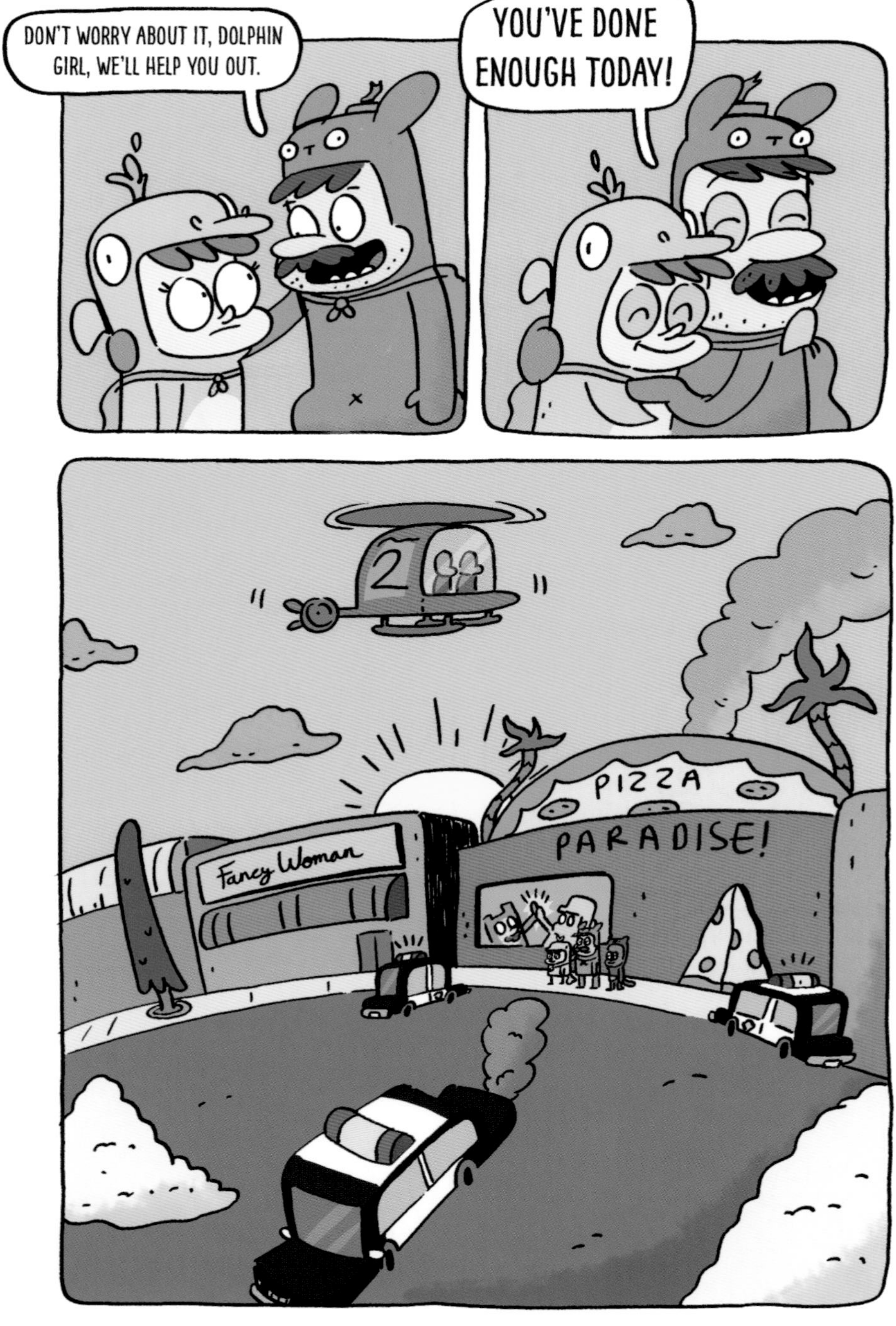
DON'T WORRY ABOUT IT, DOLPHIN GIRL, WE'LL HELP YOU OUT.
YOU'VE DONE ENOUGH TODAY!
Fancy Woman
PIZZA PARADISE!

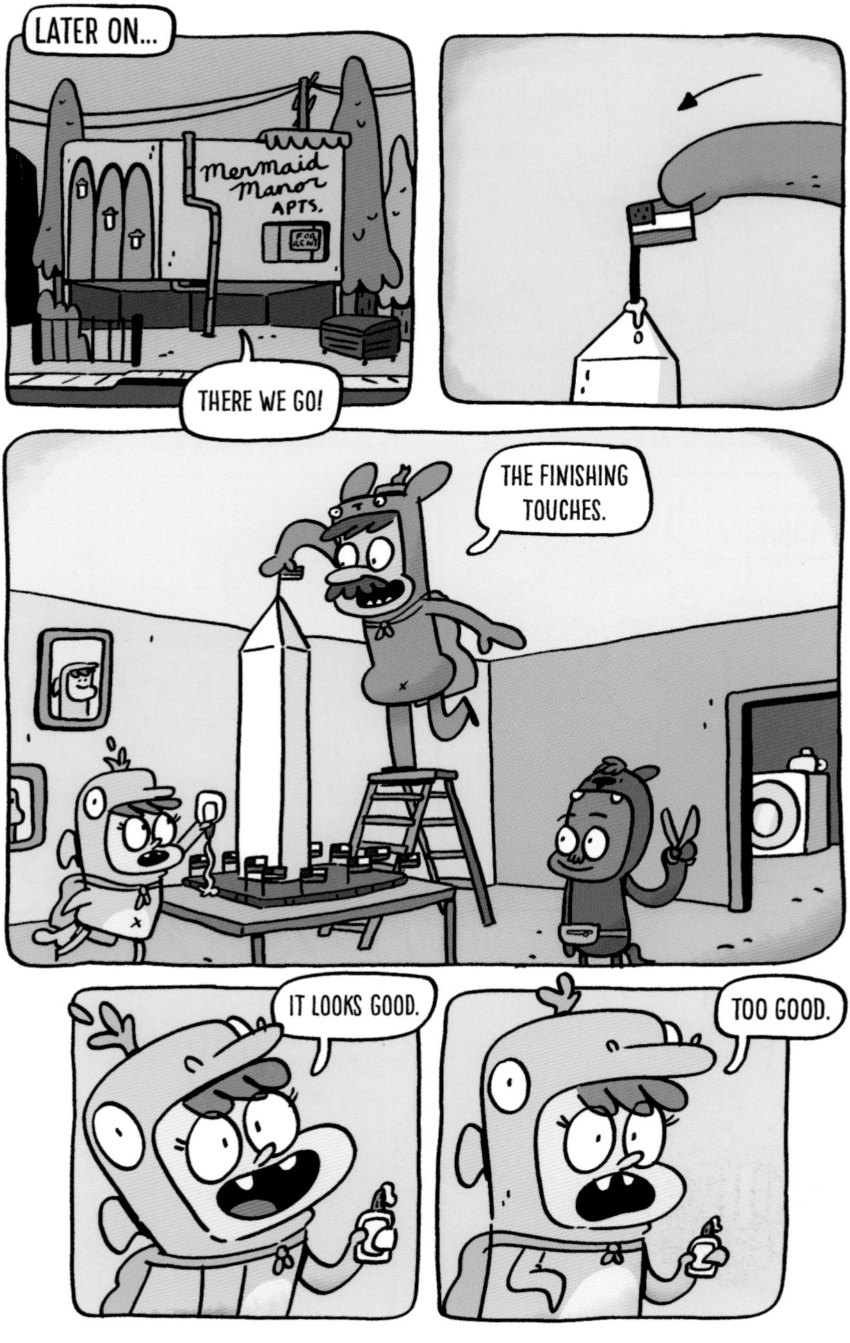
LATER ON...
Mermaid Manor APTS.
FOR RENT
THERE WE GO!
THE FINISHING TOUCHES.
IT LOOKS GOOD.
TOO GOOD.

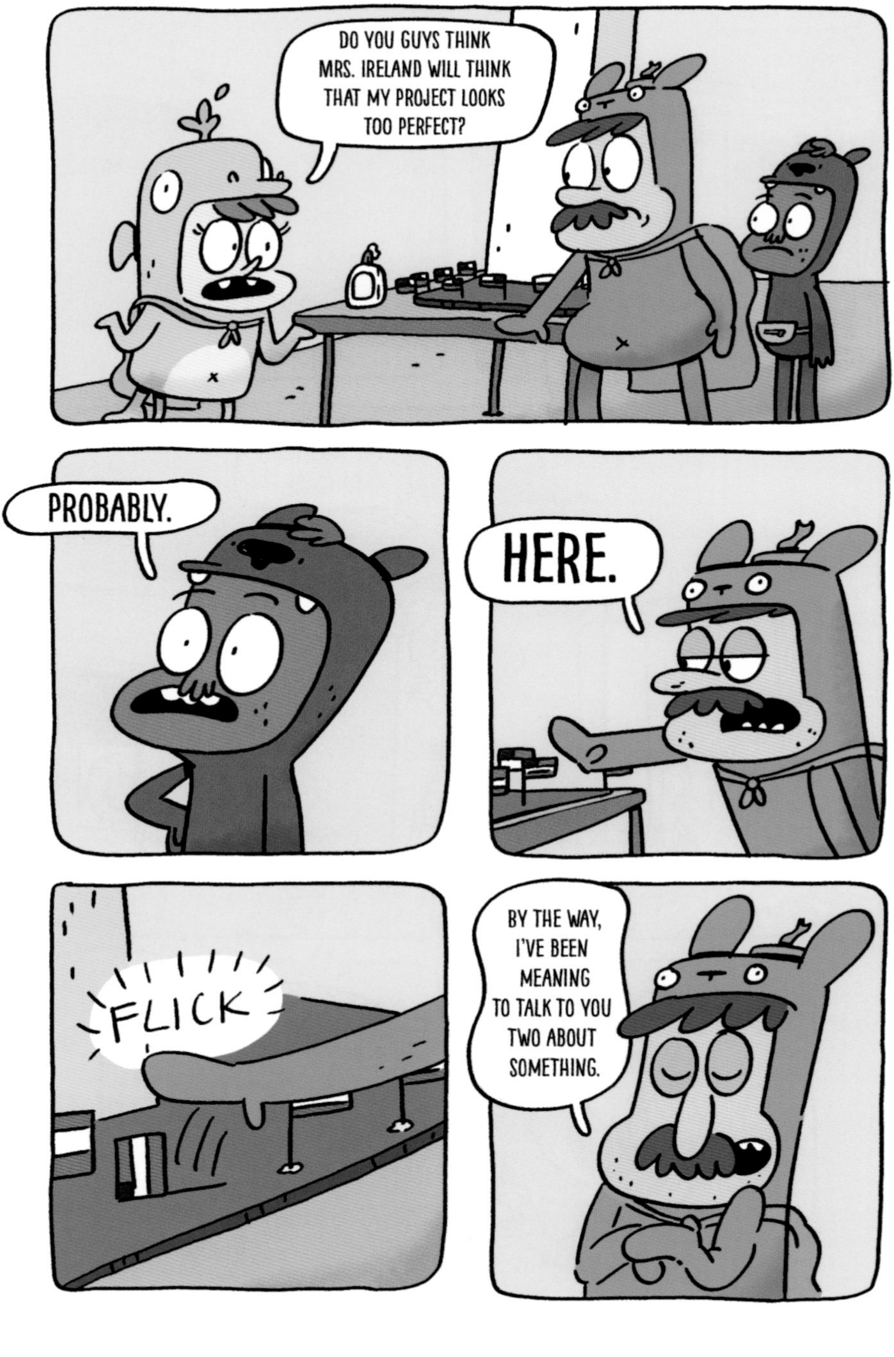
DO YOU GUYS THINK MRS. IRELAND WILL THINK THAT MY PROJECT LOOKS TOO PERFECT?
PROBABLY.
HERE.
FLICK
BY THE WAY, I'VE BEEN MEANING TO TALK TO YOU TWO ABOUT SOMETHING.

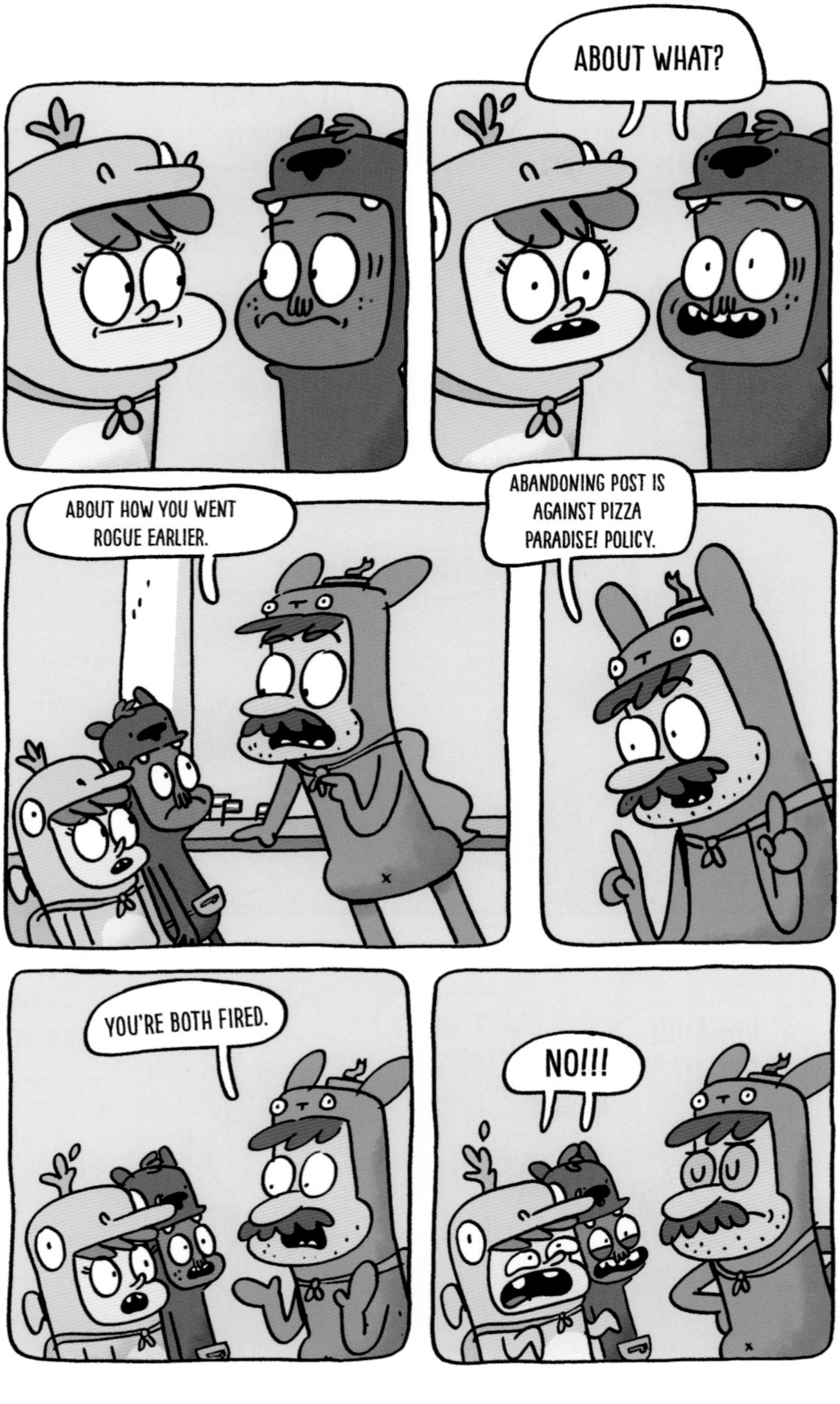
ABOUT WHAT?
ABOUT HOW YOU WENT ROGUE EARLIER.
ABANDONING POST IS AGAINST PIZZA PARADISE! POLICY.
YOU'RE BOTH FIRED.
NO!!!

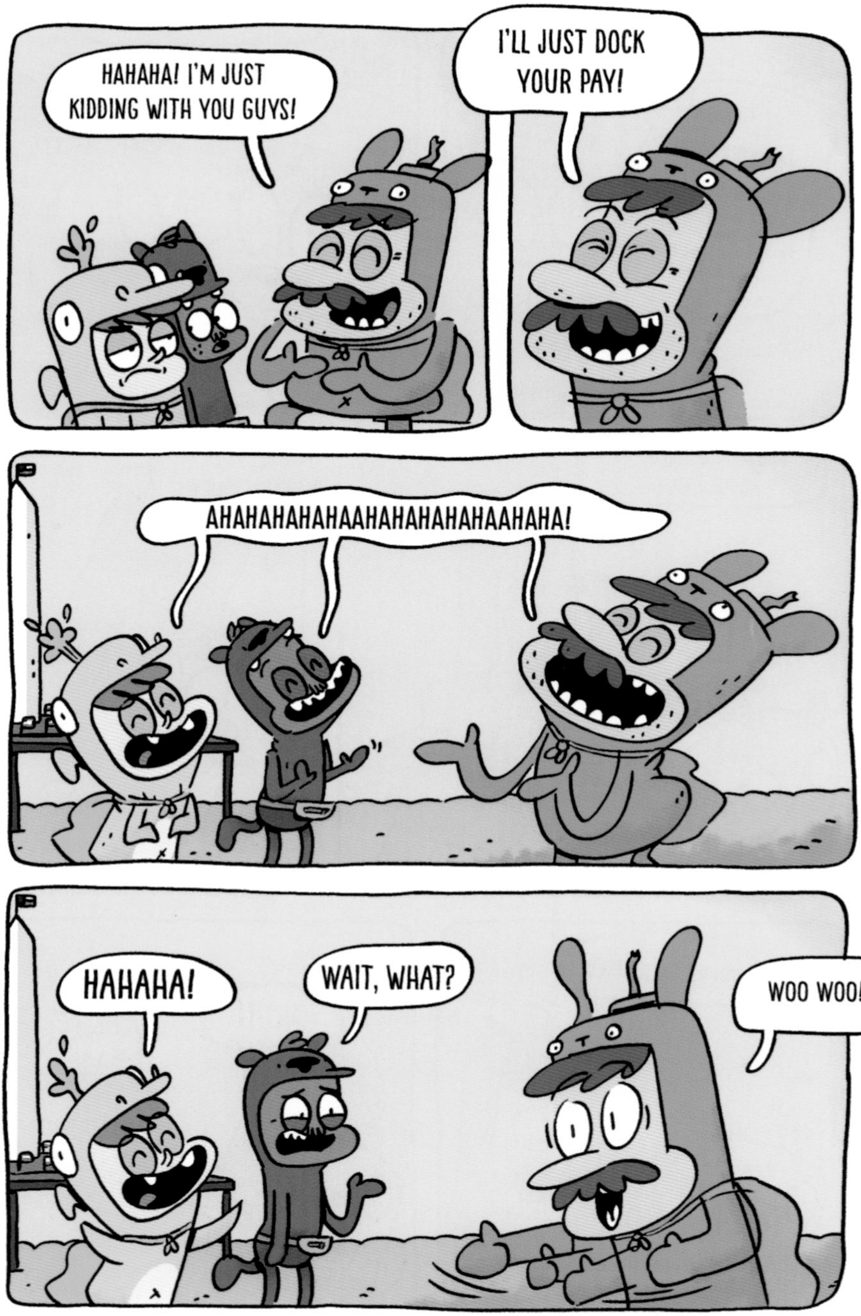
HAHAHA! I'M JUST KIDDING WITH YOU GUYS!
I'LL JUST DOCK YOUR PAY!
AHAHAHAHAHAAHAHAHAHAHAAHAHA!
HAHAHA!
WAIT, WHAT?
WOO WOO!!!

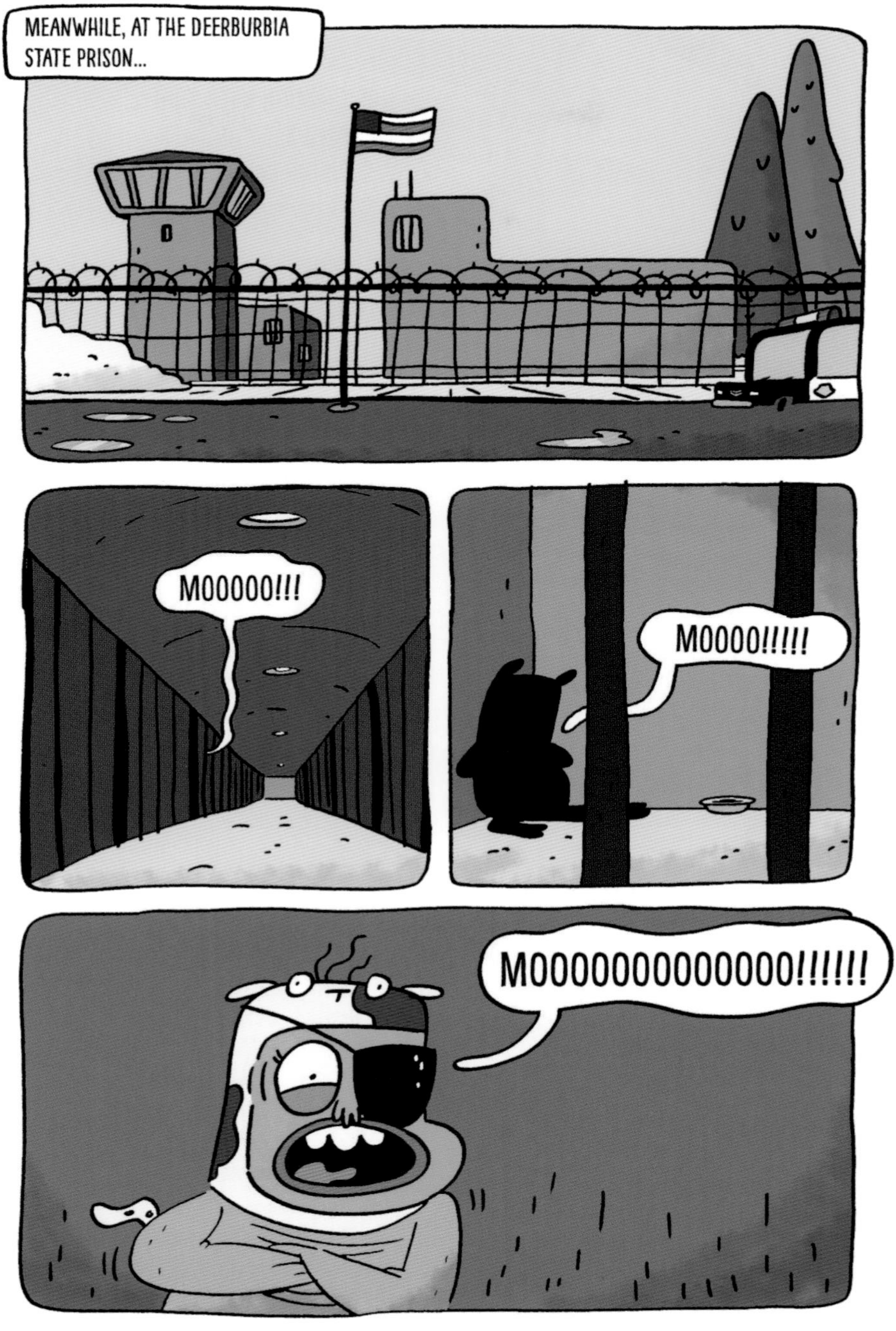
MEANWHILE, AT THE DEERBURBIA STATE PRISON...
MOOOOO!!!
MOOOO!!!!!
MOOOOOOOOOOOOO!!!!!!

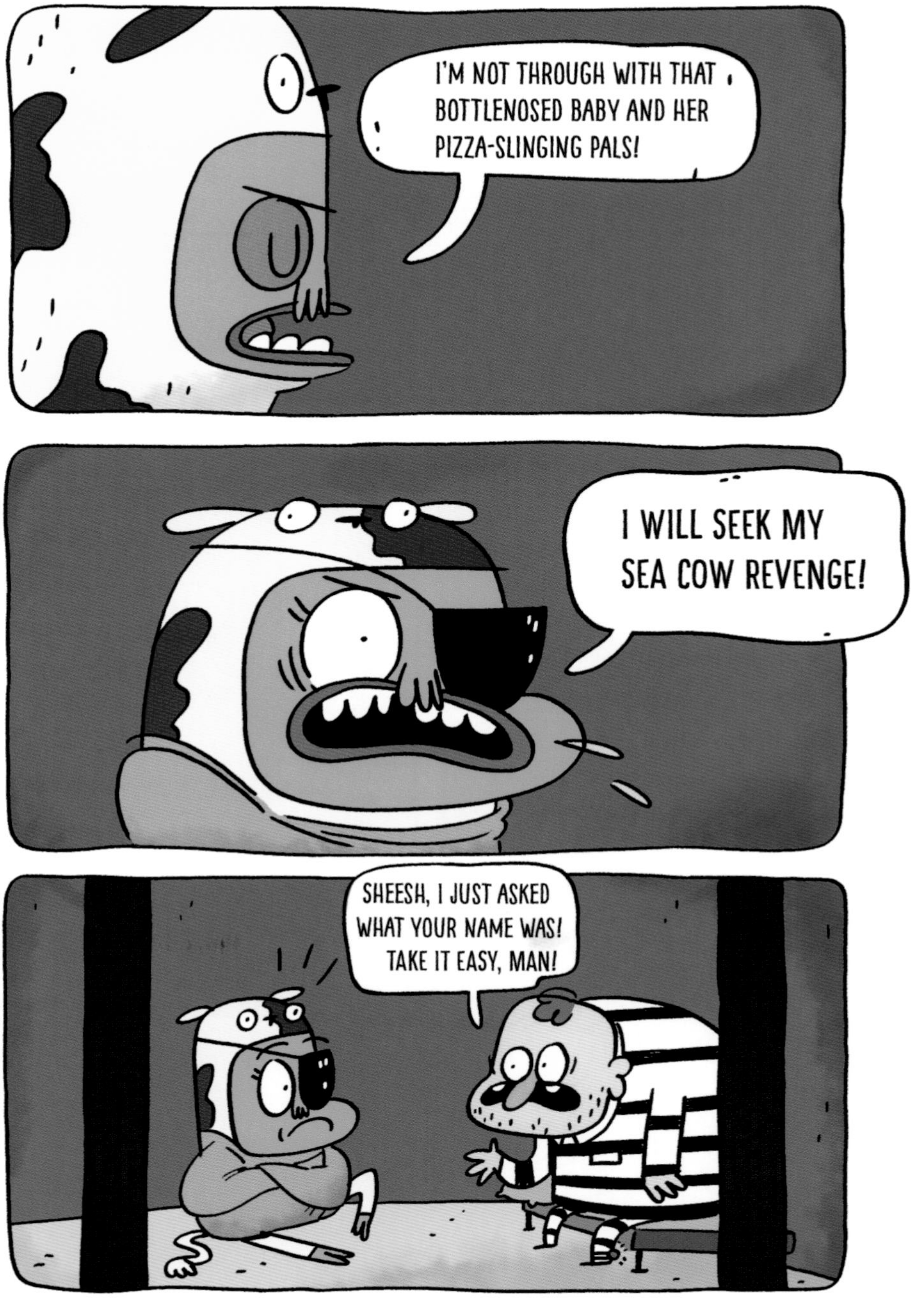
I'M NOT THROUGH WITH THAT BOTTLENOSED BABY AND HER PIZZA-SLINGING PALS!
I WILL SEEK MY SEA COW REVENGE!
SHEESH, I JUST ASKED WHAT YOUR NAME WAS! TAKE IT EASY, MAN!

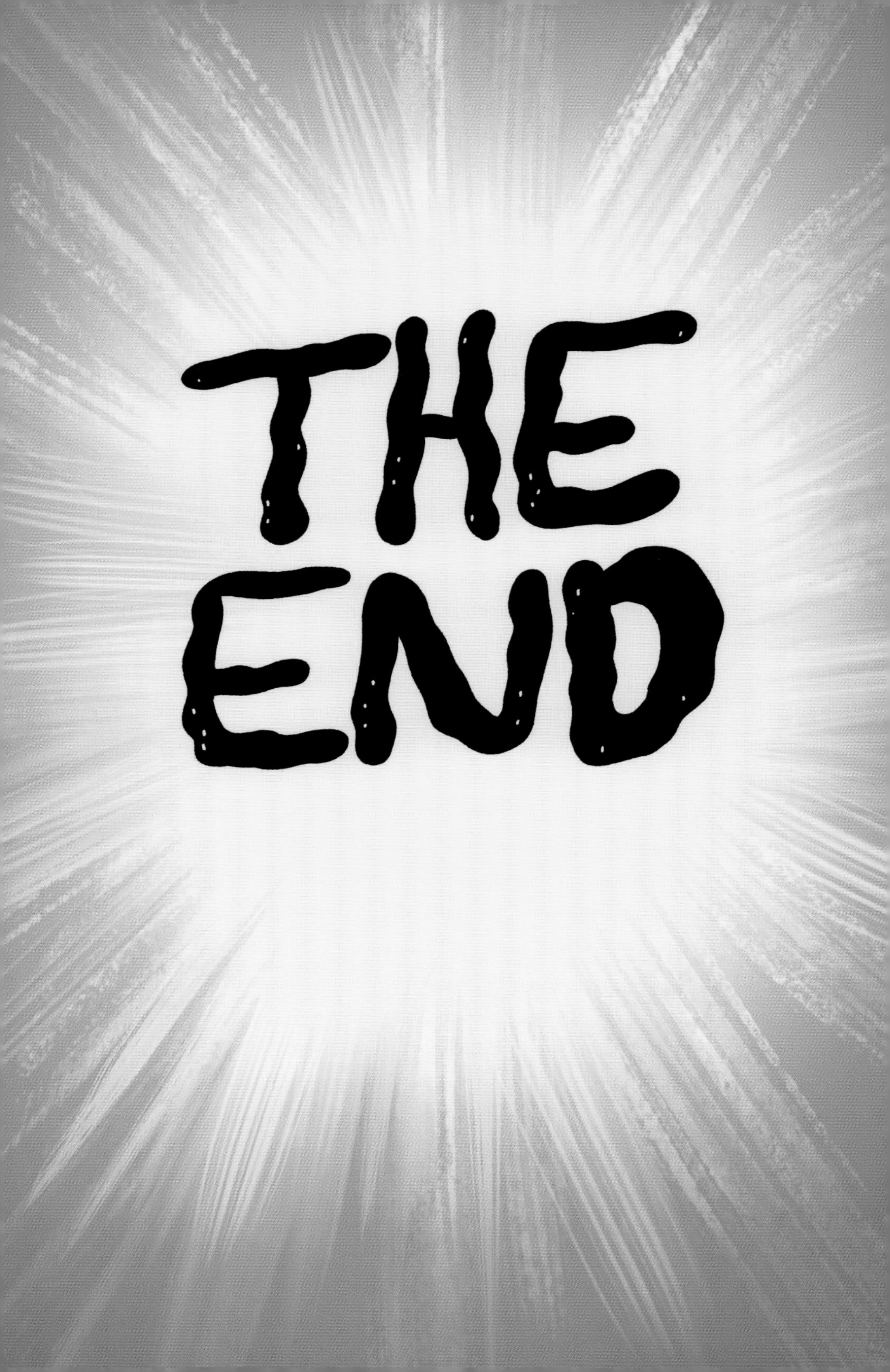
THE END

ACKNOWLEDGMENTS

To all the people who helped with the book: Bethany Buck for the amazing input and belief in these characters, and for holding my fresh baby author hand and guiding me through this process. Carol Chu for putting the book together and teaching me what a bleed is. Leticia Lacy for the beautiful mind-altering color you provided, you brought everything together like a hearty dolphin stew. To the rest of the team at Pixel+Ink; Kyra Reppen, Raina Putter, Lisa Lee, Terry Borzumato-Greenberg, Michelle Montague, Emily Mannon, Nicole Benevento, Cheryl Lew, Derek Stordahl, Adrienne Vaughn, Julia Gallagher, and Miriam Miller; Thanks for makin' this puppy sing.

To all the people who helped (but maybe didn't know that they helped): Monique Smith for dealing with my bonkers work schedule, being a joke tester-outer, and dealing with my general insanity on a daily basis. I tried to write a lot of these jokes to make you laugh. Mom and Dad for supporting me and dealing with me lugging my computer equipment to Palm Springs to work on this during our family vacation. Mary Harrington for always pushing me to do new projects. Matthew Saver for being a real-life super hero. Ashlynn Anstee, Chloe Bristol and Johnny Ryan for answering my questions about how to make books in the first place. Brooke Keesling, Lisa Dunn, and Gary Schwartz, the teachers that encouraged me to keep drawing weird stuff. The Skatalites, whose music was the unofficial soundtrack to the making of this book. Also, to all of the fast food workers, food delivery drivers, and grocery store workers that provided me with life-sustaining energy I needed in order to write this book, I don't know how many chicken nuggets were consumed during the making of Dolphin Girl, but it was a serious amount.

ABOUT THE AUTHOR

ZACH SMITH IS A CARTOONIST THAT WORKS AS A DIRECTOR AND STORYBOARD ARTIST IN THE ANIMATION INDUSTRY. HE GREW UP IN MICHIGAN AND INDIANA BUT NOW LIVES IN SOUTHERN CALIFORNIA WITH HIS WIFE, KIDS, AND EVEN TWO DOGS! WHEN HE'S NOT DRAWING THINGS FOR MONEY, HIS PASTIMES INCLUDE, BUT ARE NOT LIMITED TO, EATING FAST FOOD ALONE IN HIS CAR.

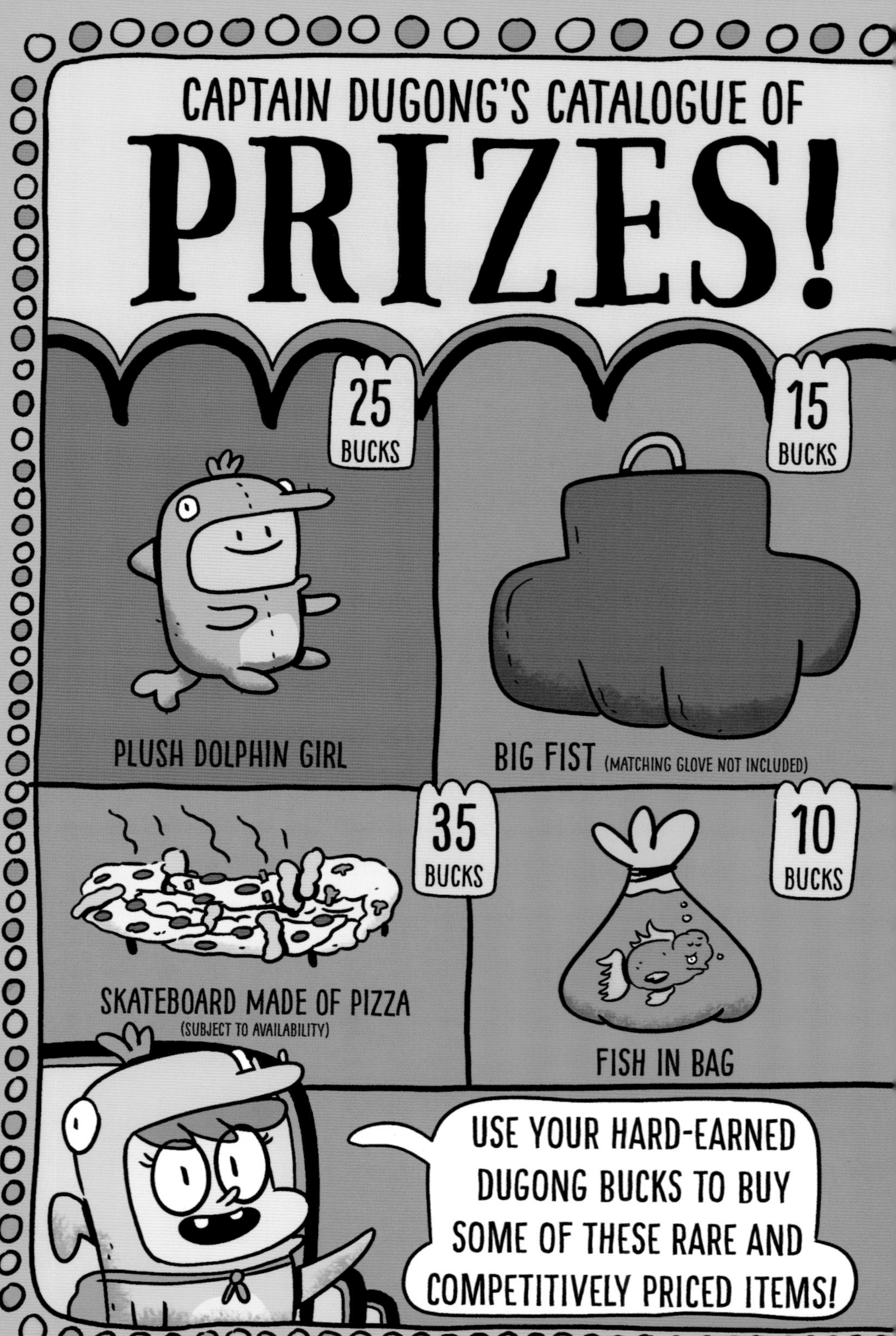

CAPTAIN DUGONG'S CATALOGUE OF
PRIZES!
25 BUCKS
PLUSH DOLPHIN GIRL
15 BUCKS
BIG FIST (MATCHING GLOVE NOT INCLUDED)
35 BUCKS
SKATEBOARD MADE OF PIZZA (SUBJECT TO AVAILABILITY)
10 BUCKS
FISH IN BAG
USE YOUR HARD-EARNED DUGONG BUCKS TO BUY SOME OF THESE RARE AND COMPETITIVELY PRICED ITEMS!

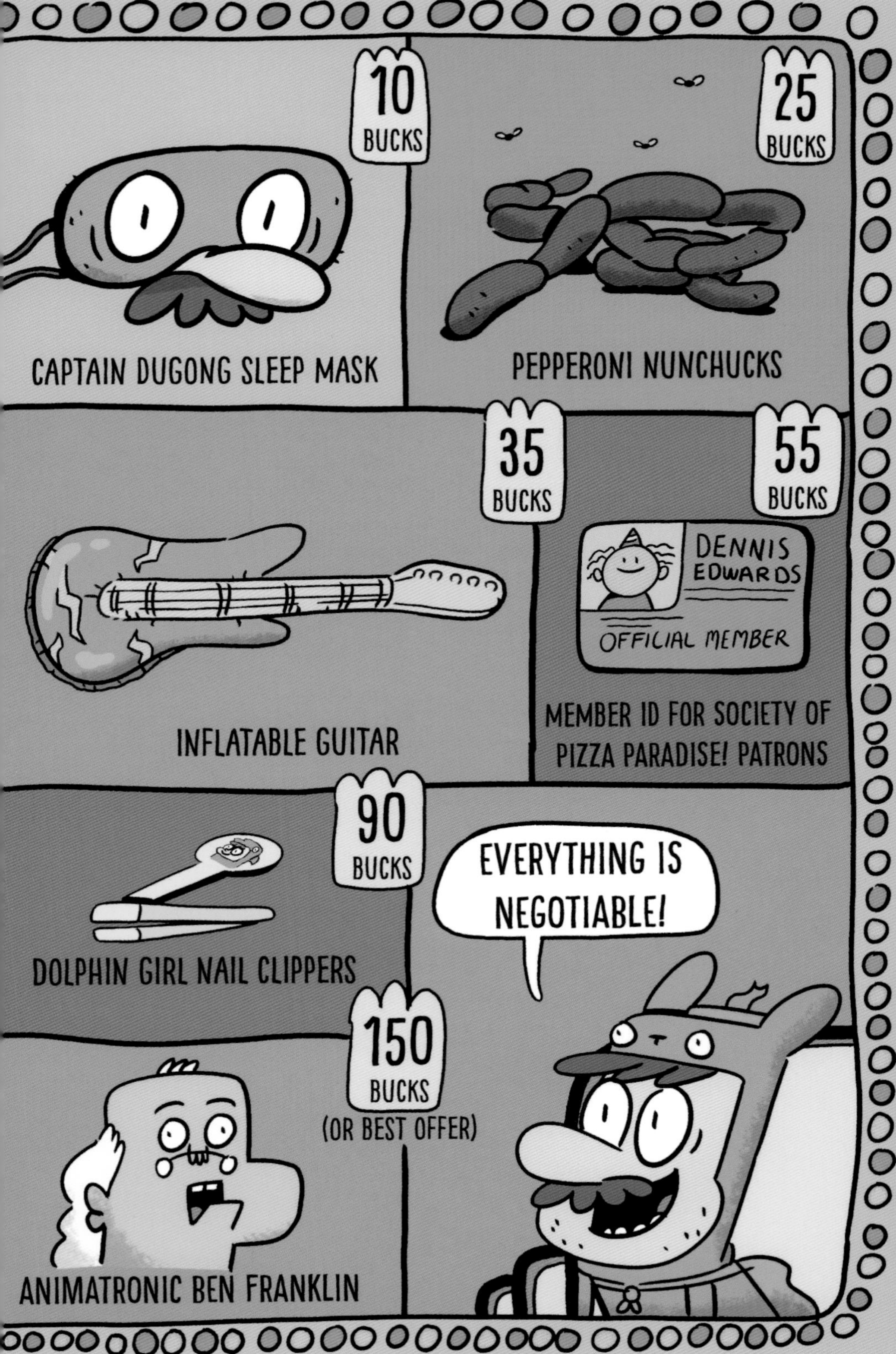
10 BUCKS
CAPTAIN DUGONG SLEEP MASK
25 BUCKS
PEPPERONI NUNCHUCKS
35 BUCKS
INFLATABLE GUITAR
55 BUCKS
DENNIS EDWARDS
OFFICIAL MEMBER
MEMBER ID FOR SOCIETY OF PIZZA PARADISE! PATRONS
90 BUCKS
DOLPHIN GIRL NAIL CLIPPERS
EVERYTHING IS NEGOTIABLE!
150 BUCKS (OR BEST OFFER)
ANIMATRONIC BEN FRANKLIN